CHASING THE *Wind*

a novel

PAMELA BINNINGS EWEN

B&H
PUBLISHING GROUP

Nashville, Tennessee

978-0-8054-6431-3

Published by B&H Publishing Group,
Nashville, Tennessee

Dewey Decimal Classification: F
Subject Heading: MYSTERY FICTION \ SPIRITUAL LIFE—
FICTION \ NEW ORLEANS (LA)—FICTION

1 2 3 4 5 6 7 8 • 16 15 14 13 12

For Scott, Andrea, Lex, and Lucia,
my beloved children.

In memory of Anna Marie Catoir

Acknowledgments

Thanks to everyone at B&H Publishing Group for their friendship and hard work in bringing this book to readers—Kim, Matt, and the whole sales team, Diana, Jennifer—all of you, without you, *Chasing the Wind* would just be a manuscript sitting on my desk. Special thanks to Julie Gwinn. Thank you for your constant, loving support. During good times and hard times I have learned that your inner strength is awesome.

Thanks to David Webb, my editor. Your ideas enhanced the story—you make the editing process painless.

Thanks, again to Jacques and Wendy Michell for sharing your memories of life in Pilottown and on the river, and the colorful history of the Associated Branch Pilots. Jude thanks you too!

Thanks to my friend Barbara Ray for reading numerous drafts of this story and for your insightful comments. Thanks to my friend and former partner, Bill Stutts, for enduring endless wandering conversations and abstract questions. And thanks to my friend David Skarke for being a sport and helping D. B. out at the end—even though it's purely fiction, my friends.

And to my mother, my favorite critic who loves every word I write—thanks, Mom! To Scott, Andrea, and Lex and Lucia—Remember, one person can almost always make a difference. And, to my husband, Jimmy, I could never have written the story of Jude and Amalise's love without you in my life.

Prologue

BINGHAM MURDOCH FLEW INTO TOWN ON a star one day. At exactly 8:47 a.m. on Wednesday, October 19, 1977, he banked the silver Lockheed JetStar at such an angle that the rays of the sun glanced off the wing and shot a glint of silver through the city of New Orleans. Bingham sat in the first pilot's seat, peering through the wide, curved glass at the metropolis spread out below him. He took in the snaking, brown Mississippi River, the heavy old buildings holding each other up in the central business district, marked by Canal Street and, on the other side of Canal, the distinctive peaked roofs of the *Vieux Carré*, the French Quarter. Smiling, Bingham then swooped toward the broad expanse of Lake Pontchartrain and the small private airport there, smiling. He'd never felt such kindred spirit with a city before. This was a town with open pockets and an attitude.

Downtown a young lawyer with the firm of Mangen & Morris stood at the window of her office on the sixteenth floor of the First Merchant Bank Building for the first time in many months. Amalise Catoir felt good because, instead of the gray walls of hospital rooms and the winding vines of pink roses on the wallpaper in her old bedroom back home in Marianus, she was back at work and looking out over the teeming city again. Automobiles crawled through the narrow streets below, people milled on the sidewalks like ants, and a man in a suit on a bicycle ducked in and out of pedestrian traffic and cars. Almost as if nothing had changed.

It was *life*.

Across the street her view of the city was blocked by another high building with rows of windows looking back at her. But to her left Amalise could look past the hospitals and domed stadium to where New Orleans stretched all the way to the lake. She couldn't see the water from this distance, but her imagination filled in the details, the breeze whipping the clouds like marzipan on this October day and ruffling the blue water below. There would be a few sailboats out to enjoy the weather, even on a weekday.

As she took in the view, a quicksilver glint in the sky drew her attention. For a moment she tracked the small plane as it descended toward Lakefront Airport, sunlight winking off a wing like a shooting star aimed straight for her. She wondered if she were the only person in the world who had just seen the momentary flash of light.

But someone else saw it, too. About a mile away, a small boy with delicate oriental features sat alone on the front porch of a sagging house in the Faubourg Marigny, watching the other children play. He was somehow different, he knew, from his foster brothers and sister. Yawning, he looked up at the clear blue sky. In the distance he saw a small plane shining in the sun. He watched it for an instant, shading his eyes with his hand and squinting. Then a bright flash of light came at him like a burst of gunfire, and he flinched, remembering.

When he looked up again, the plane was gone.

In her office Amalise shivered with the odd fancy that the flash somehow signified a fateful connection between the giver and recipient of the light.

Chapter One

AMALISE TURNED FROM THE WINDOW, LEANED back against it, and surveyed her office. It was good to be back. Her eyes caressed the leather-upholstered furnishings, the vintage mahogany desk and bookshelves, the *Black's Law Dictionary* given to her by the firm after her second year of law school, the rows of thick volumes bound in rich, colored leather—red, green, and black with gold lettering across the spines—records of corporate transactions she'd worked on during her first year with the firm, plus a few borrowed from other associates to occupy the spaces she would one day fill with more of her own.

Her eyes landed on a framed photograph on a shelf above the books, and a flood of emotions—anger, pity, fear, sorrow—hit her all at once. She walked over and picked up the photo of her and her former husband. Phillip Sharp's dark eyes glowered at her from under his brows, as if he had known even then how things would end. In the picture they sat at the Café Pontalba, across from Jackson Square, where she'd waited tables every day for three years during law school.

She closed her eyes, and the memories rushed in, swirling and mingling—Phillip's slow descent into madness, his hatred of her, his death, and then the accident and the blessed loss of memory in those last few moments. Twenty minutes, gone. Retrograde amnesia, the doctors said.

She'd been trapped in a nightmare with Phillip. Jude had warned her. And Jude had saved her in the end.

Amalise moved along the bookcase, plucking each picture of Phillip from its place among those of Mama and Dad, Jude, Gina, and one of Rebecca and her in caps and gowns at graduation from law school. Tucking Phillip's pictures in the crook of her arm, she crossed to the long credenza behind her desk that held the telephone, her daily appointment book, some new yellow legal pads, a box of sharpened number-two pencils, and more photographs.

She picked up a box of business cards and pulled one out. Embossed in shining black letters across the center of the card, just above her contact information at the firm, was the name "Amalise Catoir." *Sans* Sharp. Good. Pushing the card back into the box, she set it down and trailed her fingers across a framed photograph of Mama and Dad at home in Marianus. And another one of Jude.

Jude, her oldest dearest friend. Since childhood, from the time she was six years old and he was ten, they'd been inseparable. She'd tagged along behind him everywhere. She smiled and picked up the photograph, studying it. He'd taught her to swim and fish, tutored her in math, taught her how to dance. Here, he stood on deck aboard a ship at the mouth of the river, poised to climb down to the pilot boat waiting below. His skin browned by the sun, he shaded his eyes with his hand as the camera caught him by surprise.

Her Jude.

And then a question rose against her will: Was he really hers?

Rebecca came to mind. Beautiful, glamorous Rebecca. How casually she'd introduced Jude to Rebecca, never thinking. Amalise remembered the two of them as they were on that day, two years ago, when she married Phillip. Standing on the veranda, Rebecca had looked up at Jude, green eyes sparkling as he took her hand and led her to the dance floor.

They had been dating ever since. Yet Amalise had never given much thought to their relationship—until now. For one thing, Jude was too fine a man and too old a friend to discuss his love life. And Rebecca was focused on her career. *Driven* by her career, in fact.

Amalise's smile slowly faded. These new feelings for Jude were complicating things. During the past few months, while he'd spent so much time at her side as she recuperated, she'd grown conscious of a longing for something more than friendship with Jude, something deeper and different. She felt a connection with him that went way beyond their childhood companionship.

Was this love?

But how could anyone fall in love with her oldest, dearest friend? He was there in her every memory of youth. Could a person know someone so completely, their every little fault and wonderful thing, and then accept, or even understand, such a fundamental shift in their friendship and then just segue on to romance? Imagining the expression on Jude's face if she were ever to tell him of her feelings, she put the picture back on the credenza, setting it by the telephone where one of Phillip used to stand.

Jude probably still thought of her as that child.

And then there was Rebecca.

She set her mind to putting these thoughts aside. Jude was her best friend, but Rebecca was a good friend too. They had gone to law school together, becoming the first two women ever hired as attorneys by the prestigious firm of Mangen & Morris. They were the Silver Girls.

Amalise knew she should be happy for Rebecca. And yet, as she turned to her desk, pulled out the chair, and sat down, an empty space opened inside at the possibility of losing Jude to her. She set the pictures she'd gathered up of Phillip face-down on the desk and pushed them aside. She couldn't imagine life without Jude. He'd had girlfriends over the years, of course. Women loved Jude. But she had always come first, she'd thought, at least since the time she was too young to think otherwise.

And recently, she'd again come to take for granted her supreme spot in Jude's heart. She hadn't wondered once about Rebecca during her recuperation and Jude's ministrations. Indeed, she'd been so shaken by Phillip's death, the accident, and the amnesia that sheltered her from knowing what had happened at the end, that she had readily slipped into that old familiar intimacy with Jude, almost as if they'd traveled back in time.

But what about Rebecca?

Amalise reached out, running her hands over the dark, solid desk, steadying herself, reminding the nagging voice inside her head that, since the accident, Jude had spent every moment away from work on the river at *her* side instead of here in the city with Rebecca.

Enough! She was determined to enjoy her first day back at work.

She leaned down and pulled out the bottom drawer and then swept the pictures of Phillip Sharp inside. One night soon she would take them home and store them in some dark place. For now, she turned and put her hands flat before her on the desk, ready to go to work.

She recalled once more the glittering prize: partnership at Mangen & Morris in six more years. The unacknowledged fact that hung between Rebecca and Amalise—their competition for that prize—drifted just below the surface of her conscious thought.

She shook off the ruminations and glanced at the stack of files Raymond had left on the corner of her desk. As she reached for the folder on top, she found a note clipped inside. A surge of energy shot through her as she read it. She was ready to jump back into life, into her work. In Raymond's cryptic scrawl the note read: *Welcome back, Amalise.*

❦

The corporate jet skidded down the Lakefront runway and taxied to the gate. "Thanks for the ride," Bingham Murdoch said to the pilot, removing his hat and slapping it down on the man's head where it belonged. "Tom was right. This baby's smooth." Only the best for Tom Hannigan, Morgan Klemp's hottest banker on Wall Street. Bingham stood. "You're going on to Houston?"

The pilot nodded and bent over the instrument board. "Picking up Mr. Hannigan and the rest over there. Then back to New York."

"Well, tell him thanks for me."

The pilot nodded as Bingham turned and ducked through the cockpit door. His new partner, Robert, was waiting in the cabin, briefcase in one hand, looking like the rest of the Morgan Klemp lifers, of whom he'd been one until two weeks ago when Bingham's proposition had jelled. The stewardess arrived with Bingham's coat, holding it out for him. With a nod, Bingham slipped it on.

"Sandra," he said, pecking her cheek before he stuck his arms through the sleeves. "It was a pleasure to meet you, dear. I hear you're heading home this afternoon."

"That's right," she said, adjusting the shoulders of his coat. She gave him a sly smile. "Unfortunately."

She stepped back, and he turned around to face her. "Call me when you're in the neighborhood again." He crinkled his eyes and chucked her under the chin.

Bingham started down the stairs to the tarmac, with Robert following behind. "We'll be here a few weeks," he said over his shoulder. "Five, maybe six. I'll be staying at the Roosevelt."

"I'll remember," she said.

Her look made him smile, given the wear and tear he was feeling.

A black Town Car idled nearby. Bingham stood watching as the driver stored his suitcase and Robert's garment bag in the trunk.

Despite the sunshine, wind blew off Lake Pontchartrain and across the tarmac with a vengeance. The damp, cold wind surprised him. Wasn't this place supposed to be temperate? Bingham looked around. The terminal was a two-storied, featureless cement-block building with bricked-up windows. There were a few Cessnas around, and a single-engine plane was parked by a hangar. He spotted a woman in the tower looking down at him. He waved. She waved back and disappeared.

The driver adjusted his cap, walked toward Bingham, and opened the door. Robert went around to the other side of the car, while Bingham sank down into the deep, soft leather. A soothing melody played on the radio. "Begin the Beguine." His kind of music. The driver closed the door and followed Robert.

"May I take that for you, sir?" the driver said to Robert, nodding toward the briefcase.

"No thanks." Robert placed his briefcase on the middle seat and slid in beside it.

The driver got behind the wheel and looked over his shoulder. "Roosevelt Hotel?"

"Yes."

"I'll need a car while we're here," Bingham said to Robert as they started off.

"The hotel's got that covered."

The driver rolled the window partition down an inch. "Mind if I smoke?"

Robert: "Yes."

Bingham: "No."

With a shrug, the driver rolled the window up again, and they sped away from the airport. Bingham looked out the window, smiling, thinking of the expression on Tom Hannigan's face the first evening they'd met in Grand Cayman and he'd mentioned the Black Diamond project. They'd been sitting at the open bar on the beach, thatched hut and all. Powdery white sand everywhere you looked. Blue sky stretching over the water for miles, the water turning from green to blue to emerald as the sun sank.

They'd sat for hours under that same thatched roof a few days later, working through the prospect of Black Diamond, even after the sun went down and all you could glimpse of the sea in the darkness was the phosphorescent foam atop each wave as it rolled in, the white froth turning to lace on the sand before disappearing. Bingham took a deep breath. He could almost smell the salty air, could almost taste the ice-cold margaritas. It had all been so easy, really.

Gliding above the city now on Interstate 10, Bingham could see for the first time the dense cluster of buildings downtown and, straight ahead, the rise of the bridge over the Mississippi River. Off to the left they passed the new Superdome, a place built for sinners and saints, he'd read. He asked the driver about it.

The driver nodded. "That there dome was finished about two years ago. Thirteen acres and twenty-seven stories of bad luck you lookin' at there."

"Bad luck? Why?"

"Because it's built atop the Girod Street Cemetery, that's why." Beside him, Bingham heard Robert snort. "There's graves under that there stadium," the driver went on. He glanced at Bingham in the rearview mirror.

"My buddies and I used to play around in them tombstones when we was kids." He beat a rhythm on the steering wheel, shaking his head. "There're some restless souls under that Dome." The driver exited the interstate, stopped at a light, then turned right toward downtown. "We was just kids, but still, you gotta' have respect." He shook his head. "Can't go buildin' ball fields over graves."

Bingham grinned. He felt that connection again with the magic of this city.

The suites were ready when they checked in at the Roosevelt. As Bingham and Robert followed the white-gloved assistant manager down the hallway to the elevators, the left side of Bingham's brain sorted through the curves and swirls of the elaborate décor: The long, narrow lobby. Vaulted ceilings trimmed with red and green Italian tile work. The enormous glittering chandeliers lined up from one end of the block-long hallway to the other. The gilded chairs and tables grouped outside the fountain court, the Sazerac Bar, and the Blue Room.

But the right side of Bingham's brain remained focused on the task ahead. So far, so good. Robert would make some calls, assemble the team, set a meeting with the lawyers. Bingham smiled to himself as they crowded into the small elevator with the bellman. With one last glance at the glittering lobby as the doors slid closed, he decided that he'd chosen well.

Chapter Two

AMALISE LOOKED UP AND SMILED AS Rebecca Downer swept into her office. Rebecca came toward her, swooping her thick red hair up from her neck, looping and twisting it and then, with another twist, anchoring it with a pencil. Closing the file she'd been reading, Amalise rose. Rebecca stretched out her arms, grinning, and they met halfway around the desk in a hug.

"It's been so long. When Jude said you'd be here today, I didn't believe him."

"Three months."

"I wish I could have gotten out to Marianus to see you, Amalise. But you know how things are around here." Rebecca held her at arm's length, inspecting her.

"Sure. I got your flowers and cards. All of them."

Rebecca slipped her fingers through Amalise's hair, held it out to the side, and let it drop. Then she took one step back, looked her up and down, and shook her head. "We have work to do, friend. You need a good haircut. Looks like you've been lying in bed for three months."

"Well, I practically have." Amalise lifted a hand and smoothed the short, straight hair, still smiling as she sat back down. Rebecca took the chair just in front of her desk, the only other chair in the room. Associates' offices were small. She saw Rebecca's eyes flick to the picture of Jude beside the telephone.

Without turning, Amalise said, "I've always liked that picture."

"Jude cannot take a bad photo."

Amalise dropped her eyes. She picked up the file she'd been reading and held it up for Rebecca to see. "I just got this from Raymond. A new one: Project Black Diamond. Looks like an interesting deal. Are you on it?" She tilted her head and arched her brows as she spoke. "I hope we're working together again. "

But a fleeting look of disappointment crossed Rebecca's face as she reached for the file, and Amalise slid it over to her. Rebecca picked it up, glanced at the label, and began flipping through the pages. When she looked up, her expression was inscrutable.

Amalise sat back, a little unsettled. She flipped a pencil from hand to hand wondering what Rebecca was thinking. "It's Doug Bastion's transaction. First Merchant Bank—"

"I know." Rebecca closed the folder and handed it back. "The whole firm's talking about this one. It's a financing. A resort hotel, I've heard." She pushed back her chair and rose. "But that's just through the grapevine. Everyone's being very secretive."

Amalise blinked, looking up. "Then you're not on it?" They'd always worked together on transactions.

Rebecca hiked one shoulder. "It seems not. Looks like you got the baby."

Amalise grimaced. One of those tiny plastic baby dolls that bakers insisted on hiding in Mardi Gras King Cakes as a prize had gotten stuck in her throat once. Mama had pulled it out, but she'd had a sore throat for days.

Amalise shook her head. "I'm disappointed. I was hoping . . ."

Rebecca folded her arms. "We're not the baby lawyers anymore, Amalise. Our time's more valuable now. Three new associates started in September while you were gone." She leaned forward, bracing her hands on the desk, lowering her voice. "And one of them's a woman."

Amalise's eyes widened. "That's great!"

Rebecca sat back again, raised her hands and yanked the pencil from her hair, letting the curls fall loose around her shoulders. A worm of envy crawled through Amalise at that moment, thinking again of Jude.

"Her name's Sydney Martin. " Rebecca tipped back her head and shook out her hair. "You'll like her. Let's take her to lunch one day soon."

"Yes, let's do that."

But when their eyes met, she saw something in Rebecca's that told her other things had changed while she was gone, too. Friends or not, they'd suddenly become competitors for the best work in the firm. Eventually, perhaps, for a partnership.

And, it suddenly occurred to her—maybe even for Jude.

Rebecca smiled, rose, and flicked her hand in the air as she turned toward the door. "This is good for you, this transaction. You'll show everyone you've bounced back, just like we knew you would."

"Thanks."

As she reached the door, Rebecca turned. Leaning back into the office with one hand on the door and one foot poised for flight, she looked at Amalise. "That deal's moving fast, though, I'll warn you. They're planning to close Thanksgiving week. Are you up to that? Jude's worried you've come back too soon."

Amalise straightened, stretched her arms down the arms of the chair and smiled. "Sure I am," she said firmly.

Rebecca nodded. "Well let me know if you need help. I'm working on a transaction that's stalled right now. Things are slow."

Amalise smiled and nodded. "I'll call you if an opportunity comes up."

Rebecca held herself erect as she strode down the hallway from Amalise's office, arms swinging by her side. With a smile for Ashley Elizabeth, Amalise's secretary, she focused on the middle distance, a signal to the world that she was deep in thought and not to be disturbed. She turned the corner at the end of the hallway and, three doors down, entered her own office.

There, she closed the door softly and leaned back against it, squeezing her eyes shut. She had hoped for the Black Diamond assignment from the moment she'd heard that the firm had been hired to represent the lending group, the syndicate. But Raymond had mentioned earlier, casually, as if it were nothing important, that Amalise had been chosen instead. She didn't really know what she'd thought she might accomplish by voicing her desire to work on the transaction with Amalise, but she just *had* to work on this deal!

She opened her eyes and with a shudder, pushed off the door. Frowning, she crossed the room and dropped into her chair. How had it happened that Doug Bastion had picked Amalise right out of her sickbed for this project? This was the plum. The prize. Project Black Diamond was the biggest piece of work the firm had won in a year, a definite show-case piece for a young associate.

Rebecca dropped her face into her hands. She was the one who'd worked nights, weekends, and holidays all through the hot summer months while Amalise was home recuperating. She hadn't complained when Jude had spent his time off from Pilottown eighty miles away in Marianus. She glanced at the photograph of Jude that she kept on her desk. Yes, she understood, given the circumstances of the accident. And, of course, Amalise was his childhood friend. Amalise had introduced the two of them.

Still . . .

Rebecca felt a flush of guilt thinking of her friend this way. She stiffened, chastising herself. But then again, she was the one who'd spent days doing due diligence in that steaming warehouse in Atlanta in the middle of August because Raymond had wanted to go on vacation. And she was the one who sent flowers to Preston's wife when he'd announced last month that twins were on the way.

And, really, Amalise didn't have Rebecca's presence, her style. She opened the drawer where she kept her purse and pulled out a mirror. Holding it up, she stared at her reflection. She'd seen Doug watching her in the conference room last week. Not that he'd ever acknowledge an attraction. Smiling to herself, she touched each corner of her lips. She pushed back a strand of hair and thought, not for the first time, that her skin looked flawless even under the ubiquitous fluorescent lights.

With a prick of conscience, she stuck the mirror back in the drawer and slammed it shut. Amalise was still her friend. She pressed the button for her secretary's desk. Perhaps there were messages waiting. Maybe one of them would be from Doug Bastion, asking her to work with the team on Black Diamond. They could be the Silver Girls again. They could work on the project together.

"No messages," her secretary said.

❦

The phone on the credenza behind Amalise buzzed as Rebecca disappeared. Amalise swiveled and pressed the red blinking button connecting her phone to Ashley Elizabeth's desk, hoping this was the call she'd been waiting for.

"Doug Bastion wants to see you in his office right away."

"Thanks." Amalise grinned. She gathered up the file and a clean yellow legal pad to write on. Someone rapped on the door double time.

Raymond was standing in the hallway, arms braced between the door frames. "Hey. Welcome back. Doug wants us in his office *tout suite.* Preston's on his way."

"Okay, okay." Amalise shoved back her chair and stood. Smoothing her jacket and skirt, she raked her fingers through her hair, and grabbed the file, the legal pad, and two sharpened pencils. "I haven't had time to read anything. What's this one about?" she asked, hurrying to keep up with Raymond's long stride.

"Don't know the details yet. Something about a hotel or a resort." Rounding the corner, they passed the long row of secretaries' desks just outside the lawyers' offices.

The elevator took them two floors up to eighteen, where the senior partners had offices and the conference rooms were located. As they entered Doug's office, he rose and came around from behind the antique desk, holding his arms wide. "Amalise! Good to have you back." He took her hands in his and studied her face, assessing his investment. "You're all right, then."

She nodded, with an enthusiastic smile. "Ready to get to work."

Releasing her, Doug rubbed his hands together and motioned toward a large round table in a corner near the wall of windows. "Wonderful! Fine, that's fine. We'll sit over here."

Amalise took a scat while gazing out at the vista she loved, the power view. As in the main conference room, Doug's office looked over the business district, Canal Street, the French Quarter, and to the far right, a portion of the river. From here she could see where the Mississippi began to curve around the Quarter near the old Jax Brewery. She smiled to herself, remembering the small apartment she'd lived in during law school, only a few blocks from there, off Jackson Square.

Preston strolled into the room, tapped Amalise on the shoulder, and said, "Welcome back," as he pulled out a chair and sat.

When they were all settled, Doug took a chair with the sun to his back, crossed his arms, stretched his legs out before him, and looked around. "Ever heard of Bingham Murdoch?" No one had. "You'll meet him soon." A mysterious smile crossed his face. "He's a character. A player. Got big plans for this city, and we're going to make them happen. We represent the bank lenders, a syndicate led by First Merchant Bank. The borrower is a Delaware corporation, Lone Ranger, Incorporated, wholly owned at the present time by Bingham Murdoch." He looked at Preston. "Morgan Klemp brought the deal to First Merchant through Tom Hannigan. Murdoch is Tom's contact. You know Tom, Preston."

Preston nodded. "I've worked with him before."

Doug flipped the gold Cross pen he held and caught it in the palm of his hand. "Initially, we're financing a construction project—a resort hotel, thirty-three stories. And later on," he shrugged, "when the time's right, maybe more. Our clients, the senior lenders, are committing four million under a one-year bridge loan and three million revolving-credit working capital for three years." He looked around. No one spoke, and he went on.

"Actual purchase of the properties and construction will be financed by twenty million in fifteen-year convertible notes. The borrower is Lone

Ranger. The notes are subordinated to the syndicate's senior debt, of course, but will be guaranteed by Lone Ranger's Cayman Island subsidiary."

He gave Preston a look. "Murdoch's in charge of the companies until the closing. At the closing, he resigns and Robert Black from Morgan Klemp takes over. Murdoch earns a good-sized placement fee, I presume. Tom Hannigan and Robert Black have put together a group of investors for the subordinated notes, and they're putting in their own money too."

Preston scribbled something on his notepad.

"Tom Hannigan's team will handle the investors' documents, although we'll assure they're consistent with our bank syndicate agreements. Raymond," he pointed his pen at Raymond, "stay on top of their placement memorandum when they draft it."

Raymond nodded.

Amalise listened, elated. Representing the financing of a major new hotel in the city right now was job security for an associate. With the economy waffling and investors walking a tightrope after the summer slowdown, the firm would go all out for this one. Oil prices were still jacked up, and unemployment hovered around seven percent, so this was a coup for Mangen & Morris.

"Preston, get someone on the environmental work right away," Doug continued. "I understand Murdoch's contractor is handling permits, so coordinate with him as well." He looked around. "And whatever plans any of you have for the next six weeks, including Thanksgiving, cancel them." Doug gave Amalise a quick glance. She nodded, setting aside thoughts of Mama's certain reaction back home in Marianus.

Doug leaned forward, bracing his arms on the table. "All right, now. Bingham Murdoch is somewhat of a mystery. Like I said, he's Tom's friend, Morgan Klemp's contact. Low key, shuns publicity. Tom says he's a silent investor behind some major developments in the Florida Keys, California, and Atlanta." He paused for an instant and leaned back. "There's some talk casino gambling's on the way down here. This hotel would be the perfect fit."

Raymond rolled his eyes. "Legalized gambling won't be permitted in Louisiana."

Preston hunched forward. "Look around you, Raymond. Been out to the track lately? You can hardly find a seat in the stands. And the state needs the revenues. It's inevitable."

"We're getting ahead of ourselves." Doug gave Raymond and Preston a look. "What happens with the hotel in the future isn't our concern. Not yet. So keep the speculation to yourselves. Frank Earl Blanton at First Merchant got the pitch exclusively, and he's impressed with Morgan Klemp's presentation as it stands. He doesn't want to bring up the subject of a casino just yet." His eyes swept the table. "This project is highly confidential. Soon as we close, Lone Ranger will begin purchasing business and residential property in the target area under agents' names. If word gets out, it could inflate prices, slow down negotiations."

He looked about and everyone nodded.

"So." Doug straightened in the chair and shot his sleeves. "We have to be circumspect, move fast. Make this happen."

Preston clasped his hands on the table and studied them. "What's our target date for closing?"

Doug's brows flattened. "Murdoch insists on the last business day before Thanksgiving. He's got something else going after that, Tom says." He flipped open a leather calendar and studied it. Stabbed his finger on a date, thought about it a minute, then looked up. "That's six weeks away. November twenty-third." His voice hardened as he pushed the calendar aside. "The firm has given assurances that we can meet that schedule." Leaning back, he spread his arms over the back of his chair and looked around. "Any questions?"

"What's the location?"

There was a split-second hesitation before Doug answered. His tone held a touch of defiance. "It's a portion of the Marigny District, between Esplanade, Royal, and Elysian Fields."

Amalise stopped writing and looked up. She couldn't have heard right.

The room had fallen silent. The Faubourg Marigny was a piece of history, the first area settled in New Orleans back in the early 1800s. Almost an extension of the French Quarter, the area was colorful, eclectic, though run down in parts, one had to admit. The portion of the district that Doug described was a triangle of small businesses and wooden cottages, old architecture, the kind of neighborhood beloved by the city. Besides homes, there were funky shops, blues bars, sidewalk cafes, a park, and several good restaurants in that corner of the Marigny.

Amalise tried to hide her distress. She couldn't imagine the place being demolished to build a gaudy hotel that would loom over the French Quarter.

"You'll recall, of course, that this is confidential information." Doug's voice was firm.

Raymond pushed out his bottom lip. He tapped a pencil on his notepad. "Ah, isn't the Marigny designated historical in the National Register?

It should be, Amalise thought.

"No. And the project permits are set. That's under control. It's not a concern at this point."

Raymond looked down and began writing, and Amalise took a deep breath.

Doug stood, adjusting his tie. "Let me remind you all. There's a lot riding on this for the firm. And for us." He leaned over and braced himself, hands flat on the conference table. "Any more questions?" The question was a dare.

No one spoke.

"Good then. That's all." Doug straightened, shot his cuffs, and strode across the room toward his desk. "Preston." He picked up a piece of paper from his desk and waved it in the direction of the table. "Here are the parameters of the financing, the deal points. We'll meet with Frank Earl Blanton from First Merchant Bank at one, and after that, I'll need you to draft a term sheet."

"Right."

"Amalise and Ray?"

Their heads popped up.

"You two check out the status of Lone Ranger and the sub. Check public records in Cayman, Delaware, Louisiana. Run a search. Get organizational records, the usual. And check SEC filings, check the *Reporters* and litigation reports. Find whatever you can on the companies." He frowned and ran his hand across his forehead. "And see what you can find on Murdoch too. We don't know much about him. Morgan Klemp's bringing him to the table, but let's do a little of our own due diligence. Just basic background."

Chapter Three

JUDE SAT AT A TABLE WAITING for Amalise. On the phone earlier, Rebecca said she had looked fine when she'd seen her this morning and that Amalise had already been put on a major transaction. He'd caught a hint of something in Rebecca's voice that he'd not heard before. A touch of discontent, or disappointment maybe. He wondered if Amalise's new assignment was the same transaction Rebecca had been talking about all week, the one she wanted to work on. If so, she would find a way to get assigned to it too, he'd wager. This was a big deal for the firm, she'd said, road-to-partnership material for an associate.

Jude glanced at his watch. It was eight o'clock. Franky & Johnny's was slow tonight. He wondered how Amalise had managed on her first day back. She'd been ill for so long. He pressed his hands over his eyes and slid them down his cheeks, fingers splayed as the memories intruded. Jude saw himself behind the wheel, peering down the narrow dirt road, searching the darkness for Amalise—and for Phillip, who he knew would harm her. Suddenly Amalise had appeared from around the curve, looming in the beams of his headlights. He'd slammed on the brakes, the car skidding toward her.

He could still see the terror in her eyes just before she fell.

Jude had stumbled from the car, fallen to his knees, and gathered her to him, praying, willing her to live—desperately *willing* her blood to pump on through her veins—realizing in that moment that he wouldn't want to live without her. The understanding of what it would mean to lose Amalise had hit him then like a blow to his solar plexus, a bludgeoning glimpse of long gray years ahead without her.

He'd known then that he loved Amalise Catoir. He'd loved her since they were children, but this feeling was new, transformative—different from the way he'd felt with any other. This was something deeper, more profound.

He hadn't told her yet. Soon he would. He longed to tell her, and not for the first time he wondered how it would feel to kiss this girl whom he'd practically helped to raise. But Amalise was no longer a girl. She was a woman now—and a widow.

In the time they had spent together during her recuperation, it had been tempting just to lay things out for her, to tell her how he felt. But better judgment had prevailed. Not while she was on the mend and still vulnerable. Remembering Phillip. Remembering that night.

So he'd kept silent. So far. Waiting for just the right time.

Tonight she'd be focused on her return to work. He glanced around at the room, at the other customers, the bright lights overhead, the linoleum floors. No. Not yet, but soon. A pit lodged in his stomach at the thought. *How do you tell your oldest friend that you're in love with her?*

He steepled his hands and tipped his fingers against his lips. Years of piloting ships over the sandbars in the passes south of the river had taught him how to navigate dangerous currents and ghost-like shoals. He studied the soundings, the weather, reports from other pilots. The ships were equipped with radar to guide the way. But even with that wealth of information at hand, still he knew that the surest decisions were those based on experience—the touch of the wheel, the feel of the keel, and the chop of the Gulf.

The waitress arrived and he shook his head. "I'm waiting for someone," he said, and she disappeared. His fingers rap-tapped the tabletop in a rhythm only he could hear. Seconds passed, then he sat back in the chair, arms stretched out before him. Cacophonous sounds of madness came from the kitchen nearby, a clashing of pots and pans and ribald laughter. The jukebox blared. Behind the bar a glass shattered.

He looked up and over his shoulder saw Amalise enter the restaurant. Her face lit when she saw him. She waved and smiled, and her confident stride told him everything he needed to know. She'd weathered her first day back. He lifted his hand and pushed back his chair.

She slipped off her coat, and he took it from her, laying it across an empty chair. "You look great," he said as she raised up on her toes to plant a kiss on his cheek. Without thinking he stepped back and away. Things were different now.

She gave him a fleeting curious look as he pulled out a chair for her, and she sat. "It's windy out there," she said. She turned her face up to his as she brushed back her hair. Strands of fine, dark silk hair drifted barely to her shoulders, so different from Rebecca's long red curls. Men turned to watch Rebecca. But Amalise . . . if they only knew. Amalise was the one to watch.

He smiled and sat down beside her. "Weather's coming in. But we're in the middle of October, chère, and hurricane season's almost over. And best of all," he leaned over and patted her arm, "you've escaped the doctors at last."

She gave him a wide smile. "First day back on the job, Jude. Done."

Checking off her list. "Was it difficult?"

"No. It's as if I'd never been gone." She fluffed her hair with both hands and looked around the room.

Jude caught the waitress's eye and signaled her.

Forearms squared on the table, Amalise leaned forward. Her eyes sparkled. Her tone was triumphant. "I've been put on one of Doug's deals. They want to close before Thanksgiving, so it will move fast."

"That sounds restful. It's what any doctor would prescribe for a patient who's been laid up for months with a concussion and partial amnesia."

She threw up her hands. "I know."

He smiled. She was healthy at last and happy. *Thank you.*

Reaching for the basket at the center of the table, she pulled out a saltine cracker wrapped in plastic. "I couldn't have handled one more day as an invalid, Jude, wanting to get back to the city. To hear the sound of streetcars, to be part of the crowds downtown. To work, to eat in busy restaurants."

Absently he watched her fighting with the plastic paper around the cracker, twisting the corners.

"Not that I don't like Marianus," she added quickly. "But I've got to catch up now."

"Catch up to what?" Jude took the cracker from her, tore the wrapper off, and handed it back. He eyed her as she bit into the cracker. Amalise's calendar wasn't like others'. For her, days were mile markers. Life was a race, though he wasn't sure of the goal.

The waitress appeared and handed them menus. "Iced tea, please." Amalise tilted up her face. "Unsweetened. Plenty of ice. Plenty of lemon."

The waitress nodded. Hand on her hip, she eyed Jude's empty glass. "Same for me," he said, and she picked up the glass.

When she'd gone, Amalise lifted the menu and scanned it. "I'm restless, Jude. Since the accident, I've felt an urge, a need to do something with my life that's . . ." She gave him a self-conscious look. "I don't know. Something that's lasting, I suppose. Something with a clear purpose." She set the menu down and leaned toward him, looking at him. "But I don't know what it is."

He watched as she unwrapped the napkin from around the knife and fork, placed the napkin across her lap and the flatware side by side on the table. He sensed that something had changed in her after the accident, early on while she was still in the hospital. She'd confided in him in those early days that her brush with death, and what she called this second chance, made her understand more deeply the value of life. She wasn't afraid of death, she'd said. She knew what lay beyond. But now she thought there was a reason that God, her Abba, had spared her—for a purpose she didn't yet understand.

He entertained the notion of suggesting that life was meant for love. He longed to put his hands on her shoulders so she'd have to look straight into his eyes, and then he would explain how the friendship they'd shared for so many years had—for him—grown into something else that would last a lifetime. He wanted Amalise and children and a home.

But it was too soon. So instead he slung an arm over the back of his chair and half-turned to her and said, "What about your job? Isn't that enough?"

"Oh, I love practicing law. I'd never think of giving that up." She laughed at herself. When the iced tea arrived, she squeezed lemon into her drink. Sliding the sugar bowl over, she added two teaspoons to the tea and stirred. "I was like a sponge in law school, you know, soaking everything up." She looked at him. "But you come out of it thinking differently, analyzing problems in a new way."

Jude dropped his arm and turned back with a sideways look. "Yes. I saw that in your relationship with Phillip."

Instantly he regretted the sarcasm. For a split second she looked down, gave all of her attention to unwrapping a straw, sliding the paper down, rumpling it. She tossed it at Jude.

He shouldn't have joked. "I'm sorry for that, Amalise."

She nodded and he watched as she moved the fork closer to her plate. Slid the knife parallel again. "I know. Don't worry." She looked up. "But sometimes thinking of Phillip makes me wonder how I got so far off the path."

Amalise didn't give into moods often. Even at the worst times of her marriage to Phillip, she'd seemed able to compartmentalize, to set worries aside and enjoy a good moment.

Jude straightened. Reaching across the table, he nudged her chin with his knuckle and put more gusto than he felt at this moment into his voice. "Let's change the subject. This is your first day back at work. Take things easy for a while and have fun."

She picked up another cracker and, without fighting the plastic wrapper this time, handed it to him. He opened it, crushed the paper, and handed the cracker back. "You're on a great transaction, Rebecca says. Be thankful for the good things."

"I will." She bit into the cracker and looked at him, and his heart melted at the trust in her eyes. "After Phillip died, I suddenly understood how important it is to get things right." With a wan smile, she added, "But sometimes I'm still a little blue."

The only times he could remember Amalise sinking into gloom were the last few years of the Vietnam War, when they were assaulted every night with scenes of young soldiers fighting and dying, the brave and scarred, the dead, the wounded, night after night. Misery was all around, it seemed, tightening about the nation like chains. Jude closed his eyes, remembering the lottery for the draft. In the beginning, planted in front of the television, waiting for the numbers to be drawn, they had been struck dumb with helplessness by the randomness of it all. If your number was pulled, you were shipped out to those jungles. He'd been one of the lucky ones.

Then came the news of American troops withdrawing from Southeast Asia. The images were powerful, imprinted forever on the minds of his generation. Worse was the memory of the many left behind—numerous of America's own, the dead and captured South Vietnamese who had fought alongside them, and the most vulnerable, the elderly and the children of a war-torn land. The shadow children, Amalise had called them, orphans struggling to survive in the burning villages of Vietnam and Cambodia. Cambodia had simply vanished under a black veil in 1975 after the Khmer Rouge moved in. The killing fields, they were calling them now. Amalise had never been able to forget.

She sat silent beside him now in Franky & Johnny's, waiting for some kind of response. He sipped his iced tea. It was the futility that had gotten her down the most back then, he thought, problems that were too big to solve, even for a girl who'd grown up thinking she could fix anything given enough effort. Amalise could do nothing but watch. That was the blessing and curse of nightly television news.

He remembered one Thanksgiving in Marianus—1974, he thought it was. They'd had a long day, a good meal followed by an afternoon of fishing together. The Judge had gone to bed, and Amalise had disappeared to her room to study, so he'd thought. He'd shooed Amalise's mother, Maraine, off to bed. He could see how tired she was. He told her he'd clean up the kitchen before going home. Maraine had given him a grateful look with those eyes of hers, so like Amalise, and then she'd kissed his cheek and patted his shoulder and disappeared.

But when he finished the dishes, turned out the kitchen light, and headed for the door, he'd halted as he entered the darkened living room lit only by the flickering glow of the television set. Amalise was curled up in the cushioned armchair the Judge claimed as his own, alone, eyes riveted to the pictures on the silent screen, the orphaned children of the wars on the other side of the world, children searching the midday sky in eerie silence for the Air America planes to come and leave pallets of food on the airstrip.

He'd moved toward her and then halted when he realized that she was weeping. Her lips were moving. She was praying for those children in the shadows of the war, he realized. As she swiped tears from her cheeks with the heel of her hand, he'd backed out of the private moment before she saw him. He left through the back door.

Jude looked at her now. She was searching for meaning and purpose, wanting to get things right this time. But with all that had happened in the past two years . . . well, it was no wonder she felt a little down.

So he sat up straight while he formed the words she was waiting for, hands clasped before him, conscious that she watched him carefully, as she'd always done. He gave her a reflective look. "You've had a hard time the last few years, chère, between Phillip and everything else. But it's time to let old problems go, to put them in God's hands." He slid his own hands over the table so that their fingertips met.

She nodded but didn't say anything.

"Well, here's my advice for what it's worth." He paused. "Take each day as it comes. Use the mind God gave you, keep the faith, and you'll make right decisions." He shrugged. "If there's more . . . if you're meant for a particular purpose, you'll know it when you see it." He gave her a long look.

She slid her hands back into her lap. "All right."

Fighting the urge to pull her into his arms and comfort her, he let out a short laugh. "Prioritize," he said. "You've always been good at that."

A smile broke through. Seconds passed, then she leaned back, drawing in a long breath. "I'm starving. I'll have red beans and rice."

He pushed his own menu aside. He had it memorized by now.

"What are you having?" she asked.

"A bowl of gumbo."

"That's all?"

He laughed. "You'll order enough for two. I'll have some of yours."

When the waitress returned, Amalise ordered red beans and rice with sausage and ham, French bread on the side with garlic butter, and greens. He watched, amused, wondering again how she managed to stay slim.

She caught his look. There hadn't been time for lunch, she said. Bundling his menu with hers, she handed them to the waitress, and settled back. "When do you leave for Pilottown?"

"I've got a while." And he wasn't sorry about that because he needed time. He planned to tell her everything before he left. He envisioned the isolated hamlet where he lived with the other pilots on watch two weeks out of every month at the mouth of the Mississippi. Usually he loved the place, but recently it had begun to strike him as lonely.

Amalise sipped her tea and passed on the latest news from work. Her secretary, Ashley Elizabeth, had found a new boyfriend and was still playing tennis. Preston's wife was having twins, due in February. Raymond was billing seventy hours a week on a regular basis now, he bragged. He was up for partner year after next.

"Will Rebecca be working on this transaction with you?"

"No." She looked at him from under lowered lids. "That was a surprise. We've always worked together before." She stirred her tea and took a sip. "I guess our time's more expensive now after a year at the firm, so they'll split us up and use newer lawyers for the work we used to do together." She smiled. "Rebecca called it the 'drone work.'"

"Well that's too bad. I know she wanted it too."

Amalise nodded. "I could tell that. And she's right, this is an important project."

He hooked his arm over the back of the chair and let his eyes roam. He'd have to clear things up with Rebecca soon. He knew where things stood with her, though, unlike with Amalise. Rebecca was consumed with her work, her career. And she hadn't seemed fazed when he'd spent most of his off-duty time over the past few months in Marianus, helping the Judge and Maraine with Amalise, instead of staying in the city.

The waitress arrived, and Jude realized that Amalise had continued detailing her day at work and he'd lost track of the conversation. He knew she was working her way back to the sun as she talked in that excited, revved-up way, and half-listening, he made all the right sounds while looking for signs that she might have reentered the fray too soon. The doctors had been split on that decision, so she'd made it herself.

But he shifted his attention to the thick, fragrant gumbo when the waitress set it down before him. The gumbo was dark and spicy, thick with chicken, okra, and Andouille sausage. He ate and watched as Amalise scooped up the red beans and rice as though she hadn't eaten in a week.

She looked at him. "Is the gumbo good as Mama's?"

"Not a chance." He leaned over and scooped a bite of beans and rice from her plate. Savored it for a moment. Nodded. "That's good."

Amalise gave him a sideways look, fork hovering over the plate. "The schedule on this deal will be grueling, but I'm excited about being on the team."

He glanced at her and worked the worry from his expression. Their earlier conversation still lingered. Still, he couldn't help but ask the question. "You sure you're ready for this?"

"Yep." Lifting the glass of tea, she smiled. "I've got energy to spare after all that bed rest. I've stored up my nuts for the winter."

He looked at her, thinking of the squirrels darting over the branches of the oak tree just outside Amalise's bedroom window in Marianus. Year after year they scurried around preparing their nests for winter, and the next year they did it all over again. Again and again, an endless circle in the same old search.

He bent over the bowl of gumbo. Amalise was looking for something more than that, as she'd made clear. If she was right, she'd find out what that was in time. Perhaps her purpose in life would end up having something to do with those shadow children, the ones she'd fixed on in Phnom Penh back in '75.

Chapter Four

Phnom Penh, Cambodia 1975

SAMANTHA BARLOW LOOKED UP AS THE office door opened and Oliver Murna walked in. Outside the U.S. Embassy she could hear panic rising in the street, shrill voices and the incomprehensible chatter that came with terror and the unknown—shouts, curses, screams. In the distance she could hear the muffled sound of artillery fire. Refugees came on foot, in oxcarts, rickshaws, automobiles, Jeeps, trucks, all pushing into the city and jamming things up, stirring the dust, stirring the fear. President Lon Nol had fled weeks ago. Wealthy families had followed. Politicians, foreigners, even some of the aid workers had left.

"Roads are blocked." Oliver shut the door behind him and lowered his voice. "We're leaving, Sam. Evacuating."

"When?"

"Three hours. That's all the time we've got, and there are only two planes. Not much room." He looked at her and repeated, "We have only three hours."

Impossible. "At the airport?"

"No. Pochentong's already shut down, under fire." His face shone with perspiration as he gave her directions to an old airstrip outside the city. He stuck his hands in his pockets, walked to the window, and gazed at the mass of humanity streaming toward the center of Phnom Penh. When he turned back, she saw the fear in his eyes.

"The Khmer Rouge are moving in. We're cutting it close, Sam. Now look," he crossed his arms and locked his eyes on hers, "if you're not there . . ." He jutted his chin out. "You have to be there on time. I'd go with you now, but there's too much to be done here, so you'll have to make it on your own. Don't pack much—just the essentials."

She nodded.

"I'll be waiting for you at the airfield. But you will be left if you're not there in three hours when the planes take off. It's not me—there are others." He paused. "Do you understand?"

She nodded again and stood. Her heart was racing; she couldn't think. She'd read of the atrocities. The Khmer Rouge were mindlessly cruel. She waved her hand over the room. "The records a-a-and the families."

"We're taking care of things here. We'll burn what we can't bring. Just make sure you get to the airstrip on time." He glanced at his watch. "It's two o'clock now."

His words were like pieces of a jigsaw puzzle she couldn't put together. She'd thought they'd have weeks to prepare if evacuation became necessary. "And what about them?" She turned her head to the window behind her, to the thousands crowding the streets outside the embassy gate. "What about the families? The children? We can't leave them behind."

He lowered his eyes. She watched in silence as he seemed to gather himself, and when he looked back up at her, his face was hard, unreadable, his lips pressed into a straight, tight line. "Orders, Sam. No one else comes along. We have limited space. U.S. citizens only." His eyes gleamed moist, and he turned away toward the door. "You have to keep this to yourself. And remember, no more than one bag—a small one."

"What about CARE? USAID?"

He stopped and nodded. "They're evacuating, too. Some are coming with us." He turned back and fixed his eyes on her again. "The planes lift off at five. No one else, Sam, I mean it. If you bring others, they won't get on. It'll only make things harder if you do. More difficult for everyone."

She stood behind the desk, dazed, as he closed the door. Three hours to pack, to leave Cambodia forever, to leave behind the hundreds of people who depended on her for food, clothing, and medicine. Once she left, there'd be no contact with the outside world for these people she'd come to love. She had prayed this time would never arrive. Honestly, she'd never been able to contemplate the possibility and couldn't bear to think of it now.

Samantha pulled her purse from a drawer in the desk. She closed the folder she'd been working on, lists of thousands desperate for help, the elderly, the sick, the hungry, the lost, and all the new ones flooding into the city every day just ahead of the approaching army. She imagined the Khmer Rouge, now just hours away, imagined their relentless march toward Phnom Penh, swarming like an army of red ants over everything and everyone in their path.

She didn't know if she could do this. She would be abandoning everyone here who needed her.

Her hand rested on the folder for a moment, and the words of the report came back to her. The pillaging of villages, rape, torture, murder. Slowly she lifted her hand. She was afraid to stay. She was a coward, she realized.

Digging into her purse, Sam pulled out her wallet. Whatever money she had would go to someone that needed it. She opened the wallet and counted out riel notes. She had only the equivalent of about ten U.S. dollars of her own, not even enough to buy passage out of the city to get to the airfield.

Her eyes lit on an envelope on her desk that had arrived two days ago. Inside was a stack of worn ten-dollar bills, U.S. currency. One hundred dollars cash. Who would send cash through the mail like that, addressed to no one particular, just U.S. Embassy, Phnom Penh, Cambodia? It was a fluke that it had arrived intact. *To be used to help the children*, the note had said, with no signature.

She snatched up the envelope, glanced at the name and address on the back, and stuffed it into her purse. With a last glance at the folder on the desk, Sam turned and walked toward the door, struggling to hold on, not to let the horror reach into her soul because if it did, she would surely fall apart.

Not yet. Not yet.

Samantha exited the gates of the U.S. Embassy and ran into the swarm of humanity at the corner of Norodom and Sothearos Boulevards. She looked around before pushing into the crowd. Bodies shoved her one way and then the other. Hot sun. Dust. A fury of sharp elbows, knees, hands shoving, pushing. Children wailed, and women wept. Men with empty faces, knowing eyes, pushed forward. The Khmer Rouge were coming.

A bicycle rammed past, and she moved aside just in time, clutching the purse as she pushed into the bicycle's draft before the crowd could close around her again. The body heat and stench were smothering. Her toe struck a cement curbstone and she tripped, caught her balance, and fought her way onto the sidewalk, moving against the surge of humanity. Suddenly she was pressed against a building by the panicked crowd moving in the other direction, and she flattened herself against it, catching her breath.

After a moment the crush lessened. Samantha straightened, took a deep breath, and looked back through the crowd at the embassy gates across the street, to the building beyond. Tears rolled down her cheeks as she thought of all that she was leaving behind.

And then a small hand slipped into hers, curling to fit her palm.

Sam started and looked down. A child stood beside her, staring straight ahead into the crowd. No more than three feet tall, he stood there pressing against her leg. She gripped her purse—children could be vandals, too, in this city. But the child only clung to her hand not moving or looking at her or speaking. After a moment, she stooped, sitting on her heels, twisting so that she faced him.

He looked at her, expressionless.

"Hello," she said in Khmer. She was proficient after five years here.

He was silent. She tried again. "Are you lost? Where's your family?"

As if afraid she'd leave, he inched closer, still grasping her hand. He was thin, like a bag of fragile sticks, but as with all children alone in this city, his belly was round and distended.

"Where is your mother? Your family?"

But she saw no flicker of recognition. His eyes were flat, emotionless. In them she saw no reflection of happier days—not even questions or hope. She looked around for someone to claim him, but no one seemed to notice them standing there. Every face, every mind was focused on one thing only: survival.

Sam shifted her purse, feeling hysteria rise. *Oh God, oh God. Tell me what to do now. What do I do with this child? I can't leave him alone in this mob, fodder for the Khmer Rouge. And I can't take him with me. What do I do?*

Glancing at her watch, she saw twenty minutes had passed since she'd left the office. She closed her eyes. Two hours and forty minutes, that's all that was left to get home to retrieve things she couldn't leave without—some photographs, some jewelry that Mother had left when she passed on—precious things.

Artillery fire in the distance startled her, and she opened her eyes, suddenly realizing the enormity of her problem. She might not even make it through this frenzied mob to reach the airstrip by five o'clock. Meanwhile, the Khmer Rouge army continued to push forward into the city.

She stood, preparing to flee, preparing to work her hand free of the child's. She refused to let her mind dwell on this. She would *do it,* leave the child right here, sheltering against the wall. As if reading her mind, the boy tightened his grip. She fell back against the cement wall again and stared at the embassy building across the street, feeling the fragile, bird-like bones in her hand. She knew she couldn't leave him behind, and there were only two hours and forty minutes left before the last plane took off from Phnom Penh.

The minute hand was ticking, and still the child clung to her.

Chapter Five

New Orleans—1977

BINGHAM LOOKED AROUND THE ROOM AND smiled to himself.
The first meeting for Project Black Diamond. Two lawyers from Mangen
& Morris were there representing the group of banks that would finance
the venture, and another lawyer, Adam Grayson, had just arrived from
New York to represent Robert Black and the other investors. And, of
course, there was Robert. They were in the Mangen & Morris offices, in
a conference room on the eighteenth floor. The large corner room was
bright with sunshine streaming in through the row of windows.

"Gentlemen," he said in a cheerful tone. He stuck his hand out
on the table, arm stretched, loose fisted. "We're going to scatter some
stardust over the city of New Orleans. From what I understand, this
is a town that likes a little glitter. When we're finished, this tower, this
hotel that we're building, will be the first thing everyone sees when they
drive into town. You'll be able to see it from every point in the city." He
gestured toward a long roll of paper on the table next to Robert. "Take a
look at the architect's drawings when you have a minute, and you'll see
what I mean."

The bankers and lawyers looked back at him, expressionless—one of their specialties, he thought. Most of them were men with no imagination, no sense of adventure, and except for Robert, no appreciation for the thrill of embarking on a new venture. He'd be glad when Tom Hannigan got down here. Now *there* was a young man who saw things in the right light.

His eyes stopped on the lead lawyer for Mangen & Morris and the bank group. Doug Bastion, a good Louisiana name. And next to him was his double—same suit, same tie, same smile. Bingham probed his memory for the name and came up with Preston Something-or-other.

Ah, well. He wasn't good with names. There were so many in the old cranium already, he'd have to get rid of some. Details were Robert's job. Cold, precise Robert—Morgan Klemp's finest, Tom had said when he'd introduced them back in New York. Robert who, ensconced in the investment banking department, was still too far down the food chain at Morgan Klemp to have qualified for the boondoggle down in Cayman. Far enough down, in fact, that he'd jumped at *this* opportunity.

Tom's rapid shift of loyalty from Morgan Klemp to his own investment in Black Diamond had amused Bingham at the time. Robert would run the hotel, Tom had argued, and later on, the casino. Bingham thought this was a good choice. Robert had two invaluable qualifications for the job: a killer instinct for business and zero empathy. And Robert had a long memory—unlike Bingham, he could take a name and a face and impress them on his mind forever.

Robert handed him a draft of the term sheet, the principal business points, that Mangen & Morris had prepared. Five pages, stapled at the top left-hand corner. Bingham shuffled through the pages and set it down on the table before him. He had the contacts, the glitz to get things done, and—he smiled to himself—the connections. It was Robert's job to run the deal. Robert's ambition would carry them through the next six frantic weeks to the closing—he wanted that hotel and the power and money. The hotel would be built because Robert willed it. And later on, when gambling was voted in, Robert would have the casino and the tax-free skim off the top that would send him running down to Cayman every month to do his laundry. Ever since

Atlantic City had voted in legalized gambling last year, people had been looking at New Orleans.

But Bingham was the first one here.

Doug Bastion had agreed to the accelerated deadline he'd demanded. They'd be working hard, long hours and moving fast. Too bad they couldn't just sign a note and be done with it. Bingham looked at the term sheet Doug held up and sighed, imagining the number of documents these lawyers could generate in six weeks.

At Doug's instruction, everyone looked down at the first page of the so-called term sheet. Once the outline of the transaction was agreed upon and signed, work would begin in earnest. As they began to discuss the provisions, Bingham folded his arms and let the hum recede. The hotel was just the beginning. Gambling was the elephant in the room, although it wouldn't be mentioned in the documents. The impetus: bags of untraceable cash, if they handled it right.

Robert and Tom had rounded up the other investors. Dominick Costa, Bingham's contractor for the project, had reported on his talks with the men in the back rooms of the capitol building down in Baton Rouge. Gambling legislation was a sure thing, he said. Once Baton Rouge got on board with the idea of a casino in the hotel after the closing, Robert planned to call on the suits on Wall Street, the high-yield guys who could juice a sale of bonds even after the squeeze went dry.

Bingham smiled to himself. Every one of the investors thought they understood the economics of risk and reward. But this idea was *his* baby.

"Can you live with that?" Robert's voice broke into his thoughts. He and Frank Earl were arguing now about push-back from the investors against limits demanded by the more conservative bank lenders.

Robert nudged him, and he snapped to. "Can I live with what?" He picked up the term sheet and ran his eyes down the page.

Doug broke in. Cool. Controlled. "The banks, the Senior Lenders, are ready to sign the commitments on the terms you see here, assuming . . ." Doug shot a look at Robert, "assuming that the investors are fully subordinated. The bank's bridge loan is paid back first, in one year."

"One year?"

They began to argue again.

Bingham skimmed through the term sheet. They knew their business all right, but none of them really understood money. He'd set up his first Swiss franc account before these dollar-mongers had grown fuzz on their cheeks, before the franc had given the U.S. the old razoo and turned thumbs down on the international fixed exchange rate, even before the Swiss could slap a negative interest tax on their foreign accounts because the franc was the strongest currency in the world. Bingham calculated the appreciation in dollars of his current account in Swiss francs, up sixty-four percent since his first deposit, while inflation had devalued the U.S. dollar every year during the same period.

Not that he minded taking a walk on the wild side once in a while.

Robert turned a page of the term sheet, and Bingham backed up, following, looking at the acronyms and numbers on page after page. *Bankers.* He thought about the last time he was in Zurich in the cold sharp light, the brisk feel of the air so unlike this closed room slowly filling up with smoke. He'd like to be there right now. Or on the beach at Grand Cayman, where this whole thing began.

Pages turned again. Doug Bastion droned on, and Bingham suppressed a yawn. They'd go through the paces, tweak a provision here or there, argue over a word or two, but he knew this was a done deal. For the bankers, the fees were too good to pass up. For the investors—from the corner of his eye he studied Robert's expression, inscrutable now, but Bingham knew that Robert and the other investors hungered, truly hungered, for this hotel.

Beside him, Robert sat, back straight, ready to ignite, to push, to press, to trade right to the brink, if he had to.

The voices receded once more. Bingham's gaze wandered to the windows, and in his mind he saw the sun sliding over the clear green waters of the Caribbean, slowly deepening at the end of the day. Without thinking, he waved off a stream of smoke, inhaling to catch the scent of island air as he sat at the little thatched-roof bar on the beach, waiting for the Morgan Klemp bonus babies to show up.

That trip had paid more than he'd hoped. He'd done his homework on those year-end incentive trips awarded to Wall Street's top arbitrageurs, brokers, and corporate finance guys. Year-end cash bonuses were the bread of life for bankers like Robert and Tom. But the annual testosterone-fueled bonus boondoggle in the warm Caribbean at the height of winter in New York almost trumped the money for these guys. The trips were exclusive—only the big dogs were invited. Some, like Tom, got the company jet. They all got the ritziest hotels, all expenses paid. And best of all, there were no questions asked when they returned to the office a week later, suntanned, smiling, eager and pumped up, ready to tear back into the market.

The chosen few from Morgan Klemp had checked into the hotel a little after five, just off the plane. He'd spotted them when he'd walked up to the desk for his keys, and Marvin, the desk clerk had done the rest. One hundred bucks U.S. go a long way in the islands.

"Yes sir, I'll get right on it," Marvin had said to Bingham as the Morgan Klemp guys strutted up. "No sir, your secretary picked up the wires an hour ago." Marvin's face had crinkled then into that famous wide smile.

He'd strolled off slow enough to hear Marvin whispering to the new-comers, "That man, gentleman, is a genuine ghost, a man you won't often see around." He could feel their eyes boring into his back as he stood at the elevator door, waiting, and he didn't have to turn and watch to know what would happen next.

Essentially, they were salesmen, these deal-makers. They knew how to ask. And when they went on asking, Marvin would plant his elbows on the counter and lean toward them, looking contrite. "Sorry, I can't give out the name, sir," he'd say. "I could lose my job." Then, ducking his head, he'd lower his voice and tell how Murdoch's private security guards laid down the law when he came down, that he always took the presidential suite, no matter who was in the house at the time.

Then he'd wink, straighten up, turn around, and get their keys.

The bankers finally wandered through the open lobby and out onto the beach in their flip-flops around 5:30, blinking in the full glare of the beach, knobby knees exposed under their new shorts, their pale city skin turning pink on arrival.

Bingham was ready.

There were five of them, but he kept his half-closed eyes on the most gregarious of the group as they stumbled across the sand to the open bar. Tom took the empty stool beside him, and when someone commented on the straw hat Bingham wore, Bingham took it off and slapped it down on Tom's head.

Tom turned to him, surprised, and although they'd never met, there was species recognition in his eyes. Bingham saluted.

Tipping the hat to Bingham, Tom smiled and kept it on. Bingham had known he was picturing himself in that hat right then, as he'd done all year back in New York, dreaming of this trip, watching himself sitting under the thatched roof of the beach bar as if it were an out-of-body experience. Tom had ordered drinks all around.

Bingham bought the next round, ordering margaritas. Jimmy Buffet music was playing in the background—something about Havana—and Bingham said they all looked like they needed one. When the sun slipped to the horizon, the bankers fell silent. They were thinking of the snow and ice back home, he knew, and how good they had it here, how they'd earned this trip. They'd brag about it for the next twelve months, casually bringing it up in conversations with buddies who hadn't made the cut.

He spotted the glimmer in Tom's eyes an hour later when he mentioned his latest investment, a big development in Fort Lauderdale that got a write-up in the *Journal.* Another hotel on another lovely beach.

Tom remembered the story. "That was you?" He lifted his brows.

Bingham shrugged one shoulder and stared off to sea.

"Real estate's the way to go with inflation on the rise," Tom said. "I heard those bonds went fast. Did you use Milkin's boys?"

"I can't discuss it." Bingham said with a half smile. Tom nodded and pulled out his business card. Bingham took it, carefully turning it over, and read out loud, "Morgan Klemp, L.P." He looked at Tom.

Tom nodded. "We'd have gotten you better pricing."

"You like poker?" Bingham slipped the card into his pocket.

"Do you like salt on your margarita?" Tom said. Bingham could see Tom's adrenaline starting to flow. Tom clearly thought he'd found a treasure map under this thatched roof.

By the end of the evening, Bingham was acknowledged as a grand old man, a soldier of fortune—in more ways than one, he was careful to let them know. His tongue loosened now, and he spoke with low-key familiarity of projects they were certain they could name though he refused to identify them. "For personal reasons, you understand . . ." It became a game among them, like guessing the titles of favorite songs.

He regaled them with real war stories too, such as his adventures back in WWII. He had been a paratrooper, he said, 82nd airborne, 504th Parachute Infantry Regiment. He told them about things they were too young to remember, and he could see it in their eyes, how they'd retell the stories when they got home, how they'd heard it all from one who'd stepped right out of history. The next afternoon Bingham secured quickie native certifications for everyone and they all went scuba diving. They dove an old wreck he'd found out there years ago.

Two days before they left, he swung his arm around Tom and guided him off to one side, splitting him from the herd. They sat down in long chairs in the cool shade of a coco palm tree and looked out over the clear green sea. Tom rattled the ice in his glass. "What's next on your agenda, Bingham?" he asked. "After this, I mean."

Bingham told him. He gave Tom the short version, but it was enough. New Orleans, right on the river, overlooking the French Quarter. Bingham leaned close, looked about, lowered his voice: A resort hotel, permits in the works. And best of all, the probability was high for some long-run razzle-dazzle because casino gambling was on the way.

Tom's brows had shot up. A ground floor opportunity. Two years, three at most.

Bingham could see Tom was thinking about Atlantic City, where gambling had just been approved.

"I want in," Tom said, sipping his drink.

But Bingham shook his head. "Sorry, old boy. I've got other plans."

Tom stuck to his guns. He would put his own money in, he said. He had friends who'd do the same.

When the Morgan Klemp jet took off at the end of the week, Bingham was on it, looking out over the clear blue sea, tongue working his cheek. Tom had a round of meetings scheduled before the flight even landed.

Now, in the conference room in the offices of Mangum & Morris, Bingham studied the faces around the table. This transaction would close in six weeks, and he knew it would happen because every person here was determined to collect their fees in time to be included in year-end hero-sheet calculations and the bonuses that went with them.

They wanted to be on the inside.

⟨~⟩

Hours passed. Bingham glanced at his watch. One o'clock and he was hungry, and when he was hungry he grew irritable. In fact, he'd felt claustrophobic for hours. Stiff-arming the growing stack of papers in front of him, he pushed them out toward the center of the table. After all, he was the client.

"It's time for lunch," he announced. He softened the interruption with a smile. His smile was contagious, he knew. He'd been aware all his life that this smile of his was a valuable tool, and he used it as such. So he looked around the room, caught each eye and twinkled, catching them off guard, breaking the connections. Otherwise they'd sit here all day, billing him.

"Let's go eat," he said, rubbing his hands together. "Let's get out of here and find some good Creole food. What do you suggest? Galatoire's? I've heard a lot about that place."

Doug glanced at Preston. "We've ordered lunch in," Preston said, scooting back his chair. "I'll go check on that."

"Nope." Bingham's voice was firm. He leaned forward, forearms on the table. "No catered food. I want to try out all your great restaurants. Let's start with Galatoire's. We'll come back here and work after."

Preston looked at Doug.

"There'll be a long line," Robert murmured to Bingham.

"So what?" He looked at Doug. "Can't we do something about the line?"

Doug nodded. "Sure."

"Get someone to stand in for us. Have them call us when they've got a table."

"No problem," Doug said again. Preston rose. Left the room and nodded when he returned. "All set."

"Good," Bingham said.

❧

Amalise stopped at Ashley Elizabeth's desk. "I'm going to lunch," she said.

Ashley Elizabeth looked up from her typewriter though her fingers continued to fly across the keys. She worked for Amalise and two other associates, so she was always busy. "All right." Ashley Elizabeth smiled. "I'm going too. Soon."

When the elevator doors opened, Doug Bastion stood there with several others. He surprised her by swinging an arm around her shoulders. "Amalise, there's someone I want you to meet." He turned to a tall, lean man with a craggy face. The man wore a gray suit that, from the fit, appeared custom made, as well as a crisp white shirt with French cuffs, a burgundy tie, and wingtip shoes. He looked about fifty-five, perhaps sixty years old.

"Bingham," Doug said, "this is one of our finest young lawyers. She'll be working with us on your transaction. Amalise, this is Bingham Murdoch."

"Well, look at this," Bingham exclaimed, opening his arms and smiling. "From the tenth circle of hell an angel has appeared." He turned to two men standing behind him and introduced them as Adam and Robert. "One's a banker," he said, "and the other's a Wall Street lawyer, angel. Don't you singe those wings."

She said hello as Doug released her from his grip.

"Amalise." Bingham glittered for her. "That's a nice name. We're all off to Galatoire's for lunch, and you're coming with us." He chuckled and shuffled beside her, slipping his arm through hers as the elevator continued the descent. "I must say, Doug, your firm has good taste. What a relief." Everyone laughed.

Preston wore a wry smile. "Amalise is a rose among the thorns."

Before she could say a word, the elevator reached the lobby and the doors opened. Bingham steered her along, leaving Doug, Preston, Raymond, Frank Earl, Adam, and Robert trailing behind.

"Call me Bingham." His eyes shone as he led her through the lunchtime crowds. Walking along, he compared in a favorable light the sidewalk crush to the streets of Manhattan this time of day. He mentioned flying into the city yesterday and how he'd felt such a bond with New Orleans the moment he saw it. He talked of a recent trip to Las Vegas and said she was prettier than any of those showgirls, and he praised the orchestra in the Blue Room at the Roosevelt the previous night.

Amalise strolled along beside him, speechless. He commanded all attention until at last they were seated around the table in the restaurant and the menu appeared, at which time he changed the subject to food.

Once Doug attempted to bring up a point under discussion in the term sheet.

Bingham's hand shot up, like a stop sign. "No business here, my boy. Not at lunch."

Chapter Six

THAT AFTERNOON AMALISE SPOKE TO COUNSEL in the various jurisdictions where Murdoch's two companies were organized and did business, arranging for organizational documents and certificates to be sent to her right away. Counsel in Grand Cayman confirmed that the Lone Ranger subsidiary guaranteeing the loans was organized under Cayman Island law. The sole shareholder was the borrower, Murdoch's Delaware Company, Lone Ranger, Inc.

"Thanks." Amalise checked that off her list. "We'll prepare forms of board resolutions and send them to you to revise under Cayman law."

Later in Raymond's office—a duplicate of hers—she and Raymond reviewed the term sheet, the deal point memo that Preston had prepared as the axis around which ongoing detailed negotiations and documents would revolve. Amalise sat in the chair in front of his desk with the term sheet propped on her lap. She made notes in the margins while they talked.

One item caught her attention, and she looked up. "Why is Murdoch providing a personal letter of credit? It's only for one million—not enough to cover the company's debt."

Raymond checked off something on his copy. "It's extra security for the banks in the syndicate. Gives them comfort. Under the terms, they'll draw any overdue interest on their loans from the credit should the company default and fail to pay." Head bent, he looked at Amalise under his brows. "It's not an insignificant amount—one million would cover your salary for forty years without investing it."

"Not yours?"

He smiled.

"I knew I was underpaid."

"Who's the issuing bank?"

"Cayman Trust."

He looked up. "I thought Banc Franck held the accounts." Flipping through the term sheet, he stopped on a page and read. "Well, Cayman Trust it is. Banc Franck just holds the borrower's primary account." He shrugged. "Doesn't matter. The letter of credit's a point of trust. It's good as cash."

"I've got the corporate due diligence started. Doug also wants us to see what background we can find on Murdoch. Where do we start?"

Raymond set the term sheet down on his desk and leaned back, folding his hands over his stomach. He looked at Amalise. "These big money men keep out of the public eye. But go ahead and get started in the case reporters, and *Barron's, Wall Street Journal*. See what you can find."

In the firm library Amalise checked regulatory opinions under both names, Lone Ranger and Bingham Murdoch. Murdoch had mentioned transactions in Atlanta, Florida, and California. His U.S. company was organized in Delaware, and he lived in New York. So she perused the *Federal Reporter*, and also the *State Reporter* for case law and other public proceedings. She searched back issues of *Barron's, The Wall Street Journal*, and *Forbes*. She also searched *Who's Who* ten years back, all with no luck, as Raymond had surmised.

At last she asked the librarian, Mrs. Plauche, if it would be possible to run a Dun & Bradstreet credit report.

Mrs. Plauche, bending over the card catalog, stuck her finger behind a card and gave her a look. "We don't do that here," she said.

"It's for a transaction." Amalise persisted. "For Doug Bastion."

"You could try accounting," Mrs. Plauche said in a vague tone, her eyes clouded. "They might have that information. But you'd need approval to even make the request." She shook her head. Her eyes bored into Amalise's as if she'd stepped over a line. "Who's the client?"

Amalise blinked. "It's First Merchant's customer, actually. We're representing them."

She went back to the card catalog. "Well, you'd think a bank would already have that kind of information, wouldn't you?"

Amalise felt the blush that rose. They would and surely did, Raymond confirmed when she reported back. A credit check on First Merchant Bank's client wasn't the firm's responsibility. He wasn't going to stir that pot.

Amalise lounged in the chair in front of Raymond's desk. "Then I guess we're at a dead end. I found nothing on either Murdoch or the companies." Thinking of the property that Murdoch would destroy in the Marigny District to build his hotel, the thought popped into her mind that she would love to see this deal die. The rogue idea frightened her, and she shook it off.

Raymond spread his hands. "Finding nothing is a good result. The Reports and SEC opinions would only bring bad news." Besides, he went on, his friend Josh Bart at Lehman Loeb vouched for anyone Tom Hannigan at Morgan Klemp recommended. He looked at Amalise, cocked his head and shrugged. "In the end, it's all about relationships."

He had plenty of work lined up for her to do. Bingham Murdoch was First Merchant Bank's concern, not a problem for Mangen & Morris.

⌥

Later that night Bingham stood at the living room window in his executive suite at the Roosevelt Hotel, gazing at the harvest moon. The full moon would cycle around once more, then wane as the closing date grew near. He was remembering a time when calculations of the moon's cycle meant to him life or death.

His heart beat faster as he thought of this, and he almost whispered the thoughts aloud. *A quarter moon is what you want, at most. The enemy would be waiting below for their chutes to open on a moonlit night, those mushrooms hanging over you like iridescent targets.* He nodded to himself. *Yes, you pick a dark night. If you're lucky, maybe the weather's acting up a little—some fog, light rain, low cloud cover. At most a quarter moon.*

Bingham smiled, shrugging off the memory. The pinnacle was now in sight. Six weeks, at most. Thanksgiving. And he had a lot to be thankful for.

He turned away from the window, adjusting his shirt collar. He licked the tips of his fingers and smoothed back his hair. Robert was waiting downstairs in the Blue Room, and he'd invited two pretty ladies to dine with them tonight. As Bingham walked into the bedroom, he sang, *"New Orleans ladies . . . they sa-shay by . . ."* Yes, he loved this city.

And Robert was doing well, so far. Bingham mused over his luck. The young investment banker was the perfect chief executive officer to run the hotel. Good with money, tough, aggressive, and smart. But Robert could stand to learn a few things. He was abrasive, and his flashpoint was low.

Bingham inspected his wardrobe, then pulled out his tux, a white shirt, a black bow tie. He untied the tie he'd worn all day and pulled it off. Despite the sorry economy, he figured the markets were poised to soar, and he sensed the kid had keen insight into the ideal ratio of risk to reward. Finding Robert was a piece of good fortune, all in all. The kid would keep the lid on things. He was hungry. And he'd chum up with the local champions of the public good.

Yes. Robert was a necessary evil.

He laid the clothes he would wear tonight out on the bed in the order in which he would put them on. When he'd finished undressing, Bingham turned on the shower and stepped inside. A rush of pleasure hit him all at once as the hot water streamed over him, a jolt of pure, unselfish joy. He always did like a good, hot shower. He dried off with a thick, soft towel and pulled on the robe with the hotel logo embroidered on the front pocket. Yes, he thought to himself while he shaved, things were moving along. He'd been told these lawyers were the best in town. Most of the banks had already committed to the project—they knew a good opportunity when one came along.

He swiped off the last of the shaving cream, splashed his face with water, and went off to dress, humming. He slipped on the white shirt the maids had washed, starched, and ironed and worked his fingers over the row of tiny buttons down the front, thinking a man needs a woman for this kind of thing. This made him think of Amalise Catoir, the pretty young associate at Mangen & Morris. Then he shrugged off the thought. She was too young and already a widow, he'd heard. He frowned, struggling with the gold cuff links. Plus, he was over the hill and better off alone. No sense in making a woman a widow twice.

Bingham pulled on the black pants and snapped his suspenders up over the shirt, thinking he wouldn't mind wearing a tuxedo every night. This was the good life. High polish on the black wingtips. He held up the shoes and sniffed the new leather. You can always tell an expensive shoe by the smell of the leather, he thought. And you can tell the quality of a man by the shine on his shoes.

There was a large mirror over the chest of drawers. Leaning close, he stretched the bow tie around his collar and snapped it. Last time he'd worn these clothes was for dinner at Le Cirque in Manhattan with Tom. That was his introduction to the other investors. Eat, drink, and be merry. The meal had cost him plenty, but it was a good investment.

Shaking his head, Bingham stepped back from the mirror. He was glad to be through with that part of the deal. He pulled on the jacket, adjusting the shoulders and sleeves, and regarded himself. He turned, checking himself from one angle, then another. Tom's tailor had done a good job. Facing the mirror again, he stood straight, studying his tall, thin frame and patted his flat stomach. Not bad for an old ace. He leaned forward and rubbed the skin on his cheeks, glad to be rid of the beard, then saluted himself and walked to the door.

Hah, he thought as he opened the door and closed it behind him, most people would've thought it couldn't be done.

Chapter Seven

THE AIR WAS CRISP AND COOL when Amalise left work that October evening. The six o'clock bells of the Jesuit church across from the Roosevelt Hotel were ringing as she stood on the corner outside the First Merchant Bank building. The fruit stand down the street was still open for business, so she crossed Common and strolled down Baronne to chat with the old lady who tended the cart. She said hello, checked out the satsumas. The sweet, pungent fragrance of the citrus fruit made her mouth water. She bought a half dozen. The old lady placed them in a brown paper bag, and Amalise, clutching the bag along with her briefcase and purse, strolled back to the parking lot on Common.

Walking into the yellow glow of the garage, she waved to Mr. Picou in the ticket booth and the security guard on duty. Once in the elevator, she pulled a satsuma from the bag, peeled it, and popped a section into her mouth, savoring the tangy burst of flavor. Jude was right: She'd take things as they came and enjoy each one.

Thinking of the small two-room suite she'd rented in a boutique hotel in the Quarter, she started the car and began the slow descent to the exit. Her place was on Chartres Street, not far from where she'd lived while attending law school. Feeling a little lonely, she reminded herself that this was only temporary, just until she located an apartment or—she smiled at the prospect—maybe even a house. Something small, uptown.

She had the money to buy. Phillip's last surprise had been a large life insurance policy.

Unintentionally he'd left her well off when he'd purchased the mutual policies. One hundred thousand dollars sat uninvested in her bank account. Her face contorted at the thought. She'd use some of it to buy a home somewhere safe; Phillip owed her that much. But the rest? Blood money sitting in her bank account. She couldn't stand to even think of it.

Resolved to put memories of Phillip behind her, Amalise planted her hands on the wheel and headed for the Quarter. As she turned onto Chartres, the narrow, well-lit street stretched ahead of her like a brightly colored ribbon running toward Jackson Square. A lone violinist played on the corner, and she rolled her window down, listening to the music and the sounds of the Quarter. She smiled, and on a whim she drove on past the hotel down to Esplanade at the downriver edge of the Vieux Carré and entered the Faubourg Marigny. She turned north on Frenchmen and drove slowly past the cafés, bars, restaurants, some of the best jazz bistros in the world.

Music permeated the entire area. On this balmy evening, locals lounged around sidewalk tables, many with their dogs. Amalise drove past homes where friends and families hunkered on stoops. They glanced up with friendly looks as she passed.

As she cruised through the old neighborhood, it slowly sunk in that all of this was marked for destruction by Murdoch's project and that she was a part of that destruction. Her hands tightened on the wheel. She told herself that it was just her job, that the world would continue to turn as it always does. She told herself that change was inevitable, that Black Diamond would provide jobs and badly needed tourist dollars.

Many streets beginning in the French Quarter crossed into the Marigny—Royal, Burgundy, Dauphine. She crossed Royal and found herself at Washington Square Park, a pretty, grassy area with spreading trees, enclosed by black iron fencing. The park occupied a small city block bordering Elysian Fields. Green iron plants and ginger clumped along the fence, forming dense, shadowy places where children like to play and hide.

Secret places. The park was empty in the twilight, and shadows deepened beyond the amber glow thrown by the old street lamps.

Was this park included in Murdoch's project area? She didn't recall.

On Kerlerec Street, half a block from Frenchmen, she slowed in front of a large two-storied house where children played in the fenced front yard. The home was pleasant looking, even though the porch and window sills sagged a bit and the paint had washed out over the years to a mere impression of green.

Watching the children, she let the engine idle, smiling, feeling again that freedom a child senses at dusk when light no longer marks time and dew forms on the grass. A pretty little girl sitting on a rope swinging from a live oak tree in the yard looked up, caught her eye, and waved. Amalise waved back. The tree was an old-growth treasure, its girth wide enough to mark several hundred years. She wondered if Murdoch would let it live.

Closer to the fence, two small boys played around the tree's bulky roots, engrossed in a grid of sticks and miniature cars. There was a fourth child on the porch, a small boy standing alone at the top of the steps. Leaning against a wooden column, he stood and watched the other children play.

Murdoch's nameless agents would purchase this house, along with all the others on this street. Bulldozers would tear down the swing and level the place where the children played in the dirt under the tree. She ducked her head, suddenly stricken by the personal impact of Project Black Diamond. She shouldn't have come here, she realized.

Seven o'clock bells chimed from St. Francis Seelos, St. Mary's, and the Cathedral of St. Louis at Jackson Square. Suddenly light flooded the yard. A woman appeared on the porch, calling for the children to come inside.

Amalise drove on. Eyes straight ahead, she told herself that Bingham Murdoch's hotel was good for the firm, good for the city, and good for her own career. The plight of that family was not her problem to solve. If she'd learned one thing from her marriage to Phillip, it was that attempts to fix other people's problems generally prove futile. Besides, the project had already taken on a life of its own. The opinions of a second-year associate were irrelevant.

Reaching her hotel, she parked the car and carried her briefcase, purse, and the bag of satsumas through the empty, high-ceilinged foyer, her heels clicking on the wooden floor. She would not think any more about the Marigny. She would not allow herself to wonder whether Bingham Murdoch intended to destroy those beautiful old oak trees or anything else in the city.

A small voice inside pointed out the public outrage that would erupt when word of Bingham Murdoch's plans got out. There would be protest marches and fiery editorials in the newspapers. But confidentiality would protect the project until it was too late—that was the key to the success of Bingham Murdoch's plans. And Amalise was bound ethically, morally, and in every other way to keep that secret.

Chapter Eight

AMALISE HAD FOUND A HOUSE FOR sale uptown she thought she'd like. She'd called Jude and asked him to come along to see it. He had said sure, and she'd made an appointment to visit the place with a real estate agent. So here he was on a Saturday afternoon, driving Amalise down St. Charles Avenue to look at a house.

He could feel her watching him. Folding her arms and cocking her head to one side, she said, "That transaction I told you about the other night is moving fast. Doug and Preston are giving me more substantive work." She settled back and looked ahead at the traffic. "We're past the drone stage at the firm now, Rebecca and I. We're on our way."

Jude smiled and nodded, only half listening as he concentrated on the traffic. They were in a hurry because she had to get back to work. She was in the office most Saturdays, but then work was Amalise's idea of entertainment.

He glanced her way, smoothing the furrows between his eyes before they formed. She'd been staying at a hotel down in the Quarter but wanted to find a real place. The apartment she'd shared with Phillip before his death wasn't an option. He'd offered to let her have the apartment on the other side of his duplex on State Street rent free and was chagrined when she'd turned him down flat.

She'd found a perfect little cottage on Broadway near the universities. She wanted a home of her own, and with the insurance money she'd received, she'd pay cash for the right one. He pondered the irony: Phillip Sharp, who'd have sucked the very life from Amalise if he could, was now financing her freedom.

So here she was, racing off in direct contradiction to his plans, as usual. But he loved that about Amalise, that determination of hers. Even with all the questions in her mind about life and purpose and meaning, about suffering in the world and those problems that were too big for one person to do anything about, still she was complete in and of herself.

And where did that leave him? He stifled a sigh. Well, he'd broach that subject soon. But he'd come to realize since the accident and all the subsequent changes in Amalise—her craving for independence, the desire to understand the purpose of her life—love, when it came to Amalise, would be the icing on the cake.

But not the cake itself.

So he kept his foot on the gas pedal and his eyes straight ahead because, again, he knew this wasn't the time or place to discuss the nature of their relationship. He glanced at her from the corner of his eye and smiled, happy for her in spite of himself. She was free of Phillip and working again.

She went on talking about that deal of hers while he concentrated on negotiating the three lanes of traffic on the two-lane avenue. Suddenly she turned to face him again, and the movement brought the scent of soap and roses wafting his way, a fragrance he'd associated with Amalise since she was a little girl. But today that scent roused emotions that had nothing to do with their childhood friendship.

"Jude, are you listening?" She leaned in close and tucked her hair behind one ear, as she always did. "I think I'm talking to myself here."

Too close. He dropped his elbow between them and tightened his hand on the wheel, covering his discomfort with a grin. "I'm listening." A battle-green streetcar rumbled by on his left, and he looked that way, creating distance between himself and Amalise.

"Just checking." She smiled and repositioned herself. "I want to talk to you about something. This new project I'm on? It's, ah . . . ," she looked off, "a development, of sorts. In an older neighborhood."

"Where?"

"I can't tell you."

He raised his brows.

"It's confidential." She sat back and folded her hands in her lap. "But it's bothering me some. Can I tell you about it, without going into detail?"

"Sure. Go ahead."

After a pause, she threw back her head, gazing at the interior roof. "All right. Picture a charming area, partly residential. Part commercial, but lots of small businesses around, like cafés, shops."

"That could be any place in New Orleans."

Her voice dropped a key. "But here's the thing. The place will be destroyed by this transaction."

"What do you mean by 'destroyed'?"

"Destroyed." She spread her hands. "As in, *demolished*."

He gave her a sideways look. "I'm assuming it's not in the Quarter."

"No."

He turned his eyes to the road again. Wheeling down St. Charles, he closed in on the University area and Broadway, tunneling beneath the canopy of live oak trees that lined the boulevard.

Her voice hardened. "They're going to level the place, Jude."

"Maybe the residents will fight it."

She shook her head. "They won't know it's happening until it's too late. That's the way it works." She looked to the right, rubbing her arms, as if comforting herself. "I've tried not to think too much about it because there's nothing I can do. But I keep imagining all those wonderful old houses, pieces of history, crushed into rubble. Old-growth trees destroyed."

He shot her a look. It wasn't easy to knock down an old house in the city of New Orleans, much less a tree. Oak trees in Louisiana even had their own club, the Live Oak Society. Trees with a certain measure of girth were members, and the only human allowed was the chairman. Certain trees were designated the president and vice president, and even Martha Washington, a member of the society, resided in Audubon Park.

"Maybe you're worrying for nothing," he said. "If the area's as you describe, there will be too many obstacles. The developers will stumble, and the city will find an excuse to halt it. City hall won't let it happen, and neither will the residents."

"No." She sounded dejected. "The groundwork's a done deal. All but the financing, and when that's completed, they'll start purchasing the properties in the target area." Blowing out her cheeks, she swiveled her head toward him. "I shouldn't be telling you any of this. You can't mention it to anyone."

"I won't. I don't even know where you're talking about. But you can trust me, you know that."

"I know."

He swerved as a car pulled out of a driveway on his right. "This city isn't fond of change. Remember that expressway proposal a few years ago? There was such a commotion, they finally gave it up. Protests, lawsuits. They stood up to the mayor, city council, congressmen, senators, federal regulators, commissions under Presidents Johnson *and* Nixon." He laughed. "They even beat back the real powers, the sewage and water board and the levee board."

"That was the French Quarter. This isn't." The look she gave him was reflective. "And that project was public, this isn't. Not even the press has gotten wind of this. It's big, but it isn't a highway or a bridge—the kind of thing where voters get to choose."

"Huh. Now I'm curious."

"And the permits have been issued, already approved." She sighed and looked to her right. "It's a huge project that will be announced one day after all the key properties have been purchased and demolition's begun."

He didn't say anything.

"The whole thing will happen without anyone realizing, one purchase at a time. The buyers will be agents of the developer, so they won't have a clue. And the first to sell will get prices they never dreamed of. So in that first phase, sellers will keep it quiet—that's part of the deal."

"Is this legitimate?"

"Sure. But there'll be huge pressure on the current owners to accept."

"What kind of pressure?"

She turned her eyes back to the road. "The pressure's in the money and the tactics. The agents will move fast, right after the closing of the financing. Purchases will be all cash, as is, no questions asked. Existing liens will be paid off." She shrugged. "Deals too good to pass up. And then, after those first properties are in, word will spread that the neighborhood's gone, though no one will understand why. And that's when prices will drop."

"What if they decide to fight then?"

Amalise shrugged. "What's left at that point will be mostly residential—individuals with average incomes, people who can't afford to go to court. And if they do try to fight it, they'll only be offered more." She pushed back a stray lock of hair. "At the end, the holdouts will realize there's nothing left to win in a lawsuit anyway. Who wants to live next door to a parking lot?"

Jude whistled. "Sounds like there's big money involved."

"Yes, there is. But the thing that makes it all work is that in the long run it'll be good for the city. The project will bring in tourist dollars and jobs." She turned to him with a confused look. "It's not supposed to be like this, Jude. I love my job, but I hate what we're doing here." She gave a helpless shrug and settled back. "I almost wish Rebecca had been picked for this instead of me."

Rebecca would no doubt agree.

Amalise sank back against the car door, facing him. She pulled up one leg and folded it under her, looking at Jude. "Where am I going wrong?"

Traffic slowed and he leaned back, one elbow propped on the window. "Well, I'll assume it's all legal. But is it moral?"

"I don't know. Are *moral* and *right* the same thing? Maybe. But either way, this is wrong." Amalise heaved a long sigh. "I grew up watching Dad dispensing justice. He made decisions in his courtroom based on principles that everyone understood. Right and wrong, good and bad, the rules made sense. If you broke a law, you went to jail. Bust the speed limit, you got a ticket. Hurt someone, you paid the price." She rapped her knuckles against the window beside her in a distracted way. "Everything was black and white in Dad's courtroom. Not shades of gray, like this."

He stopped for the light at State Street and automatically looked to his left, toward his house. That's where they should be going right now. He wanted to keep Amalise close by and safe.

Seconds passed. The light turned green, and he stepped on the gas. He looked her way and grimaced. "It doesn't sound like you have much choice, chère."

"Not really. I could leave the firm, of course. But that's not an option."

He knew that wouldn't happen. She'd worked for years to get where she was.

"Besides, Rebecca or someone else would take my place, and the deal would still go forward."

"Then you have to be practical."

She nodded. "We have a goal to reach."

He almost smiled. This was like playing *Jeopardy!* He let one, two, three beats pass and said, "Neighborhoods change all the time. People move and adjust."

She gazed through the windshield with her head turned away so he couldn't read her expression. "I know," she said, almost muttering. "And . . . I made the mistake of driving through the place the other day. Personalizing it. I put faces to the names on the list."

Jude nodded. "Probably unwise."

"I'll work my way through this," she said after a moment. "It's my job."

"Put your worry in God's hands and then just do the best you can."

She nodded. But as he drove on, the question rose in his mind: What really came first with Amalise?

◦◦◦

Amalise was looking forward to seeing the house, but right now she was just happy to be sitting beside Jude. She watched as he drove, his strong hands on the wheel, his straight back, the thoughtful way he answered her questions. A frisson ran through her, a thrill of emotion so deep and strong that it caught her off guard.

She loved Jude, she suddenly realized. In that instant, all the years they'd spent together and all the memories they'd created seemed to coalesce at this one point in time, inside this car with Jude just inches away. The subliminal feelings she'd been experiencing in the past few months took form. They had substance and a word.

Love.

She loved him! Almost holding her breath, she gave him a sideways look. He seemed like the same old Jude—and yet not. As they drove, she let her thoughts linger on this discovery. She wondered how it would feel to have him slip his arms around her. Wondered what she'd do if he stopped the car right now, turned to her, and kissed her.

And then Rebecca came to mind. Amalise turned her gaze out the passenger window and watched the trees fly by. The truth was, she had no idea where she stood in Jude's mind and heart. Or, for that matter, how he felt about Rebecca.

But you have a fair idea, said the observer, that little voice inside her, inside us all. Perhaps it was the Spirit of God, or maybe it was just the voice of human frailty. *You know how Jude feels about Rebecca,* the voice said, *if you can face the fact.*

But she didn't have to face that fact right now, she argued in response. She'd just returned to work after a long recuperation. After the death of her husband. There was plenty of time ahead to sort things out.

Yet she longed to turn to Jude and just say the words and let them hang there in the air between them. Only pride kept her from doing so.

And Rebecca.

⬬⬬⬬

They drove down Broadway until Amalise said "There!" and pointed to his left, across the street. Jude slowed the car in front of a house with a *For Sale* sign standing in the yard. A car was parked on the street, with a woman sitting at the wheel, waiting. The real estate agent, he supposed.

After making a U-turn, he looked at the small green clapboard cottage with a porch across the front, half-hidden by a neat sidewalk hedge, and his heart sank because he knew she would buy it. The yard was small, and there was a driveway on the right, leading to a garage in the back. He parked on the street behind the agent's car.

Inside, sunshine streamed in through a row of windows on the left of a long narrow hallway. Green morning glory vines crept around the edges of the windows. Amalise walked slowly down the hall in silence, stopping to examine the rooms to her right. The living room had a fireplace and ceiling-to-floor windows that opened onto the front porch. The bedroom had a set of built-in bookcases that looked like they'd been custom built for her.

The old Amalise would have spun around, eyes shining, Jude thought. She'd have been eager, would have spilled the beans to the real estate agent about how she loved the house, how she would buy it immediately and pay the asking price.

But the widow of Phillip Sharp was cooler now. Her eyes swept everything at random as they walked through the house. She strolled, finger to her lips, inspecting everything with élan, and only Jude knew that already she was imagining her furniture in this place, her books on the shelves, measuring for pictures on the walls.

At the end of the hallway they entered an octangular dining room, and beyond that was a second bedroom on the right and an outdated kitchen to the left. Another porch crossed the back of the house, the right side enclosed by a wooden lattice covered in vines.

"Good shade on a hot summer day," the agent said.

"Yes, it can get hot all right," Amalise replied in her new, distant tone.

Jude stood back as she walked casually down the steps into the back yard, a square of lush green grass enclosed by a wooden fence. She said she liked the yard without cracking a smile, and the agent gave her a nervous look. Jude watched, astounded by Amalise's aplomb.

"The asking price is sixty thousand," the agent said as they turned back to the house.

"I'll offer fifty," Amalise said, cool as you please. "Cash."

"I'll get back to you," the agent said, smiling.

By the end of the day the deal was done. They met at fifty-four. Still, Jude knew the price was high given the market downturn. She could have offered less. But when Amalise wanted something, she went for it with everything she had.

⟨☙⟩

Amalise sat at her desk late that afternoon after Jude had dropped her off, thinking. Jude had offered the empty apartment in his house, rent free. He thought she was being stubborn about buying the house on Broadway, she knew. But he was wrong. Despite this love she'd finally recognized for Jude, the years with Phillip had left her with an almost physical longing for a place of her own, a place set apart from the world. The new house would be her fortress for a while. She was sick of psychological turmoil, the kind she'd endured in her marriage with Phillip. The house she'd seen on Kerlerec Street in Marigny had made up her mind about having a home of her own.

From her desk she picked up the memorandum of transaction terms—the Black Diamond term sheet—that she should be reading, and saw instead the family in that house on Kerlerec. Everything in that scene had roots—the kind she'd had while growing up in Marianus. The children playing in the yard. The mother on the porch, calling them inside when night fell. And the father? She imagined him coming home after dark, swinging one of the boys up onto his shoulders.

Project Black Diamond would destroy all of that.

She told herself it wouldn't be so bad. As Jude had said, cities constantly grow and expand and change. That was the nature of progress.

Put things in perspective, Amalise. Prioritize. Be practical. This second chance at life was a gift of grace she couldn't waste. She told herself that Abba would lead her through this maze, even when, as now, she didn't fully understand.

Jude was right.

Jude . . .

Still holding onto the term sheet, she dropped her head into her hands. She'd seen the look in Rebecca's eyes when she'd spotted Jude's picture moved to the place of honor behind Amalise's desk on her first day back at work. And since she'd returned from Marianus, Amalise had to admit that Jude mentioned Rebecca frequently in their conversations. Were they really just friends, or had she just been deliberately blind?

Seconds passed and at last she put the term sheet down and turned to face the window. Since the accident, during her recovery, she'd convinced herself that Jude's constant attention was a sign that he preferred to spend time with her instead of Rebecca. But now . . .

Gripping the seat of the chair, she swiveled it from side to side, sensing there was something she'd missed. And then it struck her all at once: Jude was kind. He was thoughtful. But the accident had been partly his fault. That's what she hadn't seen before.

Of course that was it. The car that hit her was his own. Jude had merely done what he thought was right. His conscience had driven him to spend all that time with her over the past few months.

A hollow feeling grew inside. She stared out the window, seeing nothing. Why hadn't she realized it before?

Shaking her head at her own stupidity, she sat there turning this new thought over in her mind for a very long time. She'd been so self-absorbed, engrossed in her own little world for the past few months. And taking Jude for granted.

As the sun went down, reflections on the windows across the street turned to gold, but today she didn't care. Was Jude really in love with Rebecca? Even as she asked herself the question, she realized that she already knew the answer. Forced to imagine a future without him, she found that she couldn't. That was impossible. Shadows moved in an office across the way, and then the lights switched off and the shadows disappeared.

At last she straightened and turned back to her desk. She looked down at the term sheet. This is what she should be focusing on right now. This was her work, her future. She didn't have time right now to think about Jude and Rebecca. Hands flat, she smoothed the first of the stapled pages. Inside were complicated issues and ideas that would take time to understand, the agreed-upon terms for Project Black Diamond. This was the work she loved. Thoughts of Jude and Rebecca could wait.

Prioritize, Amalise.

She picked up the term sheet and began to read.

Focus.

Amalise paid cash and moved in right away, pending the closing. Jude had helped her move.

On the first night in her new home, she sat quietly alone in the living room. Sounds from outside—the whoosh of the Broadway bus, cars rolling by, crickets, and night birds—all seemed to surround and protect her, creating a solitary calm, a sense of starting over on her own terms. She turned her head toward the fireplace. She had no firewood, but the fireplace worked and it was hers. She studied the pictures of Mama and Dad that she'd hung on the walls, and one of Jude lifting her from the skiff. The skiff had been tied at Dad's pier in Marianus, and in the photo she was laughing as Jude swung her through the air.

There it was, that swell of emotion again.

The porch windows were open, and the long, sheer white curtains that Jude had hung for her moved in the soft night breeze. She worried her lower lip.

Abruptly she rose from the couch. The transaction at work was gearing up, gaining speed like a runaway train. She would grab something to eat from the kitchen and go back to the office for a few hours. That was one thing about being free—there was no one around to object to an unreasonable work schedule. And that's what it would take to succeed at the firm, that extra push.

She wanted to be in the engine, helping to drive the train at Mangen & Morris one day, not riding in the caboose.

Chapter Nine

Phnom Penh, Cambodia 1975

SAMANTHA DIDN'T MAKE A DELIBERATE DECISION to take the child; she just couldn't bring herself to shake him loose, to leave him alone in this mob. Clinging to his hand, she slid sideways, inching along the rough cement wall, avoiding the crush and keeping her eyes out for anyone who might be searching for the little boy. He couldn't be more than four or five years old, but if she bent down to lift him right here, there was a chance they'd both end up on the ground, underfoot and trampled.

Progress was slow. The crowd seemed to force them back a step for every two they moved forward. Despite the searing heat, the child's hand was strangely cold in hers. She looked down at him, but still he stared ahead, expressionless.

They reached the corner of a narrow side street, no more than an alley really. The street was empty, unlike the main thoroughfares that led to the city's center, toward which the mob surged like startled sheep. Rockets could be heard striking the outskirts of Phnom Penh.

"Can you run?" she asked the boy, stooping low to get his attention. She was fluent in the Khmer language, but he showed no response. Perhaps he was mute. Or deaf.

She would have to carry him, she realized, eyeing him, judging his weight. He was small and thin and should not be a heavy burden. She wondered how old he was. Four? Five? In another place, another time, she'd have guessed he was younger, but this was Cambodia where all children had that fragile, hungry look as if life had stopped them in their tracks.

She scooped him into her arms, straining thigh muscles as she stood and shifted the boy's weight onto her hip. Then she hurried down the street, carrying him that way, scurrying through alleyways and passages that she knew well, shortcuts from the embassy to her apartment. The sun's heat was relentless, and her damp dress clung to her as she worked her way through the warren of cement and stone and wood. Would Oliver really let them leave without her if she was late?

Would he have the power to delay an evacuation? Probably not.

The boy clung to her neck but made no sound. Suddenly the thought of leaving him to fend for himself in the doomed city made Sam wrap both arms around him as she began to run.

The rented two-room apartment was on the second floor of a long wooden building. She'd lived here since she'd arrived in Phnom Penh five years earlier. At the entrance she set the boy on his feet, climbed the stairs, and opened the door. For the past few months, outside doors in Phnom Penh had been left unlocked so that refugees could sleep in the hallways at night. Terrified villagers fleeing the advancing Khmer Rouge seemed to carpet every square inch of the city now, huddling at night on the steps when the hallways overflowed.

The child grasped her hand again. "Hurry," she said, pulling him along through the mass of blankets left behind on the floor of the hallway, up the sagging wooden stairs to the second floor. The building was close and dank, filled with the sour smell of humanity in close quarters. Heart racing, she glanced again at her watch. Five minutes to three. An hour already gone and no plan for getting to the airstrip.

The lump lodged in her throat grew larger. Lifting the child again, she carried him up the interior steps toward her apartment. There'd be no taxis to get them to the airstrip. No bicycle carts. Not even rickshaws.

Her living room was bright with rows of windows along the street side of the living room. Beyond that, through an open archway, was the kitchen, and to her right, a bedroom and small bath. She lowered the child to the floor and took his hand. But instead of following her, he halted, pulling her back, surprising her.

Turning, she saw that his eyes were riveted on a loaf of bread she'd left on the counter in the kitchen. Muscles worked at the corners of his mouth, suddenly convulsing, filling her with pity. Tears rose. The child was starving. Quickly she led him to a table and lifted him into a chair. His chin barely cleared the tabletop.

His eyes did not move from the bread as she moved away from him. She could feel time ticking away as she opened the old icebox and found a jar of peanut butter and some jam. The boy watched silently as she made a sandwich and cut it into four small squares. Because she wasn't sure if he'd eaten in a while, she'd give him one square at a time to slow him down a bit.

For an instant he stared at the food when she set it before him on a napkin, then he reached out and snatched it up. She poured a cup of pomegranate juice and set that down on the table too, along with another square of the sandwich. Now he watched her gravely as he chewed.

With one eye on the wall clock, Sam put the remainder of the sandwich on the napkin in front of the boy and hurried into the bedroom. Alone now, she stood for an instant, covering her face with her hands, shuddering. Then she lifted her head and looked around at the things she would leave behind, struggling to calm her thoughts. There would be time later to weep.

Irreplaceable possessions were stored in the bottom drawer of her dresser. She yanked it open. She pulled out the red silk pouch where she kept her mother's jewelry, including the wedding ring Mother had worn for over fifty years. She dropped it back into the pouch and checked inside for the silver three-leafed broach, the pearls, and the gold pendant with rubies set inside a heart. All there. She dropped the pouch into the purse slung over her shoulder and glanced around. What else, what else, what else could she not leave behind?

Pictures, she remembered. The photographs. Racing into the living room, she rummaged through drawers for the pictures. She found them along with some letters she treasured, bundled these together, and shoved them into her purse.

Then she turned and looked at the boy. For an instant she considered just leaving him here. He had managed before she'd come along. And he'd surely slow her down. Thoughts of the Khmer Rouge freight-trained through her mind, leaving no space or time for anything but flight.

Still, she hesitated. Then, holding onto the strap of her purse, she lifted the boy from the chair and his head swiveled toward the crumbs of the food as she carried him to the door, his arm reaching back around her shoulder.

At the door she halted, sighed, and returned to the kitchen for the remaining bits of the sandwich. Then she headed for the door once more, her mind sifting for names or faces of neighbors who might be willing to keep the boy.

But there was no one. A futile effort, she knew. Oliver would have to allow her to take the child aboard the plane. He would *have* to. She couldn't leave the boy standing alone on the tarmac.

With a last look around the apartment, she slammed the door behind her and raced down the stairs. In the street she halted, blinking at the blast of hot white light and dust and noise that assaulted her. She set the child on his feet and grabbed his hand.

"Come," she said. "We have to run."

One hour and twenty minutes were left before the last plane would leave.

Chapter Ten

New Orleans—1977

WORK HAD BEEN UNRELENTING FOR DAYS. Amalise arrived by eight o'clock every morning, early for a lawyer. Most nights she worked until midnight, driving home bleary eyed through the empty streets, and then falling into bed, only to start all over again the next morning.

But on this morning, something drew her back to Kerlerec Street.

She hadn't planned to go there. But on her way to the office, instead of turning toward the business district, without a conscious decision, she drove toward the Marigny. Traffic was light on this day.

Despite her prior resolve, she drove through the triangle target area, imprinting on her mind the places that Bingham Murdoch would destroy with his project. When she reached the house on Kerlerec Street, she rolled down the window beside her to breathe in the fresh morning air. There again were the children playing in the yard. Perhaps they were too young for school, or perhaps it was still too early in the day. Two of the boys played a rough version of kickball, as she and Jude had done at that age. The girl still sat on the swing, this time holding a doll on her lap, her lips moving as though talking to it.

Amalise lifted her eyes to the porch. There he was, the same small boy sitting on the top step almost hidden, one shoulder hiked, leaning against the post. She wondered why he didn't join the others.

"May I help you?" The muffled voice startled her, and she jumped.

Turning, she saw a woman standing on the street on the passenger side of the car, balancing two bulky grocery bags in her arms. The woman frowned at her. Amalise reached across the seats and rolled down the window.

"I saw you watching the children," she said before Amalise could open her mouth. She shifted the grocery bags in her arms in an irritated manner, and Amalise heard the hint of suspicion, a question in her voice. The woman's long brown hair was streaked with gray and pulled back to the nape of her neck. Fine wrinkles fanned the corners of her eyes, softening her expression despite the unfriendly tone.

Too old to be the children's mother?

"Yes, I was. They're adorable. Are they yours?"

The grocery bags slipped, and the woman hunched to grab them. A box of cornflakes tumbled to the street, and she muttered something. Amalise turned off the engine, pushed open the car door, and hurried around to where the woman stood. She picked up the box of cereal and reached for one of the bags. "Please, let me help."

Instinctively, the woman backed away. "No, thank you. I can manage." But even as she spoke, a bag slipped from her grasp. Amalise caught it as it fell.

"Whoa!" Amalise, smiling, reached out to steady the woman. "Are you all right?"

The woman closed her eyes and stood motionless for a moment, breathing deeply. When she finally looked back at Amalise, she wore a shaky smile. "Thanks," she said. Her tone was apologetic. "I think I would have fallen."

Amalise cupped her free hand beneath the woman's elbow, and they crossed the street together. When they reached the sidewalk on the other side, she let go.

"I can take it from here," the woman said.

Amalise shook her head. "I've got time. Let's get these into the kitchen."

The woman nodded, unlatched the gate, and shut it after Amalise. The boys in the yard halted their game to stare as Amalise trailed the woman up the steps. As they came close, the boy on the porch stood and slipped behind the post, as if to make himself invisible.

"This is Luke," the woman said, nodding toward him. "He's new." She rested her hand on his head as they reached the top step. "And he's still a little shy."

The child's Asian features were delicate. Up close his brown skin glowed as he stared at Amalise without expression. Dark hair framed his face, soft and shining in the sunshine.

"Say hello, Luke," the woman said, articulating her words with care, but the boy stood motionless. She turned to Amalise with an apologetic look. "He won't talk." Turning, she headed for the door, speaking over her shoulder. "He'll learn soon enough from the other children. We think he understands more than he shows."

Amalise followed, catching the screen door before it slammed behind them and feeling the child's eyes following her.

They wove their way through a living room, dodging toys and books and boxes. "Sorry about the disarray," the woman said as they entered the kitchen. Here, a rectangular table of sturdy oak stood in the center of the room, surrounded by six chairs. The woman set her bag down on the table and turned to Amalise with open arms. Amalise held out the bag, and in the instant before the woman took possession, she felt the contents shift and the bottom of the paper bag give way. They both jumped back as cans, bottles, vegetables, and the box of cereal all tumbled to the floor. Glass shattered and mayonnaise, mustard, and ketchup splattered shoes, hemlines, and walls.

With lamentations, Amalise scrambled after several rolling cans. The woman set her bag on the table and retrieved a handful of paper napkins and a wet cloth. She cleaned up the broken glass and brought out a damp mop.

"So cheap, the grocery bags they use these days!"

"And I'm so clumsy." Amalise wiped up the remaining sauces with the soggy paper napkins.

"It's not your fault." The mop swirled on the floor around Amalise. "Caroline's my name, by the way. Caroline Jeansonne."

Amalise looked up, grimacing. "I'm Amalise Catoir."

Later, with order restored, Caroline made coffee. She set a mug in front of her guest. "Amalise. That's pretty. Is it a family name?"

"It was my grandmother's." Amalise looked around the small kitchen. She could see the wood planks beneath the red, yellow, and blue striped wallpaper. The floor was linoleum. The icebox was an older model with rounded edges, with photographs of the children and crude crayon drawings taped to the door. The stove was long past any warranty, well used but spotless.

"Would you like cream? Sugar?"

Amalise looked back at Caroline. "No thanks." She picked up the mug and sipped. "I like it black. But what a mess I've caused." She shook her head. "If I hadn't come along, you'd have made two trips, and none of this would have happened."

"Don't give it another thought." Caroline filled a second cup from a shining pewter pot. She gave a little laugh. "I'd have dropped *both* bags, and it would have been worse."

Amalise smiled, studying Caroline as she set the coffee mug down on the table and lowered herself into a chair. She looked to be around fifty or fifty-five. Her blue sweater and flower-patterned rayon dress were too light for the season. The sweater had tiny moth holes around the buttonholes.

"Is the grocery far from here? I'd like to replace the things that broke."

"That's not necessary." Caroline picked up her cup and sipped. "Stay awhile. I'd enjoy having a conversation with someone over the age of six."

"Are all of these children yours?" Amalise leaned back, resolving to replace the groceries as soon as she could.

"Yes . . . in a way. We foster them, but we're hoping to adopt." Her eyes dropped for an instant.

"That's wonderful."

"Ellis and I are older than the social workers would like, especially for so many children." She shrugged one shoulder and flushed. "And income is a problem." She sipped the coffee. "But we're giving the children a home, and that counts for consideration. We're providing them stability." She set down the mug and massaged the back of her neck.

"How long have they been with you?"

Caroline lifted her hand with a little wave. "Oh, we—my husband, Ellis, and I—we took in the first two, Charlie and Nick, a couple of years ago when they were toddlers. They're the boys you saw outside." She waved her hand in the direction of the front yard. "Daisy, the little girl, joined us just last year."

Amalise nodded. "And the boy on the porch?"

"Luke." Caroline seemed to hesitate as she picked up the coffee mug again and sipped before answering. "He arrived a few weeks ago. He'd been at the home in Gentilly for a few weeks when they called us for help. Just temporarily. It's a lot to handle, but they were overcrowded."

"Poor little thing."

She tilted her head, looking at Amalise. "Yes, But at least he's out of the institutional system for a while. 'Three hots and a cot,' they call it. This is the first real home any of these children have lived in that we know of."

Amalise's stomach dropped. Murdoch's project would take care of that. She set down the coffee cup and looked at Caroline, casting around for a change of subject. "Luke looks Oriental. Is he from Vietnam?"

Caroline nodded. "From what we've been told, he was rescued from Saigon right before the Viet Cong moved in. He's been in an intake shelter on the West Coast. I guess someone just gave him the name Luke along the way. Things out there were in complete disarray, I understand. Papers were mixed up and records lost when the Saigon embassy burned after the evacuation."

"He seems lonely." Amalise dropped her eyes. What would happen to these children after Black Diamond? She told herself that she was creating drama where none existed. The family would get a good price for the house from Murdoch's agents and buy a nicer one, a newer one in another neighborhood.

Caroline nodded. "Only God knows what this child's been through. We'll warm him up soon, I hope. The social workers thought he had a sponsor here—that's why he was sent to New Orleans. But they were wrong."

"How old do you think he is?"

"It's hard to tell. He's all sticks and bones." Caroline's expression grew sober. "He doesn't eat much. Ellis says he's just not used to our food yet." She took a deep breath. "But he'll relax sooner or later, and we've been thinking about including him in our adoption petition. One more child shouldn't make that much difference, should it? But we don't know if that would hurt or help our application." She blinked and looked away.

Amalise heard the children calling to one another outside. She shouldn't have come here, she knew. She should leave. She glanced at her watch, set down the cup, and rose. "I've got to go. I need to get to work." With a rueful smile, she said, "I'm sorry for the mess, but I'm glad to have met you. I think it's wonderful what you're doing for these children." As she spoke, the front door slammed and little feet pounded through the living room and into the kitchen. Daisy raced toward Caroline, tears streaming.

Caroline reached for the girl. "Caro! Caro!" the child cried, sobbing something about her doll, the boys, and a ball. Caroline murmured to her words that seemed to soothe while she stroked the little girl's hair.

"This is Daisy." Caroline swung Daisy into her lap and looked up.

Amalise smiled but edged toward the door. She was eager to leave before she became further entangled in a problem she couldn't fix.

"Come back any time," Caroline said, stroking Daisy's hair. *Come back, come back, come back.*

Amalise nodded, heading for the door. She would, she said.

But she would not.

On the porch she found Luke still sitting alone on the top step. She looked down at the child, taking in his thin shoulders, the sharp cheekbones, the fine, straight hair, and something stirred inside. He looked so lost. Luke stiffened and stared out over the yard without moving, looking past her as if she did not exist.

Her throat grew tight as she walked to the car, realizing what she had just done. She'd put actual names and faces and stories to people sitting in the path of Bingham Murdoch's destruction. She climbed back into the car, berating herself. This had been such a mistake. The firm was counting on her to do her job, to be a productive member of the Murdoch team.

The very last thing in the world she could afford right now was to become emotionally involved with this family.

Chapter Eleven

AS SOON AS THE BLACK DIAMOND financial closing was over, Robert insisted, the agents would begin their work purchasing the Marigny properties. Bingham had a hard time convincing him to wait until the day after Thanksgiving. In the end, he'd had to issue an order to that effect. Otherwise, Robert would have charged right on. The kid would make a good CEO after the closing, but until then, he needed to understand who was in charge.

Robert sat beside him now in the Mangen & Morris conference room in a cloud of smoke. Bingham watched as he lit one Lucky Strike after the other while working his way through the first draft of the construction contract. Adam Grayson sat beside him, answering questions.

Bingham turned his attention to the blueprints of the target area spread out before him and covering the entire end of the conference table. Spidery lines outlined the properties to be purchased and demolished within the doomed triangle of the Marigny. He smiled to himself surveying the asterisks and numbers, curves, triangles and squares on the paper, and the lighter transparent overlay showing the locations of the future hotel, its grounds, and even the landscaping.

Just then the door swung open and Raymond walked in, followed by Amalise, both carrying an armload of documents. They deposited the papers at the other end of the conference table and then pulled out chairs and sat.

"Quite a load you've got there," Bingham said, eyeing the pile and hoping the papers weren't for him.

Amalise Catoir, the widow, merely smiled and gave him a little nod. Bingham dropped his eyes and tapped his fingers on the table, wondering how they'd managed to gin up so much paperwork in the past few days. Lawyers were such bores. He wished he were back in Cayman right now, sitting on the beach under a red-striped umbrella and sipping margaritas. Or flying, soaring free through the clouds to anywhere with sunshine and fresh air. He heaved a sigh and shook his head, glancing back at the stacks of paper. A necessary evil, like Robert, he mused.

Raymond caught his eye and let out a sympathetic laugh.

"I'm glad you bill by the hour and not the word." Bingham's tone was dry.

"You should be happy about that," Robert muttered beside him. "Lawyers use ten words for every one that's needed."

Stifling a yawn, Bingham watched as Amalise and Raymond split the agreements between them and began reading, consulting each other and making notes in the margins, striking out lines and sometimes whole paragraphs. Bingham glanced at his watch and frowned. It was ten o'clock in the morning and already he was half asleep. Leaning back in his chair, hands behind his head, he took a long breath and coughed in Robert's smoke, which brought to mind the fresh scent of cypress and pine from back in the days. He thought of the clean, cold wind blowing inland from the churning sea and almost shivered.

Robert stubbed out the cigarette and put down the document he'd been reading. "Coffee's low," he said to Amalise. "We've been waiting a while."

Amalise looked up and cocked one brow.

"Get us some coffee, please," Robert said. "I take cream, sugar." He glanced behind him at the empty credenza. "Napkins. And we need some spoons." Before Amalise could reply, he turned to Bingham. "And some croissants or doughnuts. Are you hungry?"

From the corner of his eye, Bingham watched Amalise's eyes grow wide. But not another muscle in the young woman's face had moved.

"No. I'll wait for lunch," Bingham said. Robert could be such an idiot. He seemed to lack even basic social skills.

Raymond pushed back his chair and rose. "I'll see what we can do. Amalise is busy here."

Amalise bent over the documents and went back to work.

Robert didn't seem to notice. He returned to his conversation with Adam, a discussion of whether to cut back some of the landscaping in favor of enlarging the parking area.

Bingham narrowed his eyes, watching his protégé. Tom had assured him that Robert was the man for the job, that if anyone could get this transaction done in the time frame Bingham demanded, it was Robert. Bingham knew he was probably right. But there'd be a price to pay because, in both business and social discourse, Robert lacked a filter most people learned to use as they matured. Then again, the kid pushed out bonds like they were free candy. And he worked well with the raucous trading desks—Salomon Brothers in New York, Milkin too—so what should he expect?

Still. He leaned close to Robert and whispered, "Get your own coffee next time, son."

Robert's chin jerked a fraction and he turned his head toward Bingham.

Ignoring him, Bingham pulled the survey over and traced the lines with his eyes. He'd keep Robert on a short leash, but Bingham had no illusions. Like the other investors Tom had brought in, Robert saw the opportunity down here: eye-popping revenues and inflated expenses, huge management fees, the tax-free skim, all tripling when casino gaming was inevitably approved. Project Black Diamond was Robert's big chance, and Bingham believed that right about now Robert was so hungry for this deal that he was capable of cannibalizing anyone getting in his way. Bingham couldn't recall ever having met a human being as purely driven by greed as young Robert.

Yes. He'd chosen the right man. Still, he was sorry for Robert's lack of social grace. Bingham studied Amalise from his end of the table. He liked the way she tackled problems, completely engrossed as she read, turning from one page to the next without looking up. She interested him.

Raymond returned with an electric coffee pot, accompanied by two young women carrying trays with cups and saucers, croissants from the deli downstairs, napkins, a few cold cans of Coca-Cola and Tab, and a bucket of ice. Robert stood, stretched, and sauntered toward the credenza.

Bingham looked down at the table again and gestured to Amalise. "Come take a look at the plans for the project. Have you seen this yet?"

With a look of surprise, she pushed her hair back behind her ears and sat up straight. "No, I haven't."

Standing, she walked over and stood behind him, looking over his shoulder at the blueprints. Beneath the translucent overlay she could see the survey lines of the properties to be purchased. She bent, watching as he traced the parameters of the triangular property, stopping just before the warehouses on the river.

"This area right here is where the hotel will face, looking out over the Quarter and the river." He moved his finger to the spot at the tip of the triangle. "Best view in town. And this"—he traced faint lines over the blocks where homes now stood—"this will be the entrance to the resort." He lifted the overlay and set it aside, revealing the survey of the properties underneath. "You see?"

He looked at her, and she nodded. He planted his finger on an area close to the river. "This is where the actual hotel will be. The rest is landscaping, gardens, terraces, two swimming pools, several fountains. It'll be nice."

"What about the park?"

"What park?"

She leaned down and pointed to a spot. "Right back here. Washington Square Park, just beyond this open area."

"Well, that borders on the parking lot—that open area." He touched a spot on the paper. Amalise was silent, and he glanced at her. "But the park won't be touched," he assured her. "We'll plant a hedge or some trees or something between the park and our lot."

Robert reappeared. Bingham sensed tension in the air as Amalise straightened and stood there while Robert took a chair on the other side of the table, facing Bingham.

Bingham looked at Robert. "How're you coming on the levee problem with the sewage and water board?"

"I'm working on that."

"Well get moving. Can we do something for them down in that area?" On the survey he placed his finger near the point where Elysian Fields and Esplanade met near the river. "Maybe donate a small strip at that end to the city for a walkway or park or something?"

Robert nodded. "There's something like that going in the Quarter, on the levee behind Jackson Square. Mayor Moon's for that one. It's in the planning stage." He grinned. "Maybe we could put a statue of the mayor, or his wife, on our spot."

Bingham nodded. He watched as Amalise walked back to her chair without saying anything. Robert went on about regulations and permits, and Bingham tuned out. Really, this transaction couldn't close soon enough, he thought.

⌐∾᷄⌐

In her office later on, Amalise frowned as she sorted through stacks of documents, looking for the draft of the syndicate's loan agreement. Despite her resolutions, despite every effort, she couldn't get the family on Kerlerec out of her mind. She made a mental note to replace the groceries she'd destroyed in their kitchen. And she thought of the child Luke. So small and timid. Malnourished, she supposed. What would happen to him if Caroline and Ellis decided not to adopt him? Or if the adoption wasn't approved? Either way, he'd be sent back into that institution.

Luke could have been any child she'd seen on the news two years ago at the end of the Vietnam War. He could have come from Cambodia, Vietnam, Laos. He could have been one of the children flown out of Saigon during Operation Babylift, just ahead of the Viet Cong invasion of the city. She frowned and tightened her lips, remembering one of the Babylift flights that had crashed on takeoff. The images came rushing back, the horror of that day, the pandemonium.

Thoughts of those shadow children had stuck with her the past few years. Was that why she couldn't let go of the family on Kerlerec Street? Was Luke a living reminder of the helplessness she'd felt, that everyone had felt watching the nightly news back then? She turned her head to the window and stared at nothing for a moment, then roused herself.

She found the loan agreement and pulled it from the pile. Pushing the rest of the documents aside, she opened this one to the first page. She told herself, as she began to read, as she had many times before, that she must focus now, that there was nothing one person could do to change things so far away. Wars, famine, orphans—that was the way of life on the other side of the globe. The only things that ever seemed to change were the names, the faces, and the geography.

Holding the agreement with both hands, she shook it, as if to focus her attention. This agreement. *This agreement!* Would it change anything for the better? Frustrated, she thumped the page and set it down on the desk before her. *Abba!* Why had she been given a second chance to make her life worthwhile, only to be stuck with this odious transaction? The question opened again that infinite void inside, the same emptiness she'd felt when she'd realized that Jude and Rebecca were in love.

Looking at the deal books on the shelf facing her desk, she knew these weren't the kind of things that could fill the empty sphere. As indicated by their elegant binders, those books, and what they represented, were important to everyone involved at the time they were negotiated and signed. But in the overall scheme of things, they were merely transient in nature. Their importance would diminish as time passed and the agreements grew outdated and, then, inevitably, were replaced or filed away, never to be seen again.

It occurred to her then that an infinite void cannot be filled with finite things.

Chapter Twelve

Phnom Penh, Cambodia 1975

FOUR O'CLOCK. THE CHILD STUMBLED, AND Samantha stopped to pick him up, hiking him so that his weight rested on her arm and he could lean against her shoulder, as you would carry an infant. He was light, but still she found it difficult to run with him as they moved against the tide of refugees stirring up the dust, shouting, sweating, many weeping. Desperation swept over her, focusing her thoughts like a beam of light from one of those plastic toy ray-guns. She had to find transportation to the airstrip. A car, a Vespa, or even a bicycle taxi. At this pace they'd never make it to the plane in time. The child buried his face in the curve of her neck and made a soft keening sound. She tightened her grip on him, patted his back.

"It's all right. Don't be afraid." She whispered the words into his ear and the keening turned to a whimper. She didn't pray much, but she found herself mumbling out loud, "Help us. Please God. If not for me, help the child."

Pushing, scrambling, Sam stepped to one side as the crowd parted for an automobile moving steadily forward, its horn blaring. An oxcart overflowing with passengers trailed in the car's wake, the driver whipping the poor animal forward before the crowd could close up again. The cart lurched from side to side, and a woman in the middle of the cart waved a white shirt like a flag.

Sam pressed on, fighting the surge. Grim faces stared out at her from the oxcart as she pushed past. Theirs were villagers' eyes, eyes accustomed to the expanse of rice fields and blue sky, to the sight of lush green banana trees rustling in the breeze. These were country eyes now opened wide to take in tall buildings they never imagined to exist and the mass of humanity around them. As the oxcart moved slowly forward, the occupants' heads whipped from side to side following the explosions of sound and smells and movement, sometimes gazing back through the blazing sunlight and dust in the direction from which they'd come as though unwilling to let that go.

A bicycle taxi following the oxcart jolted its way through the swarming mass toward Sam and the boy. She could see fury on the faces of the two passengers behind the bicycle man as they hunkered down behind him. One, a hefty man, leaned forward and shouted something she couldn't hear over the noise of the crowds, poking at the driver's back as if somehow that would move them on at a faster pace. A woman huddled beside him, clinging to his shirt and swatting wildly at people grabbing at the cycle.

The cycler spat something back at the passenger and waved one arm in the air. Closer now, Sam could hear him. "Get out if you don't like! Get out. Get out! Get out! There are others who will pay."

Fear and hope twisted inside and without thinking, Sam hefted the boy onto her other hip and began moving toward the cart, raising one arm high, shouting to the bicycle man, "Eastside airstrip! Take us to the airstrip!"

The bicycle man turned. Frowning, he glared at Sam, and she saw it in his eyes. *Ach! White woman, American woman. Don't I have trouble enough?*

Still she shoved her way toward the cart, ignoring the current passengers, seeing only a way to the plane if she could just reach the cyclist. The boy moaned and clung to her neck. The bicycle, hemmed in by the crowd, rolled to a standstill. The man in the cart pounded his fists on the cycler's back shouting for him to drive on. "Move! Now!"

The cycler swatted back, glancing over his shoulder at the attacker, and Sam, drawing closer, shouted again, catching his eye. The cyclist gave Sam a speculative look and his eyes dropped for an instant on the child before he turned away, hunching over the bicycle bars, prepared to force his way through the wall of frantic refugees blocking the road.

At that moment, with a loud curse, the hefty man in the cart half stood, leaned forward, and whacked the bicycle man's head from behind with the palm of his hand. The cyclist's foot sprung from the pedal, slammed to the ground, and straddling the bike, he whirled, his purple face contorted with humiliation and fury.

Sam glanced at her watch—only fifty minutes to reach the airstrip. There'd be no escape after that once the Khmer Rouge entered the city, she knew. To be left behind was death. She'd read the intelligence reports: Entire villages had been razed by the Khmer Rouge in the past few weeks, burned to the ground without mercy. Mass murder, torture, rape. Survivors force-marched to labor camps where they now toiled for *Ankah*, Father of the New, the Reborn, the Red State. No food, no medicine or time to sleep. She'd read of babies swung on pikes, of families torn apart, children just out of diapers pressed into work in the rice fields, young boys turned to slaves in a mindless army.

The reports hadn't yet been made public. No one was certain how much was true, but the possibility drove her forward at this moment with a vengeance.

"Fifty dollars, U.S.," she called, waving her arm at the cycler. "Fifty dollars for a ride." She had almost reached him now. Terror eviscerated any concern for the man and woman sitting behind him. "Fifty dollars for a ride."

She saw it in the man's eyes. Fifty U.S. dollars would feed his family for a year, maybe two or three, with enough left over to purchase a new cycle. It was an unimaginable sum. "Sixty," he countered, almost breathing the words, eyes riveted to hers.

The man behind him, flushed and sweating, suddenly realizing his predicament, stood, swearing and rocking the cart. The woman held onto the sides of the cart and began screaming. Sam avoided their eyes, ignoring her guilt.

"Let me see the money first," the cycler said, holding out his hand palm up, stone-faced.

Sam locked eyes with the man while digging into her purse for the envelope she'd found on her desk at the embassy. How long ago that seemed, years since Oliver had walked through the door and said they must leave. Her fingers located the envelope, and she pulled out six of the ten-dollar bills. She was careful to hide the remaining money that might be needed later on, to spur him forward if things got rough. Now she fanned the sixty dollars just out of reach of the man who could save their lives.

She saw the hunger in his eyes. He would do it.

Nodding, the cycler planted both feet flat on the ground, stood, and twisted around, shouting at his passengers, waving them off. "Get out of my cart! Out!"

Gasping, Sam held the child and watched as the woman froze, not comprehending. The man swung his fist, but the cycler raised his arm, shielding himself from the blow and the passenger, hitting muscles like stone, stumbled back, tumbling from the cart. Riveted, horrified, Sam watched bright blood streaming from the man's forehead as he lay prone on the road beside the cart wheels.

"Help!" the woman screamed, scrambling down. She looked straight at Sam, and Sam, suffused with shame but driven by desperation, looked away. "Help me!" the woman yelled again, pushing her way to the man, stiffening her arms before her as she fell, kneeling over the body. Sam glanced down at them over her shoulder.

"Help him. He'll be crushed!" Bending over the man, the woman shielded him.

The child trembled in Samantha's arms.

"Mem!" The cycler shoved Sam, reaching for the money.

Sam's head snapped up and, holding the boy with one arm, she curled her fingers around the money, fisting it, shaking her head. "When you get us there," she said, forcing herself not to look at the couple on the ground, pointing east.

The boy whimpered.

"Get in then," the cycler said, jerking his head toward the now-empty cart. Averting her eyes from the evicted passengers, the man prone on the ground, bleeding, his wife, huddled over him, Sam lifted the boy into the cart and climbed in behind him.

The cart jerked forward and swayed as the cyclist forced his way through the crowd. Sam turned back once to see the man slowly rising to his feet, supported by the woman. Wide-eyed she swiveled, face forward again behind the cyclist who was forging ahead to the other side of the street where an alley cut through the buildings. *Forgive me.* She would make herself forget this moment, block it from her memory. But despite the din of the crowd, behind her she could still hear the woman's shrill screams, and she knew those cries would stay with her forever.

The alley when they entered it was dark and a few degrees cooler. She let herself relax and took a deep breath. She knew where they were now. The alley would cut across the main thoroughfares, away from the crowds. The boy settled against her, quiet but still clinging to her neck. As the frenzy receded behind them, Sam leaned forward and gave the cyclist directions to the airstrip.

The airstrip was located at the edge of town, dangerous because the perimeters of the city were already under attack. She could hear the sound of gunfire again, closer now. Instantly the cart slowed and stopped. Over his shoulder, the cyclist studied her with a grim look. His eyes traveled down to her fist, still clutching the money, and seconds passed as she held her breath. Finally, he nodded.

As he began peddling again, Sam fell back against the seat with a strangled sob and hugged the child. The boy trembled and she patted his back gently, soothing him, as she glanced again at her watch. A chill ran through her as she realized that only half an hour now stood between escape and certain death.

At the end of the alley the bicycle turned onto a smaller, less-crowded street. Moving against traffic, they turned again and again, winding their way through a warren of alleyways and narrow streets, each one in a poorer area of town than the last.

"How much longer?" she called to the driver.

He shrugged. "Depends." Then quickly: "Sixty dollars no matter what happens, Mem. Whatever time. Sixty dollars."

"Yes," she said. No matter what happened, he'd be paid. He'd simply take it if she refused. She looked at her watch: twenty minutes to five. "Hurry, please hurry!" she cried.

The child pressed closer, silent now.

Chapter Thirteen

New Orleans—1977

ASHLEY ELIZABETH WALKED INTO AMALISE'S OFFICE and dropped a stack of mail into the wooden in-box on the corner of her desk. Amalise looked up and smiled.

"Today's mail," Ashley Elizabeth said. "And Raymond was looking for you earlier." Her eyes strayed to the pile of agreements on Amalise's desk, and she frowned, glancing at her watch. "Should I book help from the typing pool tonight?"

"Yes, four or five hours, I think. And thanks." Amalise swiveled, picked up the phone, and dialed Raymond's extension as Ashley Elizabeth left the office. He answered right away. Had she completed the due diligence they'd discussed on Murdoch and his company?

"Yes. All the corporate records check out. Cayman counsel's working with us on the subsidiary and the letter of credit. Nothing outside of that on Murdoch himself, though. And there was nothing on either company or Murdoch in our library. No litigation, no mention anywhere."

Raymond was silent for a moment. "Doug's going to want something. Let's check him out in newspaper archives, that sort of thing."

"In the public library?"

He hesitated. "Yeah," he finally said. "But don't spend too much time on it. Doug's probably not going to bill the time if we've got nothing to show."

She grimaced. "All right," she said. She'd go to the library this afternoon. Looking at the agreement she'd been working on, she said, "I'll have my comments on the latest draft of the loan agreement to you soon, and then I'll take a walk over there."

The day was sunny, though crisp and cool, and Amalise enjoyed the walk to the main branch of the library on Loyola Avenue. She'd finished marking her comments on the agreement, and Ashley Elizabeth had dropped them off to Raymond. Once he'd reviewed the changes, her secretary had promised to get them to the typing pool for revision overnight. She couldn't do the work herself, Ashley Elizabeth had said, or she'd be late for tennis. But unlike at the start of their relationship two years ago when Amalise was a new associate, Ashley Elizabeth had smiled this time when she'd made the excuse.

The librarian helped her find the newspaper microfiche tapes she needed. She pulled two years of reels for the Sunday *Times-Picayune* and *New York Times*. Sitting in a dark cubbyhole in the corner of the library where the viewers were kept, she leaned forward and began the grueling work of feeding the tape into the lighted machine, scrolling through each thin plastic reel, scanning page after page of the newspapers for any reference to Bingham Murdoch or his company, Lone Ranger.

Nothing came up on Bingham Murdoch. And the company name, Lone Ranger, Inc., turned out to be a troublesome distraction—a false lead in the news because of the cowboy connection. That fact alone nearly doubled the time it took to do the search.

An hour passed this way. Then two. She yawned, stretched, and rubbed her eyes. Her eyesight had begun to blur. Winding through a new reel of the *New York Times* twenty minutes later, her eyes stopped on a paragraph halfway down the page, on a reference to the company name. She bent closer, blinking to focus her eyes in the dim light.

The date was 1971, she saw, and then she leaned back, disappointed. The story was well known and irrelevant to her assignment. Still, it was amusing in a dark way. Raymond would like this one. A lone pirate had hijacked Northwest Orient Flight 305 out of Portland, Oregon, on Thanksgiving Eve six years ago and was never seen again. D. B. Cooper, reporters had mistakenly named him, but the name had stuck.

She smiled and decided to copy the story for Raymond. He was a fan of the Cooper caper. A quote from one of the lead detectives on the case containing a reference to Lone Ranger had caught the article in her search net. "The guy was a real lone ranger," the detective had said, referring to the hijacker.

Pressing the print button for the page, she scrolled to the next. She propped herself on an elbow and read. During a brief stop in Seattle, Cooper had released the passengers but not the crew. He'd demanded two hundred thousand dollars in ransom, plus four parachutes—two backpacks and two chest-packs. The plane took off. Midflight, Cooper jumped with the money and escaped.

The mystery of D. B. Cooper had enthralled the press for years. Police, the FBI, and thousands of volunteers had searched the forested area between Portland and Seattle for Cooper with no luck. A small cache of bills was later found in the Columbia River, but that was all. No other trace of the legend remained.

Amalise pressed the print button on the machine for a copy of the article, and then rolled the tape to the end of the reel. She returned the reels to the librarian, picked up the article from the printer, and stuck it in the folder. Glancing at her watch, she calculated the unbillable time she'd just expended. But, as stated, Bingham Murdoch was a silent investor in the nature of a phantom. He didn't want to be seen, and he wasn't.

꧁꧂

Raymond was in a foul mood when she finally caught up with him, and it didn't help when she told him she'd found nothing to shed any light on Bingham Murdoch. Sun slanted through the window in his office, and

Raymond rose to lower the shade just enough to fend off the worst of the blaze.

"Doug's not going to like this." He sat back, crossed his legs, and snapped his fingers double time. "If Bingham's as big as Tom says, there should be something on the man." He shook his head. "Somewhere."

Amalise slid the due diligence folder over to him, opened it, and pointed. "Take a look at that."

Raymond quit snapping his fingers and turned the folder toward him. He looked up. "What's this?"

"I ran across it through a reference to the company name, Lone Ranger." She leaned over, pointing to the detective's statement in the middle of the first page. "Thought you'd get a kick out of it."

He read the line she'd pointed out, then sat back and read the article. "My old friend D. B. Cooper," he said when he'd finished. Smiling, he put the article back in the file.

Steepling his hands, he rested his chin on the tips of his fingers. "That was six years ago. I wonder where he is now."

"That's the question of the decade." Amalise picked up the file and wandered over to the window. She braced her hands behind her back and looked at the clouds sliding by. "They've been looking for him ever since. He's probably on a yacht in Marina Del Rey." She turned and looked at him.

Raymond dropped his hands onto the desk. "Naw. That doesn't fit. He only got two hundred thousand dollars."

"Only!" Amalise arched her brows. "That's more than eight years of my salary. If he invested it right, he could be in Monaco."

Raymond hiked a shoulder.

Amalise walked toward the door. "See you tomorrow, bright and early. Jude's taking me out to dinner tonight." He'd called when she'd returned from the library earlier, and something in his voice had struck a warning chord. They were going to Clancy's, to celebrate a special occasion, he'd said.

She'd been struggling not to think about that call ever since. Her heart raced even now, remembering how she'd frozen when she'd heard those words. Very few things qualified as special occasions. A birth. A death. A marriage.

Rebecca and Jude?

She prayed that she was wrong. *Abba, let this not be so.* But despite the inner turmoil, she put a smile on her face for Raymond and kept her tone light.

"Better enjoy it," Raymond said without looking up. "It'll be your last night off until the closing."

Chapter Fourteen

JUDE PARKED ACROSS FROM THE SMALL restaurant on the corner. He jammed the keys into his pocket and crossed the street, thinking about the decision he'd reached. Amalise's purchase of the house on Broadway had set off an alarm, an internal warning that he'd chosen to heed. She was settling down now, planning the years ahead as she planned everything in life. He wanted to be a part of her life—her vision of the future— no matter how long he had to wait for marriage. He wanted Amalise to know that, for him, friendship had turned to love.

His heart skipped a beat at the thought of saying these things to Amalise. This conversation would change everything between them, he knew. As he opened the door, he said a silent prayer that his words would spark feelings in Amalise that she'd not recognized before. Or at least see him in a new light and then, over time, well . . . he would wait as long as it took.

His breath caught as the words ran through his mind.

I love you, Amalise.

They fit. They sounded right.

The maître d' greeted him, and Jude gave his name.

"Evening, Mr. Perret," the man said with a slight bow. He reached out and touched the back of Jude's arm, guiding him toward a table in the corner, at the front of the restaurant near a window, as he'd requested. "This way, please, sir."

As he took a seat, the maître d' smoothed the tablecloth as if wiping off invisible crumbs. In the center was a candle and one perfect red rose. The maître d' shifted the unlit candle and the flower, moving each one inch to the right. Then he turned and lifted a finger, and a waiter appeared with two glasses and a small crystal pitcher of ice water. The maître d' then smiled at Jude, nodded at the waiter, and glided off to his post.

Jude settled back, one eye on the door as the waiter lit the candle, set two menus down beside him, and filled the glasses with water. Jude ordered a soda with lime while he waited. When the waiter finished his ministrations and left, Jude blew out his cheeks, arched his fingers against the edge of the table, and looked at the door, feeling tense, as if he were waiting to climb Jacob's ladder on an up-bound ship on a stormy night in the Gulf.

The clock ticked. Jude ran his finger around the inside of his collar, picked up his napkin, then set it down again. His drink arrived, and he sipped it. Setting the glass down, he began drumming his fingers on the table in time with a song from years ago running through his head. He couldn't remember the name of the tune, try as he might, and that turned his thoughts to old age and the short measure of time we have on earth, and how long it was taking for Amalise to arrive.

And then he laughed at himself. He was waiting for Amalise, after all. Folding his hands on the table before him, Jude leaned back and gazed around the small L-shaped restaurant. The tables were close together, and there was already a crowd. He congratulated himself on reserving this one tucked away in the quiet corner. Bright, colorful pictures on the mahogany-paneled walls gave the room an elegant but festive look. Each table at Clancy's was an island of white linen, silver, sparkling crystal, roses, and glowing candles.

When the door opened and at last Amalise walked in, Jude sucked in his breath. There was something different about her tonight. Her hair was chin length in a new cut, straight and dark and shining against her skin.

She was effervescent, glowing. The maître d' took her coat, and Jude saw that she was wearing a dark-red dress with long sleeves that emphasized her hair, her skin, and her curves. When she spotted him, a smile lit her face.

She tucked one side of her hair back behind an ear and started toward him, and he stood. The only jewelry she wore was a long strand of pearls the Judge and Maraine had given her for her sixteenth birthday.

When she came close, he said she looked beautiful and held out his hand. She smiled, taking his hand, and leaned in to plant a kiss on his cheek. "Have you been waiting long?" she asked.

"No. Just got here." He pulled out the chair beside him, the one nearest the window, and stepped aside. When she turned and smiled up at him, he caught the scent she wore. The soap and roses were gone. This fragrance was something new. Simple but elegant. It was Amalise grown up.

"What a treat!" she said, hanging her purse on the back of the chair and looking about. Her voice held a note of tension, but when she turned to him she was smiling, and he thought that he'd imagined that tension. "I love this place." She touched his hand and then retreated before he could hold onto hers. "It's so cozy. I've never been here before. Have you?"

He nodded. "For Rebecca's birthday last year. The food's wonderful."

"Rebecca." She looked around. Seconds passed. "Yes. She'd like this place."

Jude picked up his glass of water and tipped it to her. "Well, this is a special night for two old friends." *And confessing for the first time that I'm in love with you is going to be a once-in-a-lifetime event.*

◦～◦

Amalise lowered her eyes. She'd seen the shine in Jude's eyes, the spray of lines around them when he smiled. He was happy tonight, and here she was struggling not to cry. Jude was straightforward and he'd get to it soon—this special occasion, why they were here. But now she knew—she'd seen it in his eyes when he'd mentioned Rebecca. He wanted to share his good news with her.

Ah, how unthinking she'd been over the last few years, how arrogant to assume that Jude was hers, that he'd always be there. Even after she'd ignored his advice and married Phillip Sharp. And now, too late, she'd recognized that what she felt for Jude was love. With her own exquisite timing, she'd sorted out her feelings just as he was moving on. Even if he'd ever been hers, had she thought he would wait forever, a man like Jude?

Driving here tonight, she'd resolved to take this evening moment by moment, feel her way through the minefield. Well, she told herself, now it was time to start.

Abba, give me strength to handle this well. Give me the words to let Jude feel happy. You know how I am, how I sometimes blurt things out before I think. Help me not to burden Jude with my own feelings.

The waiter appeared and took their orders. Redfish for her, grilled. And vegetables. Jude chose the filet, medium rare, baked potato. No salads.

When the waiter had gone, Jude held out the bread basket for her. As she reached for a piece of the crusty, hot bread, their fingers touched. The touch stayed with her when they parted, seeming to tingle as he talked about Pilottown this time of year and how the skies changed in October at the mouth of the river. He spoke romantically of the antique fall colors of the marsh reeds, the patterns of the birds and fish, the flow currents.

Jude was as solid as an old growth oak. He was fresh air and sunshine and comforting. And as he talked on without one mention of the thing she feared, despite her earlier resolutions a seed of hope began to sprout. Hadn't they loved each other since they were children? Weren't each of those years between them links in a chain that should bind them together forever?

⟡

Amalise was full of stories about the transaction she was working on, as well as the latest news from home and Maraine and the Judge. He told her about the last two weeks in P-town—this was a time of year he loved down there. But he'd decided to wait until after their meal, during coffee or dessert, to make his move.

The waiter appeared again with their plates. When he'd gone, they both dropped their heads and Amalise reached for his hand, giving thanks for the food and evening and their friendship. Her hand was warm, as soft as when she was a child, and for an instant he considered bringing up the subject now.

But when she'd finished saying grace, she released his hand and reached for her glass. Turning, she held it up to him, and he did the same. She said, "To friendship," with a smile and a tilt of her head.

He said, "To your new house and all that's in it, including you," and they both laughed.

She picked up her fork and he did too, wondering if he'd be able to eat. But the steak was perfectly cooked and tender, so that problem disappeared. "Are you settled into your house yet?" he asked. "Rebecca says the place already looks like home. Says it's just the kind of place she wants to find."

Amalise seemed to draw back at these words.

"Rebecca was a help," she said slowly, setting her fork down on the edge of her plate. She paused and looked at him in the way she had when they were kids and he would leave her sitting on the sidelines at one of his baseball games, when she wanted to play. But immediately her face cleared, and again, he decided he was going about things all wrong. He drew in his breath. Maybe he should just go ahead and tell her.

But in that instant Amalise planted both hands on the seat of her chair and sat up straight, stiff armed, looking resolute as she leaned forward. He braced himself, recognizing the launch position.

"I love my new house, Jude. I'm starting over with everything. Bought all new furniture, secondhand stuff, but it looks nice. And we, um—that is, Rebecca and I—put pictures on the walls. New rugs, linens."

He nodded, fork hovering over the plate. "That's good. You'll have a fresh start." *After Phillip.* The unspoken words lingered between them as he chewed.

"Yes."

"I want to come over and see what you've done." He grinned. "Rebecca says you need more bookcases, since you kept all the books. I've got an extra one if you want it." Books took up most of any room that belonged to Amalise.

He felt a subtle change in the atmosphere, the way things tend to go still before an incoming storm. She glanced over at him with a wooden smile.

"Yes. I've kept those." Her tone was cool. "And yes, if you're not using the bookcase, I definitely can."

He nodded, uncertain. "I'll bring it over."

She began picking at her food in a distracted manner. He lifted his own fork, but the beef tasted like cardboard now. Minutes passed.

He shifted the subject to something he knew. "There are some things to be done in that back yard of yours," he said, breaking the uncomfortable silence.

She looked up. "Like what?"

He shrugged. "Oh, fence boards that need replacing, things like that. I'll come around soon and fix them." He studied her. "Rebecca says you want a garden along the fence line. I could dig one, if you'd like."

She dug her fork into a carrot and put it in her mouth. Bemused, he watched her chew and swallow the food without looking up once at him. "No need for that," she said in an offhand tone. "Rebecca's got it wrong." She picked up the napkin and dabbed the corners of her mouth. "I don't have time for gardens right now. Not with everything going on at work."

Something was bothering her, and he hadn't a clue what it was. Feeling slightly irritable, he threw up his hands. "Fine. All right. But the fence needs work."

"Why do you say that?" She tilted her head and gave him a surprising, challenging look.

He set his fork down. Rested his hands on the table, one on each side of the plate and looked at her. "Have you checked it lately?"

"Checked the fence?" A short laugh escaped. "What would I be looking for?"

"Rotted wood."

She got a faraway look on her face and shrugged. Picked up her fork again, bent over her plate, and scooped up the last of the redfish. "It's not necessary."

Amalise could be inscrutable sometimes.

The waiter cleared their places and took off with the plates. Amalise folded her hands on the table before her and said nothing. It was time to get things back on track.

Jude pushed back his chair, angling it toward her. "There's something I want to talk about with you, chère."

She seemed to freeze. She sat very still, then dropped her hands in her lap and turned toward him. When she looked up, her face was etched with strain. "Go ahead."

He looked at her, confused, and decided that he'd just entered a no-wake zone. Women were strange; dead slow would be best in this situation. So he rearranged the plan. First, he'd make her understand his serious intent, that he wanted to settle down and create a home with her. And he needed to lighten things up—Amalise looked like she was going to a funeral.

So he slung one arm over the back of the chair, rested the other on the table, and fixed his eyes on the knife beside his plate. "I've been thinking of making big changes in my life, Amalise." Absently, he turned the knife over and over again as he spoke.

She said nothing.

Not a good start. He gave her a long look, conscious of her eyes, wide and round, fixed on him as if death had just knocked on the door. "To tell you the truth, I've been thinking of settling down here in the city."

Amalise blinked. "You mean giving up your work?"

His heart swooped in his chest. He nodded. "As a pilot. That's the idea, yes." Her lips parted, but he hurried on. No telling how Amalise could turn the conversation around if he let her jump in now. "I'm thinking of getting into real estate investment. Buying some properties, uptown at first, maybe in the Irish Channel. I've got my eye on two, for starters. I'd renovate them, fix them up, and sell them." He picked up his knife and tapped it gently on the white-clothed table, watching her.

"Why?"

That was always her first question. He almost smiled. This was the question he wanted to answer. But he reminded himself, dead slow ahead.

"Because I like the idea of living in one place, here in the city." He looked down at the knife, still tapping away. "And I like the idea of making a home."

He had plenty saved. He had learned the value of money from Dad, who'd never had a dime he didn't spend on drink. This had made him frugal. And with Amalise's long hours at work, well, he'd be around to help. His time would be flexible, and she'd have the support and freedom she'd need in the next few years for her career, if that's what she chose to do.

With children, one of us will have to change our schedules.

Amalise blinked. "I'm surprised, Jude." She hugged herself, as if she felt cold. "But there's money in fixing up old houses, and you'd be good at that." She looked off, over the table, toward the front door. "Rebecca thinks you're good at that, too."

"Yes. We've talked about it. She thinks it's a good idea."

Amalise went still, eyes riveted to the door. Jude followed her look but saw nothing to attract her attention.

Something was bothering Amalise this evening and she'd just disappeared down a rabbit hole. Her reserve put him on edge. So Jude filled the long silence by going on about his real estate idea, while part of his mind worked on putting the real question before her.

The waiter appeared. "Would you like coffee tonight?"

Still thinking about Amalise's odd behavior, he looked up at the waiter and then raised his brows toward Amalise. But her attention was fixed somewhere past him.

"Coffee, Amalise?" Jude tipped his head to one side. A busboy came and moved around them, whisking away their plates, silverware, and the basket of bread and refilling the water glasses.

She flinched. She looked up at the waiter and shook her head. "Not for me."

Jude suppressed an exasperated sigh. He looked at the waiter. "I'll have a cup, please. Cream and sugar." He turned to Amalise. "How about dessert?"

"Not tonight."

The waiter nodded, seeming to sense the tension. He scooped up their napkins, handed them to the busboy, and hustled off.

The incipient hope had died.

Rebecca. Jude kept mentioning her name. Amalise turned this over in her mind as he spoke to the waiter, moved aside for the busboy, asked if she'd like some coffee or dessert. She knew she couldn't eat a thing right now.

This new plan, this huge change in his life—giving up his pilot's license—he'd been mulling it over awhile, he'd said. He had never mentioned it to her before, but it sounded like he'd talked it over with Rebecca. Giving up the river! She could hardly take it in.

How long had Rebecca known about this, and why hadn't she mentioned it to Amalise? A wave of misery rolled through her as she tracked back over everything that Jude had said tonight, and the truth unfolded methodically in her mind.

Jude was giving up the river for Rebecca, to make a home. They were in love. And the moment the thought was articulated in her mind, she realized it was true, precise and to the mark. Once again that void yawned inside—the hollow longing for something she couldn't identify, a feeling that she'd had since the accident, an emptiness that so far she'd been unable to fill with work, as she used to do, or with the new house she'd just bought. Not even by clinging to the old friendship with Jude because, with Jude, she wanted more.

But she'd probably lost any chance of love with Jude long ago, on the day she'd married Phillip. He was Rebecca's now.

Recognition came as a brutal blow but not as a complete surprise. She turned, looking at the front door and the maître d' manning the podium there, hiding the tears that threatened, tears she'd never let Jude see, and suddenly the need to flee before she broke down pushed all other thoughts aside. She'd learned well enough from Phillip that pity was a trap. She'd never hang that kind of guilt on Jude.

Jude. Oh Jude, if you only knew.

But emotions could not be trusted now. She knew what had to be done. Hands on the edges of the chair, she straightened, saying "Hmm" and "Yes" as he talked about this new business—he'd already bid for two properties, he said—all the while calculating how far it was to that door.

Abba! Ten steps to the door. Fifteen, maybe. Help me get there!

And then he touched her arm, and that drew her full attention.

❦

As he looked into Amalise's eyes, gathering the words he'd come here to say, he felt the love inside him swell and he allowed himself to hope. Perhaps he'd misjudged her and when he spoke the words, he'd find that she loved him, too. Perhaps, perhaps . . . *Oh, just get the words out now, Perret.*

So he reached over and picked up her hands and held them in his, and then he took a deep breath. "Amalise, I realize that this may sound a little strange . . ." And then he hesitated.

What *were* the right words? How do you tell your oldest friend that you're in love with her? That you love her, not just as an old friend loves a friend, but as a man loves a woman once in a lifetime. That you long to marry her, no matter the time you may have to wait. That you will love her for the rest of your life and into eternity beyond. That you want children together.

Even as that thought came, he could see himself and Amalise and their children—three or four or five—and the Judge and Maraine, all sitting together at the table on the pier over the lagoon at her family home in Marianus.

He closed his eyes for a second. That was his dream, but how to begin?

And then he opened his eyes, looked at her, and said, "You know, chère, relationships change over time. Even friendships like ours."

Relationships change. His words tolled in her mind as a warning. She'd seen how hard the words were for him to actually say, to tell her of Rebecca. Her heart plunged, but she couldn't seem to move, to pull her hands from his. She was careful not to allow her face to betray her as the cold, heavy words sank in, words that would change her life, that would take Jude from her forever.

And underneath the words, the way he looked at her with such joy and sadness all at once, underneath those careful words she heard the unspoken name. *Rebecca.*

In that split second she looked down the stultifying years ahead, seeing the course their friendship would take after he married Rebecca. And he knew her well enough to understand that taking second place to someone else would require a huge adjustment on her part.

The observer whispered, *Remember, Amalise, he's being honest with you, respectful of your friendship. You didn't do the same for him with Phillip.*

She glanced again at the door and knew that she had to leave before he spoke the words. However their relationship was going to change, she wanted to deal with her feelings on her own. And she knew that she couldn't let him finish what he was about to say, because no matter how gently he spoke the words, how carefully he phrased them, the weight of losing him and hearing about his love for Rebecca would break her.

Yes. Relationships do change.

As he sucked in a breath and opened his mouth to go on, Amalise pulled her hands from his. Leaning back, away from him, she held up one hand, palm out.

"Stop." *Stop!*

A frown creased his forehead and he drew back, brows raised. "Amalise? What's wrong?"

And now the waiter stood before them with Jude's coffee.

Quickly, before Jude could say another word, she pushed back her chair and stood, wishing she didn't have to walk through the other diners to get to the door. Wishing that she could just snap her fingers and be at home, alone.

"Amalise!" Jude's voice again.

The waiter stepped back, getting out of the way.

Jude reached for her arm, but she was moving now, lifting her purse from the chair, slinging it over her shoulder, turning away. She had to get out of here. Now.

She left him behind at the table. Murmured something about not feeling well. She was sorry, so sorry, to ruin this beautiful night, to have to leave like this. But she wasn't feeling well.

Jude's voice, full of concern, came behind her. He would take her home. She should let him drive her.

But she shook her head, eyes fixed on the door as she managed those ten or fifteen steps through the tables in between, ignoring the upturned eyes, leaving Jude in her wake as she begged Abba for help. She asked for her coat and let the maître d' help her put it on. Then turning, she looked at the door, knowing that once she walked through it, she would be alone and Jude would be lost to her forever.

"Amalise!" He'd reached her and was holding onto her arm.

Irrational anger swung her around. Anger was her shield. She moved closer to him and spoke low. "I'm not a child. I can take care of myself now, Jude."

But when her eyes met his and she saw pain, she softened. This was hard on him, too, she realized. She looked at him and knew she had to let him off the hook.

So she managed a smile. "Like you said before, relationships do change. I'm enjoying my independence and the new house, and really . . . I don't need your help right now." She hiked one shoulder, freeing herself from his grip. "I can take care of myself."

He only stared.

Looking at him, she forced back the tears and clung to the shoulder strap of her purse. "Independence is what I need most right now, I suppose. And time."

His hands dropped to his sides. "I wouldn't interfere with that." His tone was flat.

She nodded, turned, and walked away, holding back the tears that she would later shed at home, fighting the longing to whirl around and run back to Jude and beg him to hold her in his arms just one last time.

But as he'd said, relationships change. And that's the way he wanted things.

Jude went back to the table and lowered himself into the chair, stunned by what had just occurred, feeling as though he'd slammed into a Mississippi sandbar full speed ahead.

The waiter hovered nearby, and when the black leather folder containing the bill appeared on the table, he paid it quickly. As though he were walking under water, he set his expression to neutral and managed to make his way to the door.

And then anger rose. And resentment. And he could feel the bile rising to the back of his throat as he pushed through the door and stood just outside. He simply could not understand Amalise. He'd been her bulwark for years. He'd protected her, always, helping her grow from an awkward girl into a strong young woman. He'd taught her how to swim, fish, paddle a pirogue through the swamp, how to dance, how to handle herself in a crowd. Always, he'd been there for her.

The worst thing was, he suspected that she'd known what he'd wanted to say and didn't want to hear that from him, her old friend. She wanted things to stay exactly as they were between them. She wanted no change. Status quo.

What a fool he'd been to set himself up for this without finding out first how she felt, how she might react. But a wan smile crossed his face at that idea, because Amalise was never easy to predict.

As he stood on the corner outside the restaurant, memories assailed him. Amalise in the skiff on a sun-kissed Thanksgiving Day, her hair blowing in the wind, her cheeks rosy in the sunshine and fresh air.

Maraine, her mother, as close to a mother as he'd had since his own died when he was young. And the Judge, her father, who'd helped him become a man. Standing on that corner in the darkness, alone, with Amalise gone and all hope with her, he felt a cord winding about his chest, pulling tight. And it crossed his mind that this bound, empty feeling was how he'd go through life from now on.

He would always love Amalise—he knew that.

Jamming his hands into his pockets, neck bowed, he crossed the street and headed for his car.

Chapter Fifteen

THE HOUSE ON BROADWAY WASN'T FAR from Clancy's, but the drive seemed to stretch for hours. Amalise whispered the words out loud, forcing herself to face the fact that this was real, that Jude was in love with Rebecca.

Abba, why did you let this happen?!

But she knew the answer. For the hundredth time since the moment she'd first realized she was in love with Jude, she replayed the past two years in her mind. While Rebecca and Jude had been falling in love, she had been too consumed by work—and by Phillip's needs, his demands—to notice. Yet through everything that had happened, Jude had stood by her side. Why had she never thought of losing him like this?

Relationships change, he'd said.

Turning from Magazine Street onto Broadway, she slowed the car, already regretting her abrupt departure from Clancy's. She should have given him time to speak, at least. That's what a friend would do. Should have been strong enough to listen to what he'd wanted to say and keep her thoughts to herself, let him tell her of his joy, of this big event in his life.

A tear slipped down her cheek. Everyone needs a listener for big moments. But then the muscles in her abdomen clenched as she thought of the wedding she'd have to attend. Worse, Rebecca would probably ask her to be in the wedding party, and she'd watch as the only man she could ever love married someone else. She swiped away tears from her cheeks with the heel of her hand, longing to turn the car around and drive toward Jude's house on State Street. To weep on his shoulders.

The thought of weeping on Jude's shoulders over his own wedding brought a smile through the tears. Jude was right. She was a master of the ability to compartmentalize. She was a constant victim of illusion. Indeed, she would learn to tuck away this problem, to go on without Jude. Somehow. She would have to learn to sever the friendship from the pain. Because despite the overwhelming sorrow, despite the searing pain, a little breath of wisdom told her that otherwise she'd lose Jude's friendship altogether.

She would have to be strong enough to let him go. *Abba, I know you're listening. Will you give me the strength that I don't have?*

Once home she forced herself to focus on her nightly routine. Pulled a gown from the dresser drawer, undressed, and threw it on. Hung up her clothes, turned down the cover on the bed, fluffed the pillows. She'd leave for work earlier than usual come morning.

Brushing her teeth, Amalise examined herself in the mirror, searching for reflections of the person she'd been in the days before Phillip, happier times when she and Jude were still so close that he'd seemed a part of her. The woman looking back at her had a wary look, guarded with, perhaps, a streak of new determination. She bent and splashed water on her face, reached for a towel, and patted her skin dry. Then she brushed her short dark hair and turned off the bathroom light.

It was a cool October night. Hadn't rained in weeks, she realized. She opened the windows and let the pungent scent of sweet olive fill the bedroom. Climbing into bed, she arranged the pillows neatly for her head, then lay down and pulled up the covers. She turned onto her left side, wiped away another tear, and jerking one of the pillows from underneath her head, hugged it to her chest. Minutes passed, and still hugging the pillow, she rolled over onto her right side.

For perhaps an hour she stared at the window and the branches of the sweet olive tree brushing against the screen. At last, she tossed the pillow onto the floor, rolled onto her back, threw out her arms, and stared up at the ceiling while the clock stubbornly continued its slow march toward morning.

In the early hours, just before dawn, she closed her eyes with one thought still hanging on: She would be strong. Abba would help her to be strong. Jude would never know how she felt.

Over the next few days she found that the raw pain began to diminish as she focused her energy and attention on the thousands of tasks to be performed for Project Black Diamond, leaving her little time to dwell on Jude and Rebecca. Tucked away, her misery became a melancholy vibration that was always with her, like the last piano notes of the *Moonlight Sonata* lingering even after the tune had ended.

The quiet times were the worst. That's when she let herself really listen to that music, recalling every good time she'd had over the years with Jude.

In the quiet times.

Chapter Sixteen

ONE MORNING NOT LONG AFTER THE disastrous dinner, before the music had settled in her mind, Amalise stood on the back porch of her house on Broadway and looked at the new boards in the fence. Her left hand was planted on her hip, her hip jutting out as it bore her weight. In her right hand was a steaming cup of coffee that she'd brought out to drink in the cool morning air before leaving for work. And then her eyes had lit on those three—no, she counted four. Oh! There were *five* unauthorized new boards in the fence. Jude had been here.

Rebecca's Jude.

Amalise scrutinized those boards and sipped her coffee, frowning. He'd come over and fixed the fence without even asking. Just torn out the old and replaced it with new.

Fury rose. *Things aren't as simple as all that, Jude.* One doesn't rip out the old and slam in the new without warning, not on someone else's property at least.

Nor in a heart, the observer whispered.

But this was her territory. This was *her* fence. And Jude had not consulted her before making this change.

Turning, she stormed back into the house, went to the telephone sitting on the round three-legged table in the hallway, and picked up the receiver. But even as she pressed the receiver to her ear, her anger began to cool. Seconds passed as she listened to the dial tone.

Slowly she lowered the receiver back into the cradle.

This wasn't about the fence, she knew. Not really. This anger was about her old life, about Phillip and the double bind: his weakness and her strength and acquiescence. She'd sanctioned his demands, his control over every moment of their marriage, and she wasn't about to let that happen again. Not even with Jude.

The phone rang just as she was walking out the door.

"Amalise?"

"Yes."

"This is Jude."

Of course she recognized his voice. Her thoughts scattered.

"Oh. Hello, Jude." She thought of the boards in the fence, of how she didn't need his help, and of how he was leaving her alone for Rebecca. And then his face rose before her, and she thought how, no matter what, Jude would be a part of her life. She would always love him. Yet all she could think of to say was, "Thanks for fixing the fence. It looks nice."

"You're welcome."

"The boards you added are a lighter color," she said. "I hadn't realized there were so many old ones."

"The new wood will weather. Then you won't be able to tell the difference."

She closed her eyes. "How long do you think that will take?"

"Oh, I don't know. A couple of years, maybe."

"That long?"

"Yeah. Change takes a while, but it happens over time. And then everything looks the same."

Jude hung up the phone, walked into the living room, and snapped on the television set. He fell back onto the couch and put his feet up on the footstool, crossing them. *Women!* It was as though he and Amalise were speaking two different languages. She certainly hadn't opened the door to further conversation, though. If anything, she'd sounded cool, a little distant. One thing was clear: She wanted nothing more between them than the status quo.

Standing, he went to the TV and changed the channel, tried all three stations, and clicked it off. Thinking again of the evening at Clancy's, a rise of bitterness was instantly followed by a wave of emotional pain.

The phone rang and he picked it up.

"Hi there." Rebecca's voice was cheerful, vanquishing the gloom. "I'm off early tonight. How about a movie?"

"Sure. What's playing?"

He could almost hear the shrug. "I don't know, but for $2.50 we can't go wrong."

There was work to do on the empty apartment next door before he returned to Pilottown next week. Renovations were needed before he could rent it out again. But he could stand to escape the world for a while at the Prytania Theater. "Okay, I'll pick you up. What time?"

"Seven thirty?"

"Sounds good."

Hanging up the phone, Jude pictured Rebecca's easy smile, the way she had of flipping that long red hair back over her shoulder with a little shake of her head when she laughed. She was fun, uncomplicated.

He'd be back on watch in about a week. And that was fine with him, because right about now he wanted nothing more than to forget about Amalise Catoir for a while.

Chapter Seventeen

Phnom Penh, Cambodia 1975

THE CHILD WHIMPERED, MOVING CLOSE, BURYING his face against Samantha as the cycle sped past the shanty huts that ringed the city. She held tight to the boy, wondering if the places they were passing were familiar to him. Imagined scenes haunted her. A mother weeping in the shanty warren, searching alleyways for her little boy. A desperate father calling.

But she couldn't leave him there alone. She comforted herself with the thought that the child was more likely one of the city's thousands of new orphans. He'd ravaged the sandwich at her apartment as if he hadn't eaten in days. There was no telling what horrors he had faced. Holding him against her now, she was even more conscious of his fragility, how small he was, with those big, empty eyes.

She bent her head, lips to his ear, and whispered in Khmer, "Who are you, child? Where is home?" But his only response was to press closer. Absently she stroked his hair, forcing away thoughts of a family that would be lost to him forever once they boarded that plane.

As the bicycle cart rocked along at surprising speed, she wondered where the two of them would end up. And who would care for him once she got him out of here? She'd never given a thought to the idea of raising a child. She was married to her mission work. Was there room in her life for a child?

The cyclist interrupted her thoughts, pointing. "Look there!"

He was leaving the main road, pedaling furiously at a diagonal across a burned field bordered on three sides by the thick, brooding jungle. Shading her eyes, she spotted the planes in the distance. The familiar Air America C-123s were about half mile away, she judged. But even so, she could see the propellers already spinning.

The bicycle cart bounced over the uneven field, threatening to overturn at any moment. Yet the cyclist did not slow. Sam clung to the child with one hand and gripped the edge of the cart with the other. As they grew closer, she saw cars, a Jeep, and a truck parked near the planes. And she could see people running for the ramps to board at the back of the planes.

A fresh surge of fear rushed through her as she dug into her purse for the money she'd promised the cyclist. Surely Oliver wouldn't leave her behind. She lifted her hand, waving and calling Oliver's name as the cart swayed and picked up speed.

Still, no one turned or seemed to see them.

Without slowing, the cyclist held his hand up over his shoulder, motioning. She shoved all the money into his fist—forty dollars extra, but he'd probably need it.

Now she could make out faces. She could see Oliver now. And Jason Brandt from CARE. And Margaret Bordelon from the embassy, with her girl. Others were running from their cars, arms shielding their faces from the dust raised by the propellers.

Sam called out again and again as the cart bounced across the field, but the engines roared and obliterated all other sound.

And then, ninety yards away, clutching the child with one arm, she waved and with all the power in her lungs she screamed out his name. *"Oliver! Oliver! Oliver!"*

At the foot of the ramp he halted and turned, frowning, peering into the sun, hands over his eyes, searching the field.

She half rose now in the swaying cart, grasping the child and pushing herself up. When at last he lifted his arm, waving, she broke into a smile. *Thank you, Lord. He's seen us!*

Oliver started forward, motioning, winding his arms, reeling her in, and she could hear him shouting, "Hurry, Sam! Hurry!"

That's when the cart lurched, careening from side to side as it rolled on toward the planes. A spot of bright red blood spread across the back of the cyclist, and he slumped over the handlebars.

In that instant, she heard the noise rising above the din of the engines: ear-splitting explosions—*rat-tat-tat-tat*. She recognized the sound of the Khmer Rouge AK-47s that everyone had talked about. They were here. Now.

She pushed the child down into her lap and ducked over him. Again came the stuttering, pounding sound, and dirt began shooting up around them. There was no time to think or even scream as the air around the cart turned to dust. The boy burrowed deeper, clinging to her, wailing, until at last, the cart rattled to a stop.

One thought emerged: *Get out.*

But fear rooted Sam to the seat behind the bloody cyclist, and she could not seem to move.

Suddenly a hand gripped her arm and someone pulled at her, shouting her name. Then she was out of the cart, with the child in her arms and the sun burning down on them, and they were running, running through the hiss of bullets splitting the air and the popping striping of the earth that threw up pebbles and chunks of dirt around them.

When at last they reached the ramp, a grinding hydraulic whine began. The engines revved and the last plane began slowly moving, dragging the ramp along behind it.

Amid the dust and commotion, Sam halted, panicked.

Oliver, now above her, already climbing, coaxed her up the moving ramp. "Sam! Come on, Sam!"

Then she handed the boy to Oliver, and arms reached out from the black hole behind him, taking the child and he turned back, reaching for her now and looking past her, over her shoulder, his eyes widening.

Looking back, following his eyes, Sam saw the soldiers bursting from trees and bush at the far side of the field, guns pointed, running toward them. With a scream she reached for Oliver and he grabbed her hand.

Holding her eyes, Oliver pulled her slowly up the ramp, the plane jolting them both as the engines revved.

Again came the *rat-tat-tat* followed by the *tink-tink-tink* of metal on metal this time. And that's when she felt it: just a sting at first, and then a burning, swelling, spreading pain as Oliver pulled at her suddenly dead weight.

Chapter Eighteen

New Orleans—1977

ON HER WAY TO WORK ONE morning, Amalise stopped at Langenstein's Market uptown to pick up groceries for Caroline to replace the ones she'd dropped and broken. There was a worn look to the home on Kerlerec Street, and to the family's furniture and clothing, that told her every penny counted in that household. Loading the bags into the trunk of her car, she then headed down St. Charles Avenue toward the Quarter, then on to Marigny.

She parked in front of Caroline's house, got out, and saw the children in the front yard. Daisy, wearing a pair of jeans and a red sweater too big for her, sat on the stairs with her arms wrapped around her knees, watching Charlie and Nick play kickball. Luke was nowhere to be seen. When Charlie spotted her and shouted, Daisy jumped up, waving and stamping her feet. Amalise waved back, smiling, and then hefted the two brown grocery bags and crossed the street.

Nick ran to the gate and held it open. She thanked him and made her way up the steps past Daisy, who yanked gently on the bottom of her skirt. Amalise turned, looked down, and said hello. Daisy stepped back, hooked a finger in the corner of her mouth, and smiled without saying anything.

Amalise knocked on the wooden frame of the screened door through which the interior of the house was visible. A light was on in the kitchen, and she could see Caroline hurrying through the living room toward her, smoothing her hair as she came.

"Amalise!" Caroline threw open the door and looked at the grocery bags. Her brows shot up. "Come on in," she said, stepping aside. The door slammed shut behind her. "What's that?" Caroline nodded at the bags.

"Replacements. For the mess I made the other day."

Caroline smiled. "You didn't have to do that." She leaned forward and took one of the bags balanced in Amalise's arms.

"I hope you don't mind."

"Of course not," Caroline said, as Amalise followed her into the kitchen. "It's kind of you to do this, and of course I love your company." She looked back over her shoulder. "Can you stay for a cup of coffee, or maybe some tea?" She plopped the brown paper bag she'd been carrying down on the kitchen table and turned for the other one.

"Coffee would be good. Black." Amalise handed the bag to Caroline, and then spotted Luke perched in a big chair at the other end of the table. Conscious of her attention, he slumped, chin dipping shyly to his chest. Slowly he slid his hands from the table into his lap.

"Hello, Luke," she said.

He flung his arms back onto the table and dropped his forehead, hiding his face.

Outside, the children's laughter rang out. Luke remained silent while Amalise and Caroline put away the food she'd brought. Caroline was unusually quiet. When they'd finished, Amalise sat down beside Luke while Caroline poured two cups of coffee.

But when she turned to hand one to Amalise, her face crumpled. Tears ran down her cheeks, and she sank into the nearest chair.

Amalise moved around to her, resting her hand on a shoulder. "What's wrong? Is there something I can do to help?"

Caroline shook her head, sniffling, and quickly wiped away the tears, struggling in vain to smile. "I'm sorry about this." Caroline looked at Amalise. "You've caught me at a bad time." She shook her head and wrapped her hands around the coffee cup. "It's been a rotten morning."

Amalise braced against the table, preparing to push up. "I'd better leave, then."

"No!" Caroline flushed. "I didn't mean that the way it sounded. I'm glad you showed up when you did. And—and, again, thank you for everything." But the smile on her face didn't reach her eyes. She fingered the collar of her shirt, straightening it. The tremulous smile disappeared. "It's the children, Amalise. Problems with our adoption petitions."

"Oh no." Amalise pushed back her chair, angling it to face Caroline. "What happened?"

Caroline gave her a wan smile. "The social worker handling the approval process, Francine Gebb, is worried about our ability to provide for all four children. She called yesterday. We've included Luke in the petitions, too." She glanced at Luke who was sitting up straight now, watching. "Of course, they're also looking at how the children have acclimated to us." Then she started, as if shaking herself.

"I bet things will work out. You've made a wonderful family, all of you together."

"Well, she sounded a little strange, like she was holding something back. Said she'd get back to us soon. Until yesterday we'd thought there'd be no problem, that the petitions would be approved." She spread her hands and pressed her lips together with a little sound of exasperation. "So now I'm waiting for her call."

Amalise glanced at her watch and smiled. "It's only eight thirty in the morning."

"I know." She looked about as if seeing the kitchen through the eyes of Francine Gebb. "The place is old, but it's plenty big enough. And Ellis keeps things up."

Amalise nodded and sipped her coffee, visualizing Murdoch's demolition plan. She glanced at Luke. Looked off.

Caroline sat back, arms dangling at her sides. "Surely they'll see for themselves how the children love us."

Except for Luke. Without thinking, Amalise glanced back at him.

Caroline followed her eyes, frowned, and nodded. Then she lifted her chin. "If they'll give us time, he'll come around." Seconds passed. She sipped the coffee and looked at Amalise. "It helps to tell myself that things will turn out right."

"They will." But she averted her eyes, knowing that was false consolation, given Project Black Diamond.

Luke moved in his chair, and Amalise was surprised to find his serious brown eyes fixed on her. He seemed so alone. She turned to Caroline. "Do you know what country he's from?"

"No. He arrived without any paperwork." She glanced at the child and back at Amalise. "We've no background to go on to help him get used to us. When we took him in, the children's home thought he was from South Vietnam, possibly a rural area. But we've got some Vietnamese neighbors, and he doesn't respond to them either." She shrugged. "Ellis bought home a book with Vietnamese words and pictures. He looked at them, but there was no real response."

Amalise stood, walked over to Luke, and stooped before him, folding her arms on her knees. What had the child endured to cause this withdrawal? She gentled her voice. "Hello, little one. I wish we could unlock your secret. Wish we could let you know that we want to help."

Luke's face remained expressionless, but looking back at her, he blinked. For an instant she imagined that he understood. She stood, looking down at the whorl of fine dark hair on the peak of his head. Her heart ached for the child. But remembering Black Diamond, she backed away. This was dangerous territory, getting too involved with a family living in the project's target area. In a matter of minutes she made her excuses and left.

In the office later that morning, she reviewed the last document from a stack that Raymond had left on her desk, checking for errors, flipping each one onto the growing pile beside her as she finished. These she'd take to the conference room when the meeting began a few minutes from now. She glanced at her watch. Quickly she divided the pile into sections—agreements, forms and certificates, and various checklists, all documenting Murdoch's planned destruction of the Marigny. As she worked, Amalise tucked away unwanted thoughts of Caroline and the children, especially Luke.

Luke, a reminder of the shadow children who still haunted her.

As Amalise finished and stood, Rebecca stuck her head into the office. "Lunch later on?"

Amalise looked up at the woman that Jude loved, and her throat went dry. But she forced a smile and shook her head. "No time today," she said. "The Murdoch transaction's taking off." Hugging the documents to her chest, she walked toward the door. "The closing's set for Thanksgiving Eve, only a couple of weeks away."

"Let me know if Doug thinks he needs any help." Rebecca gave a little wave over her shoulder as she walked off down the hallway.

Amalise knew Rebecca would give almost anything to take her place on Murdoch's transaction. Then Caroline's face rose before her. And Luke's. And she suddenly realized that right now she, too, would give almost anything to trade places with Rebecca.

Chapter Nineteen

THE CONFERENCE ROOM WAS CROWDED, THE air already heavy with smoke. When Bingham had arrived earlier in the morning to find lawyers and bankers already hard at work, he'd been pleased. But he'd burned through the initial exhilaration within a few hours, and now, with things huffing along, he'd grown bored. Here he sat along with everyone else, slogging through agreements line by line, paragraph by paragraph, page by page. No one could make an argument for minutiae like lawyers and bankers with their endless analysis and the surprising differences they could find between the words *and* and *or*.

Bingham sighed, wondering how they'd ever meet the closing date at this rate. Examining his fingernails, he estimated the hourly rate of the lawyers and calculated that it was costing well over a thousand dollars each hour that he sat in this chair. Not counting bankers' fees.

But it wasn't his problem. Lawyers' fees, and expenses like hotel suites and the New Orleans cooking he intended to enjoy, would be paid from the proceeds of loans to Lone Ranger after the closing. So this was Robert's concern, not his.

He dropped his hands and, threading his fingers, slid back in the chair until he was resting on his haunches. He leaned back and spread his elbows out, wishing he had the concession selling paper to these law firms. Then he thought of the magnificent trees in the Northwest forests that were fodder for these agreements and retracted the wish.

His eyes roamed over the room as he turned his thoughts to what he'd come to think of as a more purposeful destruction, Project Black Diamond. Smiling to himself, he marveled at the politicians' rationales for demolition of that piece of the Faubourg Marigny. Black Diamond would triple tourism dollars, add jobs, modernize. Dominick Costa had reported to Tom and Robert that the politicians seemed happy, even ecstatic. Dominick, the contractor he'd brought to the project, was the best at what he did.

Well, the analysis was correct so far as it went, assuming no public protests. Assuming word didn't leak to the long-haired preservationists. Assuming Robert and Tom could keep the lid on talk about plans for the casino a few years down the road so as not to rile the anti-gambling crowd. Assuming the closing occurred soon, before interest rates rose and shut the financing down.

Once again he congratulated himself for getting the jump on things. Timing was everything. Tom's investors, who would hold the convertible notes, had the traders jazzed, couldn't wait to cut up their piece of the action once gambling took hold down here. The hotel was just the beginning for them. Forget the cash-flow skim. With a casino at the end of the yellow brick road, they were talking *real* money.

Bingham smiled, thinking of the look on Tom's face that evening at the beach bar on Cayman when he'd first mentioned the plan. He'd made Tom work for it, though, made him dig out the information piece by piece over the week. He dropped his head back against the chair, thinking of those blue waves rolling in, the warm moist air, the cold margarita in his hand. His lids began to droop.

He snapped to and opened his eyes wide. He'd fall asleep if he wasn't careful. He was used to moving around during the day, stretching himself, using his muscles, working his brain. If it were up to him, he'd just sign a note for the banks. With a glance at his watch he swallowed a sigh. He ran a finger around the ring of his collar, wishing it wasn't necessary to sit in these meetings to get the job done.

Bingham reached for the cup of coffee on the table before him and took a sip, hoping the caffeine would jolt him awake. Step by step, he told himself. Patience.

With new resolve he sat up straight, put down the coffee cup, and squinted, looking down the table. Every seat was occupied by expensive lawyers on the clock. He had to stay sharp, alert, on the ball. Robert Black would do his job all right, but Bingham would keep his eye on all of them. Including Robert.

An hour passed before Doug announced they'd take a break. Except for young Ms. Catoir, who was working alone, the bankers and lawyers dispersed into huddles. Tom and Robert's attorney, Adam Grayson, sat beside him. Adam lit up a cigarette and unrolled Dominick's blueprint, spreading it out across Bingham's end of the long table. Robert and Doug were discussing a provision in the draft of the construction agreement. Bingham looked down the table, watching as Amalise flipped pages, taking notes. Just then she glanced up and caught his eye.

He winked.

She blinked, gave him a confused smile, and returned to her work.

Bingham pulled a pack of Raleigh cigarettes from his shirt pocket, tamped it against the table, and picked one out. Holding it between his fingers, he reached for a lighter, hesitated and stuck it back in, setting the whole pack down on the table. There was enough smoke in this room already. He took a deep breath and choked as thick smoke tunneled down his windpipe.

Coughing, Bingham nudged Adam. A gray stream curled from the ashtray at his elbow. "Get rid of the cigarette," Bingham said.

Bingham saw panic rising in the young man's eyes. He figured it would take maybe a minute for Adam to find an excuse to leave the room. As Adam stubbed out the butt, Bingham glanced at his watch. Yawning, he pushed back his chair, rose, and strolled down to the far end of the table where Amalise sat.

"Sorry about that wink." He lowered his voice as he sat down beside her, looking at the notes she'd been scribbling. "I'm just not used to lawyers wearing lipstick." He nudged his chin toward her notes. "What's all this?"

"I'm double-checking the list of items we need for closing."

"Don't forget to include the money."

"We'll need account numbers and wire transfer numbers."

He watched as she scanned a couple of pages and pointed out the section covering money transfers. Bingham leaned over, studying it. The largest funding would come from Tom's investors in New York—twenty million for the demolition and construction. "Here it is," she said when he asked, pointing to the middle of the page. Something in her voice made him give her a quick look.

Ignoring him, Amalise reached for the Lone Ranger subsidiary's certificate of organization from Grand Cayman. Bingham peered at it.

"Why Lone Ranger?" she asked.

He shrugged. "Because I am, I suppose."

She gave him a sideways look. He smiled.

"Where do you call home?" She ducked her head as she went back to making notes in the margins of the list.

"I have an apartment in Manhattan."

"So why did you choose Marigny for the hotel?"

He smiled. "Isn't that obvious?" He leaned back and crossed his arms. "It's close to the French Quarter. We'll have a nice view of the river." As he spoke, he envisioned the eastern shoreline of the Mississippi River from the wharves at Marigny, moving past the Quarter, crossing Canal Street into the dark warehouse district. "At the other end of the Quarter, there are too many established nuisances to contend with—the ferries, the trade center, the customs house, busier warehouse areas. Each one has its own government regulator." He spread his hands flat on the table before him. "That's expensive. Slows things down."

She nodded.

"It's easier all around to deal with small properties. Anyway, Marigny's a slum."

Amalise raised her eyes to his. "It's not."

"Not what?" The energy of her words surprised him.

"The Marigny is not a slum."

He gave her a hard look.

She arched one brow. "Have you driven through there?"

"Of course." Well, he'd driven around the Marigny once, a year ago when lightning first struck.

She tapped the pencil on the pad, and something in her expression put him on guard. "It's an old neighborhood," she went on. Was he imagining a spark of anger in her voice? "Families have lived there for generations. It's historic."

"Not designated as such."

"No. But it should be." She was doodling on the page now. Nervous? He resolved to keep an eye on her as he watched her sketch a raised square. The square became a house with a steep, shingled roof. "The architecture in Marigny is unique. Some of the cottages are hundreds of years old, but go look at the fresh paint on them. And the gardens, the children playing in the yards. Look at the old-growth trees." A porch appeared across the front of the house as she sketched. Windows across the front. She glanced at him and put down the pencil.

He shook his head. "Charm has its limits."

"People there know their neighbors. They look out for each other. They've been shopping at the same small grocery stores for years, frequenting the same cafes, attending the same churches for generations. Then there are the blues bars and the restaurants. And Washington Square Park."

"The park isn't included in our project," he said. "We're buying the land adjacent for parking. But like I told you, we'll do a little landscaping, separate the two, clean it up some."

She looked at him. "The park will change when the surroundings change, when the people are gone. *People* live in that neighborhood. They're a part of the city's soul."

He looked at her and knew he was looking at trouble. "Souls?" he snorted. "We're talking about real estate, not souls."

Instantly he saw it in her eyes: She knew she'd gone too far. Small muscles contracted at the corners of her mouth, and she turned away. Picking up the pencil, she tore off the page with the sketch and went back to her list. Bingham noted with interest the dark imprint of lead on the paper as she pressed down. Yes, something was troubling Miss Catoir.

With an abrupt but silent laugh, he looked through the windows at the cloudless sky, considering the irony of being lectured by a young associate—an associate who, by the way, was a woman, and a woman charging hundreds of dollars an hour for her time at that.

He crossed his arms, watching her write. "I'm worrying about a multimillion dollar loan, property lines, and dealing with owners who'll jack up their prices if they get even a hint that we're buying for a project." He could almost feel her hackles rising as he spoke. Good. "I'm worrying about dirt and tractors, levee restrictions, politicians, the press," he went on. Not to mention the possibility of populist revolts. He gave her a careful look. "And you're talking about souls?"

She said nothing.

Bingham shook his head, straightened, pushed back his chair, and stood. "Souls," he muttered, making his way to the door. Where was the elevator in this place? He needed to escape for a while. Outside where the air was cool. Automobile exhaust was better than the smoke and tension in this conference room.

Anonymous souls. As if he didn't already have enough to worry about. That was the trouble with people in New Orleans: The residents of this city just weren't practical.

Amalise ducked her head to hide her fury. Bingham announced to the room that he'd be back soon as he strode out the door. She fumed as she wrote, imagining his anonymous agents spreading over the Marigny like a fungus. The lead on the pencil snapped, and she felt Raymond's eyes shift her way. Expressionless, she found another sharpened pencil and went back to work.

At the other end of the table, the blueprint Adam had unrolled lay open and unattended, spread out across the table. Those plans mapped each parcel to be purchased for Black Diamond, she knew. She glanced around, but no one was paying her any attention. Doug, Preston, Raymond, and the bankers were in deep discussions. Robert was on the phone. Bingham and Adam were gone.

Setting down the pencil, Amalise pushed back her chair and strolled toward the credenza on the other side of the room. She dropped some ice into a glass, opened a Tab, and poured the drink over the ice. She leaned back against the counter. No one looked up.

Sipping the drink, she stepped over to the plans and casually scanned the squares—the spots where houses currently stood. Each square contained the street address of the property located there and the name of the legal owner of record, whether a lease existed on the property, and a few key points. A phone number was scribbled by hand under each owner's name. With a quick glance down over the surveyed area, Amalise followed the trail of lines along Frenchmen Street to Royal, curving around to Kerlerec Street where Caroline and Ellis lived.

The house was the second from a corner on the plans. The address was there, and she bent closer, looking for Caroline and Ellis's name below. Instead she found herself staring at the name C. T. Realty, Inc. She blinked and looked again.

C. T. Realty, Inc., a slumlord entity well known in this city for its cutthroat tactics.

The full impact of the information took a moment to sink in. Caroline and Ellis were only renting. There was no notation of an existing lease.

As she stood looking down at the paper covering one end of the conference table, the facts raced through her mind in the order she knew they'd occur after the closing—the sale by Caroline's landlord to Murdoch's agent, immediate notice to Caroline and Ellis evicting them from the premises, and the adoption agency's response to the loss of their home, the report citing instability and potential damage to the children. It was a classic "parade of horribles."

She thought of the worn furniture in the house, the children's secondhand clothes, and knew that Caroline and Ellis didn't have the money required to move, not to an equivalent house and neighborhood.

Such a move was well beyond their means, and the social workers, already worried about the age of the prospective parents, would realize that too.

Her heart sank. The adoptions were probably doomed. Those children, just adjusting to their new home, would be tossed out into the world again. The landlord on Kerlerec would reap the profit from the sale, and Caroline and Ellis would be left to fend for themselves.

And her job was to make sure that all of this happened.

How had things come to this?

Heart racing, she looked again at the phone number for C. T. Realty, Inc., memorizing it.

Walking back to her seat at the other end of the conference table, she sat down, pulled over her notebook, and jotted down the name and phone number of the owner of Caroline's house, all the while asking herself what she thought she was doing. When she looked up, Robert's eyes met hers. He'd been watching her, she realized. He lounged against the credenza while Preston stood beside him hammering home some point into the speaker of the telephone.

Quickly she looked off. Had he seen her take that name from the plans? She turned to Raymond and asked a question about the agreement he was working on, half listening to his answer. She'd never considered the situation she found herself in now—loving the work but hating the results. That wasn't the way things were supposed to work.

Abba. You know that all my life I've wanted to be a lawyer. I thought law was supposed to be about fixing problems, about serving justice and righting wrongs, like Dad used to do in his courtroom. Now that I've made it this far, I thought I'd have a hand in somehow making the world a better place. But things aren't working out that way this time. Only you can see the big picture, Abba. Please help me think clearly now.

When Bingham Murdoch blew back in and everyone returned to the table, still the shadows remained. Negotiations resumed and hours passed, but Amalise found that she couldn't dispatch the images of Caroline and the children. She told herself that this was just one transaction in a long career. Mangen & Morris had taken a chance in hiring her as one of the first two women lawyers in the firm. She couldn't blow it now.

She wished that she could talk this over with Jude, but she quickly shoved the thought aside. She didn't need Jude's advice. Not now. He was Rebecca's now.

Careful, Amalise, the observer said. *The path is hidden in the storm. Let the hand of God lift you up, and soon enough you'll see the truth stretching out before you.*

Chapter Twenty

A FEW NIGHTS AFTER HE'D FIXED the fence for Amalise, Jude sat on the couch, weight on the small of his back, legs splayed, watching the television set. The sound was off, and he'd been thinking. Suddenly he lurched forward, switched off the set, and went into the dining room to the telephone. Festering anger was a losing proposition. If Amalise wanted only friendship from him, at least he'd hold onto that. He picked up the phone and dialed her office. She answered on the first ring.

"Hello?" Her voice was low and tired. It was seven o'clock, and Rebecca had said the team was exhausted.

"Hi. Thought you might want to take a break, get something to eat."

There was a pause on her end of the phone. He gazed out the window. The street was dark, and he saw out there only ghosts of the children he'd hoped to have with Amalise. The others, the flesh-and-blood ones, were now all indoors.

"Sure."

Lights in the house next door flicked on, and the ghosts disappeared. Jude leaned against the wall, picturing her sitting in that office as he looped a finger through the coiled telephone cord.

"I'm still working," she said, "but I could take a break."

He slipped his finger from the cord and it sprang away. "All right. I'll pick you up and bring you back to the office afterward."

"That sounds good. What time?"

He glanced at his watch and pushed off the wall. "How about one hour?"

"See you then. Park at the corner of Baronne and Common, and we'll find a place nearby."

He went back to the living room, stretched out on the couch, hands behind his head, looking at the ceiling, and thought about the two cottages in the Irish Channel that he'd bid on earlier in the day. Should hear something on them tomorrow. He'd like to seal the deal before he left on watch next week. Then he could start planning the renovations. A thrill of adrenaline ran through him at the thought of this new venture. He'd do the work himself until he got further along.

He shifted his back and relaxed again, still staring at the twelve-foot ceiling, one reason he'd bought this duplex. He focused on the light fixture; the light up there had never worked. He'd been using lamps in this room, but he'd get after that tomorrow. Old houses like this all had some electrical problems.

Amalise had always liked old houses. He glanced again at his watch. Another half hour and he'd go pick her up, try to smooth things over after that fiasco at Clancy's the other night.

∽∾

By eight o'clock only Bingham, Amalise, and Adam were still working in the conference room, although Bingham seemed to be doing nothing more than passing time. Raymond and Preston had returned to their offices earlier to draft changes to the loan agreement. Robert was off in a meeting somewhere with the general contractor. Doug and Frank Earl had gone home, the prerogative of senior partners and their clients.

Amalise glanced at her watch and set down the pencil she'd been using, marking her place in the investor's placement memorandum describing the transaction. Consistency was the watchword with respect to the two lending group's documents, the bank syndicate, and Tom and Robert's investors. Briefly, she wondered when Tom would arrive in town.

She rose and went to a chair in the corner and retrieved her coat. "I'll be back in a while," she said when Adam and Bingham looked up.

Adam raked his hand through his hair, pushed back his chair, stretched his arms wide, and yawned. "I'll stick it out a little longer," he said.

"I'm going to eat," she said. "Would you like me to bring something back? A sandwich? Or a salad?"

"No, thanks."

But Bingham rose too and slipped on his jacket, a herringbone tweed with thick double seams that looked expensive, yet also looked as though he'd been wearing it for fifty years. He clapped his hand down on Adam's shoulder and said he'd see him tomorrow. Early. Adam nodded.

Amalise nodded toward the paperwork she'd left strewn across one end of the table. "If you finish up before I return, just leave the lights on so the night crew will know not to lock up."

"I'll be here."

Bingham pulled open the door. Amalise walked through and he followed. They stood together in front of the elevator, waiting. "So you're foraging for food?" He stepped into the elevator right behind her, punched the button for the first floor, and watched her reflection in the mirrored wall.

She nodded as the elevator descended. "I'm meeting a friend for dinner. We'll find someplace close by."

"Looking for soul food?" Bingham erupted at his joke.

Amalise gave him a weak smile.

When the elevator doors opened, Bingham tucked her arm through his, patted the top of her captured hand, and trucked toward the lobby door. She stiffened, but he'd caught her by surprise and there was nothing to do but to go along.

"Look," he said, peering down from his height. "I'm at the Roosevelt just down the street." He jerked his head in the general direction. "You and your friend come have dinner with me. Be my guests."

But she wanted Jude to herself. Besides, every time she looked at Bingham now, she saw Caroline's house torn to rubble. She shook her head. "I don't want to impose."

His voice turned insistent. "You won't find anything else open nearby. Not this side of Canal Street on a weeknight. Anyway, I could use the company. We'll go to Bailey's. Good food. Good service. Close by."

His hand pressed the small of her back as he steered her through the door and out onto the sidewalk. "You'll be doing an old man a favor." He flashed a grin. At the corner curb she saw Jude's car idling, windows down, headlights on.

From the driver's seat, Jude waved.

"Ah. Your friend has a car. I'll get in back. Save me walking a block." Her eyes widened as he freed her and headed for Jude, greeting him as if he'd known him all his life. "Hey there." He motioned back toward Amalise, trailing. "Got your girl with me." Standing on the curb, he ducked down and stuck his hand through the open window. "Bingham Murdoch." Amalise hurried up behind.

"Jude Perret. Glad to meet you, sir." They shook hands as Jude glanced behind him at Amalise. She shrugged.

Bingham walked around the back of the car, trailed by Amalise, and opened the passenger door for her. Amalise slid in. As he shut the door behind her and she looked at Jude, Murdoch yanked the back door open and climbed inside. He leaned forward between them. "I've invited you two for dinner at my hotel, Jude. The Roosevelt." He flipped his hand in the direction of the hotel. "It's just over there."

With a sideways look at Amalise, Jude shifted the car into gear. "Well, ah . . . thanks."

Bingham settled back as the car moved forward. "You're not a lawyer, are you?"

"No. I work on the river."

"I could tell by your hands, the set of your shoulders. It'll be nice keeping company with someone besides bankers and lawyers." He reached forward and tapped Amalise. "No offense."

Amalise rolled her eyes and folded her arms.

Bingham pointed ahead. "That way, son. Hang a right at the corner, on O'Keefe."

"Yes. I know."

Amalise slumped in the front and sighed as the car moved forward.

The maître d' at Bailey's lit up when he saw Bingham. He led them to a table in the corner by the windows overlooking Baronne. The waiter bustled around like a private valet. Bingham insisted on ordering steaks for everyone, medium-rare, but Amalise, feeling contrary, interrupted and ordered grilled speckled trout, with a small salad on the side.

"Drink?" Bingham looked at Jude.

"Unsweetened tea." The waiter looked at Amalise. "The same," she said.

Bingham ordered scotch. When it arrived, he closed his eyes with a sigh and took a long drink. Setting the glass down, he pulled a pack of Raleighs from his pocket and a gold lighter and looked at Amalise. "Mind if I smoke?"

She shook her head.

He extended the pack to Jude.

"No, thanks."

Bingham plucked a cigarette from the pack, lit it, and set the package and the lighter on the table beside him. With a sigh he took a long draw and turned his head aside, exhaling smoke. Then he turned back to them.

"It's been a long day in that conference room. Cooped up. I'm an outdoor man, myself. Thought I was in for a hard landing tonight before I ran into you two."

"A hard landing." Jude looked at him. "Are you a pilot?"

Bingham shook his head. Smoke drifted from the corner of his mouth. "Paratrooper. World War II." He reached to the center of the table for an ashtray and slid it toward him. "But I fly some now, too."

"What theater?" Jude squared his arms on the table and leaned slightly forward.

"Europe. France. Later on, Germany."

"That must have been something."

"Ever jump out of a plane?"

"No, sir. I stick to boats, myself."

"Call me Bingham. What do you do?"

Jude leaned back and picked up his glass. "I'm a bar pilot, guiding ships." He sipped the tea. "Wouldn't mind trying a jump, though. It sure looks like fun."

Bingham nodded. "Today maybe. But back in the day, those old chutes we had were crude. I'm lucky to be alive with no broken bones." He lifted his drink. "In those days we just jumped and prayed we'd land in the general vicinity. Now they've got toggles to steer. Ten thousand feet, land on a dime, and walk away." He lifted his drink. "Nineteen-forties, we hit the ground hard. 'Pile driving,' we called it." He chuckled. "Hit dirt and roll."

"Well, thank you for what you've done for our country."

Bingham nodded. "We had some good times, too." He lowered his eyebrows and leered at Amalise. "Prettiest girls you ever saw in France. We'd fill our canteens with wine sometimes, in case we got lucky."

They all laughed. The waiter returned with their food and moved silently around them, settling the plates.

Bingham looked at Jude. "Bar pilot, huh? Is that the same as a river pilot?"

Jude explained. As she listened, Amalise grew appalled. Jude and Bingham were getting along. *They liked each other!* Jude went on and on about life on the river and at Pilottown.

"I'd like to see that place sometime." Bingham lifted his fork and waved it toward Jude. "Maybe we could take a quick run down the river in a charter sometime when you're going down there."

Jude's brows shot up. "Sure," he said. "Anytime. It would be better than taking the bus."

Amalise stifled a groan. She didn't want to like the man responsible for destroying the Marigny triangle, and she didn't want Jude to like him either.

But Bingham's eyes glowed as Jude described the hamlet of Pilottown that had protected the river over the years from pirates, the Spanish, the French, and German U-boats in World War II. Bingham asked about hurricanes, and Jude told him how the little place was battered year after year yet still survived, isolated but determined.

"That's the kind of place I like," Bingham said. "A place with character." He glanced at Amalise, eyes crinkling. "A place, perhaps, with soul?"

She smiled. Dipped her fork into the perfectly cooked trout.

Bingham eyed her plate. He turned back to Jude. "Good fishing down there?"

Jude nodded. "Sure. You've got the Gulf and the marsh."

Bingham waved his fork in Amalise's direction, snapping her back to attention. "Give me a freshwater fish in the Pacific Northwest anytime. Coldwater stream beats a swamp, if you ask me."

She looked up. "What?"

"We're still talking about fishing," Jude said.

"I said I'd prefer a rainbow trout over your spec." Bingham nodded toward her plate. Then he looked down at his own, sawed off another piece of steak, and stabbed it with his fork.

Jude let out a laugh.

Glancing at her watch, Amalise's lips curled down. They had wasted an hour and a half sitting here when she had plenty of work left back at the office. When she pushed back her chair and said she'd have to leave, Bingham and Jude both turned to her with surprised looks.

Jude glanced at his watch. "Sorry, Amalise. I lost track of time."

"No need to break up the party. I can walk. It's just across the street." She dabbed at her mouth, folded the napkin, and placed it on the table beside her plate. When she stood, Bingham and Jude rose, too. Jude held her coat as she put it on, and Bingham waved to the waiter.

"I'll drop you off," Jude said. "I've got things to do."

Rebecca was probably waiting. The hollow inside opened again at the thought.

The waiter arrived, and Jude reached for the check. But Bingham waved him off, taking it. "I'll get it. You two run along. I'll be here awhile." Jude protested, but Bingham said, "This one's on me." He shook Jude's hand. "I like you, son. I meant what I said about flying down to Pilottown sometime."

On the short ride back to Mangen & Morris she was quiet. When Jude pulled over to the curb at the First Merchant Bank Building, he turned off the engine. Automatically she pulled back. The scent of his body, his clothing were all so familiar, and she longed to throw her arms around him as she would have done not so long ago, before that dinner at Clancy's. She ached to feel his strong arms around her.

But he didn't seem to notice. He stretched his arm across the back of his seat and looked at her. "How are you holding up, chère? Seems to me you're working awfully hard for someone just out of a hospital bed." An expression flashed crossed his face that she couldn't read—a sad, almost wounded look.

She'd hurt him, walking out of Clancy's like that. He'd planned such a fine evening, and she'd been rude. She hadn't even waited to hear the good news. "I'm fine," she said with a bright smile. She should apologize for her behavior that night, she knew. But her throat grew tight, and she couldn't work out the right words.

Jude nodded. "Well, then. I'll see you soon."

She looked at him knowing that everything between them had changed forever. She opened the door.

"Wait."

She turned her head. His voice was casual.

"See you Sunday morning?"

Slowly, she smiled. "Sure. St. Louis Cathedral?"

"Yes. It's your turn."

She entered the building and walked down the empty hallway toward the elevator, heels echoing as they clicked on the marble floor. A rush of happiness caught her by surprise. *Sunday morning.* But the joy was brief. Because relationships change, he'd said.

And then despair crept in, smothering the light, as a storm cloud will on a sunny day.

Jude watched Amalise until she was safe inside the First Merchant Bank Building. Then he turned his head, staring down Baronne through the darkness toward the bright strip of Canal Street one block away where the impressionistic scene moved ghost-like. Blurred, garish colors amid blazing lights. A streetcar rolling toward the river end of Canal. A flurry of automobiles. Two drunks stumbling on the curb, surrounded by ladies of the night taunting, teasing. The images merged and blended as he sat there.

One block closer, yellow lights glittered around the red canopy at the Roosevelt. Vaguely, he wondered if Bingham Murdoch was still at Bailey's Restaurant. He was glad the man had joined them. He'd seemed lonely.

Jude sat there for a very long time. And then he put the car in gear and drove home.

Bingham still occupied the same table at Bailey's, drinking his scotch and gazing through the windows at Baronne. He'd lived amid the razzle-dazzle for so long. But spending time with Amalise and Jude tonight had taken him back to a time when he'd been someone real, someone with hopes and dreams and values. He sat there thinking of the only two people he'd ever loved: Mother and Susan. And both were gone.

He crooked his wrist and raised the drink to his lips, remembering how it had been when he returned from the war. Made it all the way through without a serious injury. A bit more cynical and a lot poorer, perhaps, but there had been Susan. How many soldiers' girls had waited all through the war? His young wife had. He'd carried her letters in his knapsack everywhere, through France, then Germany. She'd been waiting for him in Manhattan at the Hotel Breslin on the day he returned, just as they had planned.

Bingham's eyes found the waiter's, and he lifted his finger again. One more for a nightcap.

Setting the empty glass down on the tablecloth, he turned it absently in circles, thinking of Susan, the way she would pull her hair back and tuck it into a bun at the nape of her neck. He had often kissed that sweet, soft place. Then he would pull out the barrettes and pins, and her hair would tumble down her back like water.

The waiter swapped his empty glass for a full one. He nodded at the man without looking up.

That had been thirty-two years ago, 1945. Hard to believe. Susan had been waiting for him, sitting on the edge of the bed in the corner of the dark room. Windows open to let in the warm night air. Yellow neon lights outside, just above the window, flashed on and off *Breslin, Breslin, Breslin,* just as they had on the night he'd left for the war.

But on the night he'd left, with the ships and planes and trains all waiting and the young men kissing their sweethearts good-bye behind drawn shades, there had been weeping. The streets had been dark and quiet, as though the whole city was holding its breath.

But on the night he returned in 1945, she had come running at him, arms flung wide, laughing, weeping like women will sometimes when they're happy. Car horns were honking below in the streets, with church bells ringing all over the city celebrating the end of the war.

A sheen of perspiration glistened on Bingham's skin as he recalled the touch of Susan's skin, the youth and passion and hope in her smile.

The hope.

He rattled the ice in his glass and closed his eyes again. Mother had been there for him when Susan died only ten months later. Breast cancer had taken her. He shook his head. He'd never have thought, never dreamed that happiness could disappear so quickly, like a shooting star that blazes across the sky, lights everything up, then vanishes forever, leaving you to wonder if it was ever real.

Not long after, Mother had passed on too, leaving him alone.

He took a deep drink of the scotch and rolled it around in his mouth, then swallowed. It'd been difficult at first, being on his own, after the years of adrenaline highs in Europe and then coming back to Susan. He smiled to himself. Oh, the risks they had taken, the young men, all in the prime of their lives, feeling immortal each time they jumped and walked away.

Some didn't, of course. Walk away, that is.

Bingham shook his head. Those days were gone, and he'd let the sorrow of losing Susan and Mother weigh him down for the first few years after. But after a while he'd learned how to step out into the world and take charge. How to keep moving forward, to make things happen. To change fate.

Still, seeing Jude with Amalise tonight made him wonder what his life might have been if Susan had lived.

He finished off the drink and set it down with a heavy thud reminding himself again that those days were long gone. Life was good now. In fact, he was certain that millions would trade their lives to be in his shoes. Life was a game, and he was the winner.

"Anything else before we close up, Mister Murdoch?"

He looked at the waiter and memories dissolved. "No, thanks. Put it on my room. You know the number?"

"Certainly."

"And add ten for yourself."

"Thank you, sir." The waiter picked up the empty glass. "Have a good night."

He stood, tossed the napkin on the table, and glanced through the window at the church across the street. Jesuit, they called it. Mother used to drag him to church when he was a child. He turned away, smiling. She was Baptist. He'd always thought Baptists had the best songs. Hands in his pockets, jingling coins, he strolled to the door.

A waiter stood holding the door to the lobby open for him. Bingham nodded at the waiter and headed for the elevators, still ruminating. Amalise Catoir had spirit, like his mother had. She'd have liked Miss Catoir, he mused. Mother had believed in souls, too. He wondered if it was true that life goes on after death. He wondered if Susan and Mother were waiting for him somewhere.

He hoped so.

At the elevator he pressed the button and turned, watching the activity in the lobby. Bellboys lounged near the concierge desk, and people glided in and out of the Sazerac Bar. A foursome, two couples, sat drinking at a table in the lobby just outside the Sazerac, sparkling and laughing. Chandeliers blazed a path of light the length of the city block from O'Keefe to Baronne.

Bingham turned, facing the elevator, and hummed the only Baptist song that he could immediately recall, "Amazing Grace." Back in the days when the going got rough and he'd look out the plane before jumping, when he would look out into the black space and the only light he'd see was artillery fire down below, sometimes he'd let that song run through his mind as he took the leap and then let it carry him all the way to the ground.

The bell dinged as the elevator door opened and Bingham stepped in. As it rose, he pondered something Robert had said earlier in the day. Robert had *concerns* about Amalise, he'd said. Something was wrong with her attitude. He couldn't put his finger on it, but Robert was convinced she'd developed some kind of hostility toward the deal. He wanted her taken off the transaction team.

Bingham had nixed that idea. They'd need more than vague suspicions before even considering a talk with Mangen & Morris about one of their associates. Associates were valuable investments in the future of the firm.

So he'd arranged this evening's meal to judge that very question—if you want something done right, you have to do it yourself—and he'd seen nothing to justify Robert's concern. The girl was tougher than she looked. He liked the way she'd held her own this afternoon when Raymond and Preston had questioned some points she'd made on one of the agreements.

"Put a tail on her," Robert had urged.

Not yet. Bingham would wait and see, though he understood Robert's concern. So much money was at stake. Robert would snuff his own mother's lights if she got in the way of this deal. After all, this was his chance to step out of the long line of suits on Wall Street and make his mark. He was hungry.

But over the last few days Bingham had grown kind of fond of Amalise. There was something basically good in her nature. Yet one complaint from Robert would get her taken off this deal—a career-killing move. She deserved a chance.

Tossing his coat over a chair as he entered his suite, Bingham frowned. He would certainly be disappointed if he had guessed wrong about Amalise Catoir.

Chapter Twenty-One

Phnom Penh, Cambodia 1975

SAMANTHA SCREAMED AND SLUMPED, STILL CONSCIOUS but unable to move. Oliver dragged her up the last few feet of the rough surface of the ramp, jolting another scream from her as she landed in the dark hold of the plane. She lay there panting as the plane began a laborious turn, preparing for takeoff, and she heard the hatch door grinding closed behind her.

With a lurch they started down the runway. The hold was dusty, simmering with heat and the stench of human fear. Still gasping for breath, suddenly she remembered. The child! She rolled her head to the side where Oliver sat, and peering through the dim lights she saw the boy huddled just beyond him, hunched on the floor against the fuselage, eyes wide as he stared back at her.

A sudden dizziness overcame her, then another rush of pain, and she felt limp, as if she were floating. She tried to tell Oliver about this, but his face kept disappearing, moving in close to her and then receding. She could see his mouth working, and she felt his hand on her forehead, but his voice was submerged beneath the roar of the engines. Then he faded away entirely.

When she woke, Oliver was bending over her, calling her name. He was a blur at first, as though her brain had managed to wrap the injured part of her in cotton to dull the pain. With the plane dipping and rumbling under her, nausea rose. But one thought emerged above the pain and the fear and the nausea, drowning out the others.

"Oliver," she said, and he bent, put his ear close to her lips.

It was a struggle to speak, but she forced the words up from her chest. "My purse." She turned her head and her cheek rubbed the strap still wrapped about her shoulders. "Here. It's here."

He nodded, seeming to understand.

She closed her eyes, lips tight, pressing against the pain.

Oliver put his mouth to her ear. "Be still, Sam. It won't be long now. We're headed for Saigon."

"Will I die?"

"No." He pulled back and brushed the hair from her forehead. "It's your hip. You'll be all right. Just hang on."

She had to tell him, had to get the words out while there was still time, before they landed. Before the child was discovered. "The child . . ."

He began shaking his head.

"Inside my purse. *Please,* Oliver. Look inside."

Oliver looked at her and then down at the purse that lay beside her. Gently he picked it up.

She nodded.

He twisted the clasp and opened the flap. "What am I looking for?"

"Blue envelope." She exhaled the words, watching him.

Oliver reached in and pulled out a wallet, then the red silk pouch tied at the top in which she'd stored her mother's jewelry, her keys, and a comb. He set these items on the floor of the fuselage, and each time she frowned and shook her head.

Then he pulled out an envelope and held it up. "This?"

She nodded. "Yes." Her midsection burned. "Now the jewelry."

He arched his brows, looked down at the pile he'd created beside him, pushed the things around. Then he picked up the small red pouch and dangled it over her, so that she could see. When she nodded, he untied the frayed ribbon that held it tight, and she said in a rasping voice, "The silver pin . . . need the silver pin."

Her leg was on fire, she was certain, and Oliver simply hadn't noticed. The fire would spread, and perhaps the plane would burst into flames and they'd all die a slow, torturous death in this squalid hold.

When he held up the silver pin, she looked at it and thought it must have come from another lifetime.

Suddenly the plane lurched, and she cried out again. Oliver slipped his arms around her, lifting her shoulders just inches from the floor, bracing her. She grasped his arm. "Oliver, listen to me. Listen!"

Again he leaned in close until his cheek was touching hers, and his voice was thick. "I'm listening, Sam. Just tell me what you want."

Each word was a needle of pain as she spoke, explaining what she wanted. When at last he nodded that he understood—it seemed a long time—she was able to form a smile, to let him know that she was all right, and watching. And to mask the pain so he'd let go.

"Go on," she said, nodding her head toward the boy. *"Please!"*

Gently Oliver lowered Sam back down. Holding onto the broach and the envelope, he closed the pouch, tying it tight, and stuffed it back into her purse with her other things. Sam rolled her head to watch as Oliver pushed across the floor toward the boy.

"Stay with her," Oliver barked to someone nearby. A body slid close. A soft hand, a woman's hand, stroked her forehead. Sam's eyes were riveted on Oliver and the boy. Even from here she could see the child's fear. On Oliver's approach, the boy drew into himself, like a turtle into its shell. His eyes darted to her and back to Oliver again. But he did not move. He sat very still, looking down as Oliver reached him.

Oliver slipped the folded envelope into the pocket of the boy's ragged shirt and used the silver broach to pin it to the cloth.

When he'd completed his mission, Oliver patted the child's head and swung around to face Sam. Past him she could see the boy's shirtfront pocket sagging under the weight of the broach and the envelope pinned inside. She nodded.

"Who is he?" Oliver asked when he'd reached Sam again. He rested his hand on her shoulder. The plane bucked in the wind, and a moan escaped as Sam turned her head to look at him. To thank him.

"He was lost," she said with a deep, shuddering breath. "I couldn't leave him. His . . . his sponsor's name is on the envelope. On the back. Tell them." The plane banked, starting its descent. She gripped his arm. "It's written on the back, his U.S. sponsor!" She shouted over the roar. "Tell them, will you?"

He nodded.

"Get him onto Operation Babylift out of Saigon."

Oliver frowned. "Khmer refugees go through Thailand."

Sam squeezed her eyes shut and opened them again. "Please! Just get it done." She held his eyes as seconds passed. "Please," she whispered again. "Promise. Promise."

"We'll take care of him." Oliver lifted her into his arms, buffering her from a series of rocking bumps. "But it'll be a mess."

The fire inside had spread, as she'd known it would. She closed her eyes, conscious that she'd extracted a hard promise from Oliver. Operation Babylift, already overburdened, was scrambling to ferry thousands of Vietnamese orphans from Saigon just ahead of the coming VC invasion.

"A mess. That's what I'm counting on," she murmured. Chaos would save the child. The bureaucratic nightmare of evacuation would allow for a slip here and there.

She groaned, and Oliver held her closer. "I'll fix it somehow, Sam. We'll get him on one of those planes. And to his sponsor."

She was dizzy, feeling the nausea. "Promise?" She opened her eyes and fixed them on his.

How strange. Oliver was under water now. His face wavered, swayed, and receded. "Promise," she heard him say from afar. "Don't worry, Sam. You'll be all right."

And then everything faded away.

Chapter Twenty-Two

New Orleans—1977

AT TWO O'CLOCK IN THE MORNING Amalise lay in her bed in the house on Broadway, eyes refusing to close as she stared at the ceiling, worrying about Jude and Rebecca and the deal and the conference room and the family on Kerlerec Street, everything wheeling, spinning, buzzing inside like a swarm of bees. She fought to banish the misery she'd seen on Caroline's face earlier. She fought to banish the sight of Luke's sorrowful mien and thoughts of what might have caused a child to feel like that.

She talked to Abba for a while, praying and listening for guidance. Yet when at last she finally slept, she dreamt of the wreckage caused by Bingham Murdoch's project, knowing that she'd had a hand in it.

Poets have said that startling revelations hide in the mist and shadows of time between wakefulness and sleep, those first seconds in the morning when you're lying in bed and dreams are just slipping away. Hang on to those dreams, they've said. Amalise had known since she was a child that this waking time was when Abba sometimes planted little seeds of inspiration.

When the alarm on the table by her bed urged her awake at six o'clock, she did not move at first, instead letting herself sink deeper into the softness around her. She looked at nothing as the mist drifted around in her head, slowly streaming into the ether like silken ribbons, dissolving as her mind began to clear.

That's when the idea struck.

It tiptoed in, slipping past her guard. She mulled it over for a few minutes as a sort of academic exercise. *If this . . . then that,* while sketchy details rose in her mind. She stretched long in the bed, pointing her toes under the blanket, enjoying the idea and the feel of her muscles coming alive.

She rolled onto her side and fluffed the pillow beneath her head. And all at once the mist cleared. Robert's face emerged, his obsidian eyes burrowing into her mind, searching, probing. She gave the pillow a poke and then a little punch. Then she sat up straight and kicked the covers off, swinging her feet to the cold floor.

Amalise sensed that Robert was a dangerous man. If she followed through with this idea and he found out, even though no harm had been done, it would send him into a frenzy.

She went into the bathroom and brushed her teeth. The face that looked back from the mirror dared her take the chance, to do this thing, to try to make the world a little better for one family. As she brushed and foamed and rinsed and spat, she couldn't shake the thought that this problem was very real for Caroline and her family and—perhaps—she'd just stumbled on a solution.

Discovery would be a long shot, she told herself. But on the other hand, discovery would lead to unthinkable consequences. Robert would take revenge if he found out: He'd have her job.

Shaking her head, she put on slippers and a robe and went into the kitchen to make coffee. Community brand, from the familiar red package. When the coffee was ready, she poured herself a cup and wandered out onto the back porch where the cold air and the fragrance of the coffee and the dew on the grass—her own grass—revived her smile.

At 6:30 on the dot she went inside. Time to get to work. She put the coffee cup in the kitchen sink and headed for the bedroom. She resolved to think no more of this will-o'-the-wisp idea from an impractical dream, one she could barely remember now. She turned on the shower, stepped in, and let the hot water clear her mind.

Even if the idea worked, the consequences if she were found out, the price she would have to pay, would be too high.

But as she dressed, locked up the house, and drove downtown, the thought lingered, reminding her of those leeches in Mama's strawberry patch back home. Once they got hold of you, they stuck until you burned them off.

⟨✒⟩

During a break that morning, Bingham beckoned Amalise over to where he and Robert had again spread the survey across the table. These were the final plans, he said. Bingham asked Robert to give her a guided tour. Together, they bent over the blueprints with a new translucent overlay. Everything was much more detailed than before. She was conscious of Bingham watching as she followed Robert's finger tracing the fine lines that mapped out the hotel, the pool, and the parking area.

The parking area backed up directly adjacent to Washington Square Park. She looked over at Bingham. "You said you'd do something to separate them, to preserve the ambience of the park." She ran her finger down the line demarking the two areas. "You said there'd be landscaping here." She looked up and met his eyes. "Some trees, gardens?"

It was Robert who answered. "There's not room. The pool area's on the other side of the lot. That's where the landscaping goes."

But she fixed her eyes on Bingham, shaking her head. "The park will be worthless butting right up against a parking lot. There'll be fumes, dust, noise. And here," she swept her hand over the residential areas to be demolished, "what about the oak trees over here? Some of them are hundreds of years old." Planting her hands flat on the table, she stared at Bingham. "If this entire area is designated for parking and a pool, what happens to those old-growth oaks?"

Beside her, Robert clicked his tongue against his cheek.

Bingham spread his hands. "We'll plant new ones."

"They take hundreds of years to grow."

"And we'll have palm trees. We'll have them lit, and we'll add tropical plants."

Careful, Amalise. She straightened, arms dropping to her sides.

Robert stabbed his finger onto another spot on the map. She tore her eyes from Bingham and looked at the place indicated. "This will be the casino," Robert said, observing her, taking her measure, she knew. "Later on, when gambling is approved."

She did her best to remain expressionless, masking her dislike as Robert whisked a cigarette from his pocket and lit it, watching her under heavy lids. "This project will be big. Project Black Diamond plus the Quarter equals Vegas squared." His smile was grim as he let smoke drift in her direction. "Of course, this is all still confidential."

Bingham studied his hands.

Robert flicked an ash into a small glass ashtray. "One word gets out before the closing, and the deal's blown. We've got money invested, Bingham and I, and others. We need to know you understand that."

Amalise met his eyes. "You could have saved your breath."

He shrugged. "If you're going to do a man's job, you can't take things personally."

She lifted her chin and turned away from him. She realized that Robert had seen her write down the name of the owner of the house on Kerlerec from the plans a few days ago. Without another word, she turned and went back to her seat at the other end of the table. As she waited for the meeting to begin, she contemplated the lurid possibilities, but none made any sense. Unless Robert read minds, there was no way that he could know what she'd been contemplating.

When Doug arrived, then Adam Grayson, everyone situated themselves around the table again. Robert rolled up the plans and set them aside.

Bingham looked down the table once everyone was settled in their places, and he smiled. He waved his pen in the direction of Amalise. "Robert and I just reviewed the final plans for our target area with Miss Catoir. Everything looks good, but I'm concerned about the timing of property acquisitions." Bingham placed his pen on the table and sat back. "We're closing the financing on the Wednesday before the Thanksgiving holiday. I want our agents to be ready to approach landowners the day after Thanksgiving. What's the best way to get that done?" He looked at Adam, then Doug.

Adam answered first. "We'll need a complete set of agreements drawn up for each property owner to sign. Blanks for the numbers, of course, but everything else should be included—property description, names of the seller and buyer, and so on. Everything will be purchased 'as is,' of course. By the time we sign the purchase agreements, we'll have dealt with other problems, such as liens on the property, one way or another."

Doug looked at Raymond and Amalise. "They'll be ready." Both nodded.

Preston leaned forward, looking down the table. "How many properties in total will be purchased?"

"Couple hundred," Robert said. "We'll want the purchasing documents at the closing on Wednesday, ready to go. The agents will pick them up as soon as funds arrive that day. It's critical we get them started."

Preston said he'd call the title company right away.

Robert interrupted. "I've talked to one already."

"The one we normally use—"

"Use ours."

Doug nodded slowly. "That's not a problem."

Robert hooked his arm over the back of his chair and turned toward the Mangen & Morris end of the table. His eyes flicked toward Amalise, then settled on Doug. "Let's all get something clear: Project Black Diamond is confidential. *Extremely confidential.* No one in this room will speak to anyone outside about the transaction until after the closing."

"That's a given." Preston's tone was smooth, as always. "Let's get started, then." He turned to Raymond and Amalise sitting at his right. "Make sure the title companies understand our schedule. This is a rush job."

"Trees, too." Bingham grunted and Robert looked at him. "First she's worried about souls. Now it's trees." He stabbed out his cigarette in a paper cup on the table. He was having second thoughts about Miss Catoir.

Bingham sat alone with Robert in the coffee shop just off the lobby of the First Merchant Bank Building, near the elevators. It was only ten o'clock in the morning, but already Bingham needed a break. The conference room upstairs hummed with tension that wore him down. He couldn't wait to get this thing over and done.

"I don't trust her," Robert said. "I still think we should have her followed."

Bingham looked at Robert, his dark brows slicked, his hair swept back in a smooth slide he'd have called a ducktail fifteen years ago if it were one inch longer. He took in the starched white collar on the blue shirt. And the matching tie—silk, from the look of it. Then he raised his brows. "What for?"

"Women talk."

"That won't fly."

"You've noticed it yourself. She's not on board."

Bingham said nothing. He was right. There was something going on in Amalise's mind that made him nervous.

Robert squared his arms on the table and leaned close. "Knowledge is power, Bingham. If she lets anything slip, prices of those properties will shoot up, and we need to prevent that." He frowned. "We've got too much invested to take the chance. If the preservationists find out before we close, we're done. The commotion would scare the pants off the politicians. Our permits will be withdrawn. Reporters will go crazy. And we'll have protesters with signs and flags and people sitting in trees. The banks will go into a fugue state."

There was a cooler filled with cold drinks and ice cream bars right beside their table. Robert rose, pulled two Eskimo Pies from the cooler, and handed one to Bingham. He peeled the paper off the ice cream.

"All right, then. Hire your man." Bingham liked the girl, but this was business. Besides, Robert had a point. There was too much at stake to ignore intuition. Bingham tore the paper off his ice cream and bit into it. The cold made his teeth ache, and he made a face. "But nothing comes up after a few days," he pushed out his bottom lip and shook his head, "then we forget it."

"Tom will be down next week," Robert said. "We'll have this figured out by then." He set the Eskimo Pie stick down on the table.

Bingham watched the remaining ice cream melting on the table. Robert was like that—thoughtless, unless it involved money. Bingham got up, walked to the counter, and pulled some napkins from a holder. Bringing them back to the table, he handed them to Robert. "Take care of that before we leave."

Robert cleaned up the ice cream while looking at Bingham. "I talked to Tom this morning. He said to tell you we'll all celebrate in Cayman after we close. Back at the Sunset Bar."

"That sounds good." Bingham gave Robert a sideways look, thinking of the diving trip he'd arranged last time they were all down there. Hundreds of fish coming at them, thirty, maybe thirty-five miles an hour through the gorge, and Robert pulls out a camera. "You going back to Tarpin Alley this time?"

"What's so funny?"

"The look on that guy's face when your flash went off."

Robert shrugged. "He's lucky I didn't kill him. He grabbed hold of my fins in a panic." Robert tossed the paper wrapping, and napkins in the direction of a trash can. He missed. Then he turned back to Bingham, grinning. "But you should see the look on his face in that picture."

Bingham shook his head. "We're lucky he let us back on the boat."

"Wasn't luck, old man."

"What then?"

"Fear. It's more efficient."

Chapter Twenty-Three

AMALISE AND JUDE EXITED THE CATHEDRAL, flowing with the crowd. As they stepped into the sunlight, both stopped and blinked. A couple more days would bring the beginning of November, yet heat still rose from the cement. Jude took off his sport jacket and slung it over his shoulder, then slipped on his sunglasses.

He nodded his head toward the Café Pontalba on their right. "Coffee?"

"Sure. I haven't seen Gina or Henry since the accident." She glanced at him. "What time do you leave?" He was headed down to Pilottown this afternoon.

"The bus leaves at two."

The usual Sunday morning melee at Jackson Square swarmed around them as they made their way toward the old café on St. Peter and Chartres where Amalise had waited on tables nights and weekends during law school. "I have to get to the office, but I've got an errand to take care of before then. Work's piling up. Murdoch's deadline is coming up fast."

Jude reached for her hand as they walked. Amalise averted her eyes and shifted her purse from one shoulder to the other, putting it between them. *Careful, Amalise.* She felt rather than saw Jude's response, a subtle widening of the space between them.

One step at a time, she told herself. If that's the way he wanted it, she would distance herself one step at a time. The sunshine seemed to dim for an instant at the thought.

But children inside the park, behind the black iron post fence, still laughed and chased the pigeons. Amalise watched them, shooing away thoughts of Jude and Rebecca. The riotous group of boys and girls stalked the birds from the fountain to the grassy areas to the statue of Andrew Jackson astride his horse in the middle of the park. A cloud of birds exploded at each approach.

She smiled. "It never changes, does it?"

"No." But he looked off toward the café in a distracted manner. "You'd think the pigeons would figure it out sometime and find another place."

She looked back over her shoulder as they walked on.

Jude glanced at a spot near the fence where a friend of Amalise used to paint for tourists. "Where's that artist friend of yours?"

She pursed her lips at the thought of Mouse, a friendship cut off by Phillip Sharp. "He's moved to Key West, I think." Looking about, it struck her how all the artists, clowns, mimes, and musicians on the square now were strangers.

When they crossed St. Peter and entered Café Pontalba, Gina waved across the room from behind the cash register. Henry looked up and sauntered over from his worn path behind the bar. He shook Jude's hand and then came around the end of the bar to Amalise, arms open wide. After a brief hug, he held her at arm's length, studying her.

"You're looking good now, Amalise. We worried when we heard about Phillip and the accident." His eyes grew serious as they flicked to Jude and lit on her again. Then he smiled and dropped his hands from her shoulders, stepping back. "Want your job back?"

She laughed. "You never know."

Gina walked up, and Henry leaned against the bar, stretching a black and white striped towel between his hands, twirling it. "Our girl is fine, Gina. Just fine."

"Ready to work?" Gina stood, hands on her hips, looking Amalise up and down.

Henry snorted. Popped the towel against Gina's hip. "I already tried. Pay's too low. Hours are long. Boss is cranky. What's to love?"

Gina gave him a saucy look. "Me."

She led them to a table in the corner facing the square. The full shutter doors were open to the sidewalk, and a pleasant breeze drifted in. "Lunch is on me," she said, handing them menus.

Jude looked at Amalise, but she shook her head. "Thanks anyway," he said to Gina, pulling out a chair for Amalise. He took a seat beside her. "Just coffee. Amalise is in a hurry."

"What a surprise." Gina's tone was dry. "Coffee it is, then." Ruffling Amalise's hair, she walked off, barking the order to a waiter rushing by.

Jude settled back. "That client of yours, Murdoch, is a character."

"He's not our client. We represent the banks."

"Well, I enjoyed talking to him the other night at dinner." At last he smiled. "Those old troopers were tough."

"He still is."

"I'd take that bet."

The waiter appeared with coffee, cream, napkins, and spoons. Amalise drank hers black. "I met a family living in the area that Bingham's going to demolish." She saw his quick glance and went on, wanting his reaction but conscious that she was treading a fine line. Confidentiality was essential, but Jude didn't know the location, she told herself. An older couple with foster children. They could be anywhere in the city.

So she told him just that much, and then her shoulders slumped and she shook her head. "They're fine people. I really don't know how they do it, Jude, with four foster children. The oldest is six, I think. And they're poor. He works two jobs just to keep them fed. They live in a nice enough old house, but it's run down. So they don't have much."

"How'd you meet them?"

She gave him a look that was deliberately vague. "Oh, just driving around."

He lifted his coffee cup and stretched out his legs under the table, frowning. "What will happen to them now?"

That was a bigger question than he knew. The idea rose again before her amid flashing warning signs. Jude sipped his coffee, and she looked off, fixed her eyes on the cathedral, and kept her tone casual. "They'll have to move." She hesitated. "It'll be hard on them."

Seconds passed before Jude answered. "Do you think it's a good idea to get involved with these people, Amalise?" His brows rose and a corner of his lip curled down, giving him a quizzical look.

She clasped her hands before her on the table and threaded her fingers. "No. It wasn't a good idea in the first place, I know that. But I was drawn in, and now . . ." She spread her hands and let them fall into her lap. "Now it's too late not to care."

Jude made a sound deep in the back of his throat but said nothing.

She leaned forward, wanting to explain. Rebecca or no, he was still her oldest, dearest friend. From her point of view, he always would be that to her, she knew. Squaring her arms on the table, she fixed her eyes on Jude. "There's one little boy with this family who's so lost, Jude. He's from Southeast Asia." A lump grew in her throat, and she hesitated.

Jude looked at her. "Uh-oh."

She nodded. She knew what he was thinking. "But he seems so lonely. Just doesn't fit in with the rest."

Jude set down the coffee cup, traced the thick rim with his finger, and focused all of his attention on that effort. "What country is he from?"

She shrugged. "No one knows."

He looked up, frowning. "These people don't know what country their own foster child is from?"

"No. He won't speak. Hasn't said one word. Not to the family, not in the children's home. Not that anyone can remember." She pursed her lips. "Apparently, he's been shuffled around from place to place for almost two years."

A mule-drawn red-and-white Roman Candy wagon turned onto St. Peter Street. She watched as a crowd gathered and the cart slowed, rolling to a stop across the street. The window on the side slid back. A face looked out, and a mass of small arms reached up toward him.

When she turned back, she found Jude's eyes fixed on her. "Tell me something, Amalise." She nodded. "Won't these people just sell their house and move?" He shrugged. "People do it all the time. I'm not sure I understand the problem."

"No. They're renters, Jude. No lease. They'll be evicted."

Jude leaned back and crossed his arms over his chest. "Ah."

"And there's the child." She looked off. "Luke is his name."

He took a long breath. Picked up the coffee and took a drink, then put it back down on the table. When he looked at her, she saw such a mixture of emotions on his face that she couldn't process. Regret? The burden of nostalgia? Pity?

Ah. That last was worst. It took all of her effort to sit still and not look away as he went on. His tone held a note of warning. "This transaction is an important one for your career, Rebecca says."

Rebecca again. Of course.

But Jude held her eyes, raised his brows, and nodded.

She nodded too, mirroring him. But before she thought them through, the words escaped. "I'm not asking for advice, Jude."

He threw up his hands. "Hey, none's on offer."

In strained silence they both looked off and drank their coffee. She watched a boy about Luke's age standing on his toes at the Roman Candy cart and digging in his pocket for change. Then she turned back to Jude. "I'm sorry," she said. She pushed back her hair and tucked it behind her ear. "I didn't mean that the way it sounded."

"No need to explain." But his voice was cool.

Her face grew hot, but she went on. "And while I'm at it, I want to apologize for leaving Clancy's so abruptly the other night." She shook her head slowly from side to side. "You arranged such a wonderful evening, and I was rude."

He waved off her words. "Apologies aren't necessary." But his voice softened as he said, "It was good food. Good company."

Sitting back she felt that space opening up inside her again. She realized that, despite everything, still she yearned to hang on to Jude. She looked down at her hands, longing to turn back time. If only she'd never met and married Phillip Sharp.

But when she glanced at Jude, he was looking off again, as if just waiting for an opportunity to leave. The distance between them was real, she understood. This was a different Jude sitting beside her this morning, more constrained. Watching him under her lashes as they sat quietly, sipping coffee, she wondered if Rebecca was somewhere waiting for him.

❧

Silence, unusual for Amalise, took hold. Jude's eyes roamed over the busy square. He settled back, hooked his arm over the back of the chair and watched some street musicians unloading instruments from a rusted old red truck illegally parked in front of the Cabildo.

He congratulated himself at least on steering a steady course with Amalise. The confession of love he'd planned about ten days ago at Clancy's would have been a mistake. She was too distracted, working her way through the usual list of priorities, and so far as he could tell, he was at the bottom of that list.

Over the last few months, with God's help, he'd thought he had come to an understanding of the horror she'd lived through with the broken man she'd married. But while Jude's love for Amalise was an almost physical force, the lingering effects of her marriage to Phillip still stood between them.

She looked at her watch. "I guess we'd better go."

He nodded and stood, anchoring a couple of dollars under the coffee cup. They crossed the room to say good-bye to Henry, and then Gina in the kitchen, almost like old times. Like the times before Phillip had arrived.

Amalise had parked in a lot on Royal Street two blocks from Jackson Square. When they reached her car, she stood there for a second before unlocking it.

He wanted to reach out for her, to pull her into his arms and hold her. Standing close, she fumbled in her purse, pulled out the car keys, unlocked the door, and turned to him, looking up. His heart skipped a beat. No, this wasn't the little girl he'd known so well. He looked into her eyes, awed at the transformation of his feelings for her.

But he stepped back and his words came out harsher than he'd meant. "See you in a couple weeks."

"I miss you when you're gone," she said, then opened the door and slid in.

He thought he'd heard a slight catch in her voice. But as she rolled down the window and tilted back her head and said good-bye, he said the same and walked away.

Chapter Twenty-Four

THE ERRAND AMALISE HAD TO RUN was a visit to Caroline's house. Just a quick stop before she went to the office. Ellis worked shifts, but he'd be home this morning. Caroline wanted Amalise to meet her husband.

As she walked up the front porch steps, Amalise spotted Luke to her left, almost hidden behind a hedge of bushes that grew along the porch railing. He sat alone on a wooden bench swing.

She walked over to the swing, set her purse down, and took a seat beside him. He didn't look up. His head reached only to the level of her shoulders. Thin legs poked out from his pants, dangled over the edge of the swing like two small twigs.

"Hello, Luke." She kept her voice low and casual.

He tensed like a small, trapped animal.

So she turned her gaze forward through the clear fall light. From the interior of the house she could hear Daisy chattering to Caroline.

A dove called to its mate in the tree behind her, the oak hung with Daisy's rope swing. Seconds passed and she heard the mate's answering call. The scent of nearby banana plants reminded her of Marianus and Mama and Dad and mornings sitting outside with Jude. In that moment she was filled with an unexpected, singular peace. Thoughts of the conference room downtown were far away.

And then, in the shadowed stillness she felt Luke's hand move on the bench—a mere fraction of an inch—until the tip of his little finger touched the side of hers. With shallow breaths, she sat still beside him, waiting, feeling his loneliness. She wondered again where he'd come from. Did he mourn a mother and father? Did he have brothers and sisters in Southeast Asia?

Abba, how can a child ever understand such things? It isn't fair. Help me reach him. Let me help.

Minutes passed as they sat there, fingers touching, and then slowly she covered Luke's hand with her own on the wooden seat. When he didn't pull away, she began pushing the swing gently back and forth.

Several more minutes passed, and then, as from a primal need, Luke moved closer to her, fitting his small body to hers like small animals will do when they seek warmth.

When Caroline came out the front door, Amalise was conscious that she stopped and stood very still, watching them before she spoke.

The kitchen was full of children and a cheerful-looking, round-faced man and redolent of garlic and onions. The man stood up when she walked in, trailing Caroline, still holding onto Luke's hand. Caroline halted.

"Well, Ellis." She stretched out her hand toward Amalise. "Meet Amalise Catoir."

Ellis's face lit, and he raked his hands back through his hair in a self-conscious way. "How do?" he said, tucking his blue work shirt under his belt. He moved to reach out his hand and then quickly pulled it back, as if uncertain. "I've heard a lot about you."

His chuckle made Amalise wonder exactly what he'd heard. Nick and Charlie looked up from their places at the table and smiled. Daisy held up her doll and waggled it in Amalise's direction.

Ellis pulled out a chair, and Amalise sat down. She hiked Luke onto her lap. From the corner of her eye she saw Ellis raise his brows and give Caroline a look. With a slight shrug, Caroline picked up a large spoon on the counter and turned to a pot on the stove. Over her shoulder she said,

"I've been wanting you two to meet, and . . . Ellis, I could use a pinch of salt here."

Amalise curled her arm around Luke, and he settled back against her. Ellis rose, picked up a box of Morton salt on the counter and took it to where Caroline was stirring the huge iron pot.

"Just pour until I say to stop, please." Ellis upturned the salt. Immediately Caroline shrieked and lifted the spoon. "That's enough! Not so fast. Stop. Stop. Stop!"

Amalise laughed. "It smells wonderful. What are you making?"

Ellis put down the salt while Caroline recovered. He patted his wife's shoulder and returned to his chair. "Creole Daube. Caro's a good cook."

Amalise nodded. "Mama makes it. Takes all day to make, but it's one of my favorite dishes."

"Stay and eat with us."

She raised her eyes to the ceiling and made a face. "I wish I could. But I need to get to the office."

"Then I'll save you some." Caroline turned her head, looking at Luke, sitting quietly in Amalise's lap. She smiled. "Looks like you've made a new friend."

Suddenly aware of the attention, Luke ducked his head into the crook of her shoulder. With a sigh, Caroline glanced at Ellis and turned back to the stove. "We just can't get him to open up. We've tried everything."

"He's confused," Ellis said, looking at his wife's back. "He doesn't understand."

"I know." But Caroline's shoulders slumped as she jabbed the contents of the pot.

"Imagine what he must have been through." Amalise cradled the child, feeling the thin shoulder blades, like bird's wings, pressing against her chest. Charlie and Nick scampered out of the room, and the front door slammed behind them. Daisy stood beside Caroline, looking after them. With the doll hanging at her side, she sank against Caroline.

Amalise looked over Luke's head. "I wish we knew his language."

"Could be he just doesn't want to talk," Ellis said.

Caroline walked to the closed end of the kitchen where a cabinet stretched above a counter. "Let me show you something." She pulled out several sheets of paper, brought them to the table, and spread them out, side by side. "I asked the children to draw pictures of themselves," Caroline said, spreading her hands on the table before the pictures. She pointed to one of the sketches. "This one is Luke's."

Amalise looked up. "He understood?"

"Not at first. I gave them the basic outline of a head, then gave them a mirror and told them to fill in the faces. Told them to draw their whole bodies, and add clothes if they wanted." She looked at Amalise. "He copied the others, at least this far."

Amalise studied Luke's picture, drawn with an unsteady hand, a stick figure under the head that Caroline had drawn, with straight lines for arms and legs and slashes for hands and feet. But Luke had drawn no eyes, or nose or mouth where there should be a face. There were no ears, no attempt at depicting hair. The face was simply a blank. She looked up at Caroline. It was a shocking void.

"Compare it to the others." Caroline passed her hand over the other three sheets on the table, each containing facial features, ears, hair. Daisy had used crayons—the girl in her picture had long yellow hair.

Caroline pulled out a chair and sat, looking up at Amalise. "What do you think?"

She shook her head, curling her arms around Luke. "This breaks my heart. How old do you think he is?"

Ellis leaned back. "He's malnourished. I'd guess around six years."

"He eats and sleeps here, but he needs love," Caroline said.

"I guess when he begins to feel secure, he'll learn to trust. That's what we're hoping." Ellis's voice, directed to Caroline, was soothing.

Sweeping up the pictures, Caroline stored them away in the cabinet once again and returned to the stove. Ellis watched her with a frown as she turned down the burner. She placed a lid on the pot of Creole Daube, then untied the apron and sat across from Ellis. They looked at each other.

Luke leaned back, snuggling against Amalise as if she'd been around all his life. Looking down at him, she realized that she could come to love this child, if she let herself.

Sitting on her lap was one small survivor from the war whose televised images had haunted a nation in 1975, when she was in law school. When the shadow children had been far away, there was nothing she could do, she told herself. But this one child was here now, and that raised questions about everything.

Chapter Twenty-Five

HE HAD BEEN TOLD TO KEEP her close, so here he was, bored, beat, and with nothing much to show for the day. His new client was intense, and that made him nervous. It was almost the end of October, but with the sun blazing through the windshield, he was hot. He ran his finger around the inside of the damp shirt collar, then glanced at his watch and saw it was only 1:30. He thought about making a late lunch run but rejected the idea because it would be just his luck if his client should check in right at that time.

He yawned. Bad enough he'd had to get up at the crack of dawn. He'd been beating his feet behind Amalise Catoir all morning, and now here he was stuck sitting in a hot car with the air conditioning off and the windows down, in front of the First Merchant Bank Building on a Sunday afternoon. And if she was anything like the other suits he'd followed to this building in the past, she might not come out till *next* Sunday. What was wrong with those people? Couldn't they afford to get lives?

And what was with the Asian kid? She'd come out of the house on Kerlerec with him still hanging on, until the woman who lived there had pulled him away and picked him up.

And church? He'd felt shifty skulking in the back of the cathedral. She'd met some guy there he hadn't seen before, not at the law firm anyways. At first he'd thought the way their heads nearly touched when they knelt—you couldn't have slipped a quarter between them—that they were lovers. The way they shared the prayer book, how he'd tucked his hand under her elbow and steered her out when Mass was over. But he'd taken a table behind them at the café and decided after all that they were only friends.

Besides, she'd ditched him for the kid.

The house on Kerlerec Street was what seemed to be making his client nervous. The kid lived there, and plenty others, too. He'd kept his distance, never having been fond of children. They moved too fast with all those quick, sharp movements that catch you off guard. Like cats. He was certain if you were over twenty, any kid could read your mind. They didn't miss much, either.

With a deep sigh, he struggled out of his jacket and tossed it onto the passenger seat. He reached down, pulled off one shoe, and rubbed his foot. His feet hurt from schlepping around the Quarter. Glancing around him out the windows, he saw no sign of his client, so he took off the other shoe, too. He leaned back against the door and stretched out his legs across the seat. Good pay, but what kind of hard-luck job was this?

Robert handed Bingham the investigator's first report. "You'll want to read this," was all he said. Bingham took the report, held it up, and began to read.

They were in the living room of Bingham Murdoch's suite at the Roosevelt late Sunday night. The ceiling was high, the chandeliers hung low. The room was ornate, filled with antiques, and carpeted with a large Persian rug in rich patterns of burgundy and cream. Heavy gold draperies framed the windows. Bingham lay sprawled across a sofa with intricately carved tables at each end. Robert took a seat in a chair nearby. Leaning on one elbow, chin on knuckles, he watched Bingham.

Bingham was feeling exhausted and irritable. He'd thought from the first it was a bad idea to have an associate at Mangen & Morris followed. This was asking for trouble. Amalise had been in the conference room all afternoon, right where she was supposed to be, and they were paying an investigator to sit outside in a car and sleep. Plus, he'd wanted to relax awhile. He'd just left mountains of paper and expensive lawyers behind in the conference room and needed some time to himself.

A tap on the door interrupted them. A muffled voice on the other side called out, "Room service."

Bingham jerked his head toward the door, and Robert went to open it.

"Evenin', sir." The waiter stepped past Robert and nodded toward Bingham. "Mr. Murdoch." The waiter stood holding a tray laded with a bottle of scotch, one glass, a bucket of ice, and a plate of those little sandwiches he liked. The ones with the crust cut off, like Mother used to make.

"Hello, Joseph. Just put it down there." He indicated the coffee table in front of the sofa where he sat. "How's your grandson? Doing better?"

"Yes, sir." Joseph set down the tray. Robert palmed a bill to the old man. Bingham saw it was a ten. "His fever's down and he's wantin' to get out now." Joseph's face crinkled with a smile as he turned his gray head and headed for the door. "He's figured out how to keep his grandma on the run, that's for sure." The door closed softly behind him.

The man knew how to make an exit.

Bingham turned his eyes to Robert, wishing his guest had that same wisdom. Tossing the report down on the couch, Bingham sat up straight, plopped his feet on the floor, and picked up the scotch. He added some ice to a glass and poured himself a drink. "There're some glasses at the bar over there if you want some."

"No, thanks."

"Suit yourself." Bingham sat back, picked up the report again, and settled into the corner of the couch. "Grab yourself a sandwich. There's ham, cheese, roast beef."

"I'm fine," Robert said. He sat back down in the chair, stretching his arms down the armrests and drumming his fingers.

Bingham read through a few paragraphs about going to church, coffee with someone—probably Jude Perett—before he came to the address on Kerlerec. Holding the glass in one hand, he lowered the report and looked at Robert, brows raised.

Robert nodded.

Bingham blew out his cheeks and set the drink down on the table beside him. When he looked back at Robert, he thought the expression on the young man's face was slightly smug. Robert spread out in the chair and said nothing.

"She visited people in the Marigny District?"

Robert nodded again. "Yes, a location within the project survey."

"What's their connection?"

"We don't know. She spent some time with a kid living there. An Asian kid."

"Find out about the family. Let's hope we're not dealing with troublemakers. If she's stuck on the kid, find out what that's all about."

Bingham skimmed the rest of the report. Except for the visit to the Marigny, the rest was uneventful. When he reached the end, he set the report down in his lap and, brows lowered and drawn, looked off. "Wonder how long she's known those folks. And why didn't she mention that right off, about having friends living in the target area?" He looked back at Robert. "What do you think?"

"I've told you before. I think she's trouble."

"Coincidence, maybe."

Robert plucked some lint from his suit jacket. "Too much at stake here for speculation, Bingham." Dangling his hand over the side of the armrest, he flicked away the lint. Bingham watched it float to the floor. "Too much money involved to play games. I've sent a copy to Tom."

Bingham's mouth quirked down at the corners. Robert had a point. Amalise Catoir was a woman worrying about souls and trees. She was a potential protester. He could see it now, all that commotion. He felt the surge as his blood pressure spiked. "Who else lives at this address?"

"Man and wife, with four children, including the kid. Renters."

"No lease?"

"Nope."

Bingham frowned. Renters had nothing to gain and everything to lose when a house was sold out from under them. And the sale was a certainty, he knew. The offered price would go as high as needed to get them out of there. They'd be evicted. He picked up a sandwich from the tray and chewed without tasting it.

The telephone rang. Bingham flicked his finger at Robert and finished off the sandwich. Robert lifted the rotary phone from the table beside the chair, balanced it on his knee, and picked up the receiver. "Tom, buddy!" he said after a second.

Sipping his scotch, Bingham listened to the conversation with half a mind. Tom's investors were hungry and tough—they wouldn't accept the slightest risk of interference in this project. Funds were committed, and they needed to move fast, get some dirt dug before the public knew what had hit them.

The phone slammed down and Robert turned. "Tom thinks we should take her off the project."

Bingham set the glass down on the table. He linked his hands and rotated his thumbs. Looked at the wallpaper on the wall and followed the trace of gold-patterned vines on the bronze background around to the hallway door. He'd not noticed that before. Mulling over the problem, he continued admiring the braided woodwork on the white double door.

Amalise Catoir was young, just starting her career. He liked the girl, but that wasn't the issue. If she were fired, bad feelings would ensue in the working group and, even worse, throughout the firm. That could cause some delay. He shook his head. "Nothing's happened yet. Mangen & Morris invests time and money in their associates. Let's not ask for trouble until we know more."

Robert frowned. "Why chance it?" Bingham heard the undercurrent of exasperation in his voice.

"Follow her. But leave her alone. Understood?"

Robert's face went blank. "Tom will be here on Tuesday. He's bringing Richard Murray along."

"Well, keep your cat on our mouse. We want to know every move she makes for the next few days."

"Don't worry."

Bingham gave him a quick look. Robert's smile was cold.

"How are things going on Tom's end?"

"We've got commitments for the full twenty million."

"Good. The banks are playing chicken-and-egg. They want the twenty million in First Merchant before they wire their own money at closing."

Robert narrowed his eyes at Bingham. "No. First Merchant's in the lending syndicate. We have conflicting interests, and I don't trust them. They don't get a dime from us until the deal's complete, until the banks have funded. They'll go first." He leaned forward and reached for a sandwich. "That's not negotiable." He lifted the top piece of bread and took inventory of what was there, reassembled the sandwich, sank back into the chair, and took a bite.

Bingham rattled the ice in his glass and looked deep into the scotch, as if searching for an answer. After a moment he looked up. "We'll have to work this out. They're saying there's risk if they send their money and then something happens to kill the deal—the investors come up short, or someone changes his mind at the last minute, something like that."

Robert gave him a look. "For instance, a protest pops up in the Marigny, led by Miss Catoir's friends, and the politicians back off?"

Bingham pursed his lips. "Let's not get ahead of ourselves. We'll work out a solution."

Robert stood, linking his hands and cracking his knuckles. Bingham winced.

"It's a sweet deal you put together, Bingham, even without the casino coming along. Let's hope the woman doesn't interfere. You've got a big fee riding on things working out. Things go right, and Tom will show his appreciation." He headed for the door.

"Keep your man on Miss Catoir."

Robert didn't miss a step. "Oh, don't worry. We will."

"And push the closing along, Robert. No delays. Keep up the pressure."

"It would have been easier if it weren't Thanksgiving week."

"That's the date I want."

Chapter Twenty-Six

Phnom Penh, Cambodia 1975

THE RAMP BEGAN OPENING AS THE plane rolled to a stop at Bear Cat, just outside Saigon. For a moment the light was blinding, and Oliver shielded his eyes with his arm as he watched the silhouetted medics rushing to help. They scrambled up the ramp and lifted Sam onto a stretcher, then placed the stretcher on a gurney. Sam's lips tightened as the medics lifted her, and Oliver saw tears shining on her face. He took her hand and held on as they eased the gurney down the ramp and then crossed the tarmac to the waiting ambulance.

Oliver was climbing into the back of the ambulance to ride with Sam when he heard someone calling his name. Turning, he squinted into the sun, saw Margaret Bordelon emerge from the hold, stumbling, slipping the rest of the way. He started toward her as she righted herself, then halted, glancing over his shoulder toward the ambulance.

Raising her arm, Margaret shouted. "Oliver! What about the boy?"

Someone inside the ambulance yelled that he'd better hurry. They had to go.

Oliver tensed, frowning as Margaret reached him, halting a few feet away, bending and hugging her waist, breathing hard.

A jet engine roared to life nearby. Behind him the ambulance engine idled. He looked at Margaret. "Take the boy with you, will you?"

At that Margaret straightened, dropped her hands to her sides and stared. "What! Me?" She looked about, then turned back to him. "Me?"

"Yes." He turned back to the ambulance, shouting. "Wait for me, I'm coming!" Over his shoulder he called to Margaret, "I'm going with Sam. The boy's assigned to Operation Babylift." He stopped and turned, giving her a hard look, and she nodded.

"It's official, Margaret. He's roistered for immediate evacuation on Operation Babylift. Sam's lost the paperwork, but his sponsor's name is written on the envelope pinned to his pocket. See that it gets done. Please."

Again she nodded, mute.

Oliver turned before she could object, climbed into the ambulance, and the doors closed behind him.

Chapter Twenty-Seven

New Orleans—1977

MONDAY MORNING. EIGHT FIFTEEN. THE TELEPHONE behind her on the credenza buzzed. Amalise looked over the pile of agreements she'd left on her desk last night and swiveled to answer the phone.

Ashley Elizabeth's voice greeted her. "There's a Richard Murray on the line. Says he's working on the Murdoch deal."

"I haven't had coffee yet. Ask if I can call him back."

"He says he needs to speak with you right now."

Amalise cleared her throat. "Ashley Elizabeth, please tell him that I'll call him back." She glared at the phone. "And, hold my calls, will you."

"All right."

Amalise turned back to the pile of agreements she'd begun revising in accordance with changes that the parties had agreed on yesterday. Seven agreements in all. A paragraph here, a sentence there. She would mark the changes, have them typed, proofed, and copied. Then she would circulate the documents, hopefully by eight or nine o'clock that evening. She figured ten or so hours to finish the work.

The phone buzzed again. She picked up.

"He says . . . ah . . ." Ashley Elizabeth lowered her voice. "He says to put you on the phone pronto, or you'll be off the deal before you can pack."

"What?"

"That's what he said."

"All right. I'll take the call."

Amalise stared at the blinking light that was Richard Murray. She picked up the receiver and pressed the button.

"This is Amalise Catoir," she said in the coolest tone she could manufacture.

The answering voice was clipped, impatient. "Richard Murray here, Morgan Klemp on the Murdoch deal. We need your comments on the loan documents, and we need them yesterday."

"Ah."

She could hear rustling over the line, the sound of papers being shuffled on a desk.

"All right," he said. "Let's start with the bank Loan Agreement. We'll go page by page. You summarize the changes made over the weekend on the drafts, and I'll take notes."

"Hold it."

"Now," the voice snapped.

"Look." Amalise swiveled the chair, looking out the window. "I don't have time for this. The agreements will be revised today, and changes will be sent to you this evening by fax."

There was a pause. "We're leaving for LaGuardia at six, five your time. Flight's at seven thirty. Tom Hannigan and I are coming down there. I need the proposed changes immediately. We're not walking blind into that meeting tomorrow."

Amalise swallowed. Who was this guy? She did a quick calculation. With enough help . . . she took a deep breath. "It'll take a minimum of eight hours to work through the revisions and have the documents revised. I'll send them over to your hotel tonight."

"No good. Tom's going to want to talk them over on the plane. I need everything by five p.m." He snorted. "As in post-menopausal."

She straightened, set her jaw, but decided to ignore the remark. "Sorry, but that can't be done."

There was a long pause. "Maybe you're not the girl for the job, Amalise. Did I pronounce the name right. Amalise?"

"You sure did, Dick."

"Richard." A yawn drifted through the phone. "Look, this isn't your bridge club. My notebook is empty right now. You're going to fill it. If Tom's not briefed, it will be your fault, and he won't be happy." He laughed. *Snap. Pop.* "So I'll hold."

Gum. He was chewing gum. She looked at the phone and contemplated hanging up. On the other hand, Richard was working with Tom, and Tom Hannigan and Bingham Murdoch were the lead investors on this deal. So instead she slammed the hold button down as if it were Richard Murray himself and stared at the blinking light. She now had only eight hours.

Heart racing, she rose and walked to the door of her office, working to hide her anger. Coffee. She'd had only three hours sleep after working till two in the morning, so the first order of business was to locate a cup of coffee. A glance back over her shoulder as she reached the door confirmed that Richard Murray was still on hold. Ashley Elizabeth looked up as she trudged past her secretary's desk.

"Amalise." She halted and turned. "Did you know you've left a call on hold?"

"Yes." She gritted her teeth and walked on.

She found Rebecca in the coffee room at a table near the windows. Outside the clear, bright November light was tempting. For an instant Amalise wondered what would happen if she just left that call on hold and went out for the day. She filled a Styrofoam cup with coffee and sat down.

"What's wrong?" Rebecca asked as she pulled out a chair and sat. "You look grim."

Amalise shook her head. "You're not going to believe this."

Rebecca's eyes grew wide as Amalise repeated her conversation with Richard Murray. "And he's still holding?"

Amalise took a sip of the hot coffee and nodded. "He says he'll hold until he gets a summary of the revisions to the seven documents the banks negotiated over the weekend. We finished the session last night, and I took notes."

Rebecca grimaced. "He wants you to tutor him?" She sipped her own coffee and looked at Amalise over the rim of the cup. "It's a setup—winning through intimidation. You'll spend all day bringing him up to speed, and then while he's sleeping on the plane, you'll be working all night to get the documents revised for the morning meeting."

Amalise nodded. "Otherwise, he'll stroll into the conference room tomorrow without the information, and Tom Hannigan will blame me."

Rebecca gazed into her coffee, turning the cup slowly in circles with the tips of her fingers. Then she looked up, smiling. "Two can play that game. How about this?"

Amalise leaned forward, listening. When Rebecca had finished, they looked at each other and laughed.

The hold light on the telephone was still blinking when Amalise returned to her office. Glancing down at her watch, Amalise walked to the desk, turned her back to the phone as she pulled out the chair, took a deep breath, and sat down. Then she called Ashley Elizabeth and asked her to come in. She would need two people in the typing pool assigned to work exclusively with her. And proofreaders.

And Ashley Elizabeth's help.

❦

Ashley Elizabeth obtained the New York fax number they would need from the transaction distribution list. As Amalise worked to complete the revision of each document, Ashley Elizabeth shuffled them from the office to the typing pool, from the typists to the proofers, and after all corrections were made, back to Amalise for final review.

Then on to the fax room.

Amalise worked quickly, efficiently, and Ashley Elizabeth held all calls. Still the hold light blinked. Once in a while she'd pick up the phone and say, "Still there?" Richard would say, "Yep," and she'd put him back on hold.

Once, Raymond stuck his head into her office.

Amalise looked up. Set down the pencil and flexed her fingers. "Do you know someone named Richard Murray?"

Raymond wrinkled his brow, eyeing the blinking light behind her. "Did you know you have a call on hold?"

"Yes. What's Richard's position?"

"He's in corporate finance, an associate, I think. Two, maybe three years. He's coming in tomorrow with Tom Hannigan." He gave her a quizzical look. "Why?"

"Just wondered."

Around two o'clock Amalise turned to the credenza and punched the blinking light, listening. She heard voices in the background. *"Convertible debt . . . No, we want the equity, the equity!"* A drawer slammed. A curse. She placed the call on hold again.

As the light blinked and Ashley Elizabeth trekked in and out of her office, Amalise kept an eye on her watch. Three o'clock, then four. What was Einstein's theory? The faster you move, the slower time passes? Or was it the reverse?

At 4:30 in the afternoon Ashley Elizabeth rushed in. "Here you go." She waved a thick document and her eyes shone.

Amalise looked up. "How are we doing?"

Ashley Elizabeth brushed back her hair and dropped the document on Amalise's desk. "This is number six."

"All faxed to New York?"

"Yes."

Amalise smiled. "Here's the last one." She held it out, and Ashley Elizabeth took it with a glance at the blinking light.

Ashley Elizabeth headed for the door. "Your handwriting's getting worse," she said. "Typing's starting to grumble."

When she had gone, Amalise dropped her throbbing head into her hands.

"Richard's still waiting?" Rebecca's voice roused her.

Amalise lifted her head and nodded with the beginning of a smile. She straightened as Rebecca dropped into the chair in front of her desk. "You're just in time."

High-heeled shoes clicked double-time down the hallway, and Ashley Elizabeth burst in. With a quick nod, she gave Amalise thumbs up.

Amalise placed her hands on the desk before her, sitting in what Jude would have called the launch position. "We have a fax confirmation for the last one?"

Ashley Elizabeth smiled and did a little jig.

Rebecca rose, walked to the window. "Showtime." With a cat-like smile, she folded her arms and leaned back against the window frame. "Wish I had a movie camera. At least use the speaker, so we can hear."

Ashley Elizabeth took the chair. Amalise held up one finger. Swiveling to the telephone, she pressed the button and placed Richard Murray's call on the speaker. "Richard," she said. A crackling sound answered, plastic paper—potato chips, she'd bet. She leaned close to the speaker.

Louder now: "Richard!"

Ashley Elizabeth stifled a choking sound.

There was the sound of shuffling shoes, a slow, heavy walk coming close. The squeak and groan of a chair. "Yeah." He sounded fatigued.

"We're all set." Amalise's tone was bright, cheerful.

"We leave for the airport in thirty minutes. You're dead." His voice came through harsh but clear. "You've played Russian roulette and lost. And don't think this won't be a subject for discussion tomorrow."

"There must be some mistake, Richard." Amalise's voice was silk. She turned her head, watching Ashley Elizabeth, who nodded. "Since this morning we've been faxing each agreement to your office as I completed the revisions. You've had plenty of time to read them." Leaning back in the chair, she curled her fingers and studied her nails. "We were hoping you'd be ready with some preliminary thoughts on the changes before you leave for the airport."

"I don't know what you're talking about. You say you've sent them?"

"Of course."

There was a long silence on the other end. She turned to Ashley Elizabeth, held out her hand, and took the final fax confirmation. "Everything was faxed to this number." She read it out loud.

"That's Tom Hannigan's fax, not mine!"

"It was addressed to both of you. Don't you work together?"

"What the—"

She leaned toward the speaker, elbows on the credenza, chin in her hands. "Richard, we're wasting time." She had to work to force a hint of compassion into her voice. "There are seven agreements in all. Tom will have them. He's probably already looked at them—the changes are black-lined for you. Ask his secretary to give you copies. I'm sure he'll fill you in on the plane."

"You—"

"The meeting's tomorrow at nine. Plenty of time to catch up."

With a smile, she clicked off the phone in the middle of his splutter.

"That was delicious," Rebecca said, laughing.

Ashley Elizabeth stood, straightened her skirt, and headed for the door. "I'm off to tennis. See you ladies in the morning."

"Hey."

Ashley Elizabeth turned.

"Thanks."

Ashley Elizabeth grinned, linked her hands over her head, and executed an excellent stroll right out the door.

Raymond backed into the room, eyes following Ashley Elizabeth's trail.

Brows up, he turned to Amalise and Rebecca. "What's going on?"

Amalise opened her mouth, but Raymond interrupted, pointing to the stack of papers on her desk. "Amalise, when you finish those revisions—"

"They're done."

"Good. Distribute them to the group. And Preston's waiting."

He turned and disappeared.

Amalise stared at the empty doorway and shook her head.

"Huh," Rebecca, sauntered to the door and stood, hands on her hips, looking after Raymond. After a moment she turned back to Amalise. "I get the feeling that if we both walked buck naked down that hallway after him, no one around here would even look up."

Chapter Twenty-Eight

RICHARD MURRAY DRAGGED INTO THE CONFERENCE room with Tom Hannigan the next morning, red-eyed and ill-tempered. Tom shut him down immediately when he groused about receiving the documents two minutes before they left for the airport the night before. Doug had given her a knowing smile. Raymond must have spilled the beans.

After a long morning Bingham Murdoch insisted on taking the New Yorkers to Antoine's for lunch. When the meeting broke up, Amalise excused herself, not a difficult task for an overworked associate. Now she sat in her quiet office, summarizing the most pertinent points to be covered in the next round of negotiations.

A rapid succession of knocks on the door roused her. She looked up to see Rebecca standing there, lips curled, bright eyes flashing. "How'd it go? What's Richard Murray like?" Without waiting for an answer, she strolled into the office and fell into the client chair.

Amalise smiled. "Dick? He's just what we expected."

"Was he sufficiently intimidated?"

"I don't think so."

Rebecca slid down in the chair, resting her head on the back, studying the ceiling. "Do you want to get a quick lunch? I need a break."

Amalise glanced at her watch. It was only one fifteen, plenty of time. "All right." She stood and stretched.

"Mother's, for po' boys?"

"Takes too long. How about downstairs?"

Rebecca sighed. "That'll do." They walked past Ashley Elizabeth's desk on the way to the elevator. "Back in a half hour," Amalise said, and Ashley Elizabeth nodded without looking up.

"She works hard," Rebecca murmured.

Amalise pressed the button for the elevator. "Until five o'clock. That's our deal. I find temps for evenings and weekends."

"Do you blame her? This isn't her life. For her, it's just a job."

"I don't blame her a bit."

The coffee shop just off the lobby was small but bright, and except for the cleaning woman and a young man behind the counter, it was empty.

Amalise inspected the trays of tuna, egg salad, ham, turkey, and cheese in the glass display counter and ordered a turkey sandwich with lettuce, tomatoes, and spicy mustard. Rebecca ordered tuna. They stood waiting for the sandwiches and chatting, and through the whole conversation, Amalise braced herself for the news that Rebecca and Jude were to be married.

Still, she prayed that for one more day Rebecca wouldn't raise the subject. Once the words were spoken, it would all be true. She'd have lost Jude forever. A small tremor ran through her.

Rebecca turned just then and handed her one sandwich plate and a napkin. "Are you all right?" she asked.

"Just a little tired."

To their right was the cooler. They retrieved two cans of Tab and chose a table.

"How's the Murdoch deal going?"

"It's barreling along. Raymond's in my office every ten minutes with new work. The investors are panting. They'll make a bundle."

Suddenly, Rebecca set down her sandwich and leaned forward. Amalise blinked and swallowed. Rebecca lowered her voice, almost whispering. "I want to be on that deal, Amalise. Could you say something to Preston? Or maybe even Doug?"

Amalise stared. A quick stab of envy washed through her. Rebecca had Jude, and now she wanted Black Diamond, too. But this deal was hers. If Rebecca was added to the team, Amalise knew exactly what would happen. She'd become lost in Rebecca's vortex, the swirl of attention she commanded every time she walked into a room.

She hated herself when she thought this way. After all, they were friends.

"Would you mind?" Rebecca's eyes held hers.

"Of course not," Amalise replied a little too loud. She picked up her sandwich, glancing around. "It's a killer, though, I'll warn you. You're sure that's what you really want?"

Rebecca's face lit. She settled back and nodded her head. "Sure! It would be fun to work together again."

Of course, she had to try. They were friends, not really competitors. She nodded. "I'll talk to Preston as soon as the opportunity comes up. I've got to wait for the right time, but we could certainly use the help."

Rebecca seemed satisfied. She folded her arms, ignoring her food. "What's Bingham Murdoch like? Everyone in the firm's talking about him."

Amalise shrugged. "He's been a silent partner in several big developments. Recommended by Tom Hannigan at Morgan Klemp. Doug and Tom have been friends for years, so Tom's the connection, I guess." She smiled. "And he likes good food."

Amalise washed down the last of her sandwich with the Tab and glanced at the clock on the wall. "Time to go." She pushed back her chair.

Crossing the lobby, she said, "I came across an interesting article at the library when I was checking out Murdoch's background. Remember that airline hijacker a few years ago? D. B. Cooper?"

"Sure. The hijacker that got away in 1971?" She shook her head. "What's he got to do with Murdoch?"

"Nothing." Amalise's eyes twinkled. "I copied the story and brought it back for Raymond—he's such a nut on the subject. The detective handling the case said Cooper was a real lone ranger. Lone Ranger happens to be the name of Murdoch's company."

"Hm. I wonder where he is."

"Who?"

Rebecca gave her a look. "D. B. Cooper."

"That's what everyone wants to know."

The elevator arrived empty and they stepped in. Amalise pressed sixteen and leaned against the wall beside Rebecca. "Raymond thinks he's on an island somewhere. But Cooper's not his real name. No one ever identified him."

As they reached the sixteenth floor, Rebecca swept her hair from the nape of her neck, twisted it, and let it fall again. Her hair shone like a sunset, Jude had once remarked. Without thinking, Amalise tucked back her own short, dark hair.

"Let me know what Preston says, will you?" Rebecca said as the doors opened and she stepped out ahead of Amalise.

"Sure."

Back in her office, Amalise stood in front of the window, looking out at the building next door and the cloudless stretch of sky over the city to her left. Rebecca hadn't mentioned Jude once. A sharp pain gripped her middle at the thought of Jude. She wrapped her arms across her waist, wondering how she would survive on the day that one of them, Jude or Rebecca, actually got around to telling her their good news.

Days passed when the only sun Amalise saw glared through the windows of the hot, crowded conference room as the project working group negotiated the provisions of the documents page by page. She arrived at work before the sun came up and returned home well after dark.

As always, Amalise sat beside Raymond near one end of the long table, noting revisions and disagreements between the parties as they progressed through the provisions. Revisions to the documents would be made later once solutions were reached. Raymond sat beside Preston, and Preston sat next to Doug, the partner in charge. Doug, the lead negotiator, occupied the center seat at the long table with the windows and sun at his back. On the other side of him was Frank Earl from First Merchant Bank.

Seating arrangement in such meetings had always fascinated Amalise. She would watch executives survey the room when they entered, making a beeline for the power seats, often subtly moving others aside in the process. She needed to learn to do that, she thought, and tucked the information away for the day when she'd be leading a team.

She had broached the subject of including Rebecca on the transaction two days ago, but Preston had put her off. He'd see how things went, he said, and she knew he was thinking of fees. But she'd been swamped since by feelings of guilt over her initial reaction to Rebecca's request, and even now she felt a twinge of remorse over the satisfaction Preston's response had given her. He seemed happy enough with Amalise as the sole female presence on the team.

She'd chided herself for that and vowed to ask him again another day.

Doug and Adam were arguing yet another point. Amalise balanced her pencil on a finger and watched it seesaw over the page while she waited. When she glanced up, Robert caught her eyes, as if he had been probing for secrets. Immediately adrenaline shot through her, putting her on alert. She let her eyes roam past him, wondering if it were possible for him to have found out about her friends on Kerlerec Street?

She mulled it over and relaxed.

Impossible.

Still, Robert was intense. He was not one to cross.

The conference room door opened, and Ashley Elizabeth peeked in. When Amalise looked up, she signaled. Amalise nodded. Bingham would call a halt for lunch in the next couple of hours, she knew. They'd been working day and night on this transaction, with little time off for sleep, but the one thing Bingham insisted upon was continuing his march through the restaurants of the city.

Just then, Doug suggested a short break. Amalise pushed back her chair and went to the credenza for a cold Tab and a croissant. Turning, she found Bingham Murdoch right behind her. Chewing and smiling, she moved aside.

But he turned to her as he picked up a glass, pinning her with his eyes. "I've been thinking about what you said the other day, about the area we're purchasing for the project." Something in his tone recalled Robert's earlier scrutiny. Amalise froze, suddenly unable to swallow as she recalled the rogue plan she'd been considering. But how could they possibly know about that?

"I was watching you while Robert reviewed the construction plans with you a few days ago." He poured a Coca-Cola into a glass and watched it fizz.

"They weren't exactly what I'd expected."

"I know that." Bingham turned, facing her, standing too close. She stepped back. He tilted his head. "So you're worried about souls *and* trees now."

She swallowed. The croissant had turned to dry cotton in her mouth.

Bingham gestured toward her with the glass. "Listen, don't you worry. The place will look fine when it's finished. Lots of glitz, lots of razzle-dazzle. There'll be landscaping, flowers, and new trees—decorative trees—and special lighting."

She nodded.

He shifted his weight and sipped the drink. "I just wanted you to know I understand how you feel. You love the charm of those old places, I know, but there's nothing to worry about." He paused and looked at her. "Sometimes change serves a larger purpose." He gestured toward the map rolled up and standing in a corner of the room. "That layout over there doesn't do the project justice. Those are just flat lines on a sheet of paper." He shook his head. "We'll bring in business, jobs. The residents will find other neighborhoods and settle down." He smiled and the lines around his eyes crinkled.

But Caroline and Ellis wouldn't enjoy a smooth transition. They'd be evicted. And the children would be returned to the home in Gentilly or shuffled off to other foster homes. And Luke . . .

She looked away.

"I used to think like you. Came from a place so beautiful you'd have to hold your breath to look." Bingham's voice was reflective, as if long-forgotten feelings were seeping from him like sap from a tree. "Yes, indeed. Green forests, tallest trees in the world until the paper mills came along." Together they looked at the mountain of paper on the conference table, caught each other in the act, and smiled. His voice lightened. "But those mills created jobs. And jobs fed families. And new trees were planted." He shrugged as if it was all too much. "So who are we to favor trees over the rest of life?"

If she hadn't been so worried about Caroline's family, she'd admit he had a point. But she smiled. "Maybe all this paper will be replaced someday by computers." But she thought of the one big mainframe the firm kept off limits and doubted that.

He shrugged and sipped the drink. "Who knows? You might be right."

"You should drive through there again."

"Where?"

She looked at him. "The Marigny. The project area." Perhaps if he really thought about the neighborhood, he'd understand.

He frowned and waved his hand, as if the question was of no consequence. "Like I said, I did that several years ago, when I first looked at this project." His eyes turned to hers. "But it's bad business to get involved on a personal level."

She set down the Tab and the half-eaten croissant and excused herself, turning away.

At one o'clock Murdoch called a break for lunch, and Amalise breathed a sigh of relief. They'd be gone awhile. She'd grab a sandwich and spend her time finalizing the negotiated changes to the agreements in her office. As the men began pulling on their suit jackets, she picked up a pile of paper, nudged Raymond, and nodded toward the door.

On the sixteenth floor she stopped at Ashley Elizabeth's desk.

Ashley Elizabeth looked up. "Oh, there you are." She reached across her desk for a message slip and handed it to Amalise. "I've put your other messages in your office, near the phone, but this one sounded important."

Amalise glanced at the yellow slip and saw that Caroline had called. Could Amalise call back when she had time? Something was wrong with Luke.

"She sounded like she was crying. I couldn't really make out much of what she said. Who's Luke?"

Amalise, already turning away, hurried into her office.

"Are you coming to lunch?"

Jolted, she turned to see Raymond behind her in the doorway.

"Murdoch's temperament today requires lunch at Tujac's." When she didn't answer, he grinned. "I know. It's tough. Bingham's dazzled. I guess that's how he makes it through the day."

Something was wrong with Luke. Caroline had never called before. "I can't," she said, setting down the papers she'd brought from the conference room. "Something just came up. I'll be out of the office an hour or so, I imagine."

"We'll be awhile, too, I guess. But either way, we have another late night ahead of us." With a wave, Raymond disappeared.

She picked up the phone and dialed Caroline's number. The phone rang six or seven times before she hung up. Pinpricks rose on the nape of her neck. Amalise picked up her purse and hurried to the door.

Chapter Twenty-Nine

CAROLINE'S RED AND SWOLLEN EYES WIDENED when she opened the door and saw Amalise standing there. "I'm so glad you're here." Her voice trembled as she stepped back, beckoning. Amalise looked about for Luke. Caroline reached for her, pulling her inside. "Please. Come in."

"Where's Luke?" She slipped her purse from her shoulder, laid it on the kitchen table, and pulled out a chair.

"He's upstairs. The others are at school." Caroline stood, leaning against the stove and raking her fingers through her hair. "Would you like some coffee?"

"No, thanks." Amalise took a shallow breath and asked, "What's wrong? Is he hurt?"

"No. Oh no, it's nothing like that."

Caroline pulled out a chair and sat, as if gathering her thoughts. Amalise watched as Caroline lifted her eyes and hugged herself.

"Things have gone from bad to worse with Luke. The social worker, Mrs. Gebb, was here yesterday, and she made some comments about how withdrawn he seems."

"No. He's just . . . he's just confused. Guarded."

Caroline nodded. "I know. But in the past few days, since you last saw him, something's changed. He's practically stopped eating. Hardly sleeps." She looked off. "And sometimes he wakes up screaming."

"Maybe he's remembering." She shuddered.

"He tosses around all night." Caroline's face crumpled. "I don't mean to burden you, Amalise. But I know you care about him, and in some small way he seems to connect with you. So I thought . . :" Tears brimmed and she blinked them back. "I thought maybe you could get through to him." Caroline stood and grabbed a napkin from the counter, standing with her back to Amalise as she dabbed at her eyes and blew her nose.

Then she turned around and her voice broke. "I'm afraid we're going to lose him. I'm afraid they'll take him back to the home."

Amalise's hand dropped into her lap. *Abba, help me to help this child. I'm listening now! Just put me on the right path here.*

With a wan smile, Caroline tossed the napkin into the trash can. "I'm sorry." She leaned back against the stove. "I called your office before I thought. Didn't mean to drag you away from work. He's in bed, upstairs."

"Well, that's the first thing we'll change. Let's get him out of that bed."

Amalise stood, but Caroline lowered herself back into the chair, the tears welling up again.

She sat down again. "There's more, isn't there."

Caroline's head dropped into her hands. Amalise took a breath and waited.

When she looked back up, she blurted the words. "It isn't just Luke." Hands pressed to her lips, Caroline looked at her. "I think they're going to reject our petition—for all the children, not just Luke."

"But—"

She flung her hands onto the table. "Our ages, our financial situation—it's all against us. But I thought we had a chance until this thing with Luke. This is the final straw. I could see it on Mrs. Gebb's face."

Amalise pressed her lips together, eyes roaming over the warm kitchen, the neat countertops, and back to Caroline. "They couldn't find better parents than you and Ellis."

Caroline sat back and let her arms fall limp to her sides. She heaved a shuddering sigh. "Well she wants us to do it all again. Start over. Fill out more forms—income and expenses again, this time projected for the next twelve months. We need to show we can provide a stable home, she says." She frowned, looking down. "We'll do that, of course. Ellis will. He's good at that sort of thing."

The idea Amalise had been turning over in her mind for days rose again. There were risks if she were discovered, but what were the chances of that? Slim. If she followed through with this, it might help with Francine Gebb's evaluation for the adoptions. If she did nothing, Caroline and Ellis's hopes for adoption would end in a pile of rubble.

But above all, her heart ached for the child upstairs.

She leaned forward. "Listen. You can do this. You and Ellis get that information together and give them what they want. And I'll help with Luke." She pushed back the chair and stood. "Let's take one thing at a time, Caroline, and we can fix this."

Caroline looked up at her, eyes wide.

"I'll take him for a little walk right now. Maybe I'll find a crack in that wall he's built around himself. I'll take him to the park, get him up and out of the house."

With a slight smile, Caroline rose and Amalise followed her into the living room, waiting at the foot of the stairs as she went up to get Luke.

Amalise retrieved Luke's coat from the closet. A soft wool hat was tucked into a pocket. When Luke came down the stairs with Caroline, she helped him into the coat and gently pulled the hat down over his ears. He turned and gave her an appraising look, curiosity in his eyes.

Caroline had an old bicycle with a child's seat on back. It had fat tires and low handlebars with a basket hooked over them, reminding Amalise of the bike she used to ride when she lived and worked in the Quarter.

She lifted Luke into the child seat and buckled him in. Glancing up, she caught Caroline watching her. The light she'd seen in Caroline's eyes in the other times they'd talked was gone.

She decided to head for Washington Square Park. With Luke strapped in behind her, Amalise tucked her skirt between her legs and took off. While typewriters and telephones whirred and hummed back at the offices of Mangen & Morris, Amalise wheeled down Kerlerec with the chill wind blowing through their hair. Not a peep came from the child behind her. Overhead, sunshine filtered through the last leaves of the trees and, forgetting that he didn't understand, she called back to him, pointing up to the clouds and the shimmering autumn light as they rolled along.

In the park was a fountain, and she stopped there and planted her feet on the ground. The sun warmed her and she stood there taking in the scents of fresh-cut grass, the mildew, and the dank green moss spreading like velvet over the roots and trunks of the trees. Luke sat silent behind her on the bicycle.

The park was the size of a small city block and was quiet at this time on a school day. She pushed down the kickstand, dismounted, and reached for Luke. The boy studied her with a grave expression but didn't move. Then he let eyes rove over the playground. He tilted back his head, looking into the branches above as if searching for signs of danger. At last he turned back to her. She unbuckled the strap and lifted him from the seat, while he leaned around her to see the water splashing in the fountain. He was light as a feather as Amalise lifted him and set him on his feet.

She took his hand, and they walked toward the fountain. Playfully she dipped her fingers into the water and flipped up a spray of glittering silver droplets in the sunshine. To her surprise, he reached down into the water, splashing, imitating her, his lips curling into the beginning of a smile.

Caroline was right—they shared some connection. But she just smiled, and they walked on. He took her hand this time, holding on as they crossed the grassy lawn toward some boxy wooden swings built with crossbars to hold small children in.

He halted just before one of the swings and reached up. He'd probably seen Daisy do this many times at home. Amalise lifted him into the swing and lowered the crossbar. She began to push the swing, and Luke looked over his shoulder at her. And suddenly, there it was—she thought it was her imagination at first—the silver glissando of a child's laughter.

Listen to that, Abba! Did you hear?

Luke pumped his little legs, wanting to go higher, higher, like other children did. Her spirits soared watching him. She stood aside, wishing that Caroline was here to see, clapping for him when he reached new heights.

Later, when he'd tired of the swing, they followed a meandering trail near the fence where a well-tread path through the grass was beaten down to hard dirt. They came to a patch of dark-green clover, and squatting on her heels, she brushed her fingers over the soft clover. Luke squatted beside her and did the same, glancing up at her from under his dark lashes.

They stood and walked on. They'd almost reached the bicycle, having come full circle around the park, when she saw it lying on the path. Instinct halted her at once, and Luke stopped at her side. He followed her eyes.

A small brown bird, a sparrow, lay dead on the path, perhaps fifteen feet from them. Her instinct was to distract Luke so that he wouldn't see the bird, but it was already too late. His fingers curled in hers as they stood there, both seeing the broken wing angled like a flag of death.

A soft keening rose from Luke, and his grip tightened. She looked down, uncertain. But before she could turn him away, movement in the branches overhead caught their attention. They watched silently as another sparrow fluttered down onto the pathway, hopping around the still one, head cocked first one way, then the other, its small black round eyes shining, as if demanding, *Are you coming? Come along, come along! It's getting late and we've work to do.*

Then a breeze ruffled the feathers of the one bound to earth.

The keening beside her grew, piercing Amalise as Luke pulled back, away from the birds, inching around behind her. She twisted to look down at him and saw him peeking, face crumpling. Death was something he'd seen before, she realized. Everything comes to an end on earth. Somewhere nearby was an empty nest, a circle of dry, thin twigs not yet complete. Precarious, as is life. Promise blurred, then smudged and gone.

She turned and knelt. With a cry, Luke flung his arms around her neck and collapsed against her. He buried his face in the crook of her neck, his back heaving as he wept, sobbing, clutching her. *"Mak!"* he cried as she held on. Stroking his hair, she pressed her other hand against his back, realizing that this might be the first word he'd spoken since leaving his homeland.

"Mak. Mak." Clinging to her, he sobbed the word again and again, Luke's misery escaping at last as his shoulders heaved and shook.

Amalise, used to weighing, analyzing, and prioritizing, went numb as she absorbed the child's pain. In that instant she longed to soothe, to comfort and protect him from the hardships of this world. She held him, rocking back and forth as he cried, pressing his head to her shoulder, hugging him, and whispering that she was here, that she was here, and that everything would be all right. That she would make everything all right. Somehow.

But was it true? Was she willing to risk everything to help this child?

Luke's heart beat wildly against her own. Since the moment she'd awoken after the accident months ago, she'd been conscious that Abba had given her a second chance at life for a purpose, one which so far had eluded her. Now as Luke clung to her, she realized that perhaps she'd been looking at things all wrong. An infinite sphere of longing had opened inside her after the accident—a desire to do something while here on earth that would effect lasting change. At the center of that sphere was Abba, and reason alone would never lead her to his answers. The time had come to ditch her old priorities and trust what he spoke to her heart.

She had been raised to believe that despite the presence of evil and injustice in our world, sometimes there comes an instant, a split second, when time halts and a door is opened a crack. In this moment we can make a choice and act to change things. Her mother called it a *kairos* moment, when God shows us the way to reach out to someone else.

That's when she knew what she must do.

Struck with fear at the depth of her feelings for this child, she held him for a long time until he settled down. What did the word mean, *mak*?

She lifted him onto the bicycle seat and strapped him in, then she bent down and kissed his cheek. When you care this much, you have a lot to lose.

But she'd made the decision. She would do it because she knew that we are not only responsible for what we do in life, but also for what we do not do.

Chapter Thirty

NOVEMBER ALREADY. HE'D BEEN ON THIS miserable job for over a week. At least the weather had cooled. From behind the wheel, through the windshield, he spotted his client crossing Common Street with Murdoch. He straightened and lifted his hand up over the steering wheel as Robert Black glanced his way. Black said something to Murdoch, and Murdoch looked over at him and nodded before swerving off into the First Merchant Bank Building.

Black walked toward him.

Quickly he gathered up his handwritten notes on the seat beside him, the report of his morning adventures, such as they were. Black knocked on the passenger window, and he leaned across and rolled it down.

"What've you got?" The client's voice was brusque, impatient.

He handed over the notes. "They're mostly about the kid."

Black took the notes and scanned them, then brows raised, he flipped his hand. "That's all?"

"I'll write it up in detail later, but I thought you'd want to see this right away."

He found himself staring at Black's back as the man folded the papers, stuck them inside his jacket, and walked away without another word.

Feeling the chill in the air, he rolled up the window and sat back, feeling his anger surge. He slumped behind the wheel, watching Robert Black's well-heeled self stroll back into the swank, comfortable bank building. Bitter gastric fluid rose again in the back of his throat. He rubbed his midsection. Oh, the burn. The long, slow burn.

He picked up the bottle of the thick pink stuff he kept on the passenger seat within easy reach and shook it. He should get another job. He thought about that for a while. He thought about what it would be like to work for someone who said "Please" and "Thank you" and "Good-bye" once in a while, someone who showed some respect. Someone less volatile than clients like Robert Black. You never knew what nuts like this were thinking, what they'd do when something set them off.

Fingers spread, he slid both hands down his face and sighed. Nothing would change in his life anytime soon, he knew. At least this job paid.

He unscrewed the cap from the bottle of pink stuff and swigged a few gulps. *Just choke it down,* he thought. *Get rid of the burn.*

The door was flung open, and the conference room came alive as Murdoch strode in from a long lunch with his entourage, which seemed to have expanded. Following in Murdoch's wake were two strangers, each with a briefcase in one hand and a leather garment bag hanging on his shoulder. The new arrivals wore tailored black overcoats made of expensive wool, too heavy for the mild winter months in New Orleans, Amalise thought.

"Ran into these jokers in the lobby," Tom announced as he took his seat. "Lawyers representing the investors," he said.

A rotund, red-faced man marched around the table introducing himself. "Steve Hendrick," he said in a jovial tone, eyes already moving on as he shook each hand. His jacket stretched wide as he moved. His white shirt was wrinkled, and smoke permeated his clothing.

Steve was followed around the table by Lars Elliot, a man who appeared to have grave things on his mind. He wore a quiet gray suit from Italy, as evidenced by the slim fit, and his expression was impassive as he shook hands, lightly, with just a brush as he breezed by. Still,

Amalise decided, Lars had presence. Like Rebecca, he was someone who commanded attention.

Briefcases were slammed onto the table as Lars and Steve finally pulled out chairs and sat, Lars at the end of the table, Steve beside him. Amalise picked up her pencil, sensing a gradual shift of power in the room toward Lars. Lars leaned back and spread out over the chair as if he owned the place.

Sitting directly across the table from Amalise was Richard Murray with his furrowed countenance. Worry lines between his brows were deep, and deep folds bracketing his mouth forced his lips into a permanent snarl. With their standoff still fresh in her mind, she kept her face deliberately blank.

When everyone was settled, a brief discussion ensued over the issues still on the table. "The clock's ticking, everyone," Bingham's voice rang out. "D-day is in three weeks. What have we got left?" He turned to Tom.

Tom hunched over the pile of paper before him and recited the open issues from the investors' point of view, a few contract points, including who would fund first on the closing date—the chicken-and-egg question again—and the funding mechanisms on the closing day. Then he gave a little shrug, his voice casual as he flipped his hand and added something about the interest rates on the investors' notes, things like that.

Doug tapped his pen against his bottom lip and then pointed it at Tom. "You agreed to thirteen-point-five percent convertible subordinated notes. We're not opening up that discussion again."

"Our guys think it's too low."

"Effective fed funds rate is only four and a half." Doug gazed across at Tom.

"Yeah, but it's going up. Fast and soon. We need another hundred and fifty basis points, an add-on of one-and-a-half percent—that's fifteen percent notes to cover the risk."

"Not negotiable."

"We'll see."

Doug went on to the banks' unresolved concerns, Frank Earl beside him nodding at each point. As he talked, Amalise saw Robert lean back and, reaching behind Tom, hand something to Bingham. Bingham looked down, scanned it quickly, and nodded. It could have been just her imagination, but she thought she'd seen Bingham's eyes flick in her direction as he folded the paper and stuck it inside his jacket.

Just then, the door opened and Rebecca walked in, yellow pad in hand. She wore a fitted navy-blue suit that emphasized her slim figure and the color of her hair. Chin high, she looked at Doug and smiled, halting just inside the door. Raymond lifted his hand and motioned her over to an empty chair on the other side of Amalise, near the end of the table. Tom glanced over his shoulder, and then with a look at Robert, half turned in his seat, watching her stroll across the room. Robert stared.

Raymond leaned over and cupped his hand, whispering to Amalise. "She's on the team now. With the timing on this thing, Doug thinks we can use the help. And Bingham's approved the extra fees."

Amalise held a smile, nodding, as Rebecca set her notebook and pencils down on the table beside her.

"Well, New Orleans *lay-dies*," Bingham said, gazing at Rebecca.

Rebecca glanced at him, cocking her head to one side with a slight smile as she sat down. Without getting up, Doug introduced her to everyone, said she was joining the working group. From the other end of the table Lars said someone in his office had mentioned her and asked him to say hello if they ever met.

"We're on page seventy-five of the investors' note agreement," Raymond said. "We wanted to talk about conditions for drawing funds during the construction period."

"Skip that." Lar's voice was low, but the room went silent. Every person around the table looked at him. He leaned back and spread his hands on the table. "The first order of discussion today will be interest rates on the notes. Without agreement on that, there will be no funding. We need another hundred and fifty basis points to do the deal." He paused and looked at Frank Earl. "Our high-yield guys tell us rates are going up."

Doug said, "We have a deal. Earnings—"

"Earnings." Lars scowled. "Earnings are irrelevant. We're looking at cash flow here."

Across the table from Doug, Tom pulled a cigar from his jacket and turned it between his fingers, rolling it. The crackle of the paper resounded through the room. Amalise prayed he wouldn't light it.

Beside him, Bingham smiled. "Yes. The cash flow is significant."

Lars said, "We bear the risk."

"You can always convert," Doug replied. "We'll give you the option, no trigger. Take the equity, and the cash flow's your upside."

With a reflective look, Lars said, "I'd have to run that by New York."

"Are you telling me the decision maker isn't in this room?"

"I'm telling you I have to call."

Doug frowned. Looked at Frank Earl and shook his head. Frank Earl slowly pushed back his chair, stood, and asked Doug to please call him in the office downstairs when someone with authority was in the room. Tom flushed red, and Lars rose, leaning forward like a tiger ready to spring, hands spread flat before him on the table.

Frank Earl walked out and closed the door behind him.

Lars looked from Tom to Bingham and jerked his head toward the door. Amalise watched, stunned, as Bingham, Steve, Tom, Robert, and Richard all rose as one.

"We'll be in the small conference room," Tom said. Doug spread his hands and shrugged.

When the door closed behind them, Amalise turned to Rebecca. "Looks like you joined us just in time."

Rebecca laughed. "That was wild."

Raymond said, "This could take a while. Amalise, we need the status of the title commitments. Give them a call and push them, tell them to get on the ball. If there are problems, liens, or leases, we'll need a few days to deal with those." He jutted his face toward her. "So push them."

"Will do." She kept her voice cheerful as she picked up her notepad and pencils, feeling grim. Title commitments were boring and time consuming.

"And get some first-year lawyers to help you with that."

Amalise breathed a sigh of relief.

"Rebecca. Come with me. I'll help you catch up, walk you through the deal points."

Amalise looked at Rebecca—beautiful self-confident Rebecca, Jude's future wife—and felt the axis of their friendship slip a few degrees off center.

Jude sat in a rocking chair on the front porch of the station house in Pilottown, sipping a cup of coffee and looking out over the river. The night was dark, the moon hidden by thick fog. He'd been assigned to a ship down-bound from New Orleans that reached safety in Pilottown just after the fog descended. Now Pilottown, the river, the passes—all were socked in by a whiteout fog. The red light was up, and he knew that out in the gulf, up-bound ships were anchored, waiting.

He sat back in the chair. The rest of the watch was inside, playing poker or bourré and eying that old rabbit-ear TV even though the signal had been swamped by the weather. Some, the smart ones, were catching up on sleep. He was out here alone because he wanted to be alone, wanted to think.

As the mist drifted over the water, Jude could almost see the first settlers here, guarding the entrance to the Mississippi after LaSalle claimed it for France in the early 1700s. There had been tall French sailing ships at first, sails blooming in the wind, and years later the Spanish and English, all crossing the bar at *La Balize*, the wickedest, bawdiest spot in all Louisiana before the pilots' families moved in. He imagined pirates slipping in and out of the swamplands and bayous; hunters and trappers in flatboats, skiffs, and pirogues; fishers and merchant ships; then later on, the war vessels—Confederates, Yankees, and in the not-so-distant past, German U-boats.

What a history! With a half smile he knew that if Amalise were here, they would swap stories and she'd invent every detail about those early settlers—where they came from, what they wore, what they ate, and how they lived.

He caught himself. *Enough.* Since the night at Clancy's, Amalise had been too much on his mind. He couldn't allow himself to become preoccupied while on watch. He wouldn't think of her right now.

Leaning back in the rocking chair, he strained to see the stars—any star—through the thick soup. In good weather Pilottown was blanketed with stars at night. He and Amalise had spent many hours contemplating the stars in Marianus when they were kids. He smiled at the recollection. Sometimes at night in the summertime, when the air was hot and thick and he couldn't sleep, he'd throw acorns at her window and she'd crawl out on the branch of the oak tree in her nightgown. And they'd sit there, looking at the stars and talking about the future. Possibilities had always excited Amalise.

He was doing it *again.* Staring out at the river, he rubbed his chest, as if to ease the hurt inside. Always before, when he'd looked down through the years, Amalise was right there with him. She'd become a part of him, and what once was friendship had evolved into such a strong bond that it was almost overwhelming. He'd thought he had loved before, several times. But this was different.

What if he'd really lost her?

One thing he knew: This yearning had to stop, one way or the other. Amalise had made her feelings plain. He could either wait or start to plan for life without her.

Phillip Sharp had changed her. The predator—that's how he thought of Phillip. Emotions like empathy, compassion, love—these had proved powerful weapons in the hands of a master manipulator like Amalise's dead husband. He closed his eyes as old feelings of dread and loss swept over him. What was he up against, loving Amalise? Would she ever risk herself again?

Jude doubled over at the thought, elbows slipping to his knees and face in his hands as memories of the night Phillip died ran unbidden through his mind. Amalise running from the scene. The long dark road. His headlights catching her, too late. The seemingly eternal drive to the hospital in St. Tammany Parish, with Amalise unconscious. The ragged fear that she might not make it, that he'd lost her.

Lifting his head, he looked out over the river and rubbed his hands together. If Phillip weren't already dead, he'd want to kill him. Slowly he leaned back in the rocking chair.

Amalise had made it clear that their friendship was status quo, at least for now.

And he had a job to do.

Through the eerie fog on the river he could just make out the ghost ships now gliding past the old quarantine station, down-bound ships, their river pilots rounding up for anchor in the fog, moving blind with the current toward the station. As he watched, the routine ran through his mind and voices carried over the water, shouts from pilot to captain to mate.

"Slow now, slow! Windless in gear—back out."

"Watch it! Only one, only one. Now anchor up!"

Jude sat there rocking and watching the round-up, as one by one the ships arrived, turned about, and anchored. His turn would come tomorrow when the fog lifted and the ships moved on over the sandbars and into the Gulf.

Then a thought came to him. If these large, hulking vessels could beat the weather and the current, holding fast, couldn't he do the same? Wasn't his love for Amalise just as strong? Wasn't it worth the fight? He ran his hands over his eyes, feeling tired.

I'll put that in your hands, Lord. This one's in your hands now.

Love for his oldest, dearest friend welled within him again, a sweet feeling, deep and strong, too precious to release. He would give her time.

And he would wait until she came to him.

Chapter Thirty-One

WITH THE FRANTIC PACE BINGHAM MURDOCH had set for Black Diamond, the days and nights ran together for Amalise. One afternoon, when Bingham and his entourage were at lunch, she left her office and walked through the Quarter toward Jackson Square. Cathedral bells tolled the noon hour as she reached the square.

She hurried passed Gina's café on the corner and crossed St. Peter Street, dodging a stream of cars as she headed toward the Cabildo, the state museum and one-time seat of the Spanish colonial government. She turned left at Pirate's Alley, the narrow passage that separated the Cabildo from the cathedral. Paved with slate that jutted and dipped in places, the alleyway was shaded from the sun by the high walls on either side this time of day. She passed a bookstore in the house where William Faulkner had lived, walking on between rows of heavy wooden doors to her left and the garden of the cathedral hidden in trees to her right.

At the end of the alley, Amalise crossed Royal and stopped in front of an Oriental shop she'd always loved, listening for a moment to the tinkling of the wind chimes, glass on glass. She opened the door of the shop and was greeted by a sweet musky fragrance. She'd visited this place many times when living in the Quarter. She loved the colorful silk kimono wraps, the varieties of painted glass, the paper and silk fans unfolding their picture stories when spread, and the exquisite carved figurines.

The woman she recognized as the proprietor came forward to greet her with her usual mysterious smile. Small and dainty like the figures on her shelves, her dark hair pulled into a chignon at the back of her neck, she pressed her hands together in a Western semblance of obeisance and welcomed Amalise.

"I've come to ask some questions, if you have a little time."

"How can I be of assistance?"

Amalise suddenly felt foolish. Nevertheless, she pushed back her hair and said, "I'm concerned about a child from Asia. We don't know what country he's from." She found herself lapsing into the woman's formality as she told of Luke. "He's a foster child, living with a family here in the city."

The woman gave her a blank look. "He is an orphan, a refugee?"

"Yes."

"Ah, there are so many. So many." She lowered her eyes and clasped her hands at her waist, tucking back her elbows. "Most are from Vietnam. But, of course, you wouldn't be here if he were from Vietnam. You would know."

Amalise nodded. "His paperwork was misplaced. The children's home thought he had a sponsor here in our city, but that turned out to be incorrect."

Almost imperceptibly, the woman bowed her head and her fingertips touched her chin. "And how may I help?"

"This boy spoke a word a few days ago. It's the first thing he's said that we know of. I thought perhaps you could tell me what it means."

The woman dipped her chin but said nothing.

"*Mak.* The word was *mak.*"

The shopkeeper hesitated. "How does he say it?"

Amalise gave her a puzzled look. "Just like that." She pronounced the word again, carefully, making one flat sound. "Mak."

"Yes." The woman looked off for a moment. "It's not tonal, like Vietnamese. It's probably Khmer."

Amalise started. "Cambodia?" She still recalled every moment on the news of that terrible day in 1975 when the dead-eyed boys of the Khmer

Rouge army marched past the cameras into Phnom Penh. Even now she could see the hordes of children waiting at the burned-out airport, searching the skies for the planes that dropped food each day, not knowing that those planes would never come again. Only the bravest reporters had remained in Phnom Penh on that day, their cameras rolling even as the veil of evil fell over the city.

"Probably Cambodia. Although Khmer is spoken by some in Vietnam as well. But the dialect is different."

The shopkeeper drifted toward a table on which delicate colored boxes in various shapes and sizes were arranged, and she looked down, lightly dragging her fingers over them. "Mak," she said again. With a glance at Amalise, she added, "There are many dialects in Cambodia."

"Perhaps it's a name?"

The woman shook her head. She studied Amalise and then clasped her hands together, smiling. "*Mak*. Yes, I know. It is an intimate word. It refers to someone close, someone like a mother."

Amalise stared. *Mother?*

The woman nodded. "Did he say this to you?"

Amalise nodded. She reached out and steadied herself against a glass display case. She looked into the shopkeeper's still, dark eyes that seemed to know so much, but found she couldn't speak.

Luke had called her Mother.

⟳

As if in a daze, Amalise wandered back down Pirate's Alley, across the square, and into the Café Pontalba. She took a stool at the bar, not feeling hungry, and Henry whisked the area before her with a white cloth. He then set a cold bottle of Tab and a glass of ice down on the counter. He smiled. "Want something to eat?"

"No, thanks."

She turned her eyes to the television set fixed high on the wall at the end of the bar. It was on, but muted. She pulled her eyes away, shaking her head, trying to banish the images of the shadow children she'd seen on that set many times a couple of years ago, children limned in the mist of time.

Had Luke been one of those children?

"You look like you've just seen Jean Lafitte's ghost," Henry said. She turned to him, and his smile disappeared. He moved close and leaned on the bar, his face inches from hers. "What's wrong, Amalise? I know that look."

When she didn't answer, he shook his head. "I'll get Gina."

"No, no. I'm fine." She stretched a wan smile across her face. "I'm fine." When Henry continued scrutinizing her, she picked up the Tab and drank. The cold sweet fizz slid down her throat, lifting her from the daze. "I was just around the corner and decided to stop in."

Henry turned as someone called. With a hard look back at Amalise, he nodded to the customer and walked to the other end of the bar.

She looked about, remembering. What could anyone do in the face of such injustice? *Abba, why do you allow such things?* She'd told herself that she'd done what she could at the time, sending her tip money now and then. But the truth was, she'd looked the other way after that and gone on with her life, focused on her own problems and fought her way up the ladder at Mangen & Morris, chasing the wind.

And now here was little Luke. And he'd called out to her; he'd called her Mak. She wished that Jude were here so she could tell him about Luke. But Jude was in Pilottown, and even if he were here, he'd be with Rebecca.

She snapped to and looked around, but Henry was talking to the customer at the other end of the bar. Thoughts of Luke and Jude and Black Diamond and Rebecca being added to the team hit her all at once. Quickly she reached into her purse for two dollar bills and set them on the counter. It was time to get back to work.

They convened in Bingham's suite at the Roosevelt after a long day. They had left a roomful of lawyers still working at Mangen & Morris.

Robert leaned forward and handed Bingham the detective's report on Amalise's activities over the past few days, and Bingham frowned as he began to read. "This place she visits in Marigny, the house with all the children, she spends most of her time there with the Asian kid?"

"Appears that way. She took him to the park this time. The one that abuts our parking lot. The place she was so worried about."

"And the family, they're renters?"

"Yes."

"Have we got the owner locked in?"

"No. We've made some preliminary approaches, but only to major commercial property owners. Homeowners will be last. Otherwise, neighbors will talk, sound the alarm. We need to wrap up as many properties as possible before that point."

Bingham tossed the report on the floor. The intricate pattern woven through the carpet caught his eyes, and he followed the trail across the living room of the suite. Frowning, he looked at Robert. "What do you think she's up to?"

"Doesn't matter. She's meddling. If word gets out, we're cooked."

"Maybe it's a coincidence. Maybe they're just friends."

Robert hunched over a cigarette and lit it. Leaning back, he let the smoke drift. "I don't believe in coincidence." He looked straight at Bingham. "She's figured out a way to make some money on the side. My bet is she'll buy up some of the properties using another name as a cover. Then she'll hold us up." With a sharp laugh, he said, "Or maybe she's a protester, one of those save-our-heritage people, and she's stirring things up to halt the project." Robert took another drag and blew out the smoke. "Either way, she's trouble. I say we get rid of her."

Bingham didn't like what he was hearing. He shook his head, musing on power and its burdens. "That's just speculation. We have no proof." He gave Robert a hard look, but even as he did he again felt that shadow of doubt.

Robert gazed back at him unblinking. Bingham had seen lizards with eyes like his on the beaches of Thailand. Tokays that would fix their eyes on you and stare for hours.

"I want her off the deal team," Robert said. "Tom's going to want her off." He let his arms rest on the chair, the cigarette dangling between his fingers close to the fabric.

Bingham bristled, his eyes on Robert's cigarette. "We wait," he finally said. "If she was a rabble-rouser, we'd have seen something by now."

Robert followed his eyes and reached for an ashtray. He stabbed the cigarette into the glass, looking at Bingham. "Why wait?"

"We'll wait because the banks will get spooked if we stir things up right now. And it may not be necessary. We're still just guessing." Bingham leaned back, spread out. "Your investors are used to taking risks, especially in private deals on their own dime. But the syndicate banks have got shareholders and depositors and regulators to worry about." He shook his head. "We're less than three weeks from closing. Leave it alone unless we get something tangible." He watched Robert carefully. Robert was cold, unpredictable.

Robert picked up a pen and flipped it. "The banks aren't stupid. If she's a risk, they'll want her out."

Imprudence and impatience were a bad combination. Bingham had seen this kind of thing blow a deal before. He leaned his head back against the cushion and studied the ceiling. "Miss Catoir's not dumb. At this point she's done nothing but visit friends. Her career is her life. And she's bound by ethical rules, as well as by her ambition."

Robert said nothing.

Bingham sat up, bent and picked up the report from the floor, thumping it. "But keep the detective on her. If we find she's up to something, then we'll make the move."

Robert stood. Bingham pushed up from the couch, unknotting his tie. Walking to the door, he slapped his hand on the young man's shoulder. "We're almost there." He cranked his neck to the right, then to the left, and unbuttoned his collar.

Robert halted and turned in the doorway. "We'll put that house first on the list after the closing."

"Good. Anything happens, you let me know."

Robert's expression hardened. "One wrong step, and she's out."

Bingham felt fatigue pressing down on him. Not for the first time he wondered why he'd left his island in the sun. He yearned for the wide-open sea, the sound of waves crashing against the high craggy cliffs. The old men playing chess in the square at night. The golden glow of the harvest moon on the water. He swallowed a yawn and gave Robert a gentle nudge, but he kept his tone light. "You're a little haphazard, son."

Robert pointed a short finger at Bingham, just inches from his chest. "Don't mess around with this, Bingham. There's too much money at stake." His voice was low and even. "My own money. Tom's too. And others you don't want to know. *Personal* funds."

Bingham rested his hand on Robert's shoulder. "I'm going to bed. What time are we meeting tomorrow?"

Robert shrugged him off and headed for the elevator, buttoning his jacket. "Nine o'clock. We'll have a new draft of the loan agreement in the morning."

Bingham frowned at the door as he closed it. Pups like Robert didn't understand the limits of discretion, and that worried him. You never knew what they might do. He flipped off the light and went into the bedroom. Pulled out some pajamas from the chest of drawers. He'd made it a point to always wear pajamas to bed after the war, thinking of those cold wet nights when he didn't know if the next minute would be his last.

He trudged into the bathroom. Amalise Catoir could become a problem, he had to admit, though he'd never say so to Robert. If she opened her mouth and prices went up in the Marigny, or there was a march or someone sitting in a tree, Robert would see that she'd never work another day in life as a lawyer. Bingham brushed his teeth, peering unseeing into the mirror. She'd lose her job and her law license, too. If there was a mortgage on her house, Robert and Tom would buy it and foreclose. If she had a pet, the pet would disappear.

Rinsing out his mouth, Bingham put the toothbrush back into its holder and turned out the bathroom light. He couldn't figure why he liked the young woman, but he did. Stupid. He had a lot to lose if things went badly. It wasn't just the hotel at risk, but he'd lose the investors counting on the big-money casino, the easy money, tax free and a lot of it. Easy to launder, onshore or off. He stopped at the window, looking at the bright colors of the Quarter below, the lights gleaming on the river.

Climbing into bed, he pulled the smooth silken sheets up around him and closed his eyes, drifting off. He wasn't going to worry about Miss Catoir just yet. Her sights were set on a career, not making a few bucks in a property scam. And she'd fall in line with a warning, should that be necessary. They all did, that kind. She'd let nothing interfere with her career.

Bingham woke at seven the next morning. Reaching over, he shut off the alarm. Several minutes passed as he lay in bed, gazing at the ceiling and organizing his day. At last he threw off the covers, took a hot shower, shaved, and dressed. Then he picked up the telephone on the table by the bed. He'd rented a car to see the city, and now he planned to use it.

"Murdoch," he said. "Room—"

The bellman cut him off. "Yes, sir. I know the car."

Breakfast arrived at eight o'clock sharp. Orange juice and coffee; one egg, sunnyside up; no bacon, no grits; wheat toast; and a small bowl of sweet strawberries, homegrown across the lake in Ponchatoula. Bingham read the *Times-Picayune* quickly as he ate. Then, tossing the newspaper onto the couch, he adjusted his tie, shot his sleeves, and headed for the door.

Within minutes he was tooling through the Quarter toward the Marigny District while listening to Bob and Jan Carr ponder the state of the world on the radio. At Esplanade, he took a U-turn then hooked a right on Royal. He'd lied when he told Amalise Catoir he had no desire to visit this place. In fact, he did. And he would enjoy this tour of the area, he knew. He'd remember it.

He rolled the window down and drove slowly past the bars, cafés, and small shops. The bars were all closed now, their windows almost hidden behind signs advertising jazz players, blues bands, and someone called the Wolfman. The cafés, on the other hand, were open for business. Outside one, two men in work shirts sat at a round table too small for their bulk.

As he drove past he heard a voice in the building calling, and one of the men grimaced, said something to the other that made him laugh, then rose and shuffled inside. Half a block farther, a woman in a business suit and heels high enough to make Bingham wince sat alone at a sidewalk table, reading her newspaper and drinking coffee.

He was seeking the soul of the place that Miss Catoir had mentioned.

When he came to the park, he slowed, watching children play in a sandbox, overseen by a woman on a shady bench nearby. She was engrossed in her reading. The bucolic scene was a contrast to the scheme of Black Diamond with its parking lot abutting one side. He drove around that way, paying special attention to the trees and the houses, the rows of wood-frame homes that Amalise had described, some built right up against the sidewalk. Were there no setback restrictions?

There was nothing singular in this neighborhood that cried out for historic preservation, not in his opinion. But he'd had his fill of this life long ago. So he drove on, checking each cross street for a sign that indicated it was Kerlerec. Looking about as he drove, he bet himself the old wood houses were cold in winter, the wind off the river seeping through cracks between the wood planks. He was equally certain that in the summer the heat would bottle up in there.

He recognized the house on Kerlerec Street as soon as he saw the children in the yard. He wanted to see the kid that Miss Catoir seemed to favor, but there wasn't an Asian child around.

The dull green paint on the house was worn and peeling, though a neat white trim had been put around the windows not long ago. The roof sagged where it was overhanging the porch. One side of the porch was hidden by a bank of bushes, their branches now stripped of leaves in the November chill. Windows looked out over the porch on either side of the door, like eyes.

He pulled to the curb across the street and let the engine idle, watching the children play and remembering how a spot of dirt under a tree could transform itself into the wild west when he was about that age. If his mother were there on the porch, she'd be rocking back and forth in that old chair of hers, hands folded over her waist. He remembered how strands of her hair would slip from the clips she wore at each side of her forehead, and how the unruly stands would lift and blow across her cheeks in a breeze. Suddenly it occurred to him how young she must have been at that time, in her mid-twenties perhaps. Feeling old, he shook off the memories and drove on.

Wheeling back down Decatur toward the business district and the offices of Mangen & Morris, he realized that the Marigny had reminded him in some way of home, a home he'd not thought of in years. Not since Susan and Mother had passed away. But you can choose to forget some things. If he couldn't have Susan and Mother in his life, then he didn't want any second-rate substitutes. He'd changed everything in his life since then, and he liked it that way. Those old memories could take a rest. Without attachments, a man was free.

He drove up to the O'Keefe entrance of the hotel, where the valets stood waiting. An old song ran through his mind as he got out of the car and handed the valet the key and a couple of bucks.

Freedom's just another word for nothing left to lose.

Wrong. In his opinion, that was just razzle-dazzle wrong.

Chapter Thirty-Two

IT WAS WEDNESDAY, NOVEMBER 16, ONE week to the closing day, and the hot box was popping. Tom and Doug were squaring off over the old issue of who would fund their money first, the bank syndicate or the investors. Amalise doodled on her legal pad. Rebecca, sitting beside her, did the same. Jackets and coats were thrown across chairs. Briefcases were on the floor beside the owners' feet or stowed against walls, their contents scattered across the conference table creating mountains of paper, pencils, pens, legal pads, paperclips, along with half-empty cans of warm Coca-Cola and Tab, cups of cold coffee, crumpled napkins, and ashtrays full of cigarette stubs. Smoke hung over the room like a heavy fog.

They'd been arguing for hours.

"Negotiating," Raymond had muttered when Amalise made the comment.

Across the table Tom sprawled in his chair, facing Doug, his face red, arms folded over his chest, and head tilted to one side, listening. Doug leaned forward on his arms, making his case. Tempers were rising fast.

Today was the day to act, she'd decided. The room would soon erupt once more over this issue. And when that happened she'd make her move, escaping for a few hours while the principals pulled themselves together. No one would even notice her absence.

So far as she could see, the problem arose from the timing of the closing. The federal wire system was usually jammed the day before a national holiday. So if anything went wrong during the closing and a lender or investor had already wired funds, that money was stuck in a non-interest-bearing account for thirty-six hours in a dead deal while the nation sat down for Thanksgiving dinner.

And no one wanted to take that chance. The banks insisted that the twenty million be sent to First Merchant Bank first. The investors refused. They had the same concern—and more to lose.

Robert leaned over and whispered in Tom's ear. From the corner of her eye, Amalise glanced at Bingham, sitting on the other side of Tom. She'd caught him watching her several times this morning, just like Robert, as though she were a specimen he didn't quite recognize.

Tom nodded, then looked at Doug, tapping his chest. "Our position isn't negotiable, Bastion. We're putting in twenty million to the banks' seven. They'll fund first."

Doug shrugged and slowly pushed up from his chair. He turned to Preston. "I'll be in my office. Let me know if things change."

Robert snorted.

Tom slapped the table with the flat of his hand. "Take it or leave it."

"Go make your phone call. Talk to your boss. I'll be in my office."

Tom blanched.

Robert's face turned purple. Amalise watched the mottled flush spread over his cheeks as Doug walked out of the room.

For an instant everyone was still. Then Robert shot from his chair, his fist slamming down on the table in the same instant.

"Hold it." Tom stretched his arm across Robert and said, "Let's go down to the small conference room."

❧

As Amalise left the room, Rebecca picked up a pencil and began writing on a legal pad. She was so engrossed that when Bingham walked over and sat down beside her, she was startled.

"Hello, beauty."

Rebecca gave him a half smile.

He looked down at her notepad and then up at her. "Complicated issue."

She nodded.

Arms on the table, he turned toward the door, looking for Robert and Tom, she supposed. "But it shouldn't be."

"Shouldn't be what?"

He turned back to her again and lifted his shoulder. "The chicken-and-egg problem, funding, all of it." He smiled. "It shouldn't be complicated. There's a fairly simple solution."

Robert stuck his head in the door. Bingham looked up and said he'd be there in a minute. Then he leaned toward Rebecca and spoke low, explaining what he'd meant. When he finished, he sat back, hands flat before him on the table. "Of course, I have no idea how you'd say all that in legalese. But I think it would work."

Rebecca's brows arched. "What about overnight interest on the funds?"

"I'll agree to that. The investors shouldn't lose by waiting."

He looked at her notepad and then waved the back of his hand in her general direction. "It's all yours. Consider it a gift." With a grin, he planted his hands on each arm of the chair and rose, buttoning his jacket. "Once more into the fray." With a nod, he walked off.

She sat there doodling on the notepad, thinking. What Bingham had suggested made sense. It was simple and fair. She began to sketch out the plan. It took over an hour. When she'd finished, she read over what she'd written and then rewrote the entire thing, making revisions and corrections. At last, when she was pleased with what she'd done, she picked up the legal pad and walked to the door. Preston would be in Doug's office, she knew. That would give her an excuse to present the solution to both of them at once. That way there'd be no question in Doug's mind who'd come up with the proposal. She would tell them that Bingham had sketched it out. But he'd given it to her, and she'd turned it into a real solution.

Pushing through the door, she felt a twinge of guilt at not including Amalise in this. But waiting at the elevator, she told herself that they were each on their own now and liked it that way. Still, she'd already bypassed Amalise once by getting herself assigned to this transaction. The elevator arrived and she stepped in, wondering what Jude would think of her actions.

Then she tossed her head and stabbed the elevator button with the pad of her thumb. Doug's office was on eighteen.

Tom, Richard, Robert, and Murdoch were holed up in the small conference room, talking on the speakerphone to their fellow investors in New York. Steve and Lars would be joining them shortly. Preston and Doug had retired to Doug's office. Raymond had disappeared, saying he had work to do. Rebecca had said she'd stay in the conference room to catch up on some of the documents.

Amalise walked into her office and strolled past the row of deal books on the bookshelf, running her fingers across the sequence of letters embossed on the spines. At the window she stopped and watched the swarm of people below. It was the right thing to do, she was certain.

Still. She turned around and gazed at the diploma hanging on the wall near the door. Tulane Law School, 1976. She thought of all the years that piece of parchment represented, all the work and dreams. All the hours she'd shuttled food at Café Pontalba to pay for that diploma. Working until midnight, scurrying home to study afterward, then rumbling up St. Charles Avenue on the streetcar to school every morning and back to the café at night. Had she really come so far to take a chance on losing it all for the family on Kerlerec?

Yes. Especially because of Luke.

She was excited with anticipation, but also frightened. She remembered feeling that way once when she was small. Jude was teaching her how to ride her new bike without training wheels. She must have been eight or nine years old. He'd held onto the bike at first, running alongside as she rode up and down in front of her house, weaving and wobbling.

But just when she'd gotten the hang of it and was feeling steady, he said it was time to try it on her own.

So she'd sat there, perched on the bicycle seat, feet on the pedals, waiting, anticipating. Jude said he'd warn her first. He would say, "Ready, set, go," then give her a little push and she would take off on her own.

As she'd waited for that moment, sucking in her breath, she had looked down the sidewalk ahead, and she gripped those handlebars like she'd never let go. Because she knew that she might fall, might scrape a knee, and it would hurt. But she also knew that if things went right, she would experience a new kind of freedom. She would be able to fly from now on instead of walking everywhere she went. She'd feel the wind in her hair, and something would change forever. If only she took the chance.

She looked again at the books and the Lucite trophies on the shelves beside them, mementoes of everything she had to lose. And then she thought of those childhood days when happiness turned on decisions as simple as learning to ride a bike. Of course, that bicycle was long gone, replaced in her life by other vehicles. And it occurred to her then that those books, as well as the agreements and transactions they represented, were, in the grand scheme of things, ephemeral vessels. One day other lawyers would sit in this office, at this desk, instead of her. Like the bicycle, the agreements bound in these volumes would come to an end in a couple of years and be replaced.

But there was only one Luke.

Ready. Set. She retrieved her purse from the desk drawer and slung it onto her shoulder. *Go!* She headed for the door.

Caroline and Ellis might make out somehow if she did nothing. Charlie and Nick and Daisy might, too, eventually. But Luke would not. Luke would disappear forever behind that wall he'd built around himself. His cry in the park would be his last if he were yanked from the safety of Caroline and Ellis's care and returned to the orphanage. He would give up on the world once and for all.

Amalise drove uptown to Whitney Bank on Carrollton Avenue, where she kept her accounts, and parked on the street. She stepped out into the dappled shade as sunshine filtered through branches overhead. Birds sang, and a squirrel inspected her from a nook in the tree.

The bank was on the corner. As she entered the lobby, she could see Edward Stephenson sitting in his glassed-in office across the way. He looked up, waved, and walked to the door, holding it open for her.

They shook hands and she took a seat, holding her purse in her lap. "I have an unusual transaction to work through, Edward, and I'll need your help."

He sat behind his desk and picked up a pen. "Just tell me what you need."

It took two hours to explain and a half hour more to sign the documents. But when she left, Edward had already dispatched someone to the offices of C. T. Realty and was picking up the phone. She had no doubt he'd get it done, and in time.

Later that afternoon in the conference room, Amalise's lips parted as she listened to the proposed solution for the funding problem. It was Rebecca's idea, Doug said, looking down the table past Amalise. Beside her, Rebecca shifted and looked down.

"Rebecca?" He motioned in her direction. "Why don't you explain."

Rebecca nodded, squaring the papers on the table before her as she looked up. "My idea's simple, really. Investors fund into the company's Cayman account at Banc Franck on the day before the closing, on Tuesday. Interest on the notes will begin to accrue during this period."

Tom turned. "Bingham, the company agrees?"

"Yes. We've already discussed it."

Rebecca glanced down at her notes and back up. "On Wednesday morning, the closing documents are executed, and when that's complete, Mr. Murdoch initiates a conference call with Banc Franck." She glanced at Murdoch, and he nodded. "All banks participate in the call, and Cayman will confirm the twenty million is on deposit as required."

She then fixed her eyes on Tom. "Upon that confirmation, the banks begin funding, and when the last bank funds are in, Cayman is notified. Banc Franck then promptly wires the investor funds to First Merchant Bank."

Doug interjected with a look at Frank Earl, who nodded. "That solves the problem from our point of view. For the banks. We'll take Cayman's confirmation that the money's there to start our funding and go first." He looked at Bingham, and Murdoch nodded. "And it should satisfy the investors, since they'll be earning interest even if by chance their money is stuck in the Caymans over the holiday. And funds in the Cayman account will be under Bingham's control, not First Merchant Bank's."

Amalise picked up a pencil and drew circles on the notepad, a spiral of smaller and smaller circles. The idea was simple and smart. Beside her, Rebecca was silent.

Tom said, "I think that might work. I'll have to run it by the rest of the group, but it sounds good." He turned to Bingham. "What do you think?"

Bingham nodded. "I think it works."

"Robert?"

"Yes." Robert fixed his eyes on Doug. "But we'll want the wiring memorandum to specify each step. Every detail."

"Amalise?"

Amalise just stopped herself from flinching. She leaned forward, looking down the table past Raymond and Preston to Doug. "Yes?"

"You'll prepare the wire transfer memorandum. We'll need to get wiring information from each investor and bank, get each step nailed down."

Amalise nodded.

"We'll give you what you need for the investors," Tom said.

Robert's voice came, cold, insinuating: "I'll want to approve it." His eyes flicked to Amalise and back to Doug. "And we'll want to see a draft right away."

"Not a problem." Doug looked at Frank Earl. "We'll have someone in your wire room on the closing day to confirm as each bank's transfer hits?"

"Yes. We'll leave the phone line open in here at that point."

Doug leaned forward, caught Amalise's eyes again and held them. "Got all that?"

"Yes. No problem." Why hadn't Rebecca mentioned this to her before the meeting? Immediately she checked the thought because she knew the answer: They were competitors now.

"Good. I want a first draft by tomorrow morning to circulate to the other side."

Again, Amalise nodded. "All right."

Frank Earl heaved a sigh, and a hum of conversation began. Chairs were pushed back from the table. People stood and stretched. Beside her, Raymond rose, scooping up his legal pad, and she did the same.

Rebecca pushed back her chair, looking past Amalise as Doug called her name. Standing, she sidestepped Amalise. Raymond's eyes followed her.

Preston walked up, bracing his hand on Raymond's arm, and Raymond snapped to. "Find her a good model for the wiring memo. The one we used in the Roustabout deal might work. Once we've got the wire transfer memo circulating, we'll need Amalise and Rebecca to start preparing those purchase agreements for the properties. Time's short and there are hundreds of those things."

Past Raymond and Preston, Amalise saw Frank Earl scoot his chair away from the table to make room for Rebecca. Rebecca sat and bent her head, listening to Doug, with Frank Earl looking over her shoulder.

Amalise's suddenly realized there were no longer *two* Silver Girls in the room.

Tom and Adam had returned to their hotel to call the other investors. Bingham and Robert were in the small conference room down the hall on eighteen. Robert lay the investigator's latest report down on the table between them.

"What've you got?" Bingham felt tense, short-tempered after the events of the day. The closing loomed and nothing could be allowed to interfere. He looked down at the report Robert had placed before him and turned the pages.

"Amalise Catoir left the building for a couple hours today. After we broke up the meeting this morning."

"So?"

"She went to a bank on Carrollton Avenue."

Bingham spread his hands and arched his brows.

Robert's eyes went flat. "The investigator says she was there for . . ." he reached over to the report, turned it and read, then returned it to Bingham, "two hours and thirty-five minutes."

Bingham looked at the wall across from him. "That's a long time," he said at last. Too long for making a deposit or cashing a check. He turned to Robert. "Anything new with that family in the Marigny?" Robert's face turned dark. "Or the kid?"

"No."

Amalise Catoir was drafting the wire transfer memorandum, which was crucial to his deal. Doug had assigned her to the work, and Bingham knew that he couldn't interfere without solid grounds. But a woman worried about souls and trees currently inhabiting a money spot could be trouble. Put that woman together with those kids on Kerlerec Street, and that spelled big trouble.

"Find out what she's up to. Now."

Robert nodded and rose. "I'll take care of it."

❧

Robert had given her one of his murderous looks when she'd entered the conference room earlier. But returning to her office with orders to prepare the wire transfer memorandum, she told herself that Preston wouldn't have assigned the work to her if Robert or Bingham had already complained about her. And she welcomed the thought of drafting this document. Hard, challenging work, bearing down on one thing, would absorb all of her attention. After one important phone call, she'd let nothing more distract her.

At ten minutes to five she picked up the phone and dialed the number of the Whitney Bank. "Mr. Stephenson, please," she said. "Amalise Catoir. Yes. Thanks, I'll hold."

Cradling the phone in the crook of her neck, she continued marking up the memorandum. A minute ticked by and then a cheerful voice came on the line. Amalise dropped her pencil and grabbed the telephone.

"Hello, Edward. This is Amalise Catoir. Have you received a confirmation yet?"

"Just got it, Amalise." She relaxed, hearing the smile in his voice. "We're all set."

Adrenaline shot through her. Suddenly this was real. She took a deep breath. All she had to do now was make it to the closing next Wednesday without discovery.

"So we're set for the day after tomorrow?"

"Yes. Friday. How about noon? Just bring them to my office when you get here. I'll have everything ready to sign."

Gripping the phone, she looked around her office. Would she lose all of this? "All right," she said, struggling to remain calm. "That's good. I'll see you Friday at noon. And . . . thanks, Edward." When she turned to place the phone on its cradle, the room spun. *Hold on, Amalise,* she whispered to herself. *You're going for a ride.*

Step one was complete.

Abba, are you with me? Am I right?

Chapter Thirty-Three

THURSDAY MORNING, SIX DAYS BEFORE THE closing, Ashley Elizabeth hand-delivered copies of the wire transfer memorandum that Amalise had prepared to each member of the team. She reported back that Bingham Murdoch's group was already closeted in the small conference room on eighteen, reading it. Amalise breathed a sigh of relief and thanked her.

She looked down at her desk. Ashley Elizabeth had made one hundred and eighty-six copies of the form purchase agreements, each one to be competed with individual property descriptions, the names of the buyer and sellers, and other pertinent information. Preston had instructed Rebecca and Amalise to split this work. Ninety-three agreements each.

Just looking at her allotment made her yawn. Amalise had worked on the wire transfer memorandum most of the night and had managed only a couple of hours' sleep. A sudden restless feeling made her stand up and walk over to the window, to move, to stir her blood, before she began the arduous work.

"Don't jump." She started and turned to see Rebecca.

"Hey." The smile came on its own. "Good thinking, yesterday."

"Thanks." Rebecca strolled in, eyeing the forms on Amalise's desk. She waved her hand over them. "I've got the other half. They're already putting me to sleep."

Amalise grimaced. "I think they may be reproducing." She went back to the chair behind her desk and dropped into it, arms flung out over the armrests. Rebecca lifted her hair and let it fall as she sat facing her. For a beat Amalise sensed an invisible barrier between them that hadn't existed before. She took in Rebecca's shining eyes, her glowing skin, the hair tumbling around her shoulders and told herself it was no wonder Jude loved this girl. She was smart as well as beautiful. Smart enough to have figured out an elegant solution to the chicken-and-egg problem.

"Is Jude back from Pilottown?" Amalise picked up a pencil, balancing it between the tips of her fingers, staring at the number-two yellow as if the pencil was the most intriguing thing she'd seen in a while.

"Yes. He got in last Sunday." Rebecca smiled. "My parents are having us over for Thanksgiving dinner. I came to see if you could join us."

Amalise dropped her eyes. She'd rather work on these purchase agreements for the next six months than accept that invitation. The telephone buzzed. Amalise held up a finger as if to say, *One moment,* and picked up the phone. Raymond was on the line. She breathed a sigh of relief. They were needed in the conference room *tout suite.* Both Rebecca's invitation and the purchase agreements would have to wait.

❧

During a break in the morning session, Bingham Murdoch walked into the small conference room where Robert had been meeting with Dominick Costa, the general contractor for Black Diamond. They were going over blueprints spread across the table before them.

Robert sat with his back to the door. Bingham walked around the table to shake hands with Costa. "Good to see you again, Dominick. Robert says you're making good progress."

Dominick nodded. "We are. In fact, I was with Mayor Moon last week and showed him the plans. He's excited about this. Said to give you his best."

Bingham stuck his hands in his pockets and jingled some change. "Good man. He's a good man."

Robert glanced up at Bingham. "We've had a productive morning."

Dominick began rolling up the blueprints. "The necessary permits are all approved. We'll start demolition as soon as the properties are nailed down."

"Or when we've purchased the majority of them, anyway." Robert stuck a cigarette between his lips, bent, and lit it. Inhaling, he straightened and exhaled smoke. "After that it won't hurt for holdouts to see bulldozers arriving. Give them some incentive."

When the door closed behind Dominick, Bingham looked at Robert. "We were lucky to get him. I heard he turned down a big job over in Texas to work with us. But I've worked with him before, so I'd have been surprised if he'd turned us down."

"Yes. He seems to know all the right people." Robert snapped open his briefcase. Just then the door behind him opened and Tom walked in. He took a seat at the head of the table.

Robert pulled three sheets of paper, stapled together, from his briefcase, shut it again, and slid it across the table. Another report, Bingham saw. He picked it up and looked at Robert, then at Tom.

Tom said, "I've read it."

"Well, what's it say?"

Cigarette clamped between his teeth, Robert threw his arm over the back of the chair. "Miss Catoir's been busy. Take a look."

Bingham sat back, glanced at the first page and immediately looked up. "What *is* this?"

"It's a deed."

"I can see that." Bingham ran his eyes down the first page and flipped through the other two. "But why am I looking at a deed?" He dropped the document on the table in front of him. "Give me the short version."

"Amalise Catoir has purchased one of the properties on our list."

Bingham blinked. "In the Marigny?"

Robert nodded.

A sharp pain shot down his forehead, between his eyes. Massaging the place with his thumb, he picked up the report and scanned the deed. Sure enough, Amalise Catoir was the named purchaser. The property purchased was the wood-framed, two-storied home on Kerlerec Street, old-growth oak included. "How did this happen?"

Robert gave him a sour look. "Quick and dirty."

"This seller listed here," he thumped the page, "is he the owner listed on our survey?"

"Yes. C. T. Realty."

Bingham leaned back and gazed at the ceiling. "Why?"

Robert shrugged. "I don't have any idea."

Straightening, Bingham looked at Tom, then at Robert. "I thought things were under control. What are we paying that investigator for if he can't keep track of one girl, warn us ahead of time?" Despite his rising fury, Bingham's voice was low and controlled.

Tom interjected. "He did keep track of her, Bingham. And I don't like what we're seeing."

Bingham's eyes swung back to Robert. "So give me the details."

There wasn't much to tell. Robert repeated in a monotone what the investigator had already reported. When he'd finished, he stretched his hand out on the table, cigarette burning between his fingers, and looked away. "Our guy figures she arranged this yesterday when she disappeared into the bank for two hours."

Bingham clicked his tongue against his cheek.

Tom studied his hands, clasped together on the table. "She must have offered a pretty good price to get this done so fast, more than the place was worth."

Robert sucked on the cigarette and blew smoke. "The seller probably figures he struck gold. She'd have bought it 'as is,' like we'd have. No inspection. No conditions. Minimum title work, maximum price." He rolled his tongue around in his cheek. "She'd have had to pay cash. There wasn't time to arrange a mortgage."

Tom glanced at Robert. "How'd you find the deed so fast? City records aren't usually that efficient."

Robert leaned across the table and pointed to the date stamp at the top on the right-hand side of the first page. "It was recorded yesterday, late afternoon, a couple hours after she left the bank. Our guy had a feeling whatever was going down had something to do with that house. He checked the property records this morning. The clerk still had it on her desk." The corners of his eyes tightened. "It cost us to get that copy."

Bingham gave him a reflective look. "What do you think this means?"

Tom interrupted in an exasperated tone. "It means she bought the house." He turned to Robert. "But why would she take such a risk? A deed is a public record. She must have known we'd find out sometime." Tom's voice was hard, brisk.

"She doesn't know we're looking."

"If it weren't for the fact she put it in her own name, I'd say she's looking to make some money on the deal. Hold us up for an outrageous price." Tom leaned back, extended his legs and stuck his hands in his pockets. "But this doesn't make sense. There's no way an associate at Mangen & Morris is going to try holding up one of the firm's clients and their best customers."

"Maybe she bought it for those friends of hers," Bingham said.

"So *they* can hold us up?" Tom shook his head. "Still doesn't make sense."

Bingham pursed his lips as they both looked at him. The room went silent. One minute ticked by, then two. When he spoke, his voice was firm, resolute. "It's too close to the closing to cause a commotion over this right now. We'll wait it out and deal with it later. The closing's our priority. Complaints and accusations will only stall things. We'll keep an eye on her and keep things moving."

Robert leaned toward Bingham. "I say we expose her now. We go to the management of the firm. Get her off the deal, have her fired."

"No, Bingham's right." Tom's voice was a lazy drawl. "We can't afford to shake the bushes now. Let's see what she's up to. Right now the only person with a real problem is Miss Catoir." His expression turned cold. "She needs a lesson after this is over."

Robert picked up the report and slipped it back into his briefcase. Bingham watched in silence as he stood, yanked open the door, and disappeared into the hallway. With a look at Bingham, Tom trailed him from the room.

When they were gone, Bingham turned this new problem over in his mind. He tipped back the chair in which he sat and stretched his arms lengthwise until the tips of his fingers touched the edge of the table. And then ramrod stiff, he balanced like that, mulling over Amalise Catoir's recent actions.

There was more to come, he was certain.

She was so outrageous, he could almost laugh.

Almost. But not quite.

Chapter Thirty-Four

AMALISE HAD SPENT MOST OF THE day revising the wire transfer memo according to comments received from the working group. At three o'clock Ashley Elizabeth distributed the revised draft, and then Amalise turned to the stack of purchase agreements. She wondered how Rebecca was coming along with hers.

At 8:30, with about two-thirds of her allocation still to be done, she placed the agreements and related title commitments into a large box her temp had dredged up and turned out the light. She'd work on the remaining agreements at home where she could relax. She picked up the box and left the office, smiling.

She was smiling because before she went home, she had a pleasant task before her. Driving down Decatur toward the Marigny, she almost laughed in anticipation. When she opened the gate of the house on Kerlerec Street, she left the box of work behind her in the car along with all the worries they represented. She couldn't wait to see Caroline and Ellis's faces when she told them the news.

The porch lights were on and windows glowed. Damp wind blew in from the river. Amalise shivered, pulling her coat tight around her as she walked up the steps. There was a large pumpkin on each side of the front door, and over the door, fragrant boughs of pine, and pyracantha loaded with orange berries. She took a deep breath and knocked.

Ellis answered right away. He opened the door wide when he saw her. "This is a pleasant surprise," he said, stepping aside. Pulling her in, he took her coat and hung it in the closet, alongside many smaller ones. "Caroline said you were working day and night. How'd you escape?" He went to the foot of the stairs and called up, "Caroline, we have a visitor!" Then he turned back, gesturing toward the kitchen. "I'm making coffee. It's bedtime for the children. Come join us."

"I apologize for the late hour," she said, eyes roving over paper cutouts of Thanksgiving turkeys and pilgrims and pumpkins taped to walls near the kitchen door. She wondered if any of these were Luke's, and with a rush of emotion she thought of a thousand questions she'd like answered about the child.

But now was not the time. And so, following Ellis into the kitchen, she quieted her thoughts, enjoying the moment.

"How about a cup to warm you up?"

She nodded. "That would be great." The kitchen, still full of cooking smells, was warm and pleasant against the cold, dark night.

Ellis held out a chair for her. "The kids will be sorry they missed you." He rummaged in the cabinets for cups—red enameled mugs for the coffee—and in the refrigerator for cream. He set everything down in the middle of the table, picked up the coffee pot and poured two cups.

"Thanks. I take mine black."

"I remember." He sat down and added cream and sugar to his. Then he sipped the coffee, watching her. "Is everything all right?"

"Oh, yes." She set down the cup but molded her hands around it, feeling the warmth. "I'm sorry I didn't call first."

"Caroline will be glad to see you. She enjoys this time of night, when the children are in bed and we can sit here and relax and talk without being interrupted."

"Is Luke sleeping well these days?"

Ellis's brows drew together. "Not really. Something's locked away in that little head." He looked at her over the coffee cup. "Caroline says he's taken to you."

She knew. He'd called her Mak.

Caroline swept into the kitchen. "What a nice surprise!" She squeezed Amalise's shoulders on the way to the stove. Picking up the coffee pot, she poured some into the empty mug and sat down beside her husband. "I'd have thought you'd be working all night, with that schedule of yours."

Amalise laughed, clasped her hands together, and leaned forward. "I would've, except that I have news that couldn't wait."

They looked at each other, smiling, and then back at her.

"Bear with me now."

Caroline nodded. Ellis's face went blank.

She took a deep breath. "This may take a moment to explain."

Caroline picked up her coffee cup and sipped. "Shoot."

So she began, telling how when Phillip had died she'd been the surprised beneficiary of a large insurance policy. Some of it she'd just spent buying a house uptown, in the university area.

Ellis's face lit up. "Congratulations! A house of your own. That *is* good news."

She shook her head. "That's not why I'm here." Unable to suppress a grin, she looked from Caroline to Ellis and threw up her hands.

"I'll just say it. Yesterday I used some of that money to also buy this house." When neither Caroline nor Ellis said anything, she paused and pointed down, to the floor. "*This* house."

"I don't understand," Ellis said. Expressionless, he crossed his arms over his chest and tilted back the chair. "Do you mean that you're our new landlady?"

"No." She giggled. "I mean that I've bought the house for *you*. It's yours. Or it will be after we sign some papers tomorrow."

Ellis's expression exuded patience, wisdom. He sometimes reminded her of Jude. His tone when he spoke also reminded her of Jude. He was being kind, reasonable, but firm in the face of what he saw as chaos. "Well, that's a nice thought, Amalise. But we can't do that. We don't have the money to buy a house." He gave Caroline a sideways glance.

Caroline said, "Ellis, we've been saving."

He turned and shook his head. "Don't go there. We've saved a few dollars, Caro. But not enough to buy." His face was set and his voice firm as he turned to Amalise. "No. Renting's fine."

"Wait." Amalise raised her voice and held up both hands. "I'm not doing a good job of this, I know. But I'm trying to tell you that this house will be *yours*. It's a gift." She looked from one to the other. "From me to you. I'll sign the deed over to you tomorrow."

"A gift?" Caroline's voice pitched up a key.

Amalise nodded, lit with the happy feeling spreading through her. "I did it for the children, to help with the adoptions."

But she edged back a little in the following silence.

Looking from one blank face to the other, she saw that they still didn't understand. "Don't you see?" She concentrated on Caroline, since she knew her best. "You'll own your own home now. It will be an asset on the balance sheet—the financial security Francine Gebb is looking for."

And when Bingham's agents approached Caroline and Ellis to sell, they'd get a good price, money they could use to purchase another home, in a neighborhood like this one, with good schools, and yards and parks and children to play with.

But she couldn't tell them that. So she waited.

The front two legs of Ellis's chair hit the wooden floor with a bang and she jumped. He gave her a cold look, filled with suspicion. "Is this a joke?" He banged his arms on the table, hunched over them, and turned his face to Caroline. "I don't know what to think."

Amalise's good feeling disappeared like smoke. "No. Wait!" Clasping her hands, she leaned slightly forward and willed him to look at her. "This is no joke. It's a *gift*." She emphasized the last word.

Seconds passed as she held his eyes. Then, jaw set, he slipped an arm around Caroline's shoulders. "I'm sorry, Amalise. But we can't accept your . . . ah, gift."

She stared back at him, speechless. This wasn't how things were supposed to go.

Caroline burst into tears and buried her face in her hands. Ellis bent over his wife, murmuring into her ear, eyes blazing when he looked up at Amalise.

Amalise watched, helpless. She should have discussed this with them first, she realized. But instead, as usual, she'd jumped right in. Still weeping, Caroline turned her face into Ellis's chest.

Amalise struggled to reorder her thoughts. This wasn't going at all the way she'd planned. "Please, let me explain." Her voice broke as she spoke. *Abba, help me explain. You know how it is. I can't tell them what's coming. I can't mention the project or the demolition.*

Caroline rolled her face toward Amalise, still hunched against Ellis's chest.

And then the words began to flow. Like the perennially damp moss that absorbs nutrients from a tree, she benefited from this gift as much as they, she told them. "This is, in a way, a selfish gift." She spoke softly. "Giving you this house makes me happy. That money, the life insurance money, should never have been mine. I'll never spend the rest of it on myself. I just couldn't. More than anything, I want to help the children."

Silence was the answer.

She ducked her head and dropped her hands into her lap. "Please accept my gift," she said. How many times had she seen suffering and tiptoed around it, insulating herself, guarding against intrusions, going on with her life? But not this time. Not this time.

This time there was something she could do.

She looked at Caroline and Ellis, pressing her hands over her heart. "Please," she said again. "Think of the children. Think of the adoptions."

Caroline lifted her head and looked at Ellis. Amalise sat very still and said nothing. When at last Ellis turned to her, she saw the muscles around his eyes and mouth soften. Caroline sat up straight beside him. And then he turned to her, cradling her face, and bent down to kiss his wife.

Amalise exhaled. *Thank you, Abba.*

She'd never realized that giving a gift could be so difficult.

Caroline got up to make more coffee. As she puttered about, Amalise saw a change come over her. She stood with her back long and straight.

Her steps were light and quick as if a burden had been lifted. Her voice held a new note of hope—and anticipation.

"Now," Caroline said after she'd made fresh coffee and filled each of their mugs, "tell us everything!" She pulled out her chair and sat. "Start at the beginning. How'd you manage this?"

Choosing her words carefully, Amalise explained how she'd arranged the purchase yesterday. She kept the price to herself—it was high for the place. But C. T. Realty would have had gotten that price from Bingham, too. She told them how she'd signed the documents, and how the loan officer had taken care of the rest—meeting with the seller, transferring title temporarily into her name, transferring funds to the seller's account.

"What happens now?" Caroline's eyes sparkled.

"Caro!" Ellis flushed.

"Tomorrow we meet at the bank. Can you get there around noon?" Ellis and Caroline seemed fixed on the movement of her lips while she spoke, as if to ensure this wasn't just an hallucination. "We'll transfer the deed into your names, and the house will be yours."

Caroline let her eyes roam over the kitchen.

"Sure," Ellis said. "I'll arrange it with the boss."

"Good." Amalise pushed back her chair. "Whitney Bank on Carrollton Avenue."

"No inspections or anything?" Ellis's voice was teasing now.

She smiled. "I figure the new owners are familiar with any defects."

Caroline looked about once more, wide eyed. "It's ours?"

"Yes," Amalise said. "We'll have the deed recorded tomorrow afternoon."

A noise at the kitchen door caught her attention. She turned to see Luke standing in the doorway, rubbing his eyes with the knuckles of his hands. He was barefoot. Soft white cotton pajamas imprinted with pale blue figures of a cute dog hung off him, several sizes too large.

As Caroline pushed back from the table, Luke dropped his hands to his sides and shuffled with a sleepy look over to Amalise as if he'd expected to see her there. She opened her arms, bent down for him, and he climbed into her lap. Curling into a ball, he nestled against her and closed his eyes. She held him, scarcely breathing as she looked down at his nodding head.

Caroline and Ellis looked at the two of them in silence. Amalise pulled Luke close, feeling the curve of his warm little body, his chest moving slowly with his breath in a sleepy harmonic rhythm. Resting her cheek atop his head, she gazed across the table and saw a look pass between Ellis and Caroline.

Chapter Thirty-Five

IT WAS FRIDAY AFTERNOON, AND HE was beat. He stood at the door to Bingham Murdoch's suite, shifting his weight from one foot to the other as they peppered him with questions. Murdoch and Robert Black sat in chairs. They'd left him standing.

"Yes, sir. Miss . . . ah . . . Catoir met the people from the Marigny in front of the bank about two hours ago, and they went inside together."

Murdoch looked at him hard. "The kids, too?"

"Yes." Black answered the question. His voice was cold. His eyes were splits of steel.

"Yes, sir," he echoed Black. "Four, I think. It's hard to count when they're moving around like they do."

Murdoch lips moved, but he had to lean forward to catch the words. "Go on. Did you follow them inside?"

"Yes, sir." He looked down. Dug his foot into the carpeting and looked back up again. Hitched one shoulder up a bit. "They went into an office. But that lobby's not very big. Couldn't hang around too long after that."

"That's not much help."

Confused, he glanced at Black who wore a look of disgust. He looked back at Murdoch. The old man was easier. "Ah. Well, they all came out together at the end," he added. "Miss Catoir, the parents, and the kids."

"How long were they inside?"

"About an hour." He squeezed his brows together. "The woman, she was crying, and the man just stood there shaking Miss Catoir's hand over and over like he weren't ever gonna let her go." His eyes darted between Robert and the older man. "I couldn't hear what they said. And then the woman, still sobbing away, she hugged Miss Catoir."

"And then what?" Black's voice was clipped. Impatient.

"Uh, then they got in their car, the family did. It was parked on—"

Murdoch flipped his hand. "Get to it. What did Miss Catoir do then?"

"She came back here . . . er, to the First Merchant Bank Building."

Murdoch looked down. He raised his toes and looked at the socks on his shoeless feet. He dropped his feet back onto the floor. "What do you think's going on here, Robert?"

"Simplest explanation is usually the best. She's pulling a scam—put the house in the family's name, and they'll jack up the price when we show up to buy. Figures we won't notice the history."

Murdoch tapped his fingers on the armrest. His voice when he spoke was mild, as if he'd come to some resolution. "You." He jerked his chin toward the door. "Go to city hall and take care of that clerk. Fix her up. Make sure she calls you about any property filed in the next two weeks in Marigny."

"Yes, sir."

Murdoch stood, looked around for his shoes, and found them. Dropped back down on the couch and shoved them onto his feet while he talked. "If there's another transfer of that property, we need a file stamped copy." When he looked up, his eyes were piercing. "Got that?"

He nodded.

"After the fix, you get on back here." Murdoch looked at Black. "Give the man some money. Enough to grab that clerk's attention."

Black dug into his pocket, pulled out a wallet, and handed him a crisp, one-hundred-dollar bill. "That's not enough, let me know."

He stuck the bill in his pocket and nodded again. It was more than enough. He'd keep the change for his trouble.

"You can go," Black said, looking past him to Murdoch.

Stone cold, he thought, turning away. Both of them.

"Thank you," he heard Murdoch say.

Well, all right then. The older man was easier to deal with than Black. But he was a puzzle. He'd seen that type before, and they always surprised you.

Later that afternoon, Rebecca and Jude sat at a small iron table on the front porch of the Columns Hotel in the heart of the Garden District, sipping iced tea with fresh mint leaf and looking out over St. Charles Avenue. The hotel, with its tall white columns and turn-of-the-century architecture and the wide covered front porch, was Rebecca's favorite shady place to spend an hour or two in the afternoon. Rebecca had called and asked Jude to meet her here.

She hadn't seen the sun in a few weeks, she'd said. "Need a break. Meet me at the Columns? I've got a couple of hours to steal."

"Sure," he'd said.

They had been talking for a while, or rather Rebecca had been talking about the Murdoch transaction. He'd been listening with one ear.

It was a difficult deal, she said, and everyone was on edge with the closing coming up next week. Amalise seemed especially tired and tense.

His ears pricked up at the mention of Amalise, but Rebecca went on, telling him now how she'd solved some major problem with the deal, and how everyone had thought it was a good idea. He smiled, congratulated her. Doug seemed pleased, and she hoped that would get her assigned to his next project.

Jude struggled to pay attention—he really did—to the stories of Doug the rainmaker, the partner with clout in the firm. About how the idea she'd come up with would advance her career. Still, he was distracted, because he'd decided the time had come to tell her how he felt about Amalise. She'd probably already guessed, he knew. The news wouldn't have much impact one way or another in her world. In Rebecca's world, work came first. But to be fair, to be clear . . .

Now he was waiting patiently for the right moment.

But Rebecca had more to say, and he found he couldn't get a word in edgewise. Streetcars rolled by, clattering and clanging, stopping and starting, discharging passengers and picking them up, while she went on about work.

From the sidewalk across the street, two small boys ran into the street and squatted near the streetcar tracks. Against the hum of Rebecca's voice, Jude watched as they carefully placed something on a track and then ran back to the sidewalk. There they stood, leaning against a fence, hands in their pockets, waiting.

He smiled. He knew what they were doing. Amalise would, too.

He missed her. He missed the little things—the shared secrets, the jokes. She understood his sometimes dry humor, things that flew right past Rebecca. He sipped the tea, looking at the beautiful oaks on the neutral ground, the center slice where the streetcars ran. Those trees still stood after centuries of hurricanes. Amalise would love sitting here and thinking of that. He wished she were here right now.

"It's sure noisy out here today," Rebecca said.

"Beats the foghorn back in P-town," he answered, turning back to her. He watched the condensation rolling down her glass.

"I imagine so."

Rebecca pressed against his shoulder. Like Amalise used to do. The thought depressed him, but he shook it off. He dropped his arm over the back of her chair. "Tired?" Maybe now he could bring up the subject.

She tilted her face up to his. "Not really." Rebecca sipped at her tea and set it down. "We're working long hours, but it doesn't wear me out like sitting still would. The closing's next Wednesday. There'll be plenty of time to rest after that." She straightened, and he lifted his arm. With a look at him, she pulled her hair back with both hands and let those red curls fall like silk.

No one could ever say Rebecca wasn't beautiful.

And then she launched into the deal again.

He watched the boys across the avenue. Another streetcar came along, headed toward downtown. It stopped and discharged passengers and then rolled off. The boys raced to the track and picked up their flattened nickel, inspecting it, heads ducked over the treasure, laughing. Then one kid put it in his pocket, and they sauntered off. Amalise would have laughed.

Rebecca's touch got his attention. "Speaking of Thanksgiving," she was saying. "Are you still coming over for dinner?"

For as long as he could remember, he had spent Thanksgiving in Marianus with Amalise and Maraine and the Judge. His throat grew tight. "I don't think so, Rebecca. We need to—"

He was going to say they needed to talk, but she interrupted. "Well, that's a shame. But then, I might just sleep all day. We're working on Friday, organizing things, post-closing. I'm looking forward to a day off, though." She picked up her glass and sipped the tea. "But if you change your mind, just let me know."

He looked at her and smiled. Even in the shade he could see the yellow flecks in those green eyes.

She launched into another long description of something that had happened at work, something about wiring funds or however they got the money into those banks, and he decided this was not the day for a serious discussion about his feelings. Rebecca was happy enough with her career.

And after all, Amalise had made her feelings clear.

Chapter Thirty-Six

SATURDAY. THE CLOSING LOOMED IN JUST four days. Fifteen copies of the final construction contract were stacked in the center of the conference table. Finished. Done.

The bank loan agreement was also complete, unless the investor group pulled something tricky again. The investors' agreement covering their subordinated debt was still in draft form—they were holding out on a few of the provisions. Richard Murray was back in New York drafting those new proposals.

And a small stack of purchase agreements sat on the conference table in front of Amalise. These were the ones she'd completed. The remainder of the agreements from her share—Rebecca had the other half—sat in her office, unfinished. Raymond had asked to see the ones that were done. So here she sat, waiting for Raymond to appear. That was the difference between a second-year associate and a fifth-year, she knew: She was the one to jump, and she was the one to wait. That's the way it was, but things would change for her in a couple of years. Everyone else was at lunch with Murdoch or back in their offices, working.

She chewed at the edge of her thumb near the nail because in the pile of agreements before her was one bearing the names of Ellis and Caroline Jeansonne, owner-sellers of the house on Kerlerec Street. Heart pounding, she prayed that Raymond wouldn't compare the names on the agreements to the original list taken from the survey. Unlikely as it was, this was a terrifying scenario, because the original list showed C. T. Realty as the owner of that property, and if they tracked back, her name would be found in the chain of title.

As long as he didn't match them up, she was safe.

Raymond wandered in and sat down beside her, eyeing the agreements. "I'm so glad I'm past this work," he said.

She laughed.

"How far have you gotten?"

"I'm a little more than halfway through." Well, almost. She slid the stack over to him.

He frowned.

She took a shallow breath, watching as he pulled the top agreement from the stack and set it down on the table before him. Raymond was thorough, but would he go through each one, duplicating her work as he'd used to do when she was still new to the firm? She sat very still as he carefully read the one he'd picked up, turning pages. At last he nodded and dropped it back onto the pile.

"Looks good," he said in a dismissive tone.

Her heart slowed to a normal rhythm as she let out her breath.

"You need to speed this up a little, Amalise. We'll be revising the wire memorandum shortly, and that'll require your attention."

"I'll do that."

He turned his chair toward her and leaned back, clasping his hands behind his head. "I was looking at the closing list a few minutes ago. We've got a long way to go. Better book plenty of time with the typing pool, day and night from now on—proofreaders, people to make copies."

"I've done just that." She pushed the stack of purchase agreements aside.

Behind them, the conference room door opened. Murdoch walked in, followed by Tom, Robert, and Rebecca. Tom and Rebecca were laughing together. She leaned toward him as they walked, her hair swinging forward and half covering her face.

Amalise felt her face flush. Rebecca didn't deserve Jude's love.

That's not your call, the observer whispered in that irritating way. Envy clouds judgment and smothers friendship like a kudzu vine if you let it.

Still. She smoothed her dress. Amalise had worn her favorite red dress for this all-hands meeting, and she knew she looked good, too. Not as glamorous as Rebecca perhaps, but she wouldn't fade into the shadows.

When everyone had taken their seats around the table, she glanced up to see Murdoch gazing at her. Their eyes met and held an instant too long, and then Murdoch looked away. Beside him, Robert leaned back in his chair, folded his arms, and stared at her, expressionless as usual.

Something was wrong.

She picked up her pencil and pulled her legal pad forward. Rebecca whispered something that she couldn't hear for the roaring, rushing sound in her ears, but Rebecca didn't seem to expect an answer. Was it her imagination, or did Murdoch and Robert know what she'd done?

She just stopped herself from shaking her head. Even if they were suspicious of her for some reason, real estate transfers took a while to record. Records wouldn't be publicly available yet.

"Amalise." Raymond's voice. She turned to him, conscious of Robert's eyes still boring through her. "Are we set with the Cayman bank on the language of the letter of credit?"

She nodded, locking her eyes on him, avoiding the stares of Robert and Bingham Murdoch. "We have a call scheduled tomorrow morning with the issuer."

But a covert glance down the table a few moments later seemed to confirm her worst fears: Somehow, some way, they had found out what she'd done.

❧

She'd finally escaped from the conference room midafternoon and now, in her office, she forced herself to focus on the purchase agreements, struggling against the rising fear as she recalled the fury she'd seen in Murdoch's eyes. And Robert Black's reptilian stare. Was it really possible they knew?

Sitting at her desk with the door closed, she tried to ignore the laughter in the hallway, the sounds of busy people hurrying past. She'd asked Ashley Elizabeth to hold her phone calls for the rest of the day, and not only because Raymond was pressing her to finish. If Doug walked through that door to end her career, she wanted to be alone when it happened.

Oh, Abba. Have I done the right thing? She thought again of Luke sitting beside her on the porch swing, his finger inching toward hers, reaching for her. For an instant she dropped her face into her hands. Then she picked up a purchase agreement and got back to work.

At the end of the day when she could no longer sit still and wait for whatever was to come, in those fleeting minutes between twilight and darkness, she took the elevator down to the lobby and hurried into the street, craving fresh air and movement. Anything but sitting alone at that desk right now.

Outside the rush hour crowds were already dwindling. Streetlights were lit. Mist and wind off the river whipped down Common Street, curling around her, the damp and cold penetrating the red dress. She'd forgotten her coat. Shivering, she began to run. Away from Mangen & Morris. Away from Robert and Bingham. Away from the phone call she dreaded would come. Running. Until she reached the corner of Canal and Baronne and suddenly stopped and looked back down the street at the familiar scene that had become such an important part of her life. She felt she belonged here. Would she lose this too?

Ignoring the cold now, she began walking back. Lights blazed from the Roosevelt across the street. Through the hotel windows she could see men and women sitting at tables, eating and gesturing while they talked, smiling at each other, tipping back their heads, laughing. They seemed content with their lives.

She dropped her eyes. If she'd read Murdoch and Robert correctly, this part of her life would be cut off now, surgically removed when he told the firm what she had done, that she'd interfered with the project plans. There'd be no patience for explanations, no willingness to hear excuses after a powerful client complained about an associate. Pain and misery gripped her, and in that moment the reasons for her actions gave no comfort. All she could think of was what she had to lose.

She folded her arms, shivering and telling herself what a fool she'd been. Acting on impulse. Forgetting priorities. Amalise Catoir would be shunned by the entire legal community in this city.

And then there was Jude. She'd already lost Jude.

Stopping and turning to her left, she looked at the church doors while deliberately calling up images of little Luke. Curling in her lap, falling asleep at the kitchen table. Clinging to her when they'd seen the birds in Washington Square Park. The faceless picture he had drawn for Caroline.

She let out a long breath. Yes. That's why she'd done it. And she'd do it again, she knew. Abba had said what you do for the children, you do for me.

She pushed through the heavy wooden doors of the church. She walked past the statues of Peter and the angels and toward the rows of empty pews.

In the past she'd always demanded answers in her prayers, solutions to every problem. She'd wanted roadmaps to mark the path, guidance to strengthen her will. But as she walked through the church this evening, a strange lightness of being lifted her spirit—a peaceful light that seemed to surround and fill her, warming her throughout, embracing every part of her, melting her heart.

She stepped into a pew and sank to her knees, dropping her head into her hands and letting go. This time she would leave the problem in Abba's hands.

It had been a long day. Bingham had watched Amalise Catoir carefully during the day's meetings, mulling over the situation, but he had come to no conclusion. Clearly she'd interfered, gone to great trouble to purchase the house he'd seen on Kerlerec, then transferring it to those renters. That was a fact. But things got murky after that.

Sitting at the long bar in the Sazerac, he signaled the bartender. The guy walked over and bent, cupping his ear to hear. It was Saturday night, and the place was packed. A trio played in the far corner. They weren't bad, but for some reason, tonight the noise irritated him.

"Ramos gin fizz," he said. The bartender nodded.

What was she after? Despite the confidence he'd expressed to Robert, he was worried. Had she told the new owners about Black Diamond, about saving souls and trees? That's all he needed, neighborhood protests. But there'd been no sign of an insurrection so far. He'd checked the local news sources today.

It was too late to stop the project now. If she'd breached confidence, what was her motive?

The bartender set the drink down before him. He nodded and lifted the glass, thinking about Robert Black. Robert was the wild card in the deck. This deal was Robert's big opportunity, and there was too much money involved for him to ignore Miss Catoir's activities. He'd have to keep a close eye on the boy. He suspected that if just one sign of trouble arose in the Marigny before money changed hands on Wednesday, Robert would gladly dump the girl's body in the garbage fill east of the city.

Money was one thing. A life was quite another.

Bingham sighed. He'd tamped down Robert's flame as best he could. But even if nothing unexpected happened, Robert wouldn't let this go, he knew. Robert wasn't the type to render mercy, and he didn't like the girl. She didn't fit his pattern of reasoning.

Robert was a thug, he thought not for the first time. But he was useful. Bingham reached for a glass bowl filled with Brazil nuts, large and salty, and ate one. Chewing, he glanced down at his watch and over his shoulder toward the lobby entrance. Eight o'clock and his stomach growled. Dinner was waiting, and Robert was late.

He popped another Brazil nut watching the two bartenders spin from the bar to the rows of sparkling bottles and spigots and glasses behind them, snapping their fingers, moving with the music as they slid the drinks down the long bar to customers with flair and high fives.

Christmas greenery already framed the mirrors behind them, crowding the seasons earlier every year.

Robert slid onto the empty stool beside him. Bingham turned his head and scanned his casual attire. The necessary jacket and tie for dining were missing. "I thought you were joining me for dinner."

"Nope." Robert's voice was curt, his eyes narrowed and dark, his expression flat. "I'm going back to the conference room."

"You'll eat cold pizza there."

Robert shrugged. Bingham turned to the mirror, watching as, beside him, Robert ran his hand over the gleaming bar. "Unusual wood," he said.

Bingham glanced over his shoulder at the room encased in the same seamless swirl of wood as the bar. "It's all from one tree, did you know that?" He lifted his drink. "The trees grow two hundred feet or more. They grow in Brazil, in the Amazon rain forest." He studied Robert's reflection. "Down there, they're called monkey pot trees."

Robert gave him a sideways look. "Did you say monkey pot?"

Bingham nodded and picked up a handful of nuts. "Their nuts are similar to Brazil nuts. The trees produce pods the size of a large coconut, and the nuts are inside. The whole thing weighs about five pounds." He opened his hand, as if weighing the nuts.

Robert tapped his fingers on the bar in time with the music. "So why do they call them monkey pots?"

Bingham half turned toward Robert, leaning one arm on the bar. "The name comes from an old proverb: 'A wise old monkey doesn't stick his hand in a pot.' When the pods of these trees ripen, they split open, spilling their seeds across the forest floor. Supposedly a young monkey encountering a not quite ripe pod is tempted to reach its paws into the narrow opening to get at the nuts. Guess what happens then?"

Robert gave an irritable shrug. "I'm listening."

"The young monkey grabs a handful of nuts, but finds his hand stuck because he can't pull his hand *and* the nuts back through the hole. Yet the monkey won't let go." Bingham nibbled a nut and watched Robert's reaction in the mirror. "He's trapped by his own greed."

"Huh."

"Unless, of course, the monkey drops the nuts. Or he's smart enough to take them one at a time." Bingham nibbled on a Brazil nut while eyeing Robert. "An older, wiser monkey knows it's better to be patient and wait till the pod ripens and opens and gives up the treasure."

Robert rose and patted Bingham's shoulder. "You worry about philosophy. Right now, I've got my own nuts to worry about over at Mangen & Morris."

"Too bad you can't stay."

"You wanna close Wednesday?"

Robert left, and Bingham hunkered down over his drink. He had some decisions to make, he supposed. But he was finding his judgment impaired because, he realized, he'd broken a rule he'd held fast for the last few years: Avoid personal relationships. He'd come to like Amalise Catoir. She had heart as well as brains.

Not that any of that mattered. It was *timing* that concerned him. The next four days would decide the future. Nerves were strung out in Tom's investor group back in New York. The investors were already plumped with greed like those primates down in the Amazon. Worse, he was worried about Robert—there was no telling what he would do if pushed.

He finished the drink, left some bills on the bar, and headed for the dining room. The maître d' spotted him and picked up a menu. Bingham lifted his hand, smiling, and walked with light steps into the restaurant. Today was Saturday. Next Wednesday he'd be free of all this, and appropriately, the next day was Thanksgiving.

He, for one, would be thankful indeed. Life was good.

Chapter Thirty-Seven

WELL, IT WAS 10 P.M. ON Sunday, and Doug hadn't shown up to tell her she was fired. Yet.

Raymond had stopped by on his way out to say Doug and Preston needed the revised wire transfer agreement for final review in the morning, before distribution to the whole group. Apparently Doug had already left for the night.

The wire transfer memorandum had taken all afternoon to draft, but it was almost done. She'd drop it off with the typing pool and once again take the stack of purchase agreements home to work on overnight.

Just as she retrieved her purse and was prepared to leave, the phone rang.

"Amalise." It was Jude.

"Hi." She froze at the sound of his voice. He hadn't met her at church this morning as he usually did on Sunday. Turning, she gazed through the window at lights across the way. A shadow moved through a room in the other building. Someone over there was still working.

"Rebecca says Bingham Murdoch's project is still blazing away. She says you're all pulling long hours."

"Yes." She picked up a pencil and tapped it absently on the desktop. "I think she likes it really. Everything Rebecca does is at warp speed." She could hear a smile in Jude's voice.

"Are you leaving soon? I was thinking you might stop by for a cup of coffee."

With a sudden urge to cry, she swallowed. She longed to confide in him, but she'd sworn not to lean on him anymore.

"Amalise?"

Elbow on the desk, she rested her forehead in her hand, spreading her fingers over her eyes as if to shield herself from images of Jude and Rebecca. So much had changed in the last two weeks while he was on watch. Only Jude would understand.

She looked down at her watch and heard herself saying, "Yes. I'd like that."

"Good. I'm wide awake, still on pilot time. I'll have the coffee ready."

"All right."

She set the phone down on the hook and looked at it, forcing herself to remember Rebecca. Then she slung her purse over her shoulder and picked up the stack of purchase agreements. She walked to the door and switched off the light.

❧

Jude opened the door immediately when she knocked. Grinning, he hugged her, then held her at arm's length and said she didn't look the worse for wear.

She laughed and slipped out of her coat. Jude laid it over the back of a chair. "Sit right there." He gestured to the couch. "Make yourself comfortable. I've got the coffee ready. Be right back."

Settling down at one end of the couch, she looked around. The last time she'd been here was before Phillip's death. It was the night she'd fled, the night she'd found Phillip in her home with young, blonde, beautiful Sophie. She'd come here looking for Jude, but he hadn't been here that night. And briefly she wondered, as she had often, whether things would have been different if he had.

Jude's living room was small and square, opening through an archway into a dining room about the same size, with wide-planked wood floors throughout and sparse furniture. An old fireplace in the living room housed a space heater instead of logs. Even so, the flickering light from the heater gave the room a cozy feel. Colorful pictures she'd not seen before hung on the walls—a scenic one that looked like City Park, another of a schooner cutting through foaming waves. A watercolor of some trees in a familiar-looking swampy area hung over the fireplace. She wondered if the pictures were Rebecca's idea.

From the kitchen came sounds of cabinets opening and shutting, cups clattering, and the sucking vacuum clunk of the old Coldspot door. Smiling, she leaned back against the cushions and picked up a folded copy of the *Times-Picayune* from the coffee table. She hadn't read a newspaper in days. An article quoting Anwar Sadat suggested that Egypt and Israel were making progress toward a permanent peace accord.

Jude returned, and she set the paper down beside her.

"Watch out, it's hot." He wrapped a napkin around the mug before handing it to her.

She took it with both hands, feeling the warmth, as he set his own cup on the coffee table and took a seat at the other end of the couch.

"So." He sat facing her, spread out, arms resting atop the cushions on either side. "How's Bingham Murdoch? Keeping you busy, I hear."

She kicked off her shoes, twisted around toward Jude, and sat cross-legged holding the mug. "The schedule's frantic. Murdoch is worried about interest rates moving against him, increasing his costs. And other things." Like public outcry over the demolition of a large part of the Marigny. But she held her tongue, looking at Jude over the cup and sipping the coffee.

"That makes sense, I guess."

She nodded. "But what I've done might not."

A deep line appeared between his eyes. "What's that, chère?"

She hadn't planned to tell him, he could see that much from the tense way she began, setting the coffee mug down and winding her fingers around each other in her lap. But she always told him everything, sooner or later. As the words spilled out, she seemed to relax. She didn't provide him with details, not the location of the project, nor what was being built or the names of people involved, although he knew she was talking about Bingham Murdoch's project, wherever it was.

And whatever was bothering her came from deep inside. She was placing her trust in him tonight. Here, perhaps, was an opening, a crack in the armor she'd built for herself. The first hint of hope in some time.

Jude listened, amazed when she came to the part about purchasing a home for a family of strangers then transferring title to them. He interrupted. "Why didn't you just give them the money? Wouldn't that have been more circumspect?"

She shook her head. "No. Caroline and Ellis . . ." She dipped her head, remembering Ellis's expression when she'd first broached the subject. "They have too much pride for that. They'd have never accepted the money." She looked down. "In fact, it was difficult to get them to accept the house, and I'm sure they wouldn't have if I'd asked them first. I put it in my own name to get it done quickly, then transferred it to them after, *fait accompli.*"

He nodded. "Go on."

She told him about the problems arising from her decision. She suspected that Murdoch and someone named Robert had discovered what she'd done, and now she was afraid. Her voice turned husky and deep when she said this, and he yearned to tell her that everything would be all right. How, if this came to light, it would merely be seen as an exercise of poor judgment.

But of course he couldn't say any of those things because the worlds of investment banking and law were so different from his own. And so he sat quietly, listening, as he had all his life. Not for the first time, it crossed his mind that for such a small person, Amalise could certainly manage to stir things up.

When she'd finished talking, the look she gave him wrung his heart. He longed to reach out for her, to hold her. But she'd set up the barricades that night at Clancy's and had manned them ever since, so he merely folded his arms over his chest and worked to keep his thoughts from his face. Because, as the story had grown, he realized that her fear was probably justified.

He asked, "With so much at risk, why did you do it, Amalise?"

She'd told him about the family and the adoptions that would be buried under Murdoch's rubble as the project moved forward. Still, he didn't understand. So much was on the line.

And then she mentioned a boy, a child named Luke, one of the foster children in the family. She looked at him with tears pooling in her eyes. "He's from Cambodia, Jude. Remember? And something happened to him there. He won't talk." She hesitated. "Not really. He's in pain."

Now he understood. He blew out his cheeks and looked off, remembering. The war was coming to an end. In Phnom Penh, the children on the nightly news, waiting for food, cut off from the world. He looked at her and nodded. This woman who'd thought she could fix anything—thought she could even fix Phillip Sharp—had been defeated by the enormity of the problem. So she'd gone on with her life while the children had stood there on the tarmac, waiting. And she'd never forgiven herself for that.

"You're thinking Luke might have been one? One of the shadow children?"

She nodded. "Or one like them."

She told him about a day in a park when she and the boy came across a small dead bird on the pathway, and how Luke's emotional dam had burst at the sight. How the child had clung to her, how he'd spoken out loud for the first time since arriving here. How he'd called her Mother. The word was actually *mak*, she said, in Khmer.

He heard the catch in her voice as she'd said *mak*, and he knew Amalise well enough to understand the effect that word would have. This explained it all. The seed had been planted two years ago. Perhaps this was all God's will.

He mused on that for a moment and looked at her. "For what it's worth, chère, I think you did the right thing." He studied her small oval face, her deep brown eyes swept with wings above, the graceful line of her neck, and felt the swell of love building inside. He said, "Sometimes we have to choose what's most important in our lives."

She went still.

"After the accident," he went on, "you told me once that you felt there was a reason you'd survived all of it, that you'd been given a second chance for a special purpose."

She nodded, watching him intently with those big dark eyes.

"Well, maybe this child is it."

She swallowed. "What do you think that I should do?"

He smiled. "You've already made the choice. Done the deed—no pun intended. So just keep working hard. Make yourself indispensable." He cocked his head to one side. "I say it's probably time to throw deep now, chère."

She hugged herself. He smiled.

"You can do it, Amalise. You've done it all your life."

If he could only speak the words that might change things around, if he could tell her how much he loved her. And that even if the worst happened at Mangen & Morris, he'd always be with her, always stand beside her.

But he kept silent because what she'd done carried its own momentum, and whatever consequences were to be had had already been set in motion. Sometimes Amalise was like an overloaded down-bound deep-draft vessel headed for the shallows. Sometimes a vessel like that would make it through, with a good enough pilot.

Her Abba was her pilot.

He started to rise, wanting to move down the couch and sit beside her, and then caught himself. But she didn't seem to notice. She bent forward as if some unseen cord pulled her toward him, eyes bound to his. "No matter what happens now, Luke won't be shuffled from stranger to stranger again. The adoption will go through, and he'll have a home."

Her voice held that determined quality that he recognized and he tried to picture the little boy that had captured her heart.

They talked a while longer. When she glanced at her watch and said, "Oh," he retrieved her coat and helped her slip it on. She turned to him, looking up, her curved lips only inches from his, and for an instant he imagined that this was an invitation. He could smell the lingering scent of soap and something else light and sweet, like flowers.

But immediately, she stepped back. Away.

It was only an instant, but she thought she could hear Jude's heart, beating, beating on without her as she stood there looking up at him, knowing that this was probably good-bye to their old relationship. She couldn't fool herself into believing she'd be able to go on confiding everything in him, not after he married Rebecca.

Sadly she realized that it was probably for the best, letting him go, distancing herself from him, freeing them both to go on with their lives. Years of old friendship didn't give her a claim on Jude or the right to make him feel obligated in any way—or guilty for cutting her loose. But he was standing so close, and she wished she could put her hands on his chest and lean her head there, just for a moment so she could breathe him in one last time and then freeze that moment in her heart.

No one else could ever take his place, she knew. But if she could remember this moment as years passed, she'd at least have the memory to call it up when she was down.

The effort of stepping back, pulling herself away from Jude, took all of her strength. And it didn't surprise her when Jude let her go. He was Rebecca's now. So she planted a smile on her face, turned, and walked through the door, down the steps, and opened the gate. He still watched as she started the car and drove away, she knew, and she hoped that, to some small extent, he understood.

Chapter Thirty-Eight

MONDAY DAWNED BLEAK AND GRAY. DRIZZLE fell, though not enough for a good, cleansing rain. Just enough to jam up traffic as Amalise drove to work, still half asleep. She'd worked on the purchase agreements for hours after leaving Jude's house the previous night, and there were still plenty left to be completed before the Wednesday closing.

When she walked in at 7:30, Ashley Elizabeth was already at her desk. Amalise managed to hide her surprise. In her office she found the revised wire transfer memorandum that she'd left to be typed and proofed the night before. She took it out to Ashley Elizabeth and asked her to take it to Doug and Preston for their review and to let them know she'd wait to hear from them before sending it on to Bingham and his group.

"And we'd better book someone to work this desk tonight, Ashley Elizabeth. Whoever it is will be working late."

"I'll stay," she replied, handing Amalise a telephone message slip. "It will be easier for you that way. I know this is a big transaction."

Amalise stared. Ashley Elizabeth never worked overtime—that had been their understanding for two years. "Well, thanks," she said, smiling.

"We're a team."

Amalise looked at her and nodded. Gaining her secretary's trust had taken two years. Ashley Elizabeth had never worked for a woman before, and Amalise understood how she felt. She remembered the look on her mother's face the day she announced she wanted to be a lawyer like Dad. That had become Mama's dream as well as hers, for Mama had never had the choice. Not for college. Not for earning her own money. Not to live on her own, independent and free.

An hour later Amalise was in the conference room with Raymond and Rebecca reviewing the status of documents to be signed on Wednesday. There were seventeen principal agreements to be executed, fifteen copies each.

Raymond's eyes ran down the list. "Wire transfer memorandum?" He raised his eyes to Amalise.

"Doug and Preston are reviewing it."

"Investor agreement?"

"Richard Murray's working on that in New York. Haven't heard from him yet this morning."

Raymond looked at her. "Well, they're an hour ahead of us. Get on it. Call and push him. Let him know we're waiting."

Rebecca grinned.

Amalise hid her smile as she made a note on her legal pad.

He turned to Rebecca. "Check those new revisions to the bank loan agreement from our conference call yesterday. It should be ready by now. If so, go ahead and fax it around to the syndicate." Rebecca nodded.

Amalise looked up. *Conference call? What call?*

Raymond went on, his full attention on Rebecca. "We'll give them time to review the changes, but we need their sign-offs to complete it. Set up another call this afternoon for that purpose—that'll give them a deadline, keep things moving."

Rebecca nodded. She reached across Raymond for a copy of the agreement.

Amalise leaned on her elbows and rested her chin on her hands, watching Raymond and Rebecca. It sounded as though she'd been excluded from something big.

"If we can get that done, we'll have jumped one hurdle."

Rebecca stuck her pencil over her ear. "That would be nice. I'll get on it."

He swiveled back to Amalise. "What about the Cayman banks?"

Cayman Trust was the bank issuing the letter of credit. The other, Banc Franck, was a Swiss bank in Cayman holding the company's offshore account. "They're set. Cayman Trust is ready with the letter of credit."

"Good. Are you comfortable with the language?"

"Yes. The banks have all signed off."

He looked down at his checklist. "I'll handle the rest, here. Go harass Richard Murray." His eyes swung from Amalise to Rebecca. "Both of you, I know the purchase agreements are boring work, and I know you've got a lot on your plate, but don't forget they've got to be finished by tomorrow night. Robert insists on having them on the closing table. I wouldn't put it past him to hold things up if they're not. Understand?"

"Right." Looking at Amalise, Rebecca wrinkled her nose.

She smiled at Rebecca and pushed back from the table. "No problem. I'll go call Richard Murray."

Raymond nodded as he lowered himself into a chair and began reading.

Rebecca looked up at Amalise. "Say hello to Dick for me."

Preston blew into the room and made a beeline for the coffee pot. "Good morning, campers!" he said in a cheery tone.

Amalise waved and headed for her office.

She left several messages for Richard Murray with no response. Once she returned to the conference room, the morning passed quickly, as time always did leading up to a closing. With the exception of Robert, who watched the proceedings as expressionless as the Swiss Guard, the room was a flurry of activity. Clients and lawyers appeared and disappeared, slipping in and out of the fray. Amalise raced between her office and the conference room, with the occasional side trip to the typing pool upstairs, shuttling documents for review, making changes to provisions, and shepherding them through the process.

When the group broke for lunch, she hurried back to her office once more. Ashley Elizabeth waylaid her to say that Mr. Murray's secretary was on the line. She took the armload of documents from Amalise and followed her into the office.

Amalise picked up the telephone and pressed the flashing button. "This is Amalise Catoir."

"Please hold for Mr. Murray."

Amalise frowned and pursed her lips as the phone clicked on hold. She covered the receiver with her hand and made a face at Ashley Elizabeth. "Amalise here, holding for Mister Murray." With raised brows, Ashley Elizabeth put the stack of documents down on Amalise's desk, folded her arms, and stood waiting.

A minute passed, then two. Amalise looked at Ashley Elizabeth and shrugged. Another minute and she glanced at her watch, pressed her lips together, and shifted her weight, leaning back against the credenza. Her eyes roamed past her secretary, over the bookcase, and through the window at the sun's reflection on the glass across the street. A few more minutes passed. At last, with a shake of her head she slammed down the phone.

"I just don't have time for this."

"Whose time is more valuable?"

Amalise smiled.

"Right. Do what you need to do. I'll handle this." Ashley Elizabeth picked up the phone and dialed. She placed the call on the speaker.

Amalise sat at her desk and pulled the documents from the conference room close to her and began drafting provisions to secure the banks' loans with every dollar in Lone Ranger's U.S. bank accounts. She had to finish this work quickly so she could get back to the purchase agreements.

The sound from the speaker of the phone ringing on the other end jarred her. One ring. Two.

"Mr. Murray's office." The voice came through the speaker like caramel cream.

Ashley Elizabeth modulated her voice to a lower key. Amalise sighed, straightened, put down the pencil, and turned just as her secretary said, with no vestige of that Southern accent at all, "I believe we were cut off. I have Miss Catoir on the line for Dick . . . ah, Richard Murray."

Amalise blinked.

"Excuse me?" The voice took on a combative tone.

Ashley Elizabeth repeated the request. "Mr. Richard Murray, please."

"And who shall I say is calling?"

"Amalise Catoir, Mangen & Morris."

"Oh." Amalise detected some confusion in the voice. "Just one moment please." The call was put on hold.

Ashley Elizabeth perched on the edge of the credenza, examining her newly manicured nails.

Amalise continued working, writing and turning pages. Several minutes passed before Richard finally barked over the phone, "What do you want?"

Ashley Elizabeth's feet hit the floor, but her tone when she answered was casual and cool. "Oh, yes. Richard," she said. "I'll tell Miss Catoir you're on the line. Hold just a moment, please."

"What the—?"

Ashley Elizabeth pressed the hold button. She grinned. "Miss Catoir, Richard Murray's on the line, but if I were you, I'd let him wait."

Amalise smiled, and Ashley Elizabeth's eyes danced. Amalise shook her head sadly and held out her hand. "Gotta do it."

With a frown, Ashley Elizabeth picked up the receiver and handed her the phone.

Amalise pressed down the flashing button. "Richard," she said. "I'm calling about the investor agreement. Everyone's waiting. Your time's up." She winked.

"You'll get it when it's ready."

Ashley Elizabeth circled her thumb and forefinger and left.

Amalise tilted her head back and examined the ceiling. "Well, I'd certainly hate to have to return to the conference room with that message. Bingham, Tom, Robert, the whole group—they're all waiting for it."

"You'll get it when I'm finished."

"And when shall I say that will be?" She stretched one arm out and spread her fingers, thinking of Ashley Elizabeth's shell-pink nails. She really should do something about her own.

Richard Murray went silent, and she remembered how he'd held on all day, pressing her, with that hold light blinking behind her.

"Listen," she said, dropping her hand onto the armrest. "I've been asked to pass on the message that everyone's waiting on you and they're getting irritable. You've now received the message. Call me when you're ready to fax it, so I can pass on the good news."

She pressed the button, and he was gone.

Amalise hung up the phone and swung around to the desk, smiling. For a short time the boxes of trouble jammed in her mental warehouse receded and, focusing instead on the provisions she'd been writing, she picked up the pencil and went back to work.

⌇

Richard Murray's investor agreement arrived by fax around 3:00. Amalise had copies made and took them to the conference room where the lawyers were all still at work. Robert and Tom disappeared into the small conference room with their copies. Bingham had returned to the hotel, so Amalise had his copy delivered to his suite, along with the approved wire transfer memorandum.

For an hour she worked with Raymond, Preston, Rebecca, Adam Grayson, and the mostly silent team of Steve Hendrick and Lars Elliot, who had returned for the closing. Steve and Lars paged their way through the investor agreement, parsing through provisions that had elicited the most extensive negotiations. The room was hot and filled with smoke. Tempers were frayed, as everyone was feeling the pressure of the impending deadline. Leftovers from lunch desecrated the credenza, along with crumpled napkins, plastic forks, paper plates with half-eaten sandwiches, cookies, and bags of chips. The cans of Tab in the ice bucket now floated in water, while the few remaining Coca-Colas were submerged.

At five o'clock Raymond's secretary pushed through the conference room door with a cart for the leftover food, and Robert came in behind her. Amalise looked up, and he caught her eye. He stood just inside the door, unsmiling, and crooked his finger. When she didn't move, he jerked his head in the direction of the small conference room and said he'd like to see her down the hall. Before she could catch her breath, he was gone.

"What was that about?" Rebecca asked her with a quizzical look. No one else had seemed to notice.

Amalise's limbs turned liquid. Muscles tightened in her shoulders and the back of her neck. *They knew.* She placed her hands on the table and pushed up, feeling unsteady. "I don't know," she said, surprised to hear that her voice was steady. She looked about, wondering if this was indeed the end. Had she really been complaining to herself about the disheveled room and the heat and the smoke a few minutes ago? In that moment she hated Robert Black.

Rebecca's tone was caustic. "Now we know where Richard Murray learned his social skills."

"If I'm not back in ten minutes, call the cops." Amalise smoothed the front of her skirt while seconds turned into a minute, and then, tucking her hair back behind her ear, she headed for the door.

"Amalise," Raymond called out, "where are those certificates from Cayman? I've looked everywhere."

Glad for the momentary reprieve, she picked them up from the table. "Right here," she said, handing him the certificates that bore ornate gold seals verifying Lone Ranger's business status in Cayman. As she handed them to Raymond, she wondered if this was the last time she'd be allowed inside this conference room.

Possibilities raced through her mind as she walked out the door, but she could think of no answer to the question. *How could they know?*

She stood outside the door of the small conference room looking at it. Then she took a deep breath and pushed it open. Robert Black was sitting in a chair on the other side of the oblong table, facing the door, hands in his lap, angled slightly away from the table so that she could see his legs were crossed.

Pulling out a chair, she sat without saying anything.

Robert turned his wrist, checked his watch.

She still said nothing.

He looked at her as a moray eel might watch its prey from a cave on the ocean floor. After a moment he shifted the chair and slowly lifted his hands to the table. He observed his hands for a moment, then lifted his chin and smiled. "You've been a busy girl," he said in that cold, dispassionate tone.

She waited in silence as he rubbed his thumbnail.

"I took a look at your new house yesterday." He nodded. "Very nice."

She shivered but held steady. "Thank you."

"New, I understand. You just closed on it, what, a few days ago?"

"No. One month."

He looked up, brows arched. "Not that one. The other one. The one on Kerlerec Street."

Her heart swooped, and her stomach plunged. She sat very still.

His eyes roamed past her and beyond. "I asked myself why you would buy a second home, a young associate like you. What do you need with two houses, I wondered." His hands stilled. "The one on Broadway's nice. Only one bath though. That's a handicap."

She leaned forward. "How do you know that?"

He smiled. "I know much more than that, Miss Catoir." In the pause the air around him seemed to hiss. "For instance, I know how much you care about that family living in the house you bought on Kerlerec. And the Asian boy." He pursed his lips. "Nice-looking kid. Unique. A kid you'd spot in a crowd."

At times when Phillip had been at his worst, her hands would tremble, and then the trembling would move up into her arms, into her shoulders, into her jaw so that it was difficult to even talk. The same trembling began now. It started in her fingers and ran up her arms. She sat there silent, gripping the chair. Watching him and waiting.

"And I know how dangerous those old houses can be. Fire hazards, all of them." He shook his head sadly. "Lucky thing the ones in Marigny are coming down. You take an old frame house like that, drafty, with that dried-out wood, and you add one of those space heaters?" His eyes flicked to her, and she fought to veil her thoughts. Had she seen space heaters in the house? Probably.

"And those gas pipes running under the floors." He cocked his head. "Yeah, we looked. They're liable to crack without warning on a cold night." He jabbed out his lower lip. "Fumes hit a space heater, and the whole place goes up in flames. Two-story house?" He spread his hands. "No time to get out."

"Is that a threat?" She half rose from the chair, knees bent, hands on the table to steady her. "How dare you?"

He waved his hand in an airy manner. "Sit down, Miss Catoir. This is a conversation, not a threat." He propped his elbows on the table and linked his hands. Resting his chin on his hands, he studied her for an instant. "But you might want to give some thought to listening, given your attachment to the boy."

Eyes riveted on his, she lowered herself into the chair again.

"Now, I'm just wondering out loud here. Expressing legitimate concerns." He gazed at her, his eyes half closed. "Your house on Broadway's got the same problem. Just like the one on Kerlerec. You've bought yourself a pair of firetraps—they don't seem like good investments to me." His lips stretched across his teeth in a tight smile.

She willed the trembling to stop. Set her jaw, held her eyes on him, and stood. She spoke slowly, carefully. "If you touch so much as a hair on that child's head, or anyone in that family, you'll regret it."

His eyes widened, and then he laughed. She watched him laughing, observing him as if from a distance. As if she were someone else, someplace else. What kind of man was this?

"If anything happens to their house or mine, I'll see you spend the rest of your life in jail." Fury rose through her like the fire he'd described. "I'm a lawyer, and justice is my profession. You'll regret every word you've just said here."

Robert's smile disappeared. He leaned back in the chair and looked at her with no expression, although his voice still held a hint of amusement. "You won't be a lawyer for long if you don't pay attention, Miss Catoir. Let's get this straight. We've both got better things to do." He dipped his chin and watched her under half-closed lids. "Here's the message, plain and simple: If anything happens to delay the Black Diamond closing on Wednesday, or if there's trouble afterward—an uprising of protesters, anything that looks like it's got your hand in it—or if you mention this conversation of ours to anyone, including Bingham Murdoch, if you mention any of this, anytime, you will pay. And that kid will pay."

She stared.

He struck the table with his forefinger. "We'll see you lose this job, for starters. We'll have you fired and file a complaint with the state bar, as well. We'll see you never work again, not in the practice of law."

There was a long pause, a silence that filled the room, and then he added, "And that kid," his eyes held hers, "he looks a little fragile, easily broken. Like that dead bird in the park."

She wrenched her gaze from his and turned her back, moving toward the door, thinking this couldn't be happening. They had been following her. Tiny pinpricks of fear lifted on the back of her neck.

"Miss Catoir."

She halted without turning, staring at the closed door.

"We get this thing closed on time and the demolition completed without any trouble, then you've got nothing to worry about. For that family or the kid."

Regardless, she knew, he'd see that she lost her job. He'd have his revenge. That was in his nature.

Without a word, she yanked the door open and let it close behind her. She wished that Jude was here, not for advice or protection, but just to be with him.

Walking back down the hallway to the conference room, she worked up a smile and held it. She walked with her back straight and her head up, even while she balanced on the edge of a deep, deep crevice.

Chapter Thirty-Nine

BINGHAM SAT AT THE DESK IN his suite at the Roosevelt, looking out over the tops of buildings and houses stretching through the city toward Lake Pontchartrain. He couldn't see that pleasant expanse of water, but he remembered the peaceful little boats and the double white ribbons of causeway stretching twenty-three miles from New Orleans to the north shore. The endless blue sky had seemed to melt into the water at the horizon, giving the lake a hazy, silvery sheen on that day he'd descended toward the Lakefront airport six weeks ago.

Now it was Tuesday morning, the day before the closing. He took a deep breath and stretched his arms wide, then slapped his chest with both hands, thinking of it all. Then he picked up the wire transfer memorandum he'd received yesterday afternoon, the one Amalise Catoir had prepared for the closing. He'd provided the details for the investors' funds to Rebecca himself, the matrix of transfers between Tom and his investors in New York and on the coast, culminating in a twenty-million-dollar deposit into the Lone Ranger subsidiary account in Grand Cayman. Those wires had been initiated by Tom and Robert yesterday. The money should be there by now, earning interest and waiting for the closing.

He read through the complex memorandum, feeling pleased. The bank lenders had also provided details for their side of the funding into First Merchant Bank on the closing day. These included five smaller transfers totaling seven million, each to be wired tomorrow—after the conference call with Banc Franck in Cayman—into Lone Ranger's account here in New Orleans, while the twenty million remained held offshore.

The call with Banc Franck in Cayman would commence at 9:00 tomorrow morning so that the wire transfers could be started early. The day before a holiday was usually rushed, and wires would close early. Banc Franck's confirmation that the investor funds were on deposit would trigger the syndicate's wiring of funds. The banks would have finished, or almost finished, signing the documents by then. It was a tight squeeze, he knew, but banks on the West Coast were two hours behind and they'd hold things up otherwise.

Further, the memo provided that Banc Franck would transfer the entire twenty million to Lone Ranger's First Merchant Bank account upon notice in the early afternoon that all syndicate bank funds had been received.

Bingham smiled and thumped the page. He scratched his initials on the bottom right-hand corner of each page of the memo, indicating his approval, glad that Rebecca had taken his suggestion. Had the solution come from him, the banks would have studied it for days before agreeing that it was fair—time he didn't have. He set the memorandum down on the desk beside him. Whatever else Miss Catoir was up to, she'd done a good job on the document.

Picking up the phone, he asked for an international operator. He gave her the phone number for his account officer's direct line at Banc Franck in Grand Cayman, and then began the wait. Balancing the receiver between his chin and shoulder, he gazed out over the city, humming.

The call was picked up on the first ring. Benjamin Salter had been waiting to hear from him. Salter had been recommended by Banc Franck in Zurich, with whom he enjoyed a longtime relationship. He'd lunched with Salter in Cayman last year when he'd first opened the account, and they had got along fine.

"Bingham Murdoch here, Ben."

"How do you do, Bingham?" The banker was all business today, unlike at their luncheon. "I was expecting your call."

"You've received the instructions dated November 1, 1977?"

"Yes, we have."

"Right then. Per the standing instructions, please confirm the current balance of the account." He gave the account number.

"Your security code, please."

Bingham gave it to him.

"Just one moment."

Bingham waited. If he tilted his head in just a certain way, he could almost hear the ocean rolling in toward the Cayman shoreline. He wished he were there.

"Thank you for waiting." The banker confirmed the account number and the various deposits of the investors' funds received on Monday. On current account, twenty million and two hundred thousand dollars, U.S. currency. That included Bingham's initial deposit from a year ago.

"Thank you," Bingham said. "At nine o'clock Central time, ten o'clock your time tomorrow morning, November 23, I will call you from the offices of Mangen & Morris in New Orleans. As per the instructions, you will confirm on that call the current balance on account. Representatives of the banks in the company's loan syndicate will be on the call, as well as various parties in the conference room." He paused. "I believe I sent you the list of participants."

"I have it. I'll be expecting your call."

Bingham hung up the phone. Whistling, he slid open the desk drawer and pulled out an eight-by-ten brown envelope in which he placed the wire transfer memorandum. He slipped his copy of the standing instructions into the drawer and closed it. Then he looked about for his jacket. He needed to get over to the conference room. Got a late start this morning, things being as they were.

Already wearing corduroy slacks and a light sweater, he slipped on a jacket, an old tweed one, comfortable. Good fit. At least he didn't have to worry about wearing a suit today. Staff at Mangen & Morris would be bare bones this holiday week, and Doug had proclaimed today a casual day. No ties. The transaction team would be working nonstop to make tomorrow's closing.

With a last wistful glance in the direction of the lake, he walked to the desk and picked up the envelope. He'd bring it to the conference room for Tom and Robert to initial also. Given the circumstances, that was the least he could do for Miss Catoir.

❦

In the conference room Amalise sat beside Preston as he pulled papers from a manila file folder and scanned them. Bingham, Robert, and Tom walked in together.

Robert looked at her and she looked at him.

Bingham broke the connection. "The wire memorandum," he said, dropping an envelope in front of her. "It's initialed by the three of us. I'd like you to send a copy to each of the banks, get them to initial it, too."

She nodded. "All right." She pulled out the memo, checking the initials on each page. "I'll get this out right away."

"Good." He double-tapped the table beside her and moved on.

She stood as Raymond and Rebecca entered the room, each carrying a pair of cardboard boxes stuffed with file folders. Completed documents, ready to be set out on the closing table and signed tomorrow. Tom quickly stood and relieved Rebecca of her boxes. Holding his eyes a beat too long, she smiled and let him take them from her arms.

Amalise looked away, thinking of Jude.

"Over there," Raymond was saying. "Set them there." He nodded to the credenza near the windows. "They'll be out of the way until tonight when we organize the closing table."

Setting up the table for the closing would be an all-night job, Amalise knew. She'd created a list of documents generated in the transaction in the first week, revising it as the deal moved along. Now the lawyers in the room would be responsible for assuring that when lenders and investors showed up in the morning, every document on the closing list would be in the proper place on the table and ready for their signatures.

And those clients would show up early, around seven o'clock, and start early because the fund transfers would take most of the morning, leaving the afternoon for the transfer from Cayman, the investors' twenty million dollars. She had brought clothes with her to change for the occasion. A kitty-cat bath in the ladies room would have to do. But, oh, how she wished the firm had showers.

Rebecca poked her arm, and Amalise glanced up.

"Look over there. Check the outfit."

Raymond was wearing a T-shirt emblazoned across the front with the words *Where in the world is D. B. Cooper?*

Murdoch's voice rang out. "Who's D. B. Cooper, son?"

"Don't you know?"

"Wouldn't have asked if I did."

Preston laughed. "Don't get him started."

Robert lit a cigarette and blew smoke. "He's that hijacker from a few years ago."

Raymond raked his fingers through his hair. "D. B. Cooper is a legend. How could anyone forget that story?"

"Do tell."

Raymond pulled out a chair and sat down. "It was the night before Thanksgiving in 1971—"

"From D. B.'s point of view, it was the night before Christmas," Tom's voice drawled.

"Yeah. Well, the guy hijacks Northwest Orient Airlines Flight 305 out of Portland, Oregon—passengers and crew. Demands a big ransom and gets it."

Bingham shook his head. "Lot of hijacking going on since the sixties."

"Not like this." Raymond arched his chest, gesturing, embellishing. "Cooper jumps out midflight and is never seen again. They looked for a body and the money for years. The case is still unsolved."

Robert snorted. "He's dead."

Raymond regarded his T-shirt. "Got this at one of those Cooper Caper parties held on Thanksgiving Eve."

"I went to one in the Village a few years ago," Tom said. "It was wild."

Bingham tilted his head to one side. "Celebrations for a hijacker?"

"He had style, Bingham." Raymond let out a little laugh. "Plus, he was a madman, jumping like that from a 727. He literally disappeared into thin air."

With a thin smile, Robert stabbed his cigarette into an ashtray. He arched his eyes at Raymond. Covertly, Amalise watched him pull out a package of chewing gum, select a piece, unwrap it, and pop it into his mouth.

Beside him, Bingham egged Raymond on. "So what was different about this guy?"

"His audacity, I suppose. He demanded four chutes, but used only two, a main and a reserve. The Feds tried to follow, but weather was bad. Low visibility and only a quarter moon. But he had them running. When he made the ransom demand, there wasn't time to mark the bills. No time to plan."

"How much did he get?" Bingham sounded amused.

"Two hundred thousand, the papers said. But I'm guessing it was more and they kept it quiet."

"He'd have been thinking of weight, too."

"I don't know. A good jumper can take a hundred and thirty-five to forty pounds. He could have gotten away with more. The Feds could be covering up the real number to discourage copycats."

"How do you know that, the weight and all?"

Raymond grinned. "I've been following the guy for a while."

"Well, two hundred thousand's not so much. You're probably right. It really wouldn't have been worth the risk for so little."

Amalise broke in. "If he invested in gold right away, it would be a significant sum today. Gold's up around three hundred percent since '71."

Robert popped his gum. "Private ownership of gold was against the law until 1974."

Amalise smiled. "Not in Switzerland."

As if she hadn't spoken, Robert said, "They'll find him someday hanging in a tree, caught up in his parachute."

Bingham swung his gaze to Robert. "You think so?"

"Sure. Wind from the engines would have knocked him around up there. Would've torn up those chutes."

Bingham looked thoughtful. "Boeing 727, you could jump midflight in that aircraft. It's configured with aft stairs that drop open below the fuselage and the vertical tail." He looked off, musing aloud. "Three engines, all set high, one on the fuselage in front of the tail, the others above the horizontal. The chutes would be protected from intake and exhaust."

Raymond looked up. "He knew what he was doing."

"Air pressure might be a problem though."

Raymond shook his head. "The cabin was depressurized. He held the pilot at 170 knots and low altitude, under ten thousand feet, with the landing gear down."

Bingham worried his bottom lip, nodding slowly, studying Raymond. "Smart. Reduce the risk of incoming air."

"The Feds tried to follow, but they didn't see him bail. He jumped a little north of Portland."

"And no one's seen him since?" Tom asked.

"Nope. A few of the bills were found in a stream, downriver in the forest. Not much, though."

Lines at the corners of Bingham's eyes crinkled as he looked at Raymond. "You certainly know a lot about this."

"He does." Preston's tone was wry. "We're forced to listen to the story every year." He fixed his eyes on Raymond. "Every. Single. Thanksgiving."

Amalise, wire transfer memorandum in hand, chose this time to head for the fax room.

Bingham glanced at his watch. "Where's Doug? And Frank Earl?" He turned to Robert, his voice suddenly snappish. "Find Steve, Lars, Richard, and Adam and meet me in the conference room down the hall. We need to get things moving. Time's money." With a glance at the row of lawyers, he stood up. "Speaking of hijacking."

Raymond called to Amalise and she halted and turned. "Rebecca and I have a call on the investor agreement with the bank group in ten minutes. We're going to have to give up that hundred and fifty basis points on the investor's notes. I'll let them know to expect the wire transfer memo and that they all need to approve it right away."

She nodded. *Call? What call?*

Amalise glanced back as she opened the door. Rebecca's red hair gleamed under the lights as she bent, writing. Amalise hurried toward the fax room, reflecting on how quickly she seemed to have been replaced on this transaction.

⁘

Amalise halted in the doorway of her office, frowning at the pile of purchase agreements on her desk. She'd set them aside for everything else, and now she'd almost run out of time to complete them. There were perhaps twenty-five or thirty of the agreements left. Dragging herself to her desk, she wondered if Rebecca had finished her allotment.

Focusing on the purchase agreements, Amalise reminded herself that she was working on the biggest transaction in the firm right now. Yet this work left too much time for rumination—time for thoughts of losing Jude, the new competitive edge to her relationship with Rebecca, of Luke, of purchasing not one but two houses. Now, worst of all, there were Robert's threats toward Luke and the rest of Caroline's family. And toward her.

That last stopped her cold. Regardless of a successful closing, Robert had made it clear he would lodge a complaint with the firm as soon as it was over. Emotions whipped her thoughts, and several times she was forced to backtrack and double-check her work. How could things have gone so wrong?

But through it all, as she worked, she clung to the safe harbor that Robert had offered: If the closing went well and demolition, too, then Luke and Caroline's family would be left alone. Two weeks, she figured, dreading the wait. Or maybe three.

A thought slowly formed in the deep recesses of her mind. When at last it broke through to the conscious level, she lifted her head and inspected the rows of deal books facing her on the bookshelf. Before she'd met Luke, she'd always thought of a partnership at Mangen & Morris as the glittering prize. Each one of those books and Lucite mementoes had represented a step toward that prize. But now.

Now it was all about Luke.

Chapter Forty

AMALISE HAD ONLY TWELVE PURCHASE AGREEMENTS to go when the phone rang. Grateful for the break, she turned and picked up the telephone and let her tired eyes roam to the darkened windows across the way. It was only dusk, but on a holiday week the lights were already off and everyone had gone home.

"Amalise!" She recognized Caroline's voice, and thinking of Robert's threat, she gripped the phone.

"What's wrong?"

"Wrong?" Caroline choked and laughed at the same time. "No. No! It's going to be all right. They're going to approve the adoptions!" Her voice grew thick, husky. "You're the answer to our prayers, Amalise. I—I don't know what to say." There was a pause, and Amalise could hear her weeping. Slowly she turned the chair toward her desk.

Thank you, Abba.

"That's wonderful! Tell me what happened."

Ellis's voice came on the line. "They called this afternoon, just a while ago. Last Friday we told them about the house, about your gift. I think Mrs. Gebb was moved by what you did. And so they've reviewed our petition, and now she says this changes everything. She only just called, and . . ." He paused. Cleared his voice. "The adoption petitions will be approved."

Amalise's smiled. She pictured Caroline and Ellis standing in their own home, faces lit with happiness, the kind you experience only a few times in life. And that, only if you're lucky. She remembered feeling that way when Jude's voice broke through in the hospital, calling her name as she'd regained consciousness.

Caroline came back on the line. "We're celebrating, Amalise. You have to come over and celebrate with us. You must!"

She glanced at the purchase agreements and shook her head. "It's impossible. I can't get away right now. We're preparing for a closing tomorrow, and we'll be here all night."

"Don't you people eat? Don't you take breaks?" Amalise envisioned the face she was mugging for Ellis. "*Please.* You must come. The party won't be the same without you." She hesitated. "Look. If you can't come for dinner, just come over for one hour. Come over for dessert, for ice cream. If it weren't for you," her voice broke, "we wouldn't have a family right now. Just one hour."

Amalise heard the children shouting and laughing in the background. She wondered if Luke was with them.

She glanced at her watch. She could leave when dinner was delivered to the conference room. Take a break. No one was likely to notice her absence with the constant traffic in and out of that room right now. The clients would be leaving soon, and she'd be back by then. Only the lawyers would hang around to work all night.

The very human desire to be part of the present joy at the house on Kerlerec Street was overwhelming. And she longed to see Luke, to validate the risk she'd taken. She looked down at the stack of purchase agreements and made up her mind. She'd finish them up when she returned.

She'd be there around dinnertime, she told Caroline. But just for one hour.

The front door on Kerlerec Street was unlocked, and she walked on in, through the living room and into the kitchen, following the noise. The kitchen was bright and warm and cheerful. The family was seated around the table, Caroline at one end, Ellis at the other with his back to the door. The children were arranged along each side, and every little face looked up when she appeared.

Caroline, still wearing an apron, rose and stretched out her arms, wrapping Amalise in a hug. Ellis twisted in his chair, exclaiming, and stood. She squeezed her eyes shut for a moment in that embrace, feeling the smile spreading inside, glad that she'd come. When she opened her eyes, she saw Luke sliding from his chair, arms stretched out and reaching for her.

Ellis moved in when Caroline released her. "Thanks," he whispered in her ear. Luke tugged on her skirt, and then Daisy and Nick and Charlie joined the party. After all the greetings were exchanged, she knelt and lifted Luke into her arms. Ellis offered her his chair, but Amalise headed for Luke's. "I'll sit right here."

Luke settled back against her when she sat, curling an arm around her neck. Daisy sat beside them. Caroline swept away the remains of supper, while Ellis pulled a large tub of ice cream from the freezer.

Strawberry, she saw, as the children whooped. All but Luke.

Caroline filled bowls and passed them around. Amalise and Luke shared one.

When everyone's plates were full, they held hands around the table and Ellis thanked God for their new home, for the adoption approvals, and for bringing Amalise into their lives.

A half hour passed and Caroline lifted her fork, pointing it toward Ellis. When he looked up, she nodded toward the clock on the wall behind her. He turned and frowned.

"Right," he said. Reaching for Charlie's ice cream bowl, he winked and scooped up a bite.

"Ellis's got to go in to work tonight," Caroline said to Amalise. "But he wanted to be here when you came, to thank you for all you've done for us."

Standing, Ellis looked at her and smiled. "A complete stranger comes into our lives, and look what's happened." He spread his arms. "We can't thank you enough."

Amalise wrapped her arms around Luke and rested her chin on his head. "You're welcome," she said.

Ellis dug into his pockets and pulled out his car keys. "We've got a ship coming out of Venezuela tonight."

Caroline walked with Ellis to the front door, while in the kitchen the children continued to laugh and talk. Amalise, with Luke quiet on her lap, was content to share their joy. It seemed no time at all before the clock told her it was time to leave as well, to get back to work.

When she pushed back the chair, Luke slumped back against her, and she realized that he was fast asleep.

"The children have had a big day," Caroline said, looking at him.

"May I take him up to bed?"

"Sure." Beside her, Daisy held up her spoon and insisted that she stay. Amalise laughed and patted her head as she stood, holding the sleeping child.

Caroline stood. "Bath time, children. Boys first, then Daisy." Ignoring the howls, she looked up at Amalise. "Luke can skip his bath tonight." She glanced at him. "Are you sure he's not too heavy?"

Amalise thought of Phillip Sharp's weight. "No," she said, hiking Luke up. His head rolled against her shoulder. "He's not."

Luke and Daisy's bedroom was small, with twin beds, one on each side with a window in between. The curtains were pulled back, and through the misted windowpane Amalise could see the top of the oak tree that held Daisy's swing, and above the tree, a sliver of yellow light, the moon, shining like the grin of the Cheshire cat.

Gently she lowered Luke to his bed and pulled the covers up. His eyelids flickered with dreams. She hoped they were good dreams. She hoped that some of his terrors had faded away.

She leaned down and kissed his cheek. Then she tucked the covers around him and tiptoed out the door. Robert's threat rose again, hanging over her as she hurried down the steps, resolving that from this moment on, until the closing was complete, she'd think of nothing but her work.

She'd reached the bottom of the steps when she saw Caroline's wide eyes fixed on something behind her.

Turning, she saw Luke standing on the top step, rubbing his eyes and looking down at her. Pulling his fists away, he moved forward, flinging out his arms and calling, "Mak! Mak!"

In the split second before he fell, she saw it all. As in slow motion she saw his bare foot reaching for the stair below and slipping past the edge. She saw his little body twisting, lifting in the air, arms thrashing for balance. She cried out and started forward, watching him tumbling, tumbling, tumbling down the stairs. It seemed an eternity that he fell.

She had the only car, and Charity hospital was closest. An ambulance would take too long, she said. Together, Caroline and she maneuvered Luke into the back seat, so that at last he lay curled up there, weeping, with pillows tucked along his side to brace him, and a small blanket covering him. As she drove, he quietly wept, calling to Mak, his heaving little sobs ripping through her heart. He whimpered each time the car bounced over a pothole in the street or changed speeds or turned.

"Soon," she would say each time. "We're almost there."

Later she remembered little of the race to the hospital, lights streaming by on Canal Street until at last the huge gray edifice that was Charity appeared. She followed the flashing *Emergency* signs to the rear entrance.

All thoughts of the conference room on the eighteenth floor of the First Merchant Bank building had vanished from her mind.

She wrapped the blanket around Luke, sliding and coaxing him from the back seat. Then she bent down and scooped him up into her arms. He screamed when she lifted him.

The emergency room was as busy as a Saturday afternoon at D. H. Holmes department store on Canal Street. The sick and injured were packed in rows of molded plastic chairs, and every chair was filled. More people sat on the tiled floor, slumped against the walls, waiting. Some occupied a row of stretchers and gurneys. Across the way she saw a row of small rooms sectioned off by thin walls and hidden by drab gray curtains. Treatment rooms, she supposed.

Bright lights lit the high-ceilinged room to a white haze. The walls were gray, like the curtains across the way. The waiting room was a warehouse of misery.

Amalise made her way through the mass of humanity to reach the check-in desk. A large clock on the wall over the desk read 6:45, but Amalise looked past it in a daze.

A receptionist, whose name tag read "Jackie," looked at Amalise and Luke over her glasses. She slid several sheets of paper across the counter. "Fill these out, please."

"Is there some place that he could lie down?"

The woman shook her head. "We're full." She glanced past Amalise and scanned the room. "There're places on the floor. It's good thing you have a blanket."

"But he's just a baby."

Jackie's eyes flicked up, then down, and she nodded. "If a gurney or a cot becomes available, I'll let you know." She nudged the forms again toward Amalise. "Sooner you fill these out, the faster you'll see a doctor."

Amalise took the papers. "How long will we have to wait?"

The receptionist shrugged. "You'll have to wait your turn."

"But this child is in pain."

Jackie's voice was firm. "No one's here because they're feeling well."

Amalise began filling out the forms while Luke squirmed against her.

When she'd finished, the woman tore off a sheet and handed it to Amalise. "Give this to the doctor when you see him." She sorted through the rest, scanned it, and pulled out a file.

Amalise nodded.

They found a place near the wall. She dropped her purse beside her feet, spread the blanket on the floor, and laid Luke down upon it. Once he was still, she wrapped the blanket around him, cocooning him. Then she sat down and slid him toward her so that his head and shoulders rested on her lap.

At last, she looked up at the clock. Quarter after seven.

How long until Robert noticed and sounded the alarm?

Chapter Forty-One

BINGHAM MURDOCH HAD NOT INTENDED TO spend much time in the conference room this evening, the privilege of a client. This was what lawyers got paid to do. But Robert was hanging around, and so he'd stayed to keep an eye on him. He knew Robert's type—dangerous when they're close to money and hit an impediment. Amalise was one possible impediment.

Yet there'd been no hint of trouble stirring in the Marigny. He'd sent the private investigator down there to wander around the neighborhood, sit at café tables, talk to the owners and bartenders, and pick up any rumors or gossip that might be circulating about the project. So far, nothing.

Bingham looked about, counting heads. Besides himself and Robert, Adam was there with reinforcements he'd called in from New York, two young associates whose names Bingham could not remember. Then there was that redhead Rebecca, Preston, and Raymond, still in his D. B. Cooper shirt. The others were off foraging for food or hanging out in their offices so they could breathe without fighting for air.

Bingham watched as someone he'd not seen before walked around the conference table, moving from one stack of documents to the next. "Who's that?" he asked when Raymond walked by.

"Bank of California's counsel, here for the closing."

Bingham nodded. A minute later the door swung open, and someone else came in as Preston went out. Beside him, Robert blew smoke. Bingham watched the new guy through the deepening brown haze. After time, he figured out this was the lawyer from the bank issuing the letter of credit.

At eight o'clock Preston returned with another armload of documents. Raymond stood and said something to him, and then they both turned and looked at the clock. Raymond shrugged, and Preston dumped the documents on the table.

Bingham looked about. Still no Amalise Catoir. He shot a covert look at Robert and caught him checking the clock too. Robert shifted in his chair, preparing to stand up and cause some commotion, Bingham was certain. The young man had no self-discipline. Bingham's arm shot across him. "Not yet."

Robert lowered himself back into to the chair without looking at Bingham. "If she doesn't show soon, I'm ringing the bell."

"She's in her office. You'll look like a fool."

He could feel Robert settling back. Even so, Robert muttered, "Either way, I'll have her job when this is done. Tomorrow, once the funds are in from Cayman." Robert slid down, stretched out his legs, rested his head on the back of the chair, and blew smoke at the ceiling.

"Just as long as it's not before the closing."

❧

Luke moved and let out a cry. An hour had passed since they'd arrived. He wept now, head in her lap, arms reaching up. She leaned over him, stroking his face with her fingertips. "Shh, I'm here, baby."

She smiled at him and turned her head to the right, looking along the wall where they sat. No one had moved since she'd arrived. Across the way, a nurse pushed through a curtain in one of the treatment rooms. But there were probably sixty or seventy people waiting between those little rooms and where she sat with Luke.

Luke shuddered, and she stroked his cheek. Slowly his eyes closed, and she hoped he was sleeping. She ran her fingers across his eyelids, gently, like the brush of butterfly wings, as Mama used to do. Turning her gaze to the pay phone booth, her heart fell. There was nothing else she could do. Squeezing her eyes shut, she faced the fact that she was here for the night with Luke. She'd have to call Rebecca and ask her to pass the bad news on to Doug.

Robert would explode. The phone call would end her career, she knew.

She blinked back tears. There was no choice. No other option.

Luke woke when she gathered him up. When she stood, holding him against her, protecting the leg he seemed to favor, he began again to cry. She leaned against the wall and closed her eyes. Then she took a deep breath, steadying herself. She left the blanket on the floor to save their place as she headed for the telephone booth.

❧

Rebecca looked up as Ashley Elizabeth entered the conference room. Their eyes met and Ashley Elizabeth jerked her chin toward the door. Rebecca gave a slight nod, pushed back the document she was working on, and stood. Raymond was engrossed in a final review of the investor agreement for the fifteen-percent subordinated convertible notes and their placement memorandum. Preston and Doug were arguing with Robert and the Cayman lawyer about the letter of credit. At the other end of the table, Bingham sat, arms folded across his chest, leaning back, eyes closed.

Without a word Rebecca slipped from the room. Ashley Elizabeth was holding the elevator door. Rebecca joined her and Ashley Elizabeth pressed the button for the sixteenth floor.

When the doors closed, Rebecca turned to her. "What's going on?"

"Amalise called. She needs to talk to you."

Rebecca raised her brows. "I thought she was in her office."

"*I* thought she was in the conference room having dinner."

"Is something wrong?"

Ashley Elizabeth gave a nervous shrug.

The elevator stopped on sixteen, and Ashley Elizabeth headed for her desk. Rebecca followed. "She sounds a little upset, but I didn't want to ask. She sent me to find you."

"Strange."

"You can take the call in her office. She's waiting."

In Amalise's office Rebecca picked up the telephone, pressed the flashing hold button, and took a deep breath. "Amalise! What's going on?" She heard an amplified monotone voice making an announcement in the background.

"I'll give you the short version and explain later." Her words came out in a rush, crisp, as if she wanted to rid herself of whatever she had to say. Get it behind her. "A child's been hurt, and I'm with him at the hospital."

Rebecca leaned one hip against the credenza and clicked her tongue. "I must be missing something. What child are you talking about?"

"He's the foster child of some friends. There's no one but me to stay with him. We're at Charity right now, in the emergency room." She paused, and Rebecca could hear her take a deep breath. "I think his leg's broken and I have to stay with him."

"You have to get back here, is what you have to do! Where are his, ah, foster parents? Let them handle it."

"That's not an option. Look, I can't explain. You're going to have to break the news to Doug and Preston that I won't be back for a while."

Rebecca frowned. This made no sense.

Amalise's voice broke. "Will you do that for me, Rebecca?" She paused. "I don't know how long this will take. Just . . . just tell them I'll be there as soon as possible."

Rebecca shook her head. "Have you lost your mind, Amalise?" She glanced at the door and turned toward the wall, lowering her voice to a hiss. "You're going to sit in a hospital emergency room with someone else's child in the middle of a *closing*?" She paused. "You might as well resign."

"There was no one else, and he's . . . listen, I can't explain it all now. There isn't time. I'll tell you all about it later, but I'm asking you to please do this for me."

Rebecca recognized that tone of voice: Amalise wasn't going to budge. "Please."

Rebecca pressed her hand over her forehead. "How long will this take?"

"I don't know. Maybe hours."

"As in two or ten?"

"Somewhere in between, I guess."

Rebecca lowered herself into the chair. Amalise's career would not survive this night if she passed on this message. If the injured child were Amalise's own, or there was some other close relationship to explain, things would be different. But who was this child?

"Rebecca?"

"I'm here." She dropped her elbow onto the desk and her head into her hand, shrugging the phone close to her ear. She looked at her watch. It was already 8:35. "If I do what you ask, you'll be finished here, Amalise. The firm is counting on you."

There was a long pause before she answered. "I know. I'll have to take my chances."

Rebecca squeezed the space between her brows between her thumb and finger. "Please don't do this. You've worked too long, Amalise. Too hard."

"I love this little boy, Rebecca." Rebecca heard the surprise in Amalise's voice. "I do. I don't know how this happened, but there it is."

Rebecca could hear a small child crying, then Amalise's voice low, muffled, soothing. Another announcement in the background broke the silence between them.

Amalise's voice caught. "Please do this for me." She paused. "I'll see you later."

"Wait!"

But she'd hung up.

Rebecca straightened, looked at the phone in her hand, then slowly turned around and hung it up. Swiveling back to the desk, she knit her fingers together and stared unseeing at the books in Amalise's bookcase. A part of her wanted to weep for Amalise. They had survived law school together. They'd both been summer clerks for the firm, the first women ever hired for such a job at Mangen & Morris. And they had broken barriers together as associates in the firm's class of '76.

But a part of her also thought of the slow, steady climb toward becoming the first female lawyer up for partner. She would have no competition for the spot if she passed on Amalise's message. She fought against these thoughts, struggled against the growing temptation to do exactly what Amalise had asked.

She could do her job and Amalise's part as well. She could be the heroine who saved the closing, the one who'd stepped into the gap. And after that, if she worked hard enough for two tonight, a partnership would virtually be assured.

But there was another option, she knew.

She pushed back the desk chair and stood. Drawing in a deep breath, she looked at the telephone, then released her breath and looked up at the ceiling. Reflecting. Weighing.

Then she blew out her cheeks, picked up the phone, and dialed.

Chapter Forty-Two

JUDE ARRIVED AT THE HOSPITAL AT 8:55, stood just inside the emergency room door, and looked around. It had taken twenty minutes to get here, from the moment he'd hung up from Rebecca's call to the hospital parking lot. It was a miracle he hadn't gotten a ticket. There wasn't much time, Rebecca had said. She'd cover for Amalise as long as she could, but they'd notice pretty soon.

Dividing the room into sections as he did when searching for something out on the gulf, he scanned each square of the grid, narrowing his eyes against the bright fluorescent light. Within seconds he spotted them on the floor to his right, pressed against the wall. The child was stretched out on a blanket on the hard tile floor with his head in Amalise's lap.

Charity was a big, hard-working hospital. A teaching hospital with good doctors, and the primary destination for any ambulance in the city in an emergency situation. If the occupied chairs, stretchers, and gurneys were any indication, he figured Amalise and the child could be waiting there for days.

So he adjusted his original plan and walked toward her. As he grew close, she looked up. The blank expression disappeared as her eyes widened.

"Rebecca called," he said before she could ask. He stooped down before her, eyes on the child. The boy from Kerlerec Street, he figured.

Rebecca had warned him that Amalise's clock was ticking. No time for delay or emotion right now. Jude fixed his eyes on Amalise. Dark rings circled her eyes.

Looking up at him, her mouth tightened and she hugged the child closer. His eyes traveled down and met the child's. Large and soft and brown, warily they watched him. In the instant something turned inside, a small nudge that told him to listen to the whispers in his mind: *What you do for the least of them, you do for me.*

"What happened?"

"I think he's broken his leg." She indicated the right leg. "He fell down some stairs."

He nodded. Felt along the boy's hip, his thigh, his knee, ran his hand down the shinbone, and the boy cried out. Amalise let out a small anguished sound.

Jude looked up. "It feels like a break just above his ankle." He gently nudged the boy's chin, looking at him. "I bet that hurts, Buddy."

Luke shrank back against Amalise.

"His name is Luke."

Before Amalise could object, Jude slid his arms under the blanket and Luke and picked him up in both arms.

Amalise scrambled to her feet. "Wait! What are you doing?"

He rose and looked at her, the boy cradled in his arms, the blanket hanging down around him. Luke was silent, watching them.

Jude's brows knitted. Too much time was passing. "I'll take him to Touro Infirmary. It's smaller and there won't be a wait."

Amalise's eyes opened wide, and she nodded. "Yes. Of course. I didn't think of it."

He turned toward the door, motioning her to follow. When Luke cried out and stretched out his arm for her, she took his hand and held it all the way to the doors.

As they approached the exit, Jude turned and backed through the door, holding it open. Cradling Luke against him, he could feel the rapid thud of the child's heartbeat. The door closed behind them and they stood in the November cool, just outside the waiting room, under the portico.

Amalise reached across and pulled the hanging blanket up over Luke, gently tucking it around him. Then she slid her hand over his forehead, stroking it. Jude stood still, letting her soothe the boy, until gradually he felt the little heartbeat slow.

At last a slow shuddering sigh ran through the child, and Jude felt an almost imperceptible release of tension in the small body in his arms.

Amalise met Jude's eyes and smiled. "So Rebecca called you."

"She's worried. You'll be missed soon." He looked down at Luke. The boy was light as a feather. And sound asleep.

"I had to make a choice, Jude."

Now would come the hard part. He nodded and met her eyes. "I understand. But now you have to get back to work."

"I can't leave him." Her eyes darkened as she looked at him. "He calls me Mother." Her voice was thick with emotion. "Would a mother leave her child?"

He held her eyes. "He'll have a whole lifetime with you, Amalise, if that's what you both want." He saw her quick look, saw her thinking. "But right now you have to trust me."

She looked at him. "I do."

He nodded. "You may love this child, but you also love your work, and the two don't have to be mutually exclusive. So let me help." He nodded at Luke. "Look, he's asleep. I'll take care of him tonight. And tomorrow."

She began to protest, but he interrupted. "I'm good with kids. We'll be fine."

"I can't leave him."

"God gave you a mind as well as a heart, chère. I'm offering help. Don't drop the ball."

Her eyes were fixed on Luke. "He *is* asleep."

"Right. So don't wake him."

Her eyes turned up to him, those dark eyes that he so loved. If she loved this child, he would too. Perhaps she sensed something of that thought, because he saw just the beginning of a smile hovering at the corners of her mouth. She wanted so badly to believe him, he knew.

"Rebecca's covering for you, but you don't have much time." He looked at her. "She said to tell you that."

Still she hesitated.

"Where's your car?"

Seconds passed and in the red glow of the neon emergency sign, he saw her arrive at a decision and a smile lit her face, sparking her eyes. She pointed. "It's right over there."

"Good. Now get going. I'll treat him like my own. I'll call you from Touro and take him home with me tonight."

She stood there for a minute. Then she stood on her tiptoes and kissed his cheek, and whirling, raced for her car, digging into her purse for the keys as she ran. He watched until the headlights went on, and then hugging Luke close, he headed for his own.

Sitting in Amalise's office, Rebecca glanced at her watch and pulled the next of Amalise's unfinished purchase agreements from the stack on her desk. She'd completed her own allocation this afternoon around the time Amalise had disappeared. As minutes ticked past, she bent and wrote, filling in the final information for the closing.

Beads of perspiration formed on her brow and over her upper lip as she worked, setting each completed agreement aside and picking up the next. She'd made the call to Jude about forty-five minutes ago, she guessed. Any minute Raymond or Preston would be down here looking for both her and Amalise and wanting the purchase agreements.

Amalise drove within the speed limit, stopping at every light, avoiding the delay a speeding ticket would cause her, tapping her fingers against the steering wheel and worrying about Luke, the unfinished work on her desk, and the time ticking away. Robert may have already noticed her absence. She fixed her eyes on the red light above and willed it to change.

The length of any traffic light was relative, she knew, the time stretching in inverse proportion to your panic. This red light seemed endless. She gazed at a solitary man stumbling toward her. He walked in the gutter near the curb, as if the curb would lead him in the right direction. She reached back and locked her door, then she went back to staring at that light.

There was still a chance she'd make it back to the office undiscovered.

At last the light turned green. Stepping on the gas, she drove on toward the central business district and the First Merchant Bank Building, all the while silently thanking Rebecca for calling Jude.

❧

In the conference room, Bingham watched as Doug pushed back his chair and stood. "I'm taking off," he announced. He looked at Preston. "Everything under control?"

"Yes, we're almost there."

Doug scanned the conference table and the neat stacks of documents beginning to make their way around the edges of the table, each one piled fifteen high—originals for the various lenders and their counsel.

Doug nodded. Slipping his jacket on, he turned to Bingham. "You planning to get some sleep tonight?"

Bingham nodded. "I'll be leaving soon." He glanced at Robert, then back at Doug. "Where are those purchase agreements for the agents? Are they ready? We want those guys spreading out over the area first thing Friday morning, making offers and tying things down while everyone's still in a good mood after Thanksgiving turkey."

From the other end of the table, Raymond looked up. "Amalise and Rebecca are working on those. They'll be here soon."

Doug shot his sleeves and adjusted his cuffs. "Go check on that for Bingham, will you? Timing's everything now."

Raymond pushed back his chair. "Sure thing. Right away." He followed Doug to the door.

Bingham lit up a cigarette and nodded. "Good. We'll wait. I don't want to leave until we're certain we're rolling down the final hill."

Robert snorted. Bingham glanced at the clock. He sure hoped that Amalise showed up with those agreements soon. A few more minutes and Robert would go track her down, causing a scene.

⟨∽⟩

Rebecca glanced at her watch and knew this wasn't going to work. It was 9:30, and beside her were seven, maybe eight more unfinished purchase agreements. She had left the conference room almost an hour ago, and Raymond would be looking for her. She sucked in her bottom lip, eyes on the pile of work still to be done.

Then she set down her pen and pressed the phone button for Ashley Elizabeth's desk. Standing, she picked up Amalise's unfinished agreements, bundling them in her arm, taking the finished ones in the other. Ashley Elizabeth appeared in the doorway.

"Amalise is in trouble," Rebecca said, and Ashley Elizabeth's face blanched. She handed the finished agreements to Ashley Elizabeth and asked her to take them to the typing pool. But not right away.

Rebecca tossed her head. "Now here's what we need to do."

⟨∽⟩

The car seemed to move in slow motion. By the time Amalise pulled into her regular parking spot, it seemed as though hours, not minutes, had passed since she'd left Jude and Luke.

The garage elevator was lumbering and slow. Under the harsh fluorescent light, she studied the metal walls, picturing chaos in the conference room as Raymond or Preston or, worse, Robert discovered her extended absence. As the doors slowly parted, she shot out of the elevator and dashed past the ticket booth toward the opening to Common Street. Three seconds to the corner, she figured. Three more to cross the street and reach the door of the First Merchant Bank building. She prayed the security guard would be there to open the door right away.

6~9)

Ashley Elizabeth had returned to her desk with the completed agreements from Amalise's office. Rebecca held onto the unfinished files and flew down the hallway toward her own. As she set them down on her desk, she heard the elevator bell ding, probably announcing an unwelcome arrival.

She searched her desk for the purchase agreements she'd finished up earlier that day. In the hallway, the elevator doors clunked open, scattering her thoughts. She heard footsteps and then Raymond's voice calling out to Ashley Elizabeth. Whirling, she found the completed agreements she was seeking on the end of her credenza, ready for delivery to the conference room. With a deep breath, she scooped them up and, piling them into her arms, hurried back out into the hallway.

Raymond was walking toward Amalise's office. Ashley Elizabeth stood up, holding something as she stepped around the desk directly into Raymond's path, head down, as if absorbed in reading.

Raymond raised his arms as they collided.

Ashley Elizabeth dropped the papers, and her hands flew to her face. Stumbling back against the desk, she cried out. Raymond reached out and caught her. "Steady," he said.

"Oh!" She gave a nervous laugh and shook her head. "Excuse me. I didn't see you there." She looked around. "I must have been in another world. Are you looking for Amalise?"

"Yep."

"She's in the restroom. Can I help you?"

Rebecca saw that Ashley Elizabeth had spotted her. She hurried up, clutching the armload of finished agreements.

"I need the purchase agreements she's been working on."

"Raymond," Rebecca called.

He turned on his heels as Rebecca arrived, arms full of documents. She caught her breath as she halted just beside him. "Amalise asked me to bring these up to you. They're finished. She'll be there shortly."

"Great." He took the documents from her. "And how about yours? Bingham's hanging around until they're all on the closing table."

Rebecca flushed and, despite her attempt to smile, felt tension tighten the corners of her mouth. Amalise would owe her for this one. She flipped back her hair. She'd never failed to meet a deadline before. Not ever.

But she looked straight into his eyes and said, "Mine aren't quite finished." At his frown, her face grew hot. "But I'll get them to the conference room as soon as possible."

"Bingham's not going to like that, Rebecca."

Behind him, Ashley Elizabeth grimaced.

"It won't take long." Rebecca walked him to the elevator. When he pressed the call button, she waited, praying that Amalise wouldn't step out when it arrived.

"Well, hurry it up, will you. He's not leaving until those agreements are done."

She could hear the elevator grinding up from a lower floor. *Please don't let Amalise be inside.* The bell rang and she watched the doors part.

Without another word, Raymond stepped inside. As he leaned forward and pressed the button for the eighteenth floor, Rebecca slowly began to breathe again. She watched the doors close and stood there for a moment staring at them. Then she turned toward Ashley Elizabeth's desk and signaled her.

Ashley Elizabeth picked up the purchase agreements that Rebecca had given her earlier from Amalise's desk and headed for the typing pool while Rebecca returned to her office. She figured another forty or fifty minutes to complete the rest of Amalise's unfinished work.

Chapter Forty-Three

AT ONE MINUTE AFTER MIDNIGHT, THE start of closing day, Bingham strolled the circumference of the conference table, hands behind his back. Things were taking shape, although that pretty redhead had been off the mark on the purchase agreements. He wouldn't care, except that he was tired and ready to hit the sack.

Beauty's negligence was Mangen & Morris's problem, not his. Amalise was here now, probably had been here all along despite Robert's paranoia. Still, even now Robert was watching every move she made, streaming his dislike. He felt the tension between them in this room like a physical thing.

So Bingham cruised the table, keeping his eye on Amalise and Robert under his lids and watching her worry. Well, he told himself, a little concern right now wouldn't hurt Miss Catoir, after what she'd pulled.

Robert would hang around all night, he supposed, stalking her. Because his hand was in the monkey pot, reaching for those nuts. And nothing in the world right now could free him. Bingham almost smiled at the thought.

Raymond looked up when Bingham reached him and said it would be a long night. Bingham agreed. Jingling the change in his pockets, he wandered over to the windows. To the right he watched a well-lit tug pushing a loaded barge downriver. Slowly it glided out from under the bridge, heading for the Gulf. He watched until it curved past the Quarter, then the river went dark.

A flash of *deja vu* struck him. Once again he was on the edge, looking out into a deep, dark void. But darkness was his friend.

Turning, he signaled Robert that he was leaving.

The operation at Touro Infirmary had taken almost three hours from beginning to end. Luke was asleep by the time Jude reached home. The night had turned cold, and one of the nurses had lent him a fresh blanket, which he'd wrapped around Luke.

Flicking on the living room light, Jude carried Luke upstairs to the guest room next to his own. He pulled down the quilt and gently laid him on the bed. He picked up a pillow, fluffed it, and wedged it against the casted leg. He wished he'd thought to get a teddy bear or something at the hospital gift shop, something Luke could hold onto when he woke up.

Jude went into his bedroom, picked up a straight-backed wooden chair, and brought it into the guest room. There he placed it beside the bed at an angle and sat. He stretched his legs out and rested his feet on the board beneath the mattress, clasped his hands behind his head, and leaned back.

He could hear Luke's breathing, soft and even as he slept. Jude gazed out the window. From where he sat he could see down into his neighbor's yard, a small, neat square of grass divided from his own by a mutual fence. The yard was a well-kept place, not an unruly jungle of banana leaves and ginger like his own. He yawned. Clearing that out would be his next task. Soon.

His eyes roamed past the other neighbors' yards, all quiet now and dark, to the strip of indigo sky sprinkled with silver stars above the rooflines.

Luke moved, restless in sleep, and Jude's closing eyes snapped open. His feet dropped to the floor and he bent forward. Leaning over the child, he placed his hand on the bony shoulder, studying the face of this boy whom Amalise loved. His lips were moving, as if whispering to himself in dreams. A tiny furrow had dug in between his brows. Jude patted his shoulder, wanting to take away the pain this child had endured.

Sitting back again, Jude slid down in the chair until his weight settled on the small of his back. He rested, elbows on armrests, chin braced on his hands as hours passed. Once, Luke cried out, rolling his head to the side, eyes wide and frightened.

Jude sat there watching over Luke, until at last his own eyes closed.

Two hours later Luke woke up in the big bed and stared at the ceiling. His leg felt strange. He moved and felt the weight, testing. Lifting himself from the pillow, he braced on his elbows and looked down at the leg that had hurt so badly last night. He took in the solid white bandage wrapped around it, starting just below his knee and ending just before his foot. He wiggled the toes. They worked.

So he lay back down, head on the pillow, telling himself that *she* would come. Mak would come. Tears slipped down his cheeks. He lay very, very still.

Sometimes when he waited for Mak, he got confused, remembering another face from long ago in another world. But he couldn't hold on to that face. Sometimes he could feel his hand in hers, and then her hand slipping away. Then would come a rush of fear, and he would think that maybe, this time—like then—Mak would not come back, after all. And then the drumbeat would start in his chest.

Sometimes when he struggled to remember, he could hear the voices screaming again—those high, chattering, faceless sounds—and he would feel again the forest of legs closing in, and the hot itching crust of sweat on his skin. And then he'd fight to breathe, wanting to call out, but knowing she wouldn't hear. Because she hadn't, had she?

He blinked and turned his head to the door. For a moment he was startled, seeing the man sitting there, head lolling to one side. But he was sleeping, and Luke remembered his kindness earlier that night. But where was Mak?

He thought of her eyes that smiled at him. The soft voice, the way she held him close. Yes, she would come. Slowly he began to relax, watching the open door in this strange room. If he was very still and very good, maybe she would come.

At last his eyelids grew heavy, fluttering. He fought to stay awake for Mak.

And then he slept.

Chapter Forty-Four

BINGHAM WOKE SMILING. HE'D LEFT THE curtains open in the bedroom, and he lay there watching sunshine streaming through the windows. Today was the day.

Tossing the covers aside, he stood and stretched, looking out over the expanse of the city. The city looked fresh in this first light, gilded with a rosy, golden glow. He could almost feel the cold breeze sweeping across the water on Lake Pontchartrain, chopping the small swells into frothy white lines that appear and disappear before you're sure you've seen them.

Except for the lunchtime excursions he'd directed to various exquisite restaurants throughout the city, he'd been trapped in that stuffy conference room for the past six weeks, cut off from the world. Cut off from fresh air and sunshine, from people who thought of life as a stream of boundless beauty and joy, instead of something to be described word by exacting word on endless reams of paper.

Feeling fine, he showered and dressed. Picked up the phone and ordered coffee, orange juice with lots of pulp, and toast. Nothing too heavy today—he wanted to hold onto this feeling of lightness and freedom. Wishing for a pair of khaki pants and a loose-sleeved shirt, he instead pulled a navy-blue suit from the closet, along with a stiff-collared and cuffed white shirt and a burgundy striped tie. Everyone was expected to dress for a closing. Not much longer, he told himself, whistling.

Robert had planned a celebration after the funds arrived, a late lunch for the whole team at Arnaud's that was sure to stretch into the evening. Spicy Shrimp Arnaud to start, and then pecan-crusted speckled trout, potatoes au gratin, bread pudding, and champagne. Plenty of the bubbly. Bingham smiled, turned before the mirror for a last inspection. Then he went to the desk in the living room, opened the drawer, and pulled out a sheet of paper.

Briefly he thought of Amalise Catoir. He'd left her beavering away with everyone else last night. He considered having a talk with Robert about the futility of revenge, then thought better of it. She'd be all right. The outcome was inevitable, either way.

Breakfast arrived. He gave the waiter a large tip and received a big smile in return. Gulped down the juice. Sipped the coffee and ate a few bites of toast. Then he folded the clean white napkin just as it had come and placed it carefully down on the table beside the plate.

Whistling again, he headed for the door.

⌒∽❧

Amalise had changed into the clothes she'd brought to the office Tuesday morning. A gray-skirted suit with a short jacket and pleats around the hem, a white silk blouse with pearls, and black pumps. She'd freshened her makeup and brushed her hair. Now, back in the conference room, she made one last round of the table, checking everything against the closing list.

Every piece of paper was in place. Signature lines were marked with tabs for the clients, who were now drifting in. Laid out on the credenza were sugared beignets from Café du Monde, bagels with cream cheese, a cut-glass crystal bowl of fresh fruit, a shining stainless steel pot of steaming coffee, and a silver tray with cans of Coca-Cola and Tab beside a full ice bucket. Doug had just arrived, and he and Preston now stood in the corner conferring.

Rebecca walked in and caught her eye. Amalise lifted her hand, and Rebecca came her way. Amalise admonished herself for the rivalry and jealousy she'd felt toward Rebecca in the last few weeks. Filled with remorse, she prayed to Abba to forgive her.

"Heard anything about Luke?" Rebecca whispered, standing with her back to Doug and Preston.

"Jude left a message around midnight. It's a broken leg. He's taken Luke home with him, and I'll pick him up there this evening when we're through." Amalise leaned toward her, lowering her voice. "Thank you for saving me last night, Rebecca. For calling Jude. For what you did with the purchase agreements."

Rebecca gave her a quick look.

Amalise smiled. "I'll explain everything later. But . . . I wouldn't be here if it weren't for you."

Rebecca shrugged. "We're the Silver Girls, remember?"

Before Amalise could say anything, Rebecca swept back her hair, lifting it with both hands as she looked around. Tom walked in and she turned, letting her hair fall loose around her shoulders. With a grin, he headed in their direction, eyes on Rebecca, and Amalise moved away.

Tom was a fresh reminder of Robert's threats. Amalise walked over to the windows and gazed out over the business district, wondering if this was her last day with the firm. The odds were against her, she knew. She'd involved herself in a situation that wouldn't survive a complaint from a major client. She'd fight with everything she had, but in her heart she knew Robert would have his revenge.

Squaring her shoulders, she turned around. She'd accepted the risk when she'd bought the house on Kerlerec Street, and she knew that if given the choice again, she'd make the same one.

Walking to the corner of the conference table that was nearest the telephone, she picked up a copy of the wire transfer memorandum she'd prepared. Receipt of the investors' funds from Cayman as described in the memo would conclude the transaction, and that's when Robert would make his move. Amalise's stomach clutched at the thought.

Just then, Bingham Murdoch strolled in with Raymond, and they were laughing at something. Raymond had exchanged the D. B. Cooper shirt for a rumpled suit. Bingham swerved to the credenza, and Raymond joined Preston and Doug. Rebecca, holding a cup of coffee, drifted over to her. The two of them stood together while the last players arrived. Adam Grayson entered and headed for the coffee pot. Frank Earl came in, and Doug went to meet him. Counsel for Cayman Trust came in, hesitating at the doorway, briefcase in hand. The letter of credit was inside, she knew, ready for delivery the moment the documents were signed.

Then Robert entered, one arm slung over Richard Murray's shoulders, with Steve and Lars following, all four chuckling. Richard had come in on the red-eye. Amalise looked at Robert and lifted her chin, but Robert's gaze swept past her as he greeted Doug.

Raymond and Preston walked up. "Looks like we're ready," Preston said, standing beside her with his feet spread apart, hands clasped behind his back. She saw Robert glance at his watch and put his hand down on Bingham's shoulder, steering him toward the far end of the table. "Let's get this thing moving."

Power was subtly shifting from Bingham Murdoch to Robert Black, who would become the new chief operating officer of Lone Ranger, once the documents were signed. "The confirmation call with Cayman is set for nine o'clock," he announced. "After that, the wires will take a while, but we'll get to Arnaud's by midafternoon for the serious business."

Everyone laughed.

Frank Earl took his seat at the table, and Preston handed him a pen. It was 7:30 in the morning on Wednesday. The closing had begun.

Chapter Forty-Five

AT 8:50 AMALISE TAPPED DOUG ON the arm and looked toward the telephone. The conference call with Murdoch's Cayman bank officer and the U.S. lending syndicate was scheduled to begin at 9:00. This was the call to resolve the chicken-and-egg problem. Cayman would confirm the investors' funds had arrived, the signal for the U.S. banks to fund.

Around the table clients were hunched over documents, applying their signatures, surrounded by lawyers handing them new ones each time they finished the ones before them.

Doug looked at Robert. "How's it going? The call's scheduled in ten minutes."

"We're ready." Robert looked at Bingham, and Bingham nodded. Robert leaned back in his chair. "The principal documents are executed. Only a few certificates left. Let's get them on the line."

Doug turned his head and looked at Amalise. She picked up the wire transfer memorandum and dialed Ashley Elizabeth's number. Amalise asked if everything was ready for the conference call to Cayman.

"Yes."

"Are the banks on the line?" The room went silent as eyes lifted to her.

"Yes, all accounted for. They're holding."

"Good." She was gratified to hear that her voice was steady. "Get Mr. Benjamin Salter, Banc Franck, on the line, please. His number's on the list. Call me back when he's connected."

"Will do."

Amalise clicked off the call and lounged back, gazing about, wanting to absorb each moment of this closing in case it was her last. "Looks like things are all set," she said to Raymond.

He heaved a sigh and stretched his neck, closing his eyes. "It seems like we've been working on this deal forever."

"Well, enjoy it because we'll all be bored until the next one comes along."

Raymond straightened in his chair and gave her a wry smile. With a glance at the credenza, he stood. "Want some coffee? Or a Tab?"

She shook her head. Her stomach fluttered as she waited for Ashley Elizabeth to call back. The process of transferring funds from the various banks in the syndicate, and then from Cayman at the last, was tied to the wire transfer memo she'd prepared. She looked down again at the memo, scanning it, praying that nothing had been forgotten. Praying that the investor funds were on deposit in the Cayman account as required.

The phone rang at 9:00 on the dot. She took the call on the receiver, listened, and then nodded. Banc Franck was on the line.

Doug stood and raised his hand. "Listen up, everyone. We're beginning the conference call. Banc Franck's on the line to confirm the investors' deposit." He looked at Bingham.

Bingham's expression was nonchalant.

Robert, beside him, caught Amalise's eyes as she pressed the button to place the call on the speaker, and she fought to veil the rush of fury he aroused in her.

Bingham said, "Will you do a roll call, Miss Catoir?"

Conscious of Robert's eyes, Amalise lifted the memo in hand and leaned slightly toward the speaker. Her heart fluttered. "Good morning, everyone. My name is Amalise Catoir, Mangen & Morris. We'll do a roll call first. When I call your bank's name, please let us know you're on the line."

As she read out the name of each lender on the list, each bank officer answered present. And at last: "Banc Franck."

Benjamin Salter's voice. "Present."

She let out a long breath, and Bingham stood. Long and lean, he seemed to pull himself up as he ran the flat of his hand down his starched white shirt.

"Bingham Murdoch here, Ben."

"Good morning, Mr. Murdoch."

Bingham swung his arm behind his back and rocked forward on his toes, smiling as he turned to the room. "It *is* a good morning here, Ben. As we arranged, I'm calling on behalf of Lone Ranger, Incorporated." He looked down at the first page of the wire memorandum. "I'm in the Mangen & Morris conference room in New Orleans, and we're presently closing the company financing." Folding his arms over his chest, he gazed down the table. "As you just heard, our bank lenders are on the phone with us. I believe you have the list?"

"Yes."

"With me is our new chief executive officer, Robert Black, as well as Tom Hannigan from Morgan Klemp, Frank Earl Blanton from First Merchant Bank, and others."

"That's fine."

"So." He clapped his hands together. "In accordance with prior instructions, please confirm for us the current balance, in currency, of available funds on deposit in the company's account. That is account number 13672."

Amalise heard paper rustling on a desk from the other end of the telephone.

Ben's voice again: "As per your instructions, account number 13672. The current available balance on account is U.S. $20,200,000.00."

"Confirmed." Bingham turned to Tom and raised his brows. Tom nodded.

Counsel for Cayman Trust who sat on the other side of Doug, snapped open his briefcase. Everyone watched as he pulled out the letter of credit and placed it on the table.

Bingham nodded. "The letter of credit is delivered," he announced into the phone. He looked at Tom, at Robert, at Doug, and at last, at Frank Earl, who would be speaking for the bank group. "So then, are conditions for each bank's funding satisfied at this point?"

Frank Earl glanced at Doug and then, placing both hands on the table, he half-rose from the chair and hunched toward the telephone. "This is Frank Earl Blanton, First Merchant Bank." He raised his voice. "Are there any questions from the banks?"

A voice on the line: "The documents are executed?"

"Yes."

Another: "Looks good to you, Frank Earl?"

"Yes. I believe the conditions for funding have been met." He paused. "Any objections?"

A chorus of no's responded.

Frank Earl backed into his seat. He spread his hands toward Bingham. "The bank group is ready to fund."

Doug leaned in the direction of the phone. "Doug Bastion here. Let's get those funds on the wires as soon as possible, everyone." He leaned back. Tapped his pencil on the edge of the table.

Bingham folded his arms and looked down at the speakerphone. "Thank you, Ben. That's all we need."

"You are welcome."

Bingham disconnected the call and looked around. "Congratulations, everyone. We're almost there."

Amalise looked at her watch. The call had taken ten minutes.

Chairs were shoved back, and people rose as Bingham threaded his way through them back toward Robert. Robert looked over at Amalise, and this time there was an almost imperceptible smile on his face.

She tossed her head and turned away. She wouldn't make things easy for him.

Frank Earl walked up. "Good job, Amalise." He held out his hand, and she shook it. He reached for the telephone, pulled it toward him, and dialed, turning his back to the room. Amalise waited while he spoke to someone in Merchant Bank's wire room, instructing them to call him in the conference room upon receipt of each bank's funding transfer.

"We're tight," he said. "Need to know the minute the last funds arrive, so we can get that Banc Franck wire in before the end of the day." He listened for a moment, said yes and then no, and hung up.

Raymond passed by, giving a whoop under his breath.

The hum of conversation in the room increased. She saw Bingham walking toward the door, hands in his pockets, and she longed to catch up with him, to make her case for the house on Kerlerec Street.

Bingham stopped when he reached Doug and slapped him on the shoulder. "I'm going back to the hotel," he said. "Call me when we're ready."

"Not staying for lunch?"

He shook his head. "Not today. Anyway, I just had breakfast. I'll take a nap and eat later on at the hotel, unless you call first."

Raymond arrived just then with Rebecca in tow. He looked at the two of them. "Check the documents on the table while we've got some down time. Make sure no signatures are missing." And so Bingham escaped, and Amalise began working her way down one side of the table, Rebecca the other, flipping pages to assure that all signatures were complete.

Doug sat back, winged his arms behind his head, and said, "Looks like we have a deal."

As Bingham strolled down the hallway, headed for the elevator, he inspected the pictures along the walls, looked into the familiar offices with open doors, the secretaries' desks. The sound of typewriters, telephones, copy machines grinding behind him, spitting out those endless piles of documents. He wouldn't miss this place.

He rode down the elevator, walked through the lobby, and crossed the street. At the Roosevelt Hotel, he saluted the bellman and went up to his suite. There he walked directly to the desk in the living room and dialed the hotel operator.

It was 9:20 in the morning. "Overseas operator, please."

"Yes, Mr. Murdoch."

He waited a few minutes, and when the international operator came on, he gave the number he was calling and the name. A minute passed, then two. He leaned back in the chair, feeling relaxed. At last she came back on the line.

"All circuits are busy, sir. I'll have to ring you back."

"Fine. That's fine." He had plenty to do while he waited.

Chapter Forty-Six

A SHAFT OF LIGHT SLID THROUGH the bedroom window, extending its reach inch by inch until it reached Jude, and he woke. The light was warm. And the small body curled against him was warm. He lifted his head and saw Luke. At once, everything came back—Amalise in the waiting room at Charity, Touro Infirmary, bringing Luke home.

He lay there, letting his mind adjust to a waking state, one arm still flung over Luke, the other over his head. He'd moved from the chair to the bed sometime during the night. Turning his head on the mattress—he'd left the pillow for Luke—he saw the boy was awake and watching him.

Jude moved his hand gently across Luke's back and smiled.

Luke gave him a cautious look.

"You don't know where you are, and you don't know who I am. But you remember last night, don't you?" He patted Luke's back, feeling the slight, sharp shoulder blades. "And you remember that Amalise left you in my care, so you'll trust me, just a little bit for that reason."

Luke said nothing.

Jude pushed up, propping himself on his elbow, looking down at Luke. "Remember Mak?" He saw the quick muscle movement around the corners of Luke's eyes. He pointed to himself. "Well, I am Jude."

Luke stared.

Touching his chest with two fingers, he repeated the words. "I am Jude. Jude." Then he touched his finger to Luke's chest, speaking softly. "And you are Luke."

Luke looked down at the finger, then up at Jude.

"Luke," he repeated.

Jude blinked and nodded.

Grinning, Jude swung his legs to the side of the bed and twisted around. He ran his hand lightly down the cast, then patted it. Not too bad, he thought. The doctor had said he'd be moving around on crutches soon. Jude could show him how—he'd had a broken bone or two in his time.

Luke reached down and touched the cast where Jude had touched it, then gave Jude a questioning look.

Jude nodded. "We'll work it out, Luke. Get you used to it. Come on." He stood, bent, and gently lifted the child into his arms. "Come with Jude."

Luke hooked one arm around Jude's neck and studied his face from the new angle.

Jude chuckled, then brushed Luke's forehead with a kiss. "I guess you must be hungry. Let's go find some breakfast." He turned toward the door, and as he did he saw the beginning of what he thought might be a smile on the little face.

∽❧

Bingham Murdoch went into the bedroom and pulled a small, dark-green duffel bag from where he'd stashed it in the closet, behind the shoes and under the hanging clothes. He could get comfortable now. Whistling, he wandered to the window while he untied his tie, scanning the sky in the direction of the lake. City haze muted the blaze of sunshine, softening the vista in a yellow sheen.

Bingham yanked off his tie with glee. He changed into a pair of khaki pants and a light-blue linen shirt that he'd always liked because it let the air in, kept him cool. He sat on the edge of a chair and yanked off his socks, then slipped his bare feet into a pair of well-worn loafers. No more socks either.

When he'd inspected himself in the long mirror and found everything to his satisfaction, Bingham retrieved a package from the chest of drawers, one he'd prepared yesterday. He'd wrapped it himself in slick white paper that he'd bought at Woolworth's. He'd even tied it with a gold ribbon that curled at the ends. For a moment he considered writing a note and then rejected the idea. The gift spoke for itself. He tossed it on the bed.

The telephone rang, and he picked it up.

"Mr. Benjamin Salter of Banc Franck is on the line, Mr. Murdoch."

"Thank you." He waited through a few seconds of hisses and clicks as they were connected. Gazing through the window, he envisioned himself flying through the clouds, unbound.

"Benjamin Salter here."

He snapped to and slid the sheet of paper on the desk closer to him. "Hello, Ben," he said in a cheerful tone. "Bingham Murdoch."

"Yes, Bingham."

"I'm calling to confirm my second set of standing instructions dated November 16, 1977."

"I've got it here."

"Please confirm the funds transfer order from account number 13672 in accordance with those instructions."

"May I have your security code?"

Bingham gave it to him.

Ben Salter then read the instructions back to him, word for word. Bingham looked at his watch. It was now 9:40.

"And the status?"

"One moment." There was a pause. "Right. The two transfers are confirmed, completed in accordance with the instructions."

"Thank you, Ben."

"My pleasure."

Bingham hung up.

From the closet he picked out a leather jacket, one with long sleeves with ribbed stretch cuffs and waistband. He plucked a blue baseball cap from the top shelf of the closet and jammed it into the jacket pocket. Chuckling, he tucked the package with the gold ribbon under his arm and headed for the door.

⌒∿⌒

A general feeling of celebration pervaded the conference room during the lull while waiting for bank money to roll in from the syndicate. Frank Earl had parked himself in a chair near the telephone. The line to the wire room was held open now. After a half hour, he made the first announcement of bank funds received.

Amalise and Rebecca sat side by side at the conference table, lounging and drinking coffee, struggling to stay awake. Neither had slept in more than twenty-four hours. But most of their work was finished now—all they could do was wait. Rebecca said she was looking forward to the celebration at Arnaud's. Tom was driving her there, she said, with a sideways look at Amalise.

But Rebecca's words were lost in Amalise's haze of worry. The end of the day loomed like the Berlin Wall for Amalise, with the confrontation with Robert she knew was coming.

She consoled herself with the thought of seeing Luke tonight at Jude's house. She wanted to hold him for a while, take him home to her own house on Broadway. And she longed to talk with Jude about everything that had happened, to be near him.

Rebecca nudged her. "Go call him. See how the boy's doing."

Amalise hesitated.

"Oh, go on. There's plenty of time." She glanced at Frank Earl sitting by the phone. "We've got at least a couple hours before the last bank money hits."

Amalise nodded and pushed herself up from the chair. Rebecca was right—she should call. She fixed a smile on her face as she walked to the door. Robert would never see her tears. Nor her fear.

When Amalise returned to the conference room, Rebecca flagged her. Working her way through the tired and jubilant crowd, she dropped into the chair beside Rebecca again.

"Did you get in touch with Jude?"

Amalise smiled. "Everything's fine. They're getting along, he says. He's feeding Luke breakfast."

"Just like that man."

Amalise looked about. Tom and Robert were hunched over a calculator at the end of the table, Robert's fingers racing over the keys while Tom murmured. She suppressed a sigh of relief. Right now she wasn't his main diversion.

"How many banks are in?"

"Four. The two on the West Coast are the only ones left. The holiday traffic's slowing down the wires, but we're still on schedule." Rebecca leaned back, spread her arms over the chair, and smiled. "And then the Cayman funds will arrive, and then we'll all go off to Arnaud's."

"Or home to sleep."

Rebecca gave her one of those looks. "Amalise, we've had this talk before. You've got to socialize, get to know people like Robert and Tom and Bingham. You need face time; they're players." She grinned. "We're the Silver Girls, remember?"

Right, but this one has been tarnished. Aloud she said, "You're right. I know you're right."

If Robert won, Rebecca would find out soon enough anyway.

An hour passed and then Frank Earl announced receipt of the funds from Sacramento. One bank to go. It was getting close to lunchtime. Preston said he'd order sandwiches or something, but Robert objected. It was early yet, he said. The celebration at Arnaud's was to be a late lunch.

Chapter Forty-Seven

AT TWELVE NOON AMALISE PICKED UP the phone in her office. Sitting in the conference room all morning across from Robert had set her nerves on end. She'd call Jude one more time, just to make certain Luke was safe.

A thought struck like lightning: This was mother love. In Luke's heart—and somehow her own—he was hers.

Slowly she set down the receiver and swiveled back to her desk, turning over this thought in her mind. She had never let herself think this way before. This child wasn't a toy she could borrow from Caroline to play with and then return when he became inconvenient.

Across the room the transaction books held her gaze. Deals. Excitement. Travel.

And then there was Luke.

She dropped her head into her hands. This wasn't the time to spin that web, the compartmentalizing of one part of her life from the other, as she'd done when she was married to Phillip, struggling to give one hundred percent of herself to her marriage *and* her career. Because even if Robert was successful in having her fired from Mangen & Morris, she would fight to retain her license, to continue practicing law. She would find a way, somehow.

And where would that leave Luke?

Her thoughts cleared. She saw the struggle, a single mother compet-
ing against men and women like Rebecca, whose careers were their high-
est priority. The competition in the legal profession was fierce.

No. Loving Luke was like loving Jude. An impractical, unobtainable,
but profound emotion that was better left alone.

That settled, she picked up the phone and called Jude.

"Hello?"

"Hi. How's Luke?"

"As I told you an hour ago, he's just fine." Jude's voice held a smile,
and she felt herself relax. "I've been singing to him all morning, but he's
asleep right now."

"Singing?"

"Yeah." He laughed. "Well, what can you do? Listen. I just talked to
Caroline. Luke's going to stay here a few nights. He's comfortable, and
frankly, she sounded relieved. She's worried about those stairs and how
he'll get around."

"But—"

"I told her not to worry. We'll get him some crutches tomorrow, those
little ones they make for kids. I'll teach him how to use them before he
goes back."

Amalise didn't say anything.

"Are you coming here once you're finished there?"

"Of course!"

"Good. Caroline wants you to stop to pick up some of his clothes.
She'll have them ready for you. Can you do that?"

"Oh. Ah, sure." Her thoughts spun. Everything had been flipped
upside down. She picked up a pencil and drew circles on a notepad, thinking of Robert and what lay ahead here in the office. "It might be a while."

"No problem." Jude's voice was hearty. "He's asleep right now. Like
I said, I've been singing. I think going to sleep was his way of shutting
me up."

Amalise had to laugh.

"Amalise?"

"Yes?"

"How are things at the office? Did anyone notice your absence last night?"

"No. You and Rebecca took care of everything." Her throat grew tight. She blinked back tears. Self-pity, she knew. Jude loved Rebecca. And Robert was lurking in the conference room, waiting like the Count of Monte Cristo to exact his revenge.

After providing Jude with a few more details of how she'd slipped unnoticed into the conference room the night before, they said their good-byes and she hung up the telephone.

She pulled her purse out of the drawer and applied some lipstick and powder. She brushed her hair, tucking back some stray stands, and stood. She would go back to the conference room and wait along with everyone else on the team, and when the last twenty million arrived from Cayman, she'd find out her fate.

At 12:30 Frank Earl walked into the conference room waving a piece of paper in the air. "The last bank's in. Funds just arrived. I've sent Banc Franck a fax stating that the lending group's funds have all been received."

Tom raised his fist and shook it.

Robert stood and raked his hands through his hair. "Let's get Ben Salter on the phone. Get that twenty million moving."

Amalise looked about, then leaned toward Raymond. "Where's Murdoch?"

Raymond glanced around and shrugged. "He's been gone awhile. At the hotel, probably."

Frank Earl walked over to the phone, still on the conference table and leaned over it. "What's our time look like? We're calling Banc Franck right now. How long will the transfer take, do you think?"

From the speakerphone, a weary voice: "No way to tell. It could be some time, being an international transfer and the day before a U.S. holiday."

Robert, brusk, harsh: "Then we need to get started. I'm putting you on hold. Stand by." He pressed the button and looked around at Tom.

Tom nodded. "You're the CEO now. Go ahead and make the call."

Robert pressed the second line and dialed the operator. "I need to make an international call."

"One moment, please."

Robert shook his head, glanced in Amalise's direction, and snapped his fingers, pointing to copies of the wire transfer memorandum on the desk, just out of reach. Preston, sitting nearby, picked up a copy and handed it to Robert. The international operator came on, and Robert gave her Benjamin Salter's number in Grand Cayman.

Another wait. Robert leaned against the credenza, looking out over the room.

Amalise tensed, clasping her hands in her lap and twirling her thumbs under the table where they couldn't be seen.

Tom walked over to the windows and linked his hands behind his head, looking out in the direction of the Marigny District.

"Benjamin Salter." The voice cracked through the room.

"Ah, Mr. Salter. Robert Black, new chief executive officer of Lone Ranger."

Tom turned from the window.

"Congratulations, Mr. Black."

"Frank Earl of First Merchant Bank is here with me. I believe he's sent you notice that the lending group has funded, triggering the transfer of investor funds from your bank to the parent company account here at First Merchant Bank."

"Account number, please."

"Account number 13672. Is the transfer in process?"

"May I have the security code?"

Robert frowned. His face flushed. He turned, looking at Tom. "Excuse me, Mr. Salter. What did you say?"

"I'll need the security code."

"I don't have a security code. Don't know what you're talking about. Just advise us as to whether the transfer of funds from the account has been initiated."

"Mr. Black." There was a sigh, but Benjamin Salter's tone was patient. "I'm not in a position to release that information without the security code."

Robert threw up his arms, then bent again toward the phone, lower this time, as if he could see the man on the other end. "What do you mean you can't release the information? *I'm speaking for the company.*"

"In any event, I'll need the security code. We have procedures, as you know."

Robert raised his brows.

Tom shrugged.

"We'll fax copies of the corporate certificates confirming my position in the company, if that's what you need."

"I've already received a copy. But without the security code—"

Robert broke in, leaning on the conference table and glaring at the phone. "We have a schedule to keep. Have the funds been put on the wire or not?"

The voice was measured—polite, but firm. "Mr. Black, my hands are tied. Bingham Murdoch has the code if you do not. Get him on the phone or obtain the security code from his records. In either event, once you have the code, I'll be happy to oblige."

Without another word Robert disconnected the call. "Security code," he muttered. He looked at Tom, pinching the deepening fold between his eyes. "Do you know anything about a security code for this account?"

"No. We'll have to get Bingham."

"Well, why isn't he here?"

Tom nudged his jaw toward the window, in the direction of the Roosevelt. "He's at the hotel."

Robert's voice was strained, urgent as he picked up the phone again. "Get me the Roosevelt Hotel immediately."

Amalise envisioned the firm operator's likely response to such terse instructions. She wasn't used to such rude behavior at Mangen & Morris. Beside her, Raymond sighed. On the other side of her, Rebecca said *sotto voce* that one would think Bingham Murdoch would have been here, waiting with them. Tom walked back to his chair and sat. He rapped an irritating rhythm against the table with his knuckles.

"Yes, all right," Robert was saying. "Just give me the front desk." Glancing at Richard, he jerked his head toward the door. His tone was resigned. "Go change our reservations at Arnaud's. Better make it for six thirty. Give ourselves some leeway." But then, he held up his hand.

"Yes. Bingham Murdoch, please."

Richard stood, hand on the back of Amalise's chair, listening.

"Ring again. He has to be there." He pursed his lips and turned his back to the room.

Tom said, "He's probably on the way over here."

Across the table Doug pulled his chair closer to the table and leaned on one elbow, listening.

Robert turned, threw up a hand, and shouted into the phone, "Well then, page him. Tell him to call the conference room at Mangen & Morris immediately." Pause. "He'll know. Just page him."

He slammed down the phone and turned to Richard. A white line had formed along his upper lip, and his mouth barely moved as he spoke. "Go to the hotel and find Bingham." He looked at his watch. "Check Bailey's first. Bingham's not used to waiting for lunch."

There were chuckles around the table.

"Get him back here right away."

Richard nodded and left.

"Security code." Still shaking his head, Robert fell into a chair beside Doug. "There was nothing about a security code in the wire transfer memorandum."

Amalise's heart jumped. She clasped her hands and worked to keep her expression blank as Robert picked up the memorandum, perusing it.

Doug plucked it from his hands. "No, there's not. But we received the information for the investors' transfers, including Banc Franck, from you and Bingham." He pointed to the initials on the bottom corner of the page. His voice was firm. "You approved it." He handed it back to Robert. His voice was firm.

Amalise let out her breath. Doug Bastion had defended her. So far.

Chapter Forty-Eight

AT 1:00 BINGHAM CHECKED IN AT the American Airlines counter at Moisant Field. No luggage, just a small carry-on bag. He pulled out his passport and handed it to the ticket agent upon request. The ticket agent glanced at the picture, looked at Bingham, and smiled. Then she slipped the tickets and three boarding passes into a narrow folder and handed them to Bingham with the passport.

"Your boarding passes for Miami and Rome are in here, too."

Bingham nodded his head and stuck them in his pocket.

"Have a nice trip, Mr. Skarke."

Turning away, he smiled. "Thanks, I will."

Bingham Murdoch whistled as he strolled casually to the concourse, taking his time to settle into the new identity, figure out the personality for Daniel Skarke. It always took him a little time to acclimate. He shook his head. Passports, Social Security cards, credit cards, driver's licenses. All were easy to obtain, about fifty dollars each. A little more for the passports—maybe a thousand, as he recalled.

He stopped at a newsstand to browse, find a book or magazine to read. He selected a mystery. Maybe he'd get one of those Lucky Dogs they sold from carts in the airport. He liked those Lucky Dogs. It'd be a nice change from the rich meals he'd eaten every day for the past six weeks.

Heading down the concourse with purpose now, he smiled to himself. The money had hit Zurich before the close of business there, in time for immediate wiring to accounts in the Orient and the start of a whole new day. Two hundred thousand dollars were now in the Swiss account of his "contractor," Dominick Costa, best inside man in the game. Always had been. They went way back. The remaining twenty million had hit his own account in Zurich this morning before bouncing on.

He stopped at the Lucky Dog cart and ordered a dog with mustard and chili and a Coca-Cola. He handed the man some change and took a bite, savoring it.

The twenty million dollars had moved from Cayman to Zurich in the time it took to drink a cup of coffee. Then it had been split into three sums—$6,666,666, $6,666,667, and $6,666,667—and routed through twenty-one different banks around the world, each according to the matrix provided under his standing instructions to Benjamin Salter.

He chewed the hot dog and fought with the little napkins they give you to clean up the mess, thinking the money would reunite in the *anstalt*—a corporate trust—in Liechtenstein, before bouncing back to Daniel Skarke's account in Switzerland. He'd created that account seven years ago, before the Swiss negative tax had hit.

Finishing off the hot dog, he wiped his hands and tossed the napkins into a trash barrel nearby. The Swiss franc had preserved his purchasing power against the dollar, and it was tax free for the most part. He smiled to himself. The world's most secure currency—no risk and a fat return. Perhaps he should consider purchasing some gold, after all. With the U.S. aggravating OPEC as they'd been, the price of gold was set to skyrocket.

He perked up, listening. The first boarding call for his flight was being announced. He picked up his bag and headed for the gate. He planned to sleep on this flight and dream of taking the ferry from Naples to the villa waiting for him. As he showed the gate agent his ticket, he was already thinking of the peaceful veranda high above the cerulean sea. He could almost feel the golden sun on his skin.

Daniel Skarke, a.k.a. Bingham Murdoch, smiled.

He had never liked crowds.

Chapter Forty-Nine

IT WAS 7:30, AND THE WIRES had closed long ago. Amalise sat behind her desk, still struggling to absorb the situation. Bingham Murdoch was missing, and so was the twenty million provided by the investors. Repeated attempts to convince Benjamin Salter to reveal the whereabouts of the money without the account's security code had been unsuccessful. The information was privileged under Cayman law.

By now the money could be in Singapore or just about anywhere else in the world.

Robert Black and Richard Murray had searched Bingham's hotel suite, hoping to find the code. His clothes were still there, and all his belongings. Perhaps this was all a mistake, a misunderstanding. They'd talked to the bell captain and the bellmen at the hotel. No one had seen him after the closing that morning. Tom called every number he had for Bingham, to no avail. When at last the fed wires had closed, the mood in the conference room resembled that of a morgue.

At seven o'clock the Cayman Trust letter of credit was withdrawn.

The Mangen & Morris team had gathered in Doug's office. His face was white. "At least our bank clients are safe," he'd said. "Their funds are being held intact at First Merchant Bank over the holiday. They'll be returned on Friday." He rubbed his forehead, shaking his head.

Preston, head in his hand, looked up. "Tom's investors are the losers." Slowly Doug nodded.

"It was a con." All eyes turned to Raymond. He hiked one shoulder and raised his brows. "The whole thing was a con from beginning to end. That's my take. Tom and Robert met Murdoch in Cayman. They were the marks."

They'd all stared at each other, speechless.

Now Amalise looked up as Rebecca walked into her office and dropped down in the guest chair. She braced her elbows on the armrests and linked her fingers. "What do you think?" she said after a moment.

Amalise grimaced. "I think he's gone." She glanced at the window as if seeking him there. Between buildings she could see the quarter moon. "I think Raymond's right. Bingham Murdoch was an enigma. Everyone saw what they wanted to see with him."

"Tom and the New York contingent are packing their bags. They'll be spending the holiday tomorrow with their lawyers, I'd imagine. Or the FBI." Rebecca tapped the corner of the desk with her fingers and stood. "I'm going home to get some sleep. See you on Friday morning. Preston wants us to regroup then and wrap things up."

When she was gone, Amalise sat looking at her diploma hanging on the wall near the bookcase with disbelief. Could she possibly be safe? She thought about the question from every angle and came to a conclusion: yes. The house on Kerlerec Street would be the last thing on anyone's mind right now. Project Black Diamond was as good as dead.

She took a deep breath. *Thank you, Abba.* Then she picked up the phone and dialed Jude's number. Four rings before he answered. "We're doing fine," he said. "How'd things go?"

"I'll tell you when I get there."

"All right. Don't forget to pick up Luke's clothes from Caroline."

She parked in front of the house on Kerlerec Street and looked at it, the place she'd bought and given away at the risk of her career, this plain wooden house with its two windows across the front. Robert's threats were emasculated now.

The children were nowhere in sight. When she reached the screened door, she pulled it open and shouted, "Caroline?"

She stepped in. "Caroline. It's Amalise. I'm here."

She could hear Nick and Charlie and Daisy upstairs. Caroline clobbered down the stairs, wearing an apron. She wiped her hands on it and held them out to Amalise. "What a night you've had!"

Amalise took her hands, and Caroline pulled her into a hug. "Jude told me all about the hospital and the crowds and everything." She patted Amalise's back for a moment, and then released her. "Thanks be to God he came. I worried that you'd all be there all night. And you, missing work, and Luke in all that pain."

"But everything worked out, and I made it back to work in time."

Caroline nodded. She planted her hands on her hips. "Well, I've talked to Jude, and he thinks Luke ought to stay with him awhile." She studied Amalise.

"Jude's singing to him." Amalise's smile was wry.

"Isn't that something! Ellis and I . . . well, we've just never been able to communicate with the child at all, and here you and Jude come along and he comes to life." She led Amalise to the living room and picked up a small bundle of clothes folded on the corner of the couch. "I've gotten his things together. There isn't much. Jude said you'd be coming by to pick them up."

Caroline dropped her eyes as she handed the clothes to Amalise. When she looked back up, Amalise saw something in her eyes that held her. "He's become very attached to you, Amalise."

"I know. The feeling is mutual."

Fingering a strand of hair near her cheek, Caroline glanced down at the little pile of clothes and back up at Amalise, and she smiled.

◠◡

She couldn't remember how long it had been since she'd slept. The fatigue had hit her all at once while driving from Caroline's to Jude's. With muscles still knotted with tension from the past twenty-four hours, Amalise trudged up Jude's front steps and pressed the doorbell. Once. Twice. Then she knocked.

No answer. So she turned the knob, and the door opened.

She leaned inside and called, "Jude?"

But still no one answered. She set her purse down on the coffee table in front of the couch and walked through the living room, dining room, the small hallway where the stairs went up, and into the kitchen. There she saw that the back door was open, and through the window over the sink she could see the bare bulb lighting up the yard. And she could hear Jude's voice.

Brows raised, she walked toward the door.

A ripple of high-pitched giggles, a child's laughter, made her stop. Listening, she heard Jude again, his voice deep and even. Picking up her step, she hurried to the back door and looked out through the screen.

Luke sat beside Jude on the wood-planked floor, plastered leg stretched out before him, fully engrossed. Jude said something as he handed Luke a hammer, and Luke, taking it carefully, inspected it. She could see his face shining. Smiling.

She stood still, not wanting to interrupt anything.

Then Luke leaned forward, as Jude folded his hand over the boy's hand, so that they held the hammer together. He helped Luke to lift it, and then he let go. Luke, holding the hammer up, watched as Jude pointed to a nail in the wood below.

Luke nodded, his expression turning grave. Then he slammed the hammer down on the nail. And looking up at Jude, he laughed.

Amalise's lips parted.

Jude ruffled the boy's hair, and she opened the screened door. Both Luke and Jude looked up. "Looks like you're doing all right," she said.

Luke turned sparkling eyes to her. "Mak!"

"He's been helping," Jude said.

Luke twisted around, struggling to stand but weighed down by the cast. He cried out. Jude took the hammer and scooped him up, forming a chair with his arms as he stood beside Amalise. Luke reached out, touching Amalise's chin with the tip of his fingers, as if making certain she was real. "Mak!" he said again, but softly now.

Her throat was thick as she held out her arms.

Jude's brows drew together. "He's heavier now, with the cast."

"That's all right." So Jude slipped Luke into Amalise's arms and she held him close, cradling him. Luke rested his head on her shoulder, looking at Jude. Then he pointed his finger at Jude.

"Ju," he said.

Amalise caught her breath.

Jude looked at Luke. "That's right, buddy." He touched his finger to Luke's chest, tipped his head to one side, and raised his brows.

"Luke." Luke spoke his own name.

Amalise looked from one to the other, staring.

"I figure he's been listening for a long time," Jude said, taking her arm and guiding her back into the house.

Jude went out to buy some hamburgers, and Luke ate every bite of his, looking from one to the other of them as he ate. He smiled, and he laughed when Jude teased. Sometimes he imitated a word—like *hamburger*—and then Jude would stop and repeat it, saying it over and over again with him until he got it and understood. She was amazed.

After they'd tucked Luke into bed and he'd fallen asleep, almost instantly—lingering effects from the previous night, Jude said—Jude took her hand and steered her out of the room. "Let him sleep."

"But he's alone."

"He'll be fine. We'll be nearby." He took her hand in his. His was callused and strong as it curled around hers, the hand of a working man, steady and constant. A good man, she knew.

But he was Rebecca's now. She slipped away and started down the hallway to the stairs. "I think I'll go home and bathe and change. I'll be back before he wakes."

"Wait a while," Jude said, trailing behind her. "I want to hear what happened today."

And she wanted every moment she could have with him. So in the living room, instead of heading for the door, she curled up in the corner of the couch she'd made her own from time to time and looked at him.

He sprawled beside her, facing her, arm stretched across the back of the couch, the tips of his fingers only inches from her shoulder. Images of Jude sitting like this with Rebecca came to mind, and she tucked her hair behind her ears. She wouldn't think of that right now. Jude inched closer, threading his fingers through her hair. The hair on the back of her neck rose as he did this.

"Tell me how the closing went today. I've been worried about you."

She closed her eyes, then opened them again, and a wave of dizziness overcame her. The room wavered.

Jude leaned toward her, looking into her eyes. "Are you all right?"

"Just tired."

"You were up all night. How about some coffee?"

Without waiting for an answer, he stood and said he'd be right back.

She nodded, too tired to speak. Beside her on the couch was the bundle of Luke's clothes Caroline had given her. Yawning, she reached over and picked them up. The clothes were neatly folded along with a small blanket from his bed. Enough for a few days, Caroline had said. Setting the blanket aside, she picked up each piece of clothing, inspecting it. There were three pairs of brown pants with big square pockets on the legs—little boys pants— and three small T-shirts, a sweater, some socks, and some underwear.

At the bottom of the pile she found a faded shirt, a loose cotton weave unlike the other articles of clothing. She held it up to the light. It used to be white, she could see. And it was much too small for him now—he'd have worn it years ago. She wondered if this ragged, shapeless shirt was what he was wearing when he'd left Cambodia. Folds in the cloth were bleached lines, almost white. The edges of the sleeves were frayed and the cloth worn thin.

Amalise dropped the small shirt into her lap and lay her hands upon it, trying to imagine Luke's escape. He'd been brought to America from Vietnam, but how had he gotten to Saigon from Cambodia? She envisioned him on one of the orphan rescue flights out of Saigon that she'd seen on the news two years ago, and thought of the years he'd endured since in gray institutional places, and the foster homes that had sent him away. But why had he ended up here?

She knew she'd probably never find the answers.

She turned the shirt over and spread it across her knees, and a glint of light caught her eye. She looked down and fingered a small silver broach hanging on the square shirt pocket, pulling it down into a permanent sag. She rubbed her fingers over the smooth three-leafed design. The jewelry had the heavy feel of old silver, the look of a family heirloom. Not something you'd expect to find on the pocket of an orphan from Cambodia.

And then she felt the bulge, just a slight thickness to the pocket, as if the pin were holding something hidden.

Carefully she spread the worn pocket and looked inside. There she found a faded envelope, the kind used for international air mail, pale blue paper with a thin red stripe. Carefully she unlatched the pin, sliding it from the pocket and the paper. Then she closed it and set the pin down on the coffee table.

The envelope was folded into squares. Someone who cared about Luke had pinned this to his shirt. Amalise unfolded the envelope, square by square. The envelope was empty. She saw it had been addressed, by hand in ink, to the United States Embassy, Phnom Penh, Cambodia.

That's all. How had it even gotten there with that address?

And then her heart began beating a strange, rapid rhythm as she stared at the address and the handwriting. She lay the envelope flat in her lap and smoothed the paper, noting the many official certifications and the date stamps from different countries as something stirred just beneath the surface of her mind.

Barely breathing now, she turned the envelope over to find the return address. Time stretched and twisted and turned, and then she closed her eyes, wanting to hold onto this moment, wanting to believe.

She did not hear Jude arriving with the coffee. She didn't open her eyes or say anything when he set the cups down on the coffee table before them. And when he sat down beside her and asked in a worried tone if she was not feeling well, she couldn't answer.

She merely opened her eyes and, with her heart pounding, she held up the envelope for him to see. Because written on the back in handwriting she knew so well, were these words:

Mrs. A. Sharp
5 – Dumaine Street
Apartment A
New Orleans, Louisiana

"What's this?" He took the envelope from her.

"I found it in the pocket of one of Luke's old shirts."

Then she sat very still, remembering. It was the spring of 1975. She was sitting at a table in the Café Pontalba, addressing the envelope and writing a note. The tip money she'd saved for weeks, without telling Phillip, was on the table beside the envelope. She folded the note around the ten-dollar bills and stuffed it into the envelope.

The money was for the shadow children.

From that dark place where she'd buried the images two years ago they reeled, frame by frame, through her mind. The contrast between her life and that of the children on the television screen. The urgency of their plight, with the Khmer Rouge closing in. The scorching feeling of helplessness, watching suffering from across the globe in her own living room. And the guilt, knowing that she could turn off the television set the moment the news touched too deeply.

What can one person do? she'd asked herself at that time.

She looked at the envelope, now lying in Jude's lap, and wanted to cry. *Thank you, Abba.* One person had been able to do something after all. And then slowly she felt that infinite hole inside closing up at last, the emptiness that could never be filled with finite things.

This was why she'd been given a second chance, she realized. Luke was as much her child as if she'd carried him in her womb. Looking down at the letter she'd sent on a wing and a prayer, she knew that now. With Jude still holding onto the envelope, she rose, weak with fatigue. She walked up to Luke's bedroom and lay down beside him. She didn't touch him. Just lay there watching his little chest rise and fall, not wanting to wake him. He'd had a long day, Jude had said. At last her own eyes closed, and Amalise slept.

Chapter Fifty

AN HOUR LATER SHE WOKE—SLOWLY—LINGERING IN that half world between dreams and wakefulness, not quite sure where she was. As her mind cleared, it came back to her, all of it: the envelope attached to Luke's tiny shirt, the new purpose in her life, this child. She propped herself up on one elbow and looked down at Luke, feeling all at once a new kind of love, a force that almost overwhelmed her, surpassing every emotion she'd ever felt, even instinct, even survival.

Minutes passed as she watched the child in the dark. In her heart he was her son. That's what Caroline had been trying to communicate earlier, she suddenly realized. Without even knowing about the envelope, Caroline had sensed the connection between them.

Smiling, she brushed Luke's forehead with a kiss and slipped out of the bed without waking him. She was reluctant to leave him but couldn't wait to find Jude and tell him this. Hurrying down the steps, she smiled again, thinking of Jude and Luke as she'd seen them together earlier.

Jude was sleeping on the couch in the living room when she found him. She picked up the cold cup of coffee and sipped it, then sat down and watched him sleep, thinking how natural it now seemed that—for her—their friendship had turned to love.

Yes, yes. I know Abba. For his sake, I'll keep that to myself. She would store that feeling deep in her heart so that he would never know. Love is unselfish. Love is kind. Jude should be free to love Rebecca. Yet she looked at his strong arms and longed for them to hold her. She touched his lips with her eyes and longed for just one lingering kiss.

A nostalgic feeling arose. In this moment, she was conscious that she'd always loved Jude, and she probably always would, but he would never know. Still, she would have Luke.

❧

Drifting up from dreams, he felt her eyes on him. Immediately he was alert. He opened his eyes and looked at her, and she smiled.

"I thought *I* was the one who needed sleep." Her voice tinkled with laughter.

Her face was luminous as she sat there, fingering that shirt of Luke's. Jude hadn't seen her look so happy in a while. He blinked and straightened his legs, touching her with his toes. She laughed and jumped.

She talked of Luke, and her eyes shone. He thought of Luke's sleeping face lit by moonlight last night, and of the day they'd spent together. He'd loved watching the child open up, how he'd looked up with that grin when he'd hit the first nail with the hammer. And Luke was smart. He'd take him fishing, soon. Teach him to swim.

"About the closing last night?" Her voice broke into his thoughts.

"Yes, tell me."

"You won't believe what happened."

"Why does that not surprise me?"

She laughed and told him everything. When she spoke of Robert Black's threat, Jude curled his fists, keeping them hidden down by his legs on the couch. He'd like five minutes in a room with Robert Black. Just five was all he'd need.

She thanked him for coming to the hospital. Not just for Luke's sake, but also for her own. He'd saved her job.

But when she came to the closing, and Bingham's disappearance, he could only stare. It seemed Bingham Murdoch had been a con artist all along, stringing along his investors for a personal twenty-million-dollar payday. And now he had vanished. Jude shook his head.

She was still tired, she said, but wanted to see Luke before she went home. Oh, how she wanted to take Luke home with her.

Jude invited her to stay. He'd sleep on the sofa, he said, and she could have the bed.

She looked down, smoothed her skirt, glanced at him from the corners of her eyes. And blushed.

Amalise, blushing?

Without thinking, he reached for her, but she stood up. "I'll go check on him one more time before I leave," she said, heading for the stairs before he could catch up. He followed her, telling himself she was his best friend and that's how she wanted things to stay. Status quo. And suddenly he knew that wasn't good enough. He loved this woman, and tonight he would tell her so.

So he focused on the task before him, just as he would aboard ship, charting a course one step at a time.

⟡

Amalise stood in the doorway with Jude behind her, watching Luke sleep. Like the rooms downstairs, the guest room was square as a box, but large, with two long windows on the far side. It was already eleven o'clock at night. He wouldn't wake again until morning, she guessed.

Luke lay in the middle of the big bed where she'd left him, covered with a light blanket and sound asleep. She could see the bulge of the cast under the blanket, a bulky contrast to the rest of his undernourished body. His head was turned now, facing the door, as if he'd been waiting for her.

Mak. "He's tiny in that bed."

"Yes. Light as a feather and worn out—he'll probably sleep for a while. Last night's medicine is probably still in his system." Jude touched her elbow. "Come out on the porch. We'll hear him out there if he wakes up. We need to talk."

Reluctantly she nodded, taking one last look at Luke. She was pretty certain how this conversation would go. Jude already knew what was in her heart. He would talk about Luke, about how difficult it would be for her to try to raise this child alone, how Caroline and Ellis had already taken him into their family. But she wouldn't part with Luke, she resolved. She was his mother—the envelope had told her that. He was her son. She would do whatever it took not to lose him now. She'd explain all of this to Jude, but in her mind the decision was made. She had no doubt that Caroline and Ellis would agree Luke should stay with her. *She* would adopt him.

Pulling herself away from the sight of the sleeping child, she turned and found herself standing face to face with Jude. He was looking down at her, his hands braced on either side of the door. For a moment her legs went weak, but then he slung his arm over her shoulder as he always did and smiled, and they walked through his bedroom and out onto the screened porch high up among the trees like two old friends.

There were two cane chairs out there, a small table, and an old cane couch that had seen its best days long ago. Now stripped of its leaves by autumn winds, the spreading branches of the pin oak in the yard below no longer hid the porch from the street. To her right Amalise could see State Street stretching toward St. Charles Avenue eight blocks away, solitary in the night.

She sat on one chair, and Jude took the other. The late-November air was crisp and cool, reminding her that tomorrow was Thanksgiving Day. Moonlight filtered through the bare branches. Sweet olive was in the air, the fragrance most pungent this time of year.

Amalise glanced in the direction of the guest room. "You're sure we'll hear him out here if he wakes?"

"Yes."

"You're good with him. He likes you."

"He's a good kid. And smart."

She settled back, remembering the night she'd come here looking for Jude, the night she'd left Phillip. Then as now, light ringed the lampposts in the darkness, pooling on the grass and curbstone and sidewalks below. She took this all in, mental snapshots of this evening that she'd remember later on, after he married Rebecca and this was their home.

A dog barked in the distance, breaking into her thoughts, and another one echoed the first. Back and forth they went for a few minutes, and then there was silence.

"I wonder if they understood each other," Amalise mused aloud.

Jude laughed. "When you were a kid, you wondered once how many circles and squares there are in the world."

She looked at him. "I thought you had all the answers."

He looked off. Minutes passed in silence. She studied him from the corner of her eye, wanting to hold onto this picture, too: Jude, slouched down in his chair, looking off, thinking about ships or the river or Pilottown and some report he had to finish.

He tilted his head, leaned his face on his hand.

Visions of the years ahead without him smothered rational thought. *He thinks of you only as his friend,* she reminded herself, swallowing. *But I'm not that little girl you used to know, Jude. I'm all grown up. I'm a woman now.*

As if he'd heard her, his blue eyes turned to her, catching her by surprise. Straightening up, he angled his chair toward her and bent forward, elbows on his knees, hands linked between them. In the heavy silence, she waited.

He dropped his eyes, and when he looked up again it was with an intensity she'd never seen before. She straightened, preparing herself.

"Listen," he said. His voice was low and husky. "Do you think you could ever get past this old friendship of ours?"

Oh, not even that? Tears threatened, but she fought them back. She would not cry right now. Later on, when she was alone, she'd battle things out with herself. But not now. She lifted her chin. "Of course, I understand. When you're married, things will change."

"Well, I certainly hope so."

She spoke before she thought. "Rebecca will see to that."

Seconds passed. Then he reached over and touched her knee. "Rebecca?"

Her throat felt tight, and it hurt from the tension. She wanted to be casual and smart and say something that would make him smile, but she couldn't think at all.

And then he reached across the space between them and pulled on the chair she was sitting in, tugging, turning it so that they were facing each other, and this show of physical force made her angry. She clamped her hands down on his forearms, ready to push him away. Jude was never cruel. How could he be so cruel! Her mouth quivered and she pressed her lips together as her fingers dug into those hard muscles.

"Amalise," he said. His voice was gentle. "Look at me." He reached out and touched the underside of her chin with his fingers, tilting her face upward so that she could look at nothing else but him. She felt the tears threatening again. Then he leaned close, his face just inches from hers and he said, his voice low and fierce, "I love you, Amalise."

For a moment she stared, and then she pulled back from him, not understanding. But in that instant his hands shot out, gripping her shoulders, and he held onto her so that she couldn't move, as if he would never let her go. And he said it again.

Then she sat very still, listening.

"I want to marry you. I want to spend the rest of my life with you, Amalise. And I'll wait as long as it takes for you to feel the same."

He loosened his grip, sliding his hands down her arms. His voice grew thick, and he glanced aside and back again. "I know how strange this must seem. We've known each other for so long, and it might be hard to think of me in a different way. I know you want things to remain just as they are, but they can't because I'm in love with you." Then he gathered her hands into his and pulled her close so that their hands, joined together, covered his heart.

She could feel his breath on her face as he said these words. She could feel his muscled chest, the faint movement of his heart as he held onto her hands, pressing them to him. And as she listened, the words seemed to float around her in pieces, like bits of a puzzle that she must put together to understand.

Love. I. You.

And then, he'd said her name. *Amalise.*

Not Rebecca. Amalise.

She sorted through her jumbled thoughts, through everything he'd said, rearranging, reordering the words so they made sense. Then she leaned back, studying him, looking for clues that would tell her she'd heard wrong. She waited to see if suddenly he'd turn away and laugh and tell her this was all a joke.

When she couldn't stand it anymore, all this analyzing, this process of thinking too much, she blurted out, "But Rebecca!" She shoved her fists encased in his hands against his chest. "What about Rebecca?"

Jude's hands tightened over hers, as if she might try to escape. Bracing his arms on his knees, he leaned even closer so that she could see the faint line between his eyes. She smelled the scent of his skin, his hair.

He did not blink. "Rebecca knows, I think. She's known for a long time now. She's in love with her career. And I'm in love with you."

She'd always trusted Jude. And as she watched his lips forming these words, she began to believe that perhaps something magical was happening here. She felt the first stirring in her mind and heart of something that told her this was real.

"It's not the same anymore." He smiled that long slow smile of his and waited.

Every particle of her being, every cell in her body tingled. "Not the same?" she repeated, brows raised, eyes wide.

Jude let out a sharp laugh. "Oh, my feelings for you are definitely not the same."

And in one split second everything coalesced, and a clarity and feeling of sheer joy rose up in her, a *knowing* that rippled through her and spread like stardust. She burst from the chair, flinging her arms around Jude's neck, and the chair tipped, tumbling down, taking them both down too.

"Whoa!" Jude laughed, catching her, encircling her with his arms as he lay flat on his back, cushioning her fall. "Was that a yes or a kamikaze attack?"

He was still laughing as she braced her hands on either side of his shoulders, looking down into his face. "Have you asked a question yet? I can't recall."

His look turned grave. He shook his head. "I dunno."

"Well. Ask it."

"All right. Can you cook?"

She lowered her arms, moving closer, longing for that first kiss. "I cooked a potato once, but it exploded in the oven."

He groaned. "I remember."

And then he turned into a blur, and her lips touched his, lightly at first, moving, exploring, and he pulled her down into his arms. She felt his hands cradling her face, and then he pushed her back, away, and gave her a long look. And when their lips touched again, she felt the memories streaming through the kiss: their years growing up, the things they'd learned together, how they'd laughed, a gardenia he'd once picked for her when she hadn't had a date for a dance. Every moment of their years together fed that kiss as friendship sanctified their love.

When Jude finally lifted her, pretending to groan at the weight, they sat together on the floor, side by side, leaning back against the screen and talking, planning, interrupting each other, excited like the children they'd once been. They would get married soon, he said.

In the springtime, she said. She wanted a wedding. At the cathedral.

That's a long time to wait, he said, giving her a sideways look.

She told him he'd live.

He groaned, but smiled. "We'll wait."

After a moment, she turned to him. "This is a package deal, you know. I want to adopt Luke."

He pulled her close. "We'll adopt him, if Caroline agrees. And the agency. We'll raise him together as our own."

Amalise smiled. "Caroline and Ellis won't object. And I'm sure the agency will permit us to have him. He already loves us, I think." She turned her face to him and ran her finger across his bottom lip. "And I love you, Jude. I think I've always been in love with you."

A smile lit his face as he pulled her to him slowly, pulling her into a new life with him and with Luke as she nestled her head under his chin, pulling her with him as a river slips you into its current and carries you downstream as far as the river flows.

Epilogue

FRIDAY AFTERNOON REBECCA STOOD IN THE doorway of Amalise's office and looked at her, noting the glow on her face. Amalise, bent over her work, hadn't spotted her yet, and Rebecca took the moment to compose herself.

Jude had proposed to Amalise. They had called her together from Marianus where the two of them, with the child, had spent the Thanksgiving holiday. They'd made the trip there and back in one day, but that was Amalise. And Jude.

Well, she wasn't that upset. She was happy for them, she supposed. She leaned against the door frame, watching Amalise. Jude had always figured her, Rebecca, for a woman consumed with her career, she knew. And he was right. If she'd ever been forced to choose, she'd have chosen her career. An easy call.

Not that she'd been asked.

But what she couldn't understand was what she'd heard from Amalise this morning. She'd continue to practice law after the wedding, she said. They were adopting that child, too, and Jude was thrilled. He was giving up his pilot's commission for love. He'd go into real estate here in the city, renovating old houses.

So he'd have Amalise's back while she continued on at Mangen & Morris. Amalise had found it all—love, a family, and a career. Rebecca shook her head. She'd have never guessed, and she wondered if that plan would really work.

With a sigh, she walked on into the room. Jude had always loved Amalise. Deep down inside she felt a small ache at the loss, but she'd get over it, she knew. In fact, she admitted to herself, he'd never been hers to lose.

Amalise looked up, put down her pencil, and smiled. "Hey."

Rebecca sat in the chair in front of Amalise's desk. "Fed wires close in an hour, but it's clear Murdoch's gone and the money, too. Raymond says that Morgan Klemp's having a fit in New York, but Banc Franck still won't give anyone the time of day without that security code. Raymond figures Bingham's on a beach somewhere, surrounded by women."

Amalise smiled. "He does enjoy the good life."

Rebecca stood. Wandered over to the bookshelf and fingered a Lucite deal toy given to Amalise after the closing of a transaction last spring. She had one just like it. "Have you and Jude set a date yet?"

"In the spring. We want to give it a little time. I'm a widow, you know."

Rebecca turned and looked at her.

"And I want sunshine and flowers."

"After marrying Phillip at City Hall, you deserve a spectacular wedding."

Amalise pulled out the bottom desk drawer and propped both feet on it, smiling. Rebecca could almost see the plans already running through her mind. "I agree. I think we'll do it in St. Louis Cathedral." She eyed Rebecca and her voice turned tentative. "What do you think of that?"

"Perfect."

She saw Amalise visibly relax.

"Will you be my maid of honor? It'll be a small wedding. No brides-maids."

Rebecca grinned. She tilted her head. "If you'll let me choose my dress. I'm not wearing one of those ugly dresses."

Amalise laughed. "That's a deal."

Rebecca planted her hands on her hips and sashayed to the window. She turned, scrutinizing Amalise. "You'll wear flowers in your hair. It's too short and straight to do anything fancy, but flowers will work."

"Yes, ma'am."

"And you're small. A long, slim dress fitted at the waist would look good. White?"

Amalise shook her head. "No. Something light, a full ruffled skirt in tulle, layers of flounces in peach and pink, orange, yellow, tangerine."

"I like it." Rebecca lifted her hands and hiked up her hair, then let it fall. "What kind of music?"

"The Olympia Brass Band."

Rebecca gave her a look. "In the cathedral?"

"No. After, when we come out." Amalise gestured with her hands. "I want tubas, French horns, trumpets, drums. We'll do the second line all around Jackson Square."

Rebecca burst into laughter. "Well, I hope it's a sunny day. Where's the reception?"

"The Café Pontalba. Gina insists."

"It'll be fabulous."

Rebecca yawned and stretched. Looked at her watch. She walked to the door. Hands on the door frame, she turned and looked at her friend. "I'm happy for you, Amalise. And for Jude, too. And Luke."

"Thanks, Rebecca." Amalise's eyes held hers. "For everything."

❦

Amalise pulled her purse out of the desk drawer, closed it, and stood. Jude and Luke were waiting for her. They were all going to Caroline's for dinner. She smiled, thinking of Jude with Luke. The child was stuck to him like glue. And Mama and Dad had fallen in love with Luke.

"Miss Catoir?"

She turned to see a young man standing in the doorway. He wore the braided uniform of a valet from the Roosevelt Hotel. In his hands he held a package.

"Yes?"

He stepped inside her office and walked to the desk, holding the package out before him. He set it down carefully in the middle of her desk.

"Is this for me?"

"Yes, ma'am."

"Who sent it?"

"I dunno." He shrugged and pushed a dark shock of hair back from his forehead. "My boss just told me to deliver it today. He said the guy told him you'd understand."

"Do I need to sign for it?"

He shook his head.

She opened her purse and stuck her hand inside, looking down, fumbling for cash for a tip. "Just a moment," she said.

He held up his hands, backing away. "Not necessary. It's been taken care of." Then he turned and disappeared.

Setting her purse on the credenza, she sat down and pulled the package toward her. It was wrapped in slick white paper and tied up with a gold ribbon, knotted on the top. Carefully she untied the knot and pulled the ribbon loose. She stripped off the tape at either end of the package and unwrapped the paper.

No tissue inside. Just a folded white cloth.

She picked up the cloth, held it up, and saw that it was a shirt. As she turned the shirt to see the front, her brows shot up. Then slowly her puzzled frown turned to a smile. She lay the T-shirt down on the desk before her, spreading it flat so that she could read the words emblazoned across the front.

In glittering gold lettering, almost rising from the cloth, they read like this:

Where in the world is D. B. Cooper?

She smiled and looked through the window at a beautiful sunny day. They'd never find him, she knew. And the craziest thing about the whole story was that if Bingham Murdoch, or D. B. Cooper, or whoever he was hadn't come to town, she'd never have found Luke.

She closed her eyes, for some reason remembering that flash of light from the wingtip of a plane out over the lake she'd seen on her first day back at work six weeks earlier. *Thank you, Abba.* Because suddenly she realized that this story was never about Bingham Murdoch's deal, or even Jude. It was always, from day one, all about little Luke.

Author Note

Love is all around us, but what does the word *love* really mean? *Chasing the Wind* is a love story spiced with mystery, ambition, and rivalry set against the background of a fast paced, razzle-dazzle corporate transaction in Amalise Catoir's law practice in New Orleans. This book was so much fun to write—suspense plus whimsy, bound together with streaming satin ribbons of different kinds of love.

I say that because love takes many forms . . . *I know, I know* . . . I said this is a love story and that should mean romance. But there's more. Plato and the ancient Greeks got it right thousands of years ago. Other types of love are just as binding as romance, just as consuming, sometimes more. *Chasing the Wind* continues the saga of Amalise and Jude. But then there's the circle of love binding parent and child. There are deep, profound, and lasting friendships. And shimmering through each of our lives is *agape*—God's love for us.

As we all know, love in any form is not always easy. Sometimes love brings conflict and hard choices, and then we struggle to create balance in our lives, tiptoeing past obstacles like high wire dancers on sunbeams. Sometimes I wonder if figuring out how all the different kinds of love fit together might be one reason God put us here in the first place. When we ask ourselves why bad things happen in this world, is learning to give and receive love somehow a part of the answer?

Jude and Amalise are old friends, best friends since childhood. What happens when old friendship morphs into *eros* like fruit ripening on the vine? Mix in agape and an unexpected new love striking like quicksilver, and things are really stirred up. *Chasing the Wind* is a whirlwind of surprising emotions and conflicts that some might think arise from serendipity, or coincidence, or fate.

But I like to think that like these are *kairos* moments, God's way of intervening and guiding us, opening our minds and hearts to understanding. Making us wiser and larger than we were before.

Pamela

PAMELA BINNINGS EWEN

PAMELA BINNINGS EWEN

THE
MOON
IN THE
MANGO
TREE

PAMELA BINNINGS EWEN

SECRET
OF THE
SHROUD

a novel

Dancing on Glass

a novel

PAMELA BINNINGS EWEN